OF SHADOWS
and
SIPHONS

J. L. Rosenauer

Book Two of The Sandorg Chronicles

Published by Jerrica Rosenauer

Imprint: Jerrica Rosenauer

ISBNs: 978-1-969797-08-8 (Kindle)

978-1-969797-10-1 (Paperback)

978-1-969797-09-5 (Hardcover)

978-1-969797-11-8 (S.E. Hardcover with Jacket)

978-1-969797-12-5 (S.E. Paperback Dark mode)

978-1-969797-13-2 (S.E. Hardcover)

978-1-969797-14-9 (Dark mode Deluxe Hardcover)

Author: J. L. Rosenauer

Cover & Map Design by Jerrica Rosenauer

First Edition, 2026

Printed in the United States of America

10 9 8 7 6 5 4 3 2

CONTENTS

CONTENT WARNING

This book contains depictions of violence, war, torture, death (including of young characters), grief, past sexual abuse, and sexual content. These themes may be complex or triggering for some readers.

Not every reader will be sensitive to the same things, but I want you to feel safe going in. Please take care of yourself first—if you need to set the book down, your well-being matters more than finishing the story.

Lastly, this book includes over 168 versions of "fuck" in some manner, now 169. As well as other explicit language, if this book isn't for you, that's okay, but I did warn you.

♥ in the Chapter Title indicates sexual content. You know, just in case you're in public reading.

Furthermore, all chapters are written from Auriella's POV, unless otherwise noted.

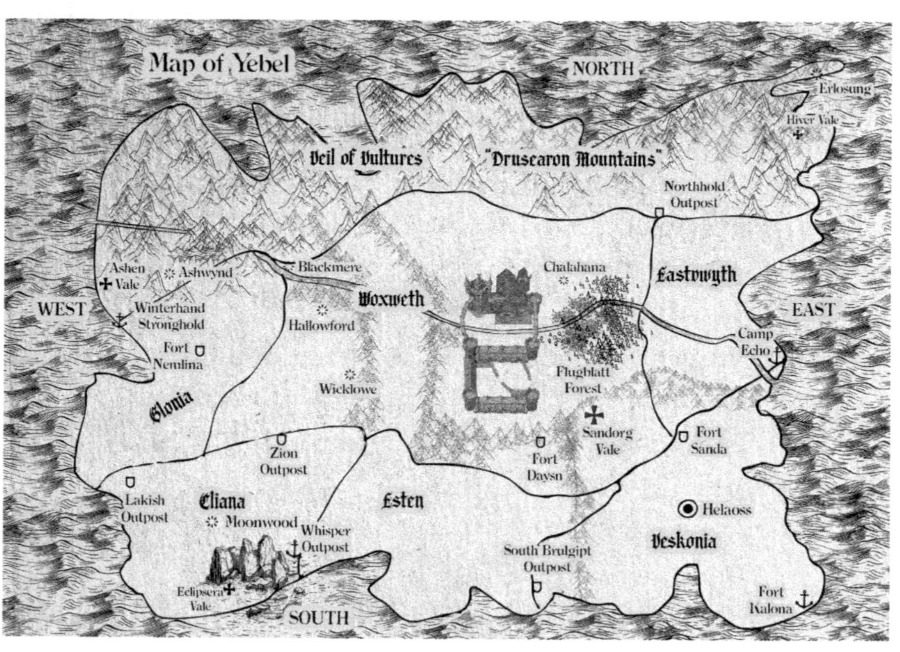

Map of Yebel
NORTH
Erlosung
Hiver Vale
Veil of Vultures
"Drusearon Mountains"
Northhold Outpost
Chalahana
Eastvwyth
Ashen Vale
Ashwynd
Blackmere
Woxweth
WEST
EAST
Winterhand Stronghold
Hallowford
Camp Echo
Fort Nerulina
Wicklowe
Flugblatt Forest
Glonia
Sandorg Vale
Fort Sanda
Zion Outpost
Fort Daysn
Lakish Outpost
Eliana
Esten
Helaoss
Moonwood
Whisper Outpost
Veskonia
South Brulgipt Outpost
Eclipsera Vale
Fort Kalona
SOUTH

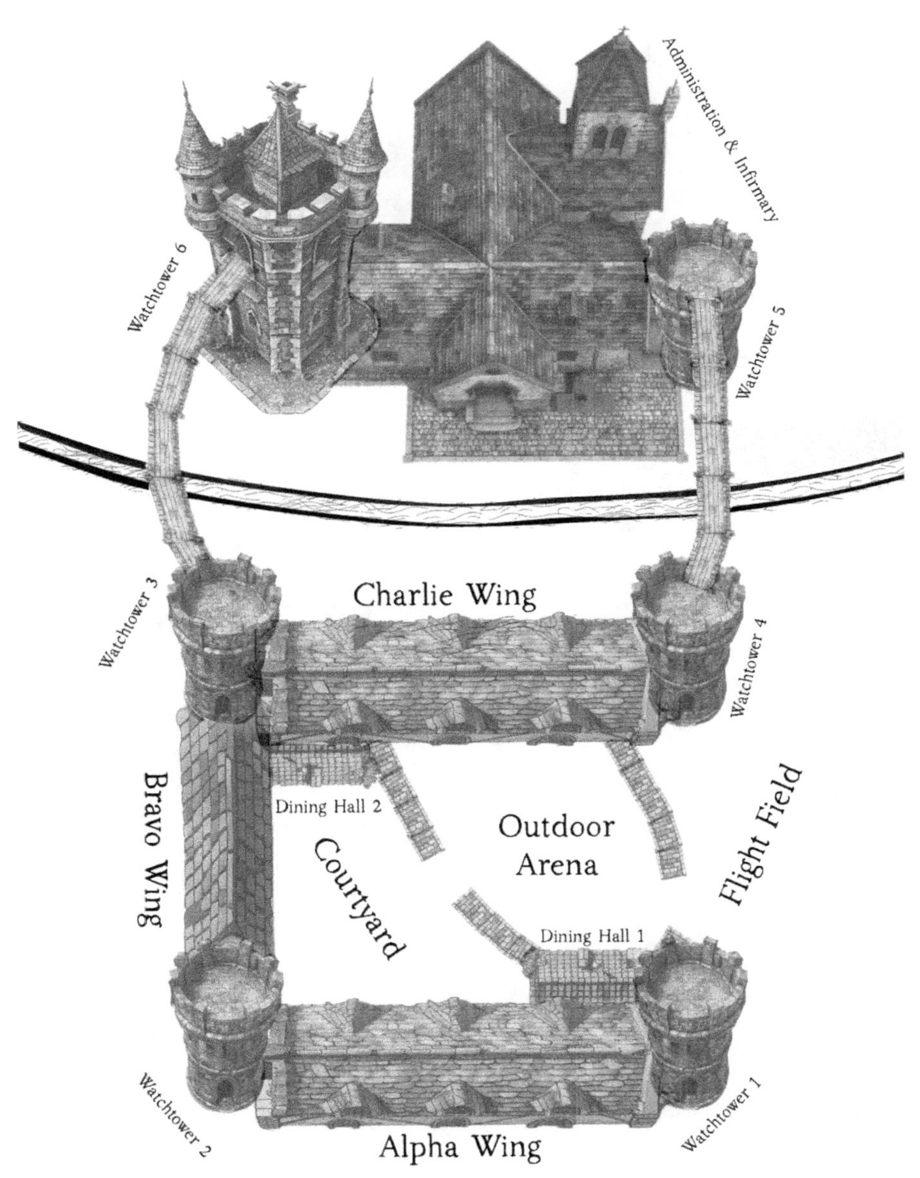

Administration & Infirmary
Watchtower 6
Watchtower 5
Watchtower 3
Watchtower 4
Charlie Wing
Bravo Wing
Dining Hall 2
Outdoor
Arena
Flight Field
Courtyard
Dining Hall 1
Watchtower 2
Watchtower 1
Alpha Wing

PREVIOUSLY IN BLACK WING AND SHADOWS

Auriella Blackcreek arrived at Sandorg Military College to complete her eight weeks of basic training. At Sandorg College, every cadet starts in basic training, no matter which branch they are in. There are seven branches one can join: Drusearons, Healers, Historians, Infantry, Riders, Shapeshifters, or Sorcerers. Every cadet except Shapeshifters is Fae, and some Fae have more magical powers than others. To join the Drusearons, you have to be winged, and not every Drusearon warrior is born with wings. Drusearons also don't have to join their own winged branch either. Shapeshifters or Werewolves are the only branch that isn't supposed to join another branch, and of course, to join them, you would have to shift.

During basic training, Auriella was put in a large platoon with mixed branches, where she was forced to face some biases that she had due to her and her best friend being sexually assaulted when she was a teenager. Being in a room with Drusearon cadets triggers flashbacks and nightmares for her.

Everything changed when she was standing in formation, and a five-nine male stood against the wall, their eyes locked onto each other, lightning coursed through her body. No matter where she turned, Zane was there.

The entire eight weeks were grueling, and during the Pass of Bête Noire, a grueling four-day mountain training, Auriella nearly dies, and two of her squadmates lose their lives, one of whom she had gotten close to. When she finally came to, Zane was there waiting for her.

He revealed to her they were mates—fated to be together for life. Not only were they mates, but he was a Drusearon. Making her come to terms with her past quickly. Their connection was instant and undeniable. Zane had known about their prophecy from an early age and had loved her from the moment he saw her standing in the field, something he hadn't shared with her. Auriella was a little more hesitant in the beginning, but quickly fell for him.

Once Auriella graduated from basic training and entered the Riders' branch, everything changed quickly. She was reunited with her best friend, Lili, and her ex-boyfriend, Alex. In a twist of events, Zane and Alex had become best friends. Unbeknownst to them, they loved the same female. Naturally, this causes friction between the three of them.

In a heated moment, Zane and Auri gave in to their sexual desires, completing the bonding process. Auri struggled with feelings of impulsivity and wondered if she was rushing too quickly, struggling with her past promiscuity. Things quickly change when Zane realizes that Auriella was the daughter of the General of the Military. Someone he blamed killed his uncles. Auri realizes that he was from the same town as the Drusearon who sexually assaulted her.

Auri opened up and shared with Zane the events that happened and led to her killing his uncle, not her father. Zane realized that he didn't know the full truth and admitted that his uncle and everyone who covered it up deserved it. Through this, Auri learns that Zane is actually the firstborn son of the Duke of Veil of Vultures, whose first name was actually Roarke. Both of them were at Sandorg because they wanted to be, not because they were required, like the majority of the others. Both of them were fighting against a destiny they didn't want.

Auri and her father hadn't been on the best of terms when she left for Sandorg. He had been busy being the General and hadn't wanted her to join the military at all. He had left her a present from her mother, who was killed when she was fourteen. It was a medical bag filled with medical supplies and a hidden letter that only left Auri with more questions than answers. Turns out her parents knew that she had a mate. Her mom warned her that once the two of them consummated the mating bond, it would be locked in, and they would have special qualities. It was too late for that letter, though. They had already figured out that they could speak mind to mind and shared feelings through their bond. Her mother's letter also implied that her father was part of something secretive and possibly a part of her own demise.

As Auri continued into her new lectures, she found herself to be hated amongst several of the cadets because of who her father was, something she hadn't realized would be so impactful on her. If that wasn't enough, professors kept hinting at her having great powers, yet she hadn't felt like she had any magic. Turns out her father kept her quite shielded, including dosing her to keep her powers from emerging.

Training in the Rider's branch, like the other branches, was brutal. Testing her strength every day. Her weeks were filled with sparring with fellow cadets, including ones who called her out personally, trying to settle vendettas with her. The rest of the time, she spent finessing her magic and obstacle courses that were trained to make them more agile and better riders.

She was promoted to flight guide, which allowed her to get her own bed chambers, but also came with more responsibilities. When one of her fellow first-year cadets fell and died during the obstacle training, Auri took it hard, going into a depressive state.

Before she could even snap out of the depressive state, she was kidnapped in the middle of the night. Her kidnappers wanted her as leverage to get to her father. She endured torture and a deadly head blow.

Zane knew right away that she was missing and started looking for her. He tried to get Auri's Wing Commander involved; however, he insisted they go through the proper protocol. Zane, not caring about protocol and only about Auri, recruited his and Auri's friends—Alex, Lili, Elijah, and Oliver—to find and rescue her. It took them two days of searching the forest before they finally found her. She was barely conscious. The group took out every captor that was in the underground cellar.

Once back at the college, the menders were able to save Auri, telling her that she was lucky; the brain wasn't an easy mending fix. All six of them were reprimanded for leaving the campus without authorization. When Auri questioned how she could control her being kidnapped, she was shut down and told that she shouldn't be a liability. Zane moves into an overprotective boyfriend, putting up a ward on her room, and no longer wanting to sleep in his own room.

When bonding day arrives, Auriella quickly finds the little silver dragon—Esme—that had talked to her months prior. They quickly bond in the forest, but not before Esme sends Auri on a wild chase, making her work to earn her place as a Rider. Most of Auri's friends all bond with a dragon, phoenix, or griffin. Bonding with a flier gave each rider unique abilities, as well as a shimmer that acted as armor over their chest and arms.

Everything seemed to be moving in a positive direction until bodies started dropping. They were murdered and laid out in gruesome displays for the entire campus. Not only that, but some of the cadets with whom Auri had conflicts. The tension around the campus started increasing.

New rules were put in place, but despite that, bodies were still dropping. It was decided that cadets would be leaving early for winter leave, without winter celebrations. First-year Rider cadets and other cadets in leadership positions stayed longer. First-year riders needed to learn how to ride their fliers before flying back to their hometowns. Leadership strategized how to manage the cadets when they arrived back. Auri's father is on campus and using his memory reader ability on the cadets to ensure all cadets who were still there weren't the murderer.

Auri made the decision to go home with Zane to his palace at Ashwynd. Her relationship with her father was still not feeling solid, with questions that Auri had that had gone unanswered. Meeting Zane's family, which included both of his parents and six siblings, was just as chaotic as she thought it would be. During the dinner the first night home, Auri is bombarded with questions. When the question came from Thea about her father killing their uncle, dinner ended quickly, with Auri and Zane retiring back to his chambers.

They didn't get to fully process everything before the two of them were summoned to his father's office, where both Auri and Zane were shocked to see Auri's father—Conri Blackcreek—sitting casually next to Zane's father, with a drink in their hands. Things escalated quickly when her father talked about her mother's murder, and Auri's ability exploded in the form of shadows. Shadows holding her up from the ground, and wrapped around her father's neck, hoisting him in the air. The revelation of a shadow summoner, something unseen in centuries, shook Zane's father.

Veni.
Vidi.
Vici.

PROLOGUE

General Conri Blackcreek

They said I was broken. I was damned. I wasn't one of them. I would never shift into the form I was born for. I expected my first shift to take my wolf form, but nineteen got closer, and it didn't happen. My pack, the ones I thought were my family, shunned me, kicked me out. I was supposed to be the Alpha. It was my right, and they betrayed me.

My grandmother—my mother's mother—welcomed me into her home. I only saw her a few times growing up, but after my parents both died when I was ten, my pack hadn't let me see her. My parents' marriage was frowned upon. My father, an Alpha, married one of the elusive Cavendish Witches. And me? Something went so very wrong.

When I arrived at my grandma Umbra's home, she sat me down and told me that my parents *knew* I wouldn't ever shift. They were going to inform me when I got older, but that opportunity never came. The priestess who saw me when I was days old told them. She also revealed that I was guarded, and she couldn't read anything else about me. I was void. Dark. My parents only wanted to protect me. With my mom being a powerful Witch, I knew I was more powerful than most. I kept it a secret, using it only when necessary.

When I was twenty-one, I joined Sandorg as a rider. I became the one thing my pack hated, to spite every one of those assholes. There I met Lucille. She was gorgeous. She was everything I dreamed of. She was a year younger than I was, but in the same year. She had told me she had a horrible childhood, and this was her fresh start. Her new beginning, I tried hard to stay away from her. She was too good for me, too pure. By year three, she treated my injuries so many times, and we grew closer. Eventually, I gave in.

We got married right after we graduated. We lost baby after baby, and both of us started to lose parts of ourselves. I am not sure we ever healed from that. I questioned the existence of every God. Watching Lucille break down more and more every time broke me down even more. I felt dark. I felt rage. I wanted to tap into the magic that would consume me, but I held on for her.

We were blessed with Auriella five years later, after losing five babies. She was the most beautiful baby my eyes ever laid on. Her existence became mine. I fought to survive for her. Lucille and I fought over taking her to a priestess. It was tradition, something most Fae did. I was terrified. Everything I buried came to the surface. I told Lucille everything. *What if she was going to shift? What if they told me she was dark like me?* Lucille convinced me—she gave me an ultimatum, really—to take her in.

Nothing prepared me for that day. It felt as though the world stopped spinning. When I handed our precious bundle to the priestess, our hands brushed against each other. She stopped, like her mind left her body. She looked confused but continued taking Auriella from my arms. She told us that she had a destined mate, a year older than her. She was beyond unique, possessing great power not just from my bloodline but also from that of Lucille's. Lucille didn't even know where she came from. A family took her in when she was a baby.

She couldn't tell us whether she would shift or not. She had a hard time reading her, just as my grandmother said happened with me. She warned us that when she and her mate found each other, they would change the world. Good or not, they would have some of the greatest power combined that hadn't been seen in a millennium.

For years, her warnings and lack of information plagued me. How powerful could she actually be? Would she inherit my darkness? Would she be a shifter?

For years, I tried to sway her from attending Sandorg. I was mostly scared of her going right as she turned eighteen, and unexpectedly shifting. From a little girl, she knew what she wanted. She wanted to be like me and bond with a dragon. She never knew about my shunned heritage. I could barely discuss it with Lucille, and definitely not Auriella.

When Auriella was kidnapped, the news didn't reach me until she had already been rescued. It came with a message stating that Shapeshifters were involved, but the pack was unknown. It didn't need to be said. I knew. Every part of me wanted to go to that village and set it on fire. I didn't, but they did pay. Anyone who would hurt someone I loved would pay if they hadn't already.

Kim and I first flew to the location where Auriella was held captive. I looked at the mess Braegon and the other cadets made and saw the cell where they kept my daughter. I investigated each body that laid slain on the ground.

Fire surged through my body, my fists clenched, and I felt flames at my fingertips. I could burn the whole damn place down myself. I stood over Franc, the Beta of the Lupine Pack. This fucking Gods-forsaken piece of shit. I hope he suffered at least some. Kim and I immediately flew east to the Lupine Pack. I didn't care if we shared blood—they made their own bleed, and for what? To get back at me? I should be the one getting back at them.

As soon as I was near, the village started scrambling as if they knew what was to come of them. Of course, it was only Omegas on the ground scurrying around. Their Alpha—Abe, my little brother—was nowhere to be found. He was in hiding, no fucking surprise, he was afraid of me growing up, and now that I stood with a dragon, he knew he wouldn't stand a chance. I set fire to several of the Omegas that came at me, sent another back with a message to Abe that he would fucking pay for what he did.

CHAPTER I

Zane

The room inverted, turning dark—candles flickered—then the shadows tore free of the corners like they'd been holding their breath for centuries.

They answered *her*.

One coiled around her father's throat and lifted him as if the air itself had hands. His glass shattered, a spray of amber and diamond across the rug. My father moved first—chair skidding back, hand half-raised—then went still as the darkness thrashed, listening to a command Auri hadn't spoken.

"Auri," I said, almost a whisper.

She wasn't touching the floor anymore. The shadows held her, skimming up her arms, fanning at her back, a cloak of night that moved with her every breath. Her eyes were wide, green absent, now dark blue, fixed on nothing.

I felt it down the bond—fear, hot and metallic. Not afraid of my father, not of her father. *Of herself.*

"Let him down," my father said, "Auriella. Release him."

She flinched at the sound.

I stepped between her and her father, raising my hands in the air. The nearest shadow curled toward me. There was a reflex inside me that rose to meet it, a familiar hunger, the part of me that knew it wanted to touch her magic.

Not now. Not here.

"Auri," I said again, softer, only for her. "Look at me."

Her father's boots kicked against the floorboards twice—then only his hands moved, weakly clawing at the band of black around his throat. The smell of scorched liquor and burning wood filled the air. I didn't spare him a glance. I could feel his panic through Auri's, like a second, frantic pulse.

"Breathe," I sent down the bond, steady, filling each word with the way my lungs moved. *"You're not alone. I am here with you."*

The shadows flared around the room, tasting the fear in the room. Feeding off of her fear, protecting *her.* Auri swayed.

"Auri." My voice cut lower. "Follow my count. One."

Her gaze snapped to my fingers.

"Two."

The shadow at her wrist pulsed, then loosened a fraction.

"Three."

I stepped closer, her eyes truly locking onto mine.

Something in the bond shifted, like a fist opening. The coil at his throat unspooled in a reluctant slide and dropped him into his chair. He bent forward, coughing, one hand braced on his knee, the other pressed to the red liquid seeping at his neck. My father took a single step toward him, then stopped and looked at Auri as if she were the darkness of the night.

"There hasn't been a shadow summoner in centuries," he said, almost to himself.

Auri flinched again. The shadows tightened around her. They were trying to shield her. To protect her.

"Easy," I murmured, closing the space between us in steady, slow steps. Every sense in my body was tingling—the tremor in her forearms, the way her breath snagged on the end of each exhale. I wanted—Gods, it didn't matter what I wanted.

What mattered was that she was breathing.

"You're in control," I told her down the bond. *"They answer you, not the other way around."*

Her lip trembled. "I didn't—" Her voice cracked, small and hoarse. "I didn't mean—"

"I know." I let the last step carry me into her reach. "Together," I said, "in. Out."

We breathed together, in sync. I moved into her space, wrapping my arms around her and pulling her in. Shadows were still wisping at her feet.

Her father coughed, ragged, swallowing air as if he'd just learned how. "Well," he rasped, voice shredded. "That... answers that."

"Answers what?" I asked, not taking my gaze from her.

"That the priestess was right." He sat back slowly, eyes bright and too sharp for a man who should have been seeing spots. "And that I was, too."

My father's gaze cut to him. "Enough riddles," he said, but there was caution under the authority—respect or fear, I couldn't tell. "It's time to speak the truth."

"Good," her father said, and dabbed the blood at his throat with his sleeve like this was a tedious part of a plan and not the moment he'd nearly died. "Because your boy is going to need clarity if he means to keep up."

My fingers paused against Auri's spine.

He smiled a fraction at that, the kind of smile that wasn't one. "Relax, Lord Braegon. If I wanted to flay you open, I'd have done it long ago."

"General," my father warned.

"I'm speaking," her father said, then looked at Auri. "You didn't lose yourself. You found it. There's a difference. Learn it."

She swallowed hard. The shadows dimmed again, like a tide pulling back from an embankment.

"May I?" my mother asked from the doorway, and I realized she and one of the household Healers stood there, silent as ghosts. Her gaze never broke from Auri's face.

"Later," my father said. "Give them a breath."

I guided Auri to a chair and helped her sit down. I lowered myself to her, locking my eyes with hers.

"You're here," I told her. "With me."

Her breath hitched. "I hurt him."

"You scared him," I said, and let my mouth curve because it was true and because she needed to see my eyes gentler than the room's. "He'll live. Unfortunately."

The anxiety coursing through the bond eased somewhat. The shadows relaxed another notch, becoming nothing more than dark spots below her feet. The shadows were calling me. The power pulled at my fingers every time I touched her. I've felt her magic before, but not like this.

A short, controlled inhale from my father. "We will continue this conversation," he said, each word placed like a chess piece. "But everyone needs to take a seat." He looked to the healer. "Salve for the General. Bourbon for the rest."

Blackcreek waved the healer away, not caring about himself. His attention fixed on me, not my father, not the room—me.

"Tell me, Roarke Junior—"

"That is not my name, do not call me that." I cut him off.

He smiled, humorless. "Yeah, whatever. How long have you known about our plans?"

"I didn't know *you* were involved at all."

"Okay, and? How long have you—"

"A couple of years," I answered him. Where the hell was he going with this? What the hell did it even matter? Auri just exploded into shadows. She sat in the chair, staring into space, like she was checked out.

"We have more pressing things to talk about." My father cut in.

"Yes, as we were discussing—before my lovely daughter showed us her new party trick..."

Auri shot her gaze to him. Was he actually trying to provoke her already heightened emotions when her power was at its most uncontrollable state?

"You both are aware of the Resurrection of Yebel?" her father said.

"Yeah... I know what I've heard around. She doesn't really know anything." I told him and turned my head to look at her. Her eyes became fixated on him, no longer green, but the darkest blue I had ever seen.

"Let me give you both the rundown, because clearly," he paused and locked eyes with Auri, "you both are now more involved than we wanted for either of you."

My dad sat in his chair, sipping bourbon. His gaze bounced from me to her, then to her father, like he was watching a spectacle. "Start at the beginning, Conri."

My eyes narrowed at my father. He used his first name, as if they were close. He had never referred to him that way. Honestly, I never heard him speak casually to anyone other than my mother and us children.

"Like the beginning, beginning?" He raised his eyes at my father.

"What the actual fuck is going on right now?" Auri shot down our bond. My eyes shot to her, and I felt instant relief hearing her voice.

"Your guess is as good as mine. I didn't realize they were friends on a first-name basis until just now—"

"Yeah... same."

"Before I begin," he started, then he stood up and moved to Auri. My entire body tensed even though I knew he wouldn't hurt her, and hell, I should be more worried about him. He knelt in front of her and placed his hands on her knees.

"My sweet Auri, I promise I never intended to keep so many secrets from you. At first it was because you were too young to understand, and then it became to protect you and—well, it doesn't matter—"

"Dad, just fucking say—"

"Auriella Reyna... please refrain from cursing at me."

She simply nodded, and anger pulsed down our bond. I sensed her magic simmering again. I could feel the urge to pull it gnawing at me. Her magic was wild and powerful.

He moved back to his seat, but his eyes fixated on her. They were drawn low, sad, almost. His right knee bounced up and down as fast as it could.

"What do either of you actually know about the mating bond?"

"Well, not much because you failed to tell me anything. I had to learn I had a mate—something you and Mom knew about—while I was at a military war college. Oh, and that once Zane and I had sex—"

"Gods, Auri!" he snapped at her. "I don't mean that..."

"I really don't know much about the bond, other than my aunt predicted ours and what she shared," I added in, not letting Auri start again.

"Figures... Well, then, it will be news to you that to have a true mating bond, one of the partners must have Werewolf blood in them, at least a quarter."

My heart started beating faster. Did I hear him correctly? What the hell did that actually mean? Was I? Did she? My aunt and uncle had a bond. Wait, what the fuck? She, too, was stunned by this revelation. Her eyes were wide with surprise at him.

"Yeah... I didn't think either of you knew that—"

"What does that—what are you trying to say?" she blurted out.

"Well... my little wolf, I am a wolf, you're a wolf—"

"I don't think I need to state the obvious here, father, but I don't fucking shift into anything." Shadows started spinning around her feet, swirling up her legs. Her cheeks turned bright red.

"Auri... listen to me. You can't lose control, you have to learn to control this..." I told her.

"You're right, you don't shift, and well, neither do I. I know I never talked about my parents much to you, and I should have. My father was the Alpha in the Lupine pack, my mother was a Cavendish Witch."

Holy shit. My mind spun around. It had never been a secret that the general's bloodline was powerful, but the specifics of its power remained a secret. And I was mated... to someone who was a part Witch, part Werewolf, and a rider... I knew if my mind was spinning, hers was too.

"If that's the case, then my aunt and uncle? Both of them were Drusearons?" I asked, my head stuck on that part.

"Of course, your uncle, my brother, was a full Drusearon. Your aunt, on the other hand, had a quarter wolf in her, and the rest was Drusearon. Until Conri didn't shift, we believed all children born to a full Werewolf would shift, because there was nothing recorded that suggested otherwise. Quarter Werewolf children shift half of the time."

"And what does this have to do with what is going on in our continent?" Auri said with a tone that suggested she didn't care, but I could feel the anger through our bond. I was watching her tap her fingers on the sides of her thighs, trying to ground herself.

"I was getting there... but I felt it was necessary to tell you about my ancestry, your ancestry—"

"Something that you should have told me years ago, you know, because what the fuck would you have said *if* I did shift?" Her voice cracked like she was holding back the tears with every ounce of strength she had.

"Given that I hadn't shifted, I didn't figure you would, or I prayed to all the Gods you wouldn't anyway."

"Well, thank the Gods I didn't then... I guess."

"Auri, I am sorry. I should have told you. Your mom didn't want to, and we had planned to when the time was right. Then she was gone, and I... I lost myself, and that wasn't fair to you, I know."

"Is there anything I should know about Mom's ancestry?"

He let out a laugh, "I wish I knew. Your mom... we know very little about her. They found her on the street as a babe, and your grandparents took her in. What we do know is that the priestess said she came from great power and possessed magic. But that doesn't tell us much. Plenty of Fae types have magic."

"Oh." Her eyes dropped to her lap.

"Let's get on with it, Conri, I don't have all night," my father cut in, "especially when we also need to discuss what the hell just woke up in this room." He shot Auri a look.

"Yeah, yeah, Roarke. I am getting there. It's not like you are sharing earth-shattering news with *your* child—"

"Because I wouldn't have held such information a secret for a long time." My dad cut him off, then turned to me. "For the record, no earth-shattering family secrets here."

"After joining the military and becoming a rider, I moved up quickly. I started paying attention and started asking questions I shouldn't have. Turns out King Fen is also a Shapeshifter. He is experimenting with creating super Werewolves. He has kept his lineage very secretive. You both heard about Nosferatu in the lecture?"

"Yes... You're not trying to say *he* is doing that to shifters—" I started to say.

"No, well, not exactly. The king has been around for a long time. He was part of the original group that helped create Nosferatu. Long ago, he was stopped. Now he is trying to apply a similar magic to Werewolves. I don't know how far he is into this. I infiltrated his group, but he hasn't shared much yet. I have also killed infected Werewolves, which is why you have a target on your back."

"Was this why I was kidnapped?" She hadn't lifted her eyes from her lap.

"Yes, and they paid for that."

"What do you mean, infected?" I asked. All of this information had my mind spinning, and I wasn't sure what was important to know, but I knew I needed to ask more questions because whatever the hell was going on was about to be at our doorsteps.

"Werewolves that they experimented on, that it didn't work. They became uncontrollable, unable to shift into their mortal form. Lucille was very close to figuring out many things. She treated some Fae that a feral Werewolf had attacked. She then came across one, and she used magic to subdue it. She started asking questions, and that is what got her killed. I pleaded with her to please drop it, but she wouldn't."

Shadows erupted from Auri again and spun all around the room. My dad sat up straight, no longer casual. Her father's shoulders tensed, eyes wide. This time, the shadows didn't touch anyone, just swirled around the room. Speaking about her mom triggered her last time. It was triggering her this time. I stood from my chair and knelt in front of her and locked eyes with her.

"Auri, my love, my Anam Cara. Breathe in with me, breathe out with me. You control them. They don't control you. If you react this way each time, he will share less the next—"

"Do you fucking hear him? How am I supposed to remain calm? He is talking about the murder of my mother, his wife."

"Yes, and this is a hard conversation. There will be many more of these. You need to learn to turn them off. You can lose control when we are in our chambers."

"Glad to see you both got the wonderful gift of telepathy," my father quipped.

Both Auri and I shot a look at him, eyes wide.

"Oh, come on, it was clear as day when your uncle and aunt did it too."

The shadows swirling around the room dissipated and retreated to Auri. She took in a deep breath.

"What is the plan, father?" she asked.

"Right now, the plan is for you two to pretend you know nothing and stay clear of any trouble," her father said.

"You're telling me that the King of Rudemont is creating Nosferatu, our King is creating super Werewolves, there is a war brewing, and cadets dropping dead at the college, and you want us to—"

"To do fucking nothing," I finished her sentence. Was he actually fucking serious?

"Yes. There is nothing for you to do, you're both cadets."

"Do the other Shapeshifters know who you are? Who I am?"

"No. Well, yes, some Shapeshifters know who I am. But most don't. When they exiled me, I took my grandmother's maiden name. My born name was Rathmore."

I've heard that name before... my mind was spinning trying to figure out where. "Where have I heard that name before?" I shot my dad a look.

"You may have heard it or seen it around your uncle's home. It was your aunt's family name." My dad said.

Auri's eyes widened and locked onto him. "Are you trying to say we are related?" Her voice was raspy.

"Not exactly. She was essentially a distant cousin, but by marriage—"

"Break it down more than that," she said.

"The Rathmore name spans wide, she was my great-great-great aunt's child. And she and Zane don't share any blood. This happens within the fates. When we see people who are mated, it's often a way of strengthening bloodlines for a greater destiny."

"That's great to know I didn't screw my cousin..." she murmured.

"Good Gods, Auri. Are you trying to give our fathers a heart attack?"

"Come on... they literally fucked our mothers to have us."

I gasped out loud. She would be the death of me. My father was laughing under his breath, struggling to contain a much louder laugh.

"Can we not mention that last bit?" Her father said.

"Ahh, Conri, stop being so uptight." My father smirked at him.

"Sorry, I'm not as open about that as you are."

Auri slumped back in her chair, her magic quieted again, but her pulse still wild through the bond. I felt it—the guilt, the anger, the exhaustion. Everything she hadn't said filled the space between us.

My father poured another drink, pretending to be calm. Her father looked like he'd aged a decade in the last hour, but I didn't care about either of them.

I only cared about her.

Whatever came next—truths, secrets, kings, or wars—I'd face it with her.

I reached for her hand. "We're done here for now. She needs time and space," I told them. "Let's get out of here," I said softly to her.

She nodded, silent.

And when she finally stood, I could feel the weight of every word unsaid between us.

CHAPTER 2

I hadn't realized how cold I was until Zane closed the door behind us. The air inside the hall hit my skin, and my hands trembled. The shadows went quiet, but I felt them pulsing under my skin, slow and steady.

Zane's hand rested at the small of my back as we walked. I didn't know if he was guiding me or holding me together. Maybe both.

The Duchess waited at the end of the hall. Her gown pooled like silver water around her feet, her fingers gripping the fabric tight enough to wrinkle it. When she saw us, she didn't speak. She just watched. Her face appeared calm, but her eyes told a different story. Worry. Fear.

Not fear of me. Fear *for* me. That somehow made it worse.

"Come," Zane said quietly, his thumb brushing against my wrist.

I nodded, but no words came out. My thoughts kept spinning too fast to catch. Nosferatu. Shapeshifters. My father's secrets. My mother's murder. Every truth he dropped in that room clawed at the next until I couldn't tell which one hurt most.

I kept seeing her in flashes. My mother, standing in every memory I had, alive and smiling. Now all I could picture was her dying in front of him.

My chest tightened. The shadows stirred again.

Zane noticed. Of course he did. "Breathe," he whispered, low enough that only I could hear. "You're safe."

Safe.

The word didn't feel real anymore.

We reached the corridor that led to his chambers. The air there felt heavier, quieter. Behind us, faint voices drifted through the stone—the

Duke, the General, and the soft tremor of the Duchess's reply—but they were only ghosts to me now.

Zane opened the door and stepped aside. His eyes never left me.

Inside, the fire burned low. The same room I fell asleep in hours ago now felt like another world. I sank onto the edge of the bed, my hands shaking against my knees.

"I don't know what to do with any of this," I whispered.

Zane crouched in front of me, the same way he had in the study. "Then don't," he said softly. "Not tonight."

His voice stayed steady, though his eyes looked as tired as I felt.

The shadows brushed at my boots, then melted back into the floorboards. I watched them disappear, too drained to be afraid.

Maybe they didn't have to be scary. Perhaps they were the only thing left that listened to me.

Zane sat beside me, our thighs pressing into each other. He was silent, and it was everything I needed in that moment. Words felt heavy right now, too heavy to hold. He brushed his thumb along the back of my hand, warmth crawling up my arm, steadying me in a way breathing hadn't.

"You did nothing wrong," he said.

"I nearly killed him."

"He's alive," Zane said. "And you didn't lose control. You stopped yourself."

Barely, I thought.

Esme's voice slid through my mind, calm but threaded with irritation. *"Barely, yes. But you did. You should give yourself credit for that instead of spiraling again."*

I let out a quiet breath. *"You always pick the best times to talk, you know that?"*

"Would you rather I let you drown in self-pity?"

"Maybe a minute longer," I muttered.

Zane glanced at me, one brow raised. "Esme?"

I nodded. "Apparently, I'm supposed to stop spiraling."

He huffed a quiet laugh. "She's not wrong."

"Thank Zane for me," Esme said, *"at least one of you listens to reason."*

"Don't encourage her," I said.

Zane leaned back against the headboard, his expression softening. "It's a little late for that."

"He's learning," Esme added.

I almost laughed. Almost.

The weight in my chest eased just enough to breathe again. The fire popped in the hearth, warm light spilling across the room. Zane drew me closer until my head rested against his shoulder.

"I don't think I can sleep," I murmured.

"Then don't," he said. "Just rest."

Esme's voice faded, her tone softer now. *"Rest, little shadow. You'll need your strength when morning comes."*

"Great... moved from little rider to little shadow."

"You're welcome for the gift."

"I am not thanking you. You gave me a gift that I... I don't even understand."

"You will understand, soon enough."

Whatever the hell that meant.

Zane slid back to the top of the bed and pulled me next to him, his arm wrapped around my shoulders. The heat from the fireplace reached the bed in slow gusts. For a while, neither of us spoke. I watched the glow of the hearth catch on the gold strands in his hair, turning them almost copper.

"Do you think about the future?" I whispered.

He shifted, resting his chin lightly on the top of my head. "Only when I have to."

"That's comforting," I muttered.

"I'm serious." His voice was calm. "I don't waste time dreaming about what I can't control. The world's already done a good job of reminding me how fast everything burns."

"So, you don't hope for anything?"

He exhaled, slowly. "Hope is dangerous. It makes people weak. But I do plan."

"For what?"

"For us."

I turned slightly, just enough to see his face. The firelight caught his eyes, darker than his normal pale blue. "Us?"

He gave a faint half-smile. "I told you. Whatever comes next, we face it together."

"You make it sound like a battle."

"It will be." His tone softened, but the certainty in it made my stomach twist. "Everything is, in the end."

I traced my fingers over the scar on his forearm, the one that cut jaggedly across his skin. "You really believe that?"

He looked at me for a long moment. "I believe peace is a lie we tell ourselves between wars. I just plan to make the next one worth surviving."

That wasn't what I expected to hear. It wasn't romantic. But somehow, it felt like a promise.

I leaned closer, my forehead pressing into him. "You think we'll make it?"

He didn't hesitate. "We'll make sure of it."

There was something in the way he said that—not fragile or naive, but like he'd already decided he'd burn the world if he had to. The thought should have scared me, but it didn't.

The room went quiet again except for the crackle of the burning wood. I didn't know how long we'd been lying there, but the tension in my chest finally began to ease, like someone lifting a stone off of it.

Zane's thumb drew slow circles on my arm. "Your brain is thinking too hard," he murmured.

"I'm allowed to think," I said, eyes half open.

"Not when it sounds like a lightning storm in there."

I smiled faintly. "You can't hear that?"

"I can feel it." His tone softened. "Your leg is bouncing a million miles an hour."

"Maybe that's just how my brain works."

"Or maybe you just like ignoring good advice."

I rolled onto my side, facing him. "Whose advice? Yours?"

He grinned. "I've been told I give excellent advice."

"By whom?"

"Myself."

A laugh escaped before I could stop it. It startled me a little.

"There it is," he said quietly. "Proof you can still do it."

"You sound proud of yourself."

"Obviously." He brushed a loose strand of hair away from my face. "I take my victories where I can get them."

"Victory? Making me laugh counts as one?"

"It's a start," he said. "Though I was hoping for something more dramatic. Maybe a full grin, or tears of joy, or spontaneous applause."

"You're ridiculous."

"I've been called worse."

"Like what?"

He thought for a second, his smile turning crooked. "Annoying. Overconfident. Dangerously handsome."

I snorted. "Who told you that last one? Yourself again?"

"Actually, that one might have been Arkin."

That made me laugh harder. "Of course it was."

He looked far too pleased with himself. "See? I knew mentioning my brother would do it."

"You're impossible," I said, still smiling.

He leaned closer, his voice a whisper against my ear. "And yet, you've kept me around."

I met his eyes. "For now."

He gave me a mock-offended look, then chuckled. "Harsh, Anam Cara. Very harsh."

"What's your favorite color?"

"That... was... random."

"We need random right now."

"Emerald, like your eyes, when you aren't seething death."

I pulled my head back to look at him. "You do know your eyes change when you're feeling murderous—"

"They do?" he cut me off.

"Yeah... to a deep indigo color."

"Hmm... okay, what is your favorite color?"

"Teal." I didn't have to think a second for that.

He brushed a thumb along my cheek, tracing a loose strand of hair back. "Teal suits you," he said. "Like the sea before a storm."

"That sounds dramatic."

"You are dramatic."

I laughed, low and quiet. "You're one to talk."

"Fair," he said, voice softening. "But I think I like your kind of dramatic better."

"Why?"

"It keeps things interesting."

He shifted, turning on his side to me. His arm stayed under my shoulders, pulling me closer until I fit against him. The firelight flickered over the ceiling, warm and lazy.

"What is your favorite subject at Sandorg?" I asked.

He let out a faint groan. "That's cruel."

"Come on," I said, smiling. "Pick one."

"Sparring," he said after a pause. "I'm able to get out a lot of frustration in there."

"That tracks."

"And yours?"

I hesitated. "Flight maneuvers, although I feel like I am toeing death's door every time."

He laughed softly. "Of course you do. You like living on the wild side."

"Don't mock me."

"I'm not," he said. "I think it's perfect."

For a long moment, neither of us spoke. The fire crackled, and his breathing grew slower, steadier. My thoughts felt heavy again, but not in the same way as before.

"You know," he murmured, eyes still closed, "if you ever wanted to fly away from all of this, I'd take you wherever you wanted."

"Even if I wanted to go hide in some no-name village where no one knows us."

"Especially then."

He laughed again, low and quiet, the sound vibrating through his chest. His hand moved absently up and down my arm, tracing lazy lines that felt more like a promise than comfort.

The warmth from the fire blurred the edges of the room. My eyelids felt heavy, my body sinking into his. The bond between us pulsed with calmness.

"You're safe, Auri," he whispered.

I wanted to answer, to tell him I knew, but the words caught somewhere between thought and dream. The last thing I felt was his thumb moving up and down my side. Then the world slipped away.

CHAPTER 3

The light filtered through the windows, lighting the room. Zane's arms still wrapped around me tightly, as if I would have disappeared in the night. I started to move, and he pulled me tighter, if that was possible.

"We don't have to get up—"

"Maybe you don't, but I have to use the restroom," I said.

He let out a laugh. "I guess I'll let ya."

His arms loosened around me, letting me get up.

The floor was cold, and the floorboards creaked as I got up.

"I wish I had more control of my magic. I could warm the floors without setting fire."

"Wouldn't that be nice?"

"Or I could use my shadows to carry me…"

He laughed. "What do you think about going to a priestess while we are here?"

He couldn't see my eyes widen while I was in the chambers. I wasn't even sure how to respond. I hadn't really thought of it. We discussed doing it, but never specified when.

"You don't have to say yes…"

"You caught me off guard. I hadn't really thought about it. What does it entail?"

"Well, we go to a priestess; we have them here in the palace. They perform a ceremony during which we both drink a tincture. They perform an aura reading and then bless it. At the end, they do a chant, and we receive matching tattoos—"

"Wait… *what?*"

"I didn't figure you knew that. The location and design are decided by fate and the Gods."

"Oh…"

He was always full of surprises. I never really thought of getting a tattoo. It wasn't something I saw many women having, aside from Shapeshifters and Drusearons. Well fuck. I was a Shapeshifter. Lovely little news my dad dropped on me. I hadn't even really had time to process it. I wasn't even sure what the hell to think either.

I stood there staring at my reflection in the mirror, trying to decide whether I looked like someone ready for a holy ritual or someone who'd just survived a small war. My hair was a disaster, my robe was crooked, and my thoughts were a mess.

A priestess ceremony. Matching tattoos. Fated markings.

The idea made my stomach twist—not because I didn't want it, but because I wasn't sure I was ready for the Gods to carve fate into my skin like it was permanent ink on parchment.

Esme's voice flickered through my mind, lazy and smug. *"It's already permanent, little shadow. The bond existed long before the mark."*

"Thank you for that comforting thought," I muttered.

"You're welcome."

Zane's laughter drifted from the other room. "Are you arguing with Esme again?"

"Maybe," I called back.

"She's probably not wrong, you know."

"She usually isn't," I said, walking back into the bedroom. "That's the problem."

He was sitting up now, the blanket low around his waist, his hair a tangle of gold and sleep. Gods, he looked too good for this early in the morning.

He smirked. "So? What do you think? Priestess or no priestess?"

"I don't know," I said honestly. "It's a big step. Magical permanence, matching tattoos, fate choosing where to ink them—kind of a lot before breakfast."

"True," he said, pretending to think. "We could get breakfast first. Maybe pancakes, then eternal bond."

I rolled my eyes. "Romantic."

He grinned. "I try."

I climbed back onto the bed, folding my legs under me. "Where did your aunt and uncle's marks appear?"

"Their inner bicep."

I raised an eyebrow. "What was it?"

"It was an ivy wrapped around a moon... which I guess makes sense after learning that the mating bond is tied to the Werewolf."

"I still can't believe I am part Werewolf, part Witch, and who knows what my mother was."

"That was a lot. I think whatever fate decides for us, you will like."

"Questionable."

"Definitely."

I laughed, shaking my head. "You really think the Gods care where they put them?"

"I think the Gods have a sense of humor," he said. "So, probably somewhere inconvenient."

"Like my forehead."

"Or your left butt cheek."

"Zane!" I threw a pillow at him, and he caught it easily, laughing.

He tossed it back, softer this time. "What? You said inconvenient."

I pressed my lips together, trying not to smile, and failed miserably. The laughter broke the heaviness that hung between us since last night. For a moment, it was just us—no shadows, no bloodlines, no politics. Just two people talking about divine tattoos.

He reached for me, fingers curling gently around my wrist. "Where would you want it, if you could choose?"

I thought for a moment. "Maybe here," I said, touching my shoulder. "Something small. Hidden."

"Hidden suits you," he said quietly, "but the Gods like to show off."

"Of course they do."

He brushed his thumb along the edge of my collarbone. "I'd still like to see it."

My breath caught, and for a second, the humor faded into something softer.

"Zane," I said, my voice quieter. "If we do this, it's real. Not just the bond we feel—it's visible. Permanent."

He nodded. "That's the point."

"Even if things change?"

His expression softened. "They'll change. That's what life does. But you'll still be mine, and I'll still be yours. Everything else, we figure out."

He said it so simply, like the world could be that easy. Maybe with him, it was.

I leaned forward, pressing my forehead against his. "You make it sound simple."

He smiled. "That's my charm."

"Charm is a strong word."

He laughed again, low and rough. "You wound me."

"Good. Keeps you humble."

I let the silence stretch a little longer, my head still resting against his. The thought of a mark chosen by fate no longer felt so terrifying. Maybe because I already carried something I didn't choose and survived that, too.

"Alright," I said finally. "We'll do it."

His eyes opened, slow, like he wasn't sure he'd heard me right. "You mean it?"

"I do."

A slow grin spread across his face. "You're sure? No take-backs once the Gods start chanting."

"Pretty sure that's how ceremonies work," I said, smiling. "Besides, if I'm stuck with you for eternity, might as well make it official."

"Official and tattooed," he said, "excellent."

Before I could answer, someone knocked on the door. Zane groaned. "Already?"

"Apparently, the universe refuses to let you bask in victory."

"Come in," he called out. A young attendant stepped through, carrying a tray balanced with fruit, bread, and something that smelled like cinnamon and butter.

"Breakfast from the Duchess, my lord," she said, bowing her head before setting the tray on the table near the hearth. "She sends her regards... and her reminder that morning meetings wait for no one."

Zane winced. "Wonderful. Tell her I adore her, but her timing is cruel."

The attendant smiled politely and slipped out again. I climbed off the bed to look at the tray.

"She sent enough to feed half your siblings."

"Which means I'll have to share," he said, following me. "Tragic."

I poured tea while he stole half the bread.

"Do you always eat like someone's about to attack your plate?" I asked.

"Yes," he said around a mouthful, "because in this family, someone usually does."

I laughed. "You're incorrigible."

"I prefer efficient."

He poured honey into two cups and handed me one. "So, when do you want to go see the priestess?"

"Later today," I said, surprising myself with how steady it sounded. "Before I lose my nerve."

He smiled, softer this time. "Then later today."

"Can I come? This should be fun," Esme asked.

"What? No. This is personal.""I literally hear your thoughts... every single dirty thought. He watched us get branded together."

"You can't fly into the city, and you will be able to hear every one of my thoughts, remember?"

I heard her grumble through the bond.

We ate in companionable silence for a few minutes. The smell of cinnamon mixed with the faint scent of smoke from the fire. For a rare, quiet moment, the palace felt almost peaceful.

Then another knock broke it.

Zane set his cup down, sighing. "If that's another breakfast tray, I'm moving out."

A deeper voice answered through the door. "Lord Zane, the Duke requests your presence in his study. Only yours."

Zane's brows pulled together. He stood, slow and deliberate, and wiped his fingers on a napkin like he needed the movement to think.

"Only mine?" he called back.

"Yes, my lord," the voice replied. "Immediately." Footsteps retreated down the hall.

Zane let out a low breath, almost a growl, then rolled his shoulders as if shrugging on armor. "Well, that sounds promising."

I tried to keep my voice light. "Sounds ominous."

"Probably just wants to talk about last night," he said, but his tone was too careful.

He reached for his tunic, which was draped over the chair. His fingers hesitated on the collar, then slid it on.

I set my cup down and stood, folding my arms to stop fidgeting. "Do you want me to come anyway?"

He shook his head, stepping closer. "No. It's better if you stay here. Whatever he says, you don't need to hear it yet."

My mouth opened, but he caught my wrist before I could argue. His thumb traced a slow circle against my skin. "I'll be fine," he said quietly. "I always am."

I searched his face. The smile he gave me looked like one of his father's knives—sharp, polished, dangerous.

"I'll hold you to that," I said.

"You'd better," he murmured, then bent to press a quick kiss to my temple. "Finish your tea. I won't be long."

He left before I could answer. The door clicked shut behind him.

The room felt different without him. The fire suddenly grew louder, and the tray of food was too large for one person. Esme hummed at the edge of my mind, not words, just a low, restless note. I sat back on the bed, staring at the lessened steam rising from my cup. The warmth had already started to fade.

I sat there for a long time, staring at the tray we'd half emptied. His cup still sat where he'd left it, a faint lip mark on the rim. Stupid, the things I noticed when he wasn't here.

My stomach twisted.

He said it like it was nothing—I'll be fine—but I'd learned how easily those words cracked under pressure. I knew his father would never hurt him, and I was being irrational with my fears. I could feel the faint hum of our bond, still warm, but faint enough to make me wonder what he was thinking.

"You're pacing again," Esme said, her tone half scold, half sigh.

I hadn't realized I had stood and started moving until she said it. *"I'm not pacing."*

"You are. Back and forth. Like a caged animal."

"I don't like that he didn't tell me what his father wanted."

"He didn't know."

"He did. I felt it." I ran a hand through my hair and sank back onto the bed. *"He just didn't want me to."*

"Sometimes that's protection, not deceit."

"Or both," I muttered.

Esme's silence after that said enough.

I leaned back on my elbows, staring at the ceiling. Shadows shifted softly along the corners of my eyes, responding to my pulse like they were waiting for orders I didn't have. They'd been different since the night everything changed—quieter, but aware, almost alive.

I stretched a hand toward the nearest one. It moved closer, like a curious cat sniffing at my fingers. Maybe I should've been afraid of it, but I wasn't. Not anymore.

"What are you?" I whispered.

It pulsed once and vanished within me.

I sank deeper into the bed. My chest felt heavy, like there was too much air and not enough oxygen. I hated waiting. Waiting meant thinking, and thinking meant replaying every word my father said, every flicker of unease on Zane's face.

The idea of fate carving something permanent into my skin felt smaller than the truth I already carried. I'd been marked long before any ceremony.

Marked by blood. By power. By him.

Esme's voice hummed low, a vibration more than words. *"He's safe."*

"You sound sure."

"You'd feel it if he wasn't."

I wanted to believe her. I closed my eyes and visualized the bond that was between us. Distant. Steady. Strong.

CHAPTER 4

Zane

I hated leaving her side, but I wasn't going to disobey my father's order to come without her. The walk to my father's study felt longer than usual, maybe because every step echoed, perhaps because I knew what waited behind the door.

Guards nodded as I passed, their eyes shifting just enough to remind me they'd seen what happened last night. The smell of oil and iron lingered in the corridor—someone had polished armor recently. Nothing in this place ever dulled for long.

I stopped outside the carved doors. They were already cracked open. Of course, he knew I was coming. My father never summoned without knowing the exact second you'd arrive.

Inside, the study was heavy with morning light. Maps covered the walls, ribbons of parchment crisscrossed with ink and old scars of spilled wax. The fire hadn't been lit yet, and the air carried that chill that made even truth sound brittle.

He stood near the desk, back to me, hands clasped behind him. The black of his coat swallowed the sunlight, a shadow that didn't need magic to dominate a room.

"Close the door," he said.

I did.

He didn't turn right away. "You slept?"

"Some."

"And she?"

"She slept."

Finally, he faced me. His eyes mirrored mine, just colder. "Good. You'll need her rested."

The phrasing set something sharp under my ribs. "Is there a reason I'm here alone?"

"Yes. Because this conversation isn't for her ears—"

"She is stronger than you think—" I cut him off.

"She nearly killed her father uncontrollably."

"Speaking of, where is he?"

"In his quarters."

"And my siblings? Should they see him? The ones who you let believe he killed their uncles, my uncles. Auri's rapist... Yeah, I'm aware. Painfully fucking aware."

His silence said everything in that moment. I could feel my pulse going faster, heat rushing to my cheeks. I immediately knew I needed to put up more of a block so that Auri couldn't sense it. I couldn't block her completely, as that would worry her more.

"I hate that you had to find that out, but it is good for you to know."

"And yet, you didn't kill him yourself?"

"No. I believed him when he denied it. I thought they had the wrong person. It wasn't until Conri shared the memory with me, after they—"

"He did what?"

"Yes, Conri can read memories, but he can also project memories. Very few people know about that, and that little gift of his isn't tied to his dragon. That is a Cavendish affinity, I'm afraid."

"Wow. He did that little mind-reading trick to me, and it wasn't fun."

"So, he said. Speaking of which, build your fucking shields better, Zane. Thank the Gods, we had been working—"

"Yeah, about that. What the fuck?"

"Tone, son... When he came to talk to me following their deaths, we had a good conversation after he did his little mind game. I've been questioning the King's motives for a while. I had heard rumors. He confirmed them. We decided to work together."

"And? When were you going to tell *me*? Back to what I said earlier, you have him in a home, where our siblings think he is the villain."

"I will be meeting with each of them this morning after you, informing them that he was not involved in their death. I will not be sharing details. That story isn't mine to share. And I *will not* force Auriella to share that ever again."

"Appreciate that, father."

In that moment, I knew my father didn't want harm to her. I never wanted her to have to share that part of her again, unless that was what she wanted. When she told me, I felt an overwhelming urge to set the entire world on fire. I wanted to bring my uncle back from the dead, to rip his heart out, to inflict the pain he deserved.

"On to some other pressing matters," he started, then he ran his hand through his hair. Something he did when he didn't want to have the difficult conversation he was about to have.

"I don't think you and Auriella should return to Sandorg—"

"No. Respectfully, no, unless you have a damned convincing reason, we are returning."

"Zane. How do you think she will be received when she returns with shadows swirling her feet?"

"I don't know, but she can't stay hidden either. I can't ask that of her."

"You're the marquess. You're the next in line. You should be here with me, learning, should anything happen to me."

"I don't want that. I never have. Arkin will make a suitable duke when the time comes."

He scoffed, his jaw tightened, and I knew what came out of my mouth was a half-life. I did think Arkin had potential, but my father needed to be sterner. I didn't want the politics and everything that came with that. I wanted to live a simple life with my wife. Did I know she was going to be a rider? No. Nor did I know her bloodline was complicated. I didn't care about any of that. Her being a rider already meant our life wasn't going to be as simple as I'd hoped.

"I've heard you tell me that for years, Zane. This was meant for you, this is your legacy—"

"But it's not. It's what I was born into, but I don't believe this is what the Gods have planned for me. I can't believe that. I have never been interested in the political bullshit like you wanted me to be. I'm just not."

"I hear you loud and clear."

"Do you? Is there anything else?"

"We could spend hours talking about everything, but you just said you don't want to hear it. It boils down to, I'm worried about you, about her."

"I have her, and I will not hesitate to end a life if hers is threatened."

"Zane—"

"I speak the truth, father. Before I go, I should also add that we will be seeing a priestess later today—""ZANE."

"I'm letting you know," I said.

"You *know* how important that is. We should be there, her father should be there."

"It's not a marriage—"

"It's more important than one," he said, cutting me off.

I knew that, but I had forgotten its true importance. Marriage was important, it was holy, and the ceremony was beautiful. Some families had ceremonies that lasted for days, whilst others were shorter. A mating bond ceremony was truly a very rare event. Something I never understood the why of until last night. I didn't know anyone other than my aunt and uncle.

I didn't know why the fates chose me for her. I didn't feel anywhere near worthy of her. She had no idea some of the demons I buried down. She had no idea that for the two years before Sandorg, I was the one who slayed traitors. Those bodies were on my hands. My hands clenched around the armrests of the chair.

"How about I talk with her and let her decide? I already shocked her by telling her there was a tattoo involved."

"At least you told her that part. And yes, please let us know asap. Your mother and I would really enjoy going. I also know it would mean a great deal to her father. We don't need the siblings, if you or she doesn't want."

I left the study with the taste of his words copper on my tongue. The door closed behind me with the soft click that meant business was done. The corridor swallowed the sound.

Guards glanced up as I passed. No questions. Their faces were a map of last night—tired, a little thin with curiosity. I kept my head down. The castle breathed the same as always: oil, polishing cloth, the faint sour smell of old wine.

The bond hummed, a thread I could feel even without thinking. Warm where hers still was, duller where my restraint sat. She was safe. That steadied me more than any command from my father.

I moved through the wing that smelled of cedar and old maps. Light cut across the floor in hard, straight lines. I remembered a winter when the snow blanketed everything, and we burned the bodies at dawn. I remembered the sound of rope and the way a man's eyes rolled when he knew the end had come. I killed them because the orders came and because the orders made sense to me in a way prayers never had.

They lived in me, quiet and patient. Every man I'd executed for treason still had a place in my memory, filed neatly under necessary. Those nights were the ones that taught me the truth about choices. They taught me the weight of keeping someone alive and the price of letting someone die.

I slowly walked, not out of hesitation, but because the stillness helped me think. My father wanted me to stay, to learn, to lead. He called it legacy. I called it a gilded cage. The title of marquess was another chain polished until it shone. What he didn't understand was that I'd already spent enough years serving causes that didn't deserve it.

It scared me sometimes—not that I'd kill again, but that I'd do it without thinking twice if it meant keeping her alive. The bond pulsed faintly, reminding me she was still safe. The warmth steadied me, even as my thoughts darkened.

I turned down the corridor, where sunlight slanted through tall windows. Outside, knights drilled in the yard, their swords catching light in rhythmic arcs. I watched them for a moment, admiring their precision and discipline.

There was a time I'd believed in that. In discipline and order, and clean lines between right and wrong. I'd learned better. Instead, it's a huge grey area. Sometimes it wasn't right, nor was it wrong. If someone came for her, I wouldn't hesitate. The only thing I questioned was how much I'd enjoy it. The thought should have unsettled me. It didn't.

By the time I reached our door, her lingering scent hit me. It calmed something profound in my chest. I pushed the door open quietly. The fire burned low, painting the room in gold and shadow. She wasn't here, but our bond told me she was safe.

I sat on the edge of the bed. The sheets still held her warmth. My father wanted heirs and politics. I wanted her. Simple as that. Legacy didn't matter if she wasn't part of it.

I leaned forward, elbows on my knees, hands clasped. The world could call me a marquess, a warrior, a monster, and it didn't fucking matter. It changed nothing about who I'd become or what I was willing to do for her. For us.

CHAPTER 5

"Where are you?" he said through our bond.

"Oh, Aeliana insisted I come to her chambers to hang out."

"Mmm. I'm sure she is giving you all the dirt."

"Maybe. Maybe not. You will never know, but she was just asked to speak with your father. I'm coming back now."

"So much to discuss."

First, Zane was pulled into his father's study. Now Aeliana? What was happening? I also wondered where my father was after last night. Was he here, in the palace?

My mind was racing with every thought, one after another rushing in. My chest began to feel tight, and my pulse started to pick up. Anxiety. That bitch was a damn bully. Aeliana's room was down another hall at the end of the hallway. This place was so large, it would take time before one remembered where everything and everyone was. Shadows encircled my feet, trailing up my legs. They felt colder, like they were trying to suck in air too.

"My little shadow, you need to breathe. You control it, it doesn't control you."

"I know... but it's so fucking hard."

"It's not supposed to be easy," Esme said, her voice quieter now, less bite and more breath. *"If it were, everyone would be walking around masters of their powers."*

I took a shaky inhale. The corridors felt longer than they had five minutes ago. The tapestries lining the walls rippled with the air I didn't realize I'd stirred. I tried to focus on something simple—my steps. The soft scuff of my boots on the stone floor. The faint warmth of the magic lamps humming above.

Each sound pulled me back from the edge.

"Better," Esme murmured. *"Keep going."*

"I'm trying."

"Try harder. The last thing we need is a hallway full of terrified servants."

A huff of air slipped past my lips, almost a laugh. *"You're such a motivator."*

"I prefer realist."

I reached the main corridor that led to our wing. The closer I got, the stronger the bond pulsed, steady and low like a heartbeat that wasn't mine. It calmed me more than breathing ever could.

The shadows that curled around my calves thinned, retreating with each step until only a faint grey lingered at my feet. I didn't banish them. They just eased back on their own, as if listening.

"That's it," Esme said. *"You're learning. Power doesn't always need a fight. Sometimes it just needs you to stop panicking long enough to listen."*

"Noted."

The door to our chambers came into view, dark wood carved with the same crest I'd touched the night before. The sight made my chest tighten again—but this time it wasn't fear.

It was relief.

"He's waiting for you," Esme said.

"I can feel him."

"Then stop talking to me and go to him."

I almost smiled. *"Bossy."*

"Always," she said.

I paused outside the door. The bond pulsed, warm and inviting, and the tension that lived under my skin since I left Aeliana's room finally loosened.

"Okay," I whispered, resting my hand on the latch. "Everything will be alright."

The door gave a quiet groan when I pushed it open. Warm air met me first, tinged with cedar smoke and the faint spice of the tea we'd left untouched.

He sat on the edge of the bed, elbows on his knees, head tipped forward. The firelight painted his hair gold at the edges and shadowed everything else.

He didn't look up right away, but the bond flared the moment I stepped inside. The steady pulse of his presence wrapped around me, low and strong, like a hand at my spine.

"You're back," he said.

"I told you I was coming."

His mouth curved faintly, but the smile never reached his eyes.

I crossed the room slowly, trying to read the silence. Something in it felt different—thicker, heavier. The kind of quiet that follows hard truths.

"Your father called Aeliana in," I said. "She was nervous."

"She'll be fine," he said, voice low. "He wants to clear the air with everyone. You, me, my siblings. It's... overdue."

I stopped a few steps away from him. "You sound like that meeting wasn't pleasant."

He lifted his gaze then, and the look in his eyes made my chest tighten. Calm on the surface, storm underneath.

"It wasn't bad," he said after a beat. "Just... layered."

"Layered?"

He exhaled slowly through his nose. "He and I see the world differently. Always have."

I eased closer until my knees brushed his. "And how do you see it?"

He didn't answer right away. His hand came up instead, resting against the side of my thigh, thumb tracing slow circles through the fabric. That slight motion said more than words could.

"I see it in shades of grey. He still wants to believe in white and black," he said, finally.

The honesty in his tone caught me off guard.

"Grey's honest," I said quietly.

His eyes met mine again, the edge softening for the first time. "It's messier."

"Life usually is."

We stayed like that, close but barely touching, the fire snapping behind us. I wanted to ask what else was said. What his father warned him about, but something in his expression told me not to. He needed quiet more than questions.

I slid onto the bed beside him. The mattress dipped under our combined weight, and his arm came around my waist without hesitation. Our bond pulsed warm again. Familiar. Home.

I rested my head against his shoulder. "You're thinking too loud, now," I murmured.

"Can't help it."

We sat for quite a bit of time in silence, both of us wanting to say something more, but neither of us wanting to ruin the moment.

"My father... he wants us to... he doesn't want us to return—"

"What? Why?"

"He feels we will—you will—be a target. Your powers will scare people."

"Oh..." I wasn't even sure what to say. My mind never shut up, and it went blank. I hadn't thought about that. When my powers exploded, his father looked at me like I was Marzana reincarnated. My father tried to pretend he was fine, but I knew he was terrified in that moment. He was great at masking, but I knew him the best.

"I'm not afraid of you, Auri."

"Are you sure?"

"If you only knew what I've done... and I know you would never intentionally hurt me—"

"But I'm not in control—"

"You are, my love... You will learn to be." He pulled me into him and tightened his arms around me.

"I'm terrified of myself..."

"You and I, we are a team."

"*And me...*" Esme purred.

That made me giggle a little bit. "Esme said not to forget about her."

"Of course, I wouldn't forget."

"What did you tell your father?" I asked, almost afraid of what he would say. Going to Sandorg was a dream, and I was a rider after all. I couldn't just quit. Could I?

"I told him that wasn't happening, we would be returning."

"Good."

"There is more—"

"Of course there is..."

"I let him know that we would be going to the priestess this evening..."

"Oh?"

"And... he would like for my mother, your father, and himself to attend?"

"Oh..."

"That was one too many *Ohs*."

"I am trying to process what your dad wanted, my own fear, my... Gods, everything is just complicated.""We can tell them no."

"No... no... We should... yeah... We should invite them. I don't know much about this, but they do, and I think this is something special our parents should be a part of. I just..." My words faltered.

I was thinking of my mom and how she should be a part of this. Zane just let the silence hang, letting me process everything. Letting everything sink in for me.

"I just always pictured my mom being a part of me getting married—"

"We aren't getting married, but we can—"

"No, I wasn't saying that. Not that I don't want that one day, I just mean I know this is important like that, and she should have been here for it."

"I'm sorry, Auri."

"It is what it is... your parents shouldn't miss this. I am sure your mom will be enthusiastic to be a part of this.""She will, very much so."

He kissed my head, leaving his lips pressed to my head. Electricity shot through me from his lips to my toes. The shadows at my feet went from light to dark in seconds. They swirled around my legs. They weren't cold this time, but warm.

"We should shower and then let our parents know. By then, my father should have finished breaking the news."

"Mmm, a shower sounds so very lovely."

"And that's my cue to shield up... ya'll are—something."

"I am sure you have some dragon friend that suits you."

"I do, actually."

"Oh, we are so talking about that later."

"Maybe," she purred, and then the bond between us dimmed to barely flickering.

CHAPTER 6

Zane grabbed my hand and pulled me to my feet. He pulled me to the bathing chamber, and I trailed behind him. I felt a tingle between my thighs, and warmth filled my stomach. My chest beat harder and faster with anticipation, building with each step I took. Electricity coursed through my hand and up my arm.

Once we reached the bathing room, he pulled me into him, gripping my face with both of his hands. He pulled me into a fiery, passionate kiss. In that moment, every single worry fled, every fear gone. All I felt was Zane, the love between us. We feverishly kissed, our tongues swirling around each other. Every couple of seconds, he would draw my tongue in, sucking on it.

I felt the warmth between my legs, tingling more with each suck. He pulled his tongue out and pulled my bottom lip into his mouth, gently sucking with teeth, slightly grazing my lip. Gods. It felt like the first time every time we kissed.

He let go of my face and reached down to pull my shirt off. I gripped his tunic, pulling it up. I rubbed my fingers slowly down his chest, taking in every moment, every detail of him.

"Let them free," I demanded of him.

"So bossy," he breathed.

He pressed his forehead against mine so tenderly before I heard his wings pop freely behind him. He started kissing me along my neck, moving down my body, slowly. I stood with my head tilted up, eyes closed. Every kiss and bite left me wetter and wetter between my legs. He circled his tongue around my nipple before drawing it in and sucking on it. I relished every single second of him worshipping my body.

He kissed me down my stomach, then he knelt before me. He looked at me, our eyes locking. Every part of me felt like I was embers burning after a wildfire. I reached down with one finger and did lazy circles on his wing. His entire body shuddered under my touch. He pulled at my pants, pulling them off of me. I moved my other hand to his wing to touch the other side. Once he pulled my pants to my ankles, he lifted each leg to pull them off.

He moved to a stand, and I reached between us to unbutton his pants. He reached back and gripped a handful of my hair along with my neck, tilting my neck back some for him to gently suck on me. I pushed at his pants, wanting him free. I wanted to actually feel him, not the bulge through fabric.

"Now... there aren't shields on this room..." he purred into my mind.

"I guess we are about to see how quiet we actually can be..."

"Un-fucking-likely."

He was probably right. I was already lowly moaning, and he was already letting little growls slip out.

His pants slid down his legs, and he quickly stepped out. His cock touching my lower stomach instantly made me moan and feel wetter. He reached between us, right between my thighs.

"Fuck, I love how fucking wet you get for me."

"I love feeling you inside of me... so fuck me like there is no tomorrow."

He turned me around and gently pushed my back forward. He pulled my waist even closer. I could feel his cock pressed against my ass. "Step back onto my feet," he demanded.

I stepped back, my heels onto his feet.

"Good girl," he growled.

He bent his knees to lower himself, while also gripping my ass to pull me a little higher. He let go of one hand and reached between us. He took a finger and did the slowest circles around my clit. Teasing me. Bringing me closer and closer to the edge.

"I'm already dripping wet, Zane. Fuck I want you in me... Now!"

"I'm just enjoying the view."

He grabbed onto himself and pressed himself into me. Slowly. I wanted him faster, deeper, harder. I knew I wouldn't last long. It felt like my clit was on fire, and he was the gas that fueled it.

"Gods. Fuck me, Zane. Grip me and have your way."

"So impatient..."

He moved deeper into me, quicker. I let out a whimper. He was letting out a low, deep moan, and damn, that did something to me. He reached forward, grabbed a handful of my hair, and thrust faster. It felt intoxicating. My entire body quivered.

"Auri... I'm... Fuck me... I'm gonna cum."

He moved faster, thrusting into me deeper. He let out a low guttural moan, and I lost every ounce of control I had. He controlled me. I let out a moan before I pulled my hand to my face and bit the side of my hand, riding the orgasm out. Shadows erupted from me, swirling around us like a tornado. He was still moving sinfully in and out, and my body felt like it was having aftershocks.

He let go of my hair, still holding me close to him. He dragged a finger down my spine, leaving my entire body to shiver. Gods. It was an incredibly intense sensation that I hadn't felt before. I took in a deep breath, closed my eyes, and went inside my mind and pulled the shadows back in. I felt them. In that moment, it was like I went whole again. I didn't realize that they created a void.

He gently pulled out of me, and then quickly pulled me around and into him. He pressed his lips into my forehead, both of us taking in the moment.

"Now, we can actually shower." He growled.

"Hmm, yes. We can do whatever now."

He pulled back and stared at me. His pure blue eyes stared straight into me.

"You really are an addiction, ya know."

"So, you say."

He moved into the shower and turned it on. Like his shower in his chambers at the college, this shower was also enormous. My dad may have been a general, but we definitely didn't live lavishly by any means. We never had a permanent home. We always leased wherever the military sent us.

Zane grabbed my wrist and pulled me into the shower with him. He pulled me into his arms, my back pressed against his chest. He leaned in, breathing into my ear. Goosebumps popped up all over my arms.

"You liked it when I gripped your hair?" he whispered into my ear.

I just nodded my head. He was right. It wasn't something that had ever happened, and Gods, it was such a turn on when he did it.

"Hmm, what else do you like?" He breathed slowly into the nape of my neck.

"I... I guess I don't really know—"

"Mmm, I guess we will find out together."

He grabbed the cloth and lathered some soap into it before washing my body, gently trailing the soap down my body and each leg. Once he stood up, I grabbed it from him and returned the sentiment. There was something wholesome about him caring for me after sex, and me caring for him. I wanted to stay in the shower with him longer. Everything outside of this room was heavy. There was conflict, something I tried hard to avoid. It always felt like it was trying to suck the happiness out of me.

As much as I protested, we left the bathing chambers and got dressed. When Aeliana came to retrieve me earlier, she also brought me some clothing. Included in that were several floor-length dresses. When I raised an eyebrow at her, she insisted that it was appropriate for women to wear dresses unless I was going into combat or flying.

There was one that was dark blue, floor length, with one slit that went up to the knee. I chose that one. I could still access my thigh sheath with that one. I didn't feel like I was in danger here, but I also didn't want to go without any weapons. I knew that my shadows were dangerous and were any weapon that I could imagine them to be, but I didn't even know how to control them yet.

"You will learn my little shadow—" Esme purred down the bond.

"Would you quit calling me that?"

"No."

"Reason?"

"I could call you my little rider, but my little shadow seems more fitting, and I'll do what I want." Then she laughed.

She was impossible. Hilarious—yes, but impossible.

Zane dressed in black leather pants and a light blue tunic top. Even here in his own home, he kept his wings hidden. Actually, now that I think about it, his entire family kept them hidden. Did his siblings even have them?

"So... who first—my mother, your father, or my father?"

"Do I actually have to decide this?"

"I could decide, yes, but I want your input."

"Your mother seems much more approachable."

He let out a loud laugh that lasted several seconds.

"I'm not sure I agree with that, but that was a good one."

"She seems very lovely, you know."

"She is... she is very lovely."

CHAPTER 7

I felt like I needed to have sex with her every single day and never get tired of it. Each time left me wanting more and more. Having her lose control and her power go wild turned me on in a way that I didn't understand. I felt the surge of her power right before her shadows erupted. Every single part of me craved that power and wanted to play with it. Every single second I was around her, my control was tested. She wasn't aware how much magic seeped from her, but I was.

I wanted to tell her about my lack of control, to tell her everything, but I was terrified she would be afraid of me. She would push me away, something I couldn't handle.

We knocked on my mother's study. During the weekdays, she spent her time here. Sometimes she read quietly, other times she was writing letters to the citizens of our province or to other provinces. Without my mother, my father would have surely faltered decades ago.

"Come in," she called.

We pushed through the door, and she lifted her head from the book in her hand. She gave us both a smile, put the book down hastily, and stood up.

"Hey there, I hope you both were able to get some sleep." She moved to stand in front of us.

"We did," I told her, smiling at her.

"Let's sit," she said, motioning to the chairs.

Auri and I sat in the chairs across from the one she previously occupied. She took her seat. She was radiating. My mother had always been beautiful with a contagious smile.

"Have you spoken with Dad this morning?" I asked her.

"I haven't. He has been in his study all morning talking with each of you."

"Well then, this shall be fresh news for you."

"Oh?"I looked over at Auri, grabbed her hand, and held it tightly. I knew she was nervous. She barely knew my mother, yet here we were, telling her we were about to get our bond confirmed.

"Auriella and I have decided that while we were home on leave, we would like to go to the priestess and have our bond—"

"Eeeeee," she squealed, a noise I'm not sure I've heard from her before.

"—and father reminded me how big a deal this was, and we would like for you, him, and her father to join us this evening."

"As well as his siblings... if they want," Auri said. My eyes darted to hers. I didn't think she wanted them to be there.

"Are you sure?" I said, my voice low.

"Yes, I know Aeliana would be devastated if she weren't there, and we couldn't very well invite her and not the others."

My mother clapped giddily, like she was a child getting her most prized wish. "I am elated by this news. Have you arranged a time with the temple?"

"We haven't," I said.

"Can I do all the arrangements for you?" She asked.

I turned my head to look at Auri, unsure of deciding on her behalf.

"Yes, please. It will be one less thing we are worried about," Auri said.

"I will get the time figured out with the priestesses. I assume you want one that favors the God of Freya?"

"No, Wymond," Auri said, with the straightest face.

My mother gasped so hard, I burst into laughter. "She is kidding, mother."

"Am I?" Auri quipped. "Okay, I am. Sorry. I almost said Panki, but then I figured you'd catch that joke."

"Oh, Gods, bless child. You fooled me for a moment."

"Sorry."

"No, you're fine. I just haven't learned your humor yet, like I have Zane's siblings."

"She catches me off guard sometimes, too," I added in. One of my favorite things about her was her sense of humor, which often came when it was needed most.

"I will arrange the time, the celebration afterwards—"

"With a lot of people?" Auri rubbed her finger in circles around her palms, her leg starting to bounce a little faster.

"No. No. Just our family, unless you want to invite friends."

"No." Auri and I both said at the same time.

"Perfect. Only our family. Would you like a dress sent up?"

"Sure, but please not so over the top. Beautiful but simple."

"Anything you want, Auriella," she told her.

"Would you let our siblings know? We have to let her father know, and let father know we decided to make it a family affair," I asked her.

"I can do that, I can also let your father know, too."

"Thank you, ma'am," Auri said to her. I dipped my head, knowing what my mother would say next.

"You can call me Mom or Kalie, short for Kaliope."

"Got it," Auri said, giving her a big smile that revealed a tiny dimple.

We headed out of my mother's study, her hand joined with mine. I could feel her anxiety through our bond, with every step down to the guest corridors. There was so much left unsaid and unanswered with her father. It weighed heavily on her.

"No matter what, you have me, you have my family," I told her.

"I know," she said. Her voice was low, unsure despite what she said.

Her father was in the guest wing, which I was sure my dad made sure was not left unattended, or that my siblings were not allowed to see him before morning conversations. The majority of us were on the east side of the palace, whereas the guest wing was on the west side.

We only knocked once before he was at the door, almost like he knew we were coming. Maybe his wolf traits. My mind was still trying to process one of the biggest secrets.

"Hey, Dad," she said, like she hadn't tried to kill him the previous day.

"Auri," he said, which sounded cold, but the smile he gave her said otherwise. "What do I owe the pleasure?"

"Just came to talk," she told him.

"With the bodyguard, of course."

"Hmm, pretty sure I showed you I don't *need* a bodyguard—"

"Yeah... something I don't think I will be forgetting for a while."

"Sorry, by the way. I reacted—"

"Poorly?" he said.

"Something like that..." she said, her eyes locked onto the floor.

"Let's sit," I suggested. It seemed that every conversation involving her dad always led to high emotions.

"Is this an attack the Dad type of conversation?" he asked.

"No, no," she said, "I'd send my shadows scattering before you sat, if so."

She laughed. I let out a half laugh, but the tension felt like cutting through frozen butter.

"Ah, Zane, you haven't learned that my dear Auri is quite the jokester?"

"I'm learning, but sometimes I still wonder what's a joke or not."

She giggled. She would be the end of me. The literal death of me.

"What did you guys want to discuss? More questions?"

"I have a lot of questions, but right now my brain is so tangled that I don't know what I should ask, what's important... I just don't know. So no, we came for something else." She was fidgeting with her fingers, her knee bouncing as quickly as it could. "So... so... Dad."

"What did you *do*, Auri?"

"She did nothing." I snapped.

"She only stutters when she is—"

"I'm sitting right here... Zane and I are going to the priestess and—"

"You two are going to get confirmed?""Yes," I told him.

"Shit."

"We wanted to know if you wanted to come," she said.

"I do. Gods, I do. I'm just... I have a lot of feelings and wasn't quite expecting this. You actually caught me off guard."

"I've been waiting my whole life for that." She let out a full laugh, deep and pure. Gods, I'm not sure I had ever heard her laugh this loud before. It was contagious, and I found myself laughing with her. Shadows started swirling around her feet. They weren't like what happened last night, but more like what happened earlier. They responded to her emotions differently. Like earlier, I could feel the pull of her magic. Just one touch. One borrow. I took the deepest breath in and focused on her laugh.

Her dad went from a slight giggle to a gasp. The shadows scared him, even if he wanted to pretend that they didn't.

"Auri, you really are going to have control of that better."

"I know." Her eyes dropped to the ground, every bit of laughter and happiness gone. Shadows dissipated.

"I never wanted to shield you, not years ago, and I don't want to now, but—"

"You're afraid."

"Yes. I can't lose you. I have been afraid of something happening to you ever since that priestess said... well, it's not important—"

"What did she say?" Her tone was no longer sarcastic.

"Does it change anything?"

"It might not, but I deserve to know."

"She told us about your mate. She also said it was tough to read you, but that when you two would meet, your powers would be something so powerful it hadn't been seen in a millennium."

"Oh, wow," she said.

I was sitting there looking between the two of them in my own state of shock. What did that mean? What did her powers have to do with me? Did the priestess say that during my blessing, as a newborn?

"It really is nothing, but it did worry me about what your powers may be. She wasn't able to tell us if you would shift. I didn't think you would because I didn't, but the fucking Gods clearly have a sick sense of humor," her dad said.

"Is that why you suppressed my powers?"

"Yes, I know it was wrong, but I was terrified of you getting magic and not being able to handle it truly. The priestess made it seem like you had extraordinary magic in you. With me being away, I was afraid of what would happen. Afraid that mine and your mom's secrets would be exposed."

"You put me at a serious disadvantage in classes."

"I don't know why your power was still dormant. I stopped giving you the power when you turned eighteen—"

"Wait, what?"

"Yes, right before your birthday, I stopped having them mix it into your tincture. I needed to know if you were going to shift. It's also why I really didn't want you to join, and was really glad you didn't go right away. The thought of you being in the riders branch and shifting, our family secrets being put on display. How would a dragon react?"

"I understand, I disagree with you keeping me in the dark, but I get it... I guess." Her eyes spoke of her pain.

"I know this year has been a lot of learning, secret after secret. I want to tell you everything, but there is a lot I can't share just yet. We also need to focus on this evening, on you two. Do you know what happens during these?" He looked at me and then back at her.

"Zane said we go in, we drink a tincture, the priestess does some magic ritual, and then there is a ceremony officially uniting our souls."

"There is also a bond mark—"

"He told me that," she said.

"Zane, anything you want to know?"

"My aunt told me some, but of course I wasn't there."

"Given it's more exclusive to shifters, it happens in our villages more than most know about," he told us both.

"Is it okay to do it here? Not on *their* territory?" she asked.

"Yes, every priestess knows how—they just do. All that matters is that it's a priestess and it's performed in a temple."

"My mother will be setting up all the details, to include a celebratory meal afterwards, family only," I added.

"Good. I may be terrified of the unknown, but this is something that should be celebrated and honored."

"Thanks for the blessing, Dad," she told him.

"Yes, thank you, sir," I said

He provided us with clarity but also raised more questions. Why did Auri's powers take two years to return, not to mention she had to take a tincture for them to ignite? Why was there such a delay? I knew her power was something most people hadn't seen, but how did that make us the most powerful couple in a millennium? Was it because of my ability?

Unlike Auri's, mine manifested earlier than usual. If a Drusearon warrior was going to have an ability, it usually manifested around the age of eighteen. Mine came at sixteen. My father is the only one who knows about my power—the magic I was cursed with. Knowing what he knows and watching Auri's ability manifest in front of him was probably the source of his fear.

I dragged Auri into the dining room for lunch. We both needed to eat and take our minds off everything else.

CHAPTER 8

We walked into the dining room for the second meal together with his siblings. With his father telling them that my father wasn't responsible for their uncle's death, the tension was less tense. Zane said lunch was a very informal meal, often with not all of them there at the same time.

Of course, all six of his siblings were sitting at the table in chaos. Their parents usually didn't attend lunch. I wasn't sure whether I should be more scared of them not being there as a buffer. My palms were feeling sweaty, and my heart kicked up a little faster. All six of them stared at us—at me—when we walked in the door.

Aeliana smiled at me, the same smile she gave me when she dragged me to her room. Thea looked up, then dropped her head down to stare at the plate in front of her. Her cheeks turned slightly pink. The rest of them looked at me and gave me a slight smile.

"Come and sit next to me," Aeliana said.

Zane pulled me along to that side of the table, and he sat between us, putting me on the end. The seat directly in front of me was empty, which I was grateful for. Thea sat on the other side next to Aeliana, which was the kind of buffer we needed at the table.

"Mama said you guys were having a special ceremony later," Elizabeth squealed out.

"Yes. Do you know what the ceremony means?" Zane asked her.

"Not really. I just know we are expected to wear the fancy dress Mama has gotten for us."

Arkin laughed and then said, "it means Zane won't be moping around the house that he never found her again—"

"Again?" I cut him off.

"Yeah... you know he found you once, but then lost you for years..."

I shot Zane a look, because wait, what?

"Oh... hmm... well, our father spoke with us all earlier, and cleared the air and some rumors," Arkin said.

"What did he mean by lose me again?" I asked Zane down the bond, because I couldn't let this go.

"Well... you see, I saw you years ago in the clearing, but then a dragon swooped down and picked you up, and you both were gone. I didn't lose you because I didn't have you then."

"Why didn't you tell me?"

"Wasn't really relevant?"

"I mean, it kind of is, but we can talk about this later."

His siblings were bantering about the upcoming ceremony, all of them throwing out theories of what would happen. None of them had been to one, and they only knew what little they heard.

"I'm sorry," Thea mumbled out.

The entire table went quiet. Zane leaned forward, looking around Aeliana to see her. His eyes were fierce and demanding.

"Say again?" he said, his voice void of any emotion.

"I'm sorry," she muttered again.

"I know our parents taught you better, say it louder, say it with purpose, say it like you fucking mean it."

"Fuck you, Zane. I *am* sorry, Auri," she said much louder.

"To think there would be a lunch without someone dropping curse words," Adrian said.

Everyone let out a laugh, including me.

"I accept your apology, Thea," I told her. I appreciated her saying sorry. I understood her anger. Hell, I would be angry if I were in her position. I always thought my father didn't have siblings, but everything I thought I knew wasn't even close to the truth. Having a Witch heritage explained why my magic was hard for me to tame, which is why Professor Vindex pushed for me to control it better. I wondered what exactly he knew. How many people knew the actual truth?

Lunch wasn't as bad as I'd expected. Maybe everyone was being careful, or perhaps they'd already heard about my outburst and decided pretending ignorance was easier.

When Zane and I returned to our chambers, the afternoon light turned warm and low, slipping through the tall windows. Two outfits waited for us, laid out with almost ceremonial care.

My gown was a soft cream color, the kind of shade that made my skin look paler. Delicate lace traced the cuffs and neckline, the fabric so light it barely seemed real. Zane's all-black clothes were laid next to mine. Someone had even polished his boots until they caught the light like glass. It all felt perfect, and yet I was waiting for the lightning storm to strike.

I rubbed my finger along my palm, trying to ease my rising nerves. What were we doing? Were we really going to do this? We would be the center of attention, while they all watched. Arms wrapped around my waist, startling me and bringing me back to the room.

"Let's get out of here for a little bit," he whispered in my ear.

"Yes, let's, but where?"

"Anywhere but here… You'll need to change and wear your flight coat."

"Come to me, come to me," Esme pleaded to me.

"It would be nice to see you, too."

"Esme wants us to go to her—"

"Deal, we can rove to the outskirts of town," he said before I finished.

Before I had the last of my coat fastened, he pulled me close, and we flashed through darkness. It felt like minutes, not seconds, like when we were at the college. As soon as our feet touched ground, the shadows spread outward and up my legs. Zane immediately stepped back. He threw his hand up.

"Auri, they are responding to your emotions, your fear. You need to control it, my love."

"I know, I am fucking living it."

I closed my eyes and took a deep breath. It smelled like pine outside, and I rubbed my leather coat between my fingers. I went deeper within. I could visualize Zane's bond, I could visualize Esme's bond, then there was another tether there, dark and intense. That was where my shadow's power held, within me. I controlled them, I took a breath, and visualized them coming up my hands. I opened my eyes to watch the swirls going around my arms, waiting for my command.

Zane was watching me, studying my movements. I turned my hand over and played with them. Then I closed my hands and turned off the power. Just like that, they were gone. Zane stepped closer and pulled me tightly into him.

"You actually kind of terrify me..." he muttered.

"Really?"

"Yeah... and I don't scare easily."

"Oh..." Hearing him say that made me a little sad. I knew he was being honest, but damn, I never wanted anyone I loved to be scared of me.

"Incoming," Esme purred.

Within seconds, I could hear her wings beating, beating through the sky, getting closer. I could feel the shimmer we shared, feeling stronger as she neared. I watched the sky for her, but her silver scales made it hard to spot her against the bright afternoon sky.

When she landed, snow had scattered everywhere.

"My little shadow and her little bat."

A loud laugh burst out of my lips. Even though it had only been a day since I saw her, my heart was filled with happiness at seeing her. I wasn't even annoyed at her little nicknames for us. It was just what I needed with how the last twenty-four hours went.

"So, where should we fly to?" Zane asked.

"He can fly wherever, by himself." Then she puffed a stream of sulfur towards him.

"She will like me eventually..."

"Maybe..."

"It's weird when you can't hear her. I don't like to be the middle person. Esme says you can fly alongside us."

Esme nudged my shoulder. *"That isn't quite what I said."*

"Hmm... tomato—tamato."

"We can fly towards the seas, near the Ashen Vale. Seeing fliers is normal on this side of the city."

"Let's go, my little shadow. I have places I want to see."

"Do you promise not to fly crazy? I don't have the saddle to hold onto."

Zane laughed, and Esme chortled at me, but didn't answer. She dropped her shoulder for me to climb on. Gods. I hope she didn't have any crazy plans today.

As soon as I got situated, she launched into the air. My thighs tightened against her, and I gripped for anything to hold onto. Zane launched right next to us and flew alongside us. My eyes looked below us, taking everything in as we flew west. We rose above the mountains, and in the far distance, you could see the sea.

"Do you want to see where I was born?" Esme purred.

"You were born at the Ashen Vale?" I said, instead of talking through our bond, I spoke out loud so Zane could hear some of the conversation.

"Yes. I was in my egg for only four years before it hatched. My mom was at Sandorg, your dad was only a second year."

"How long is a dragon normally incubated?" *"It depends upon the breed and lineage, but usually anywhere from ten years to fifty."*

"Why did you hatch so early?" *"Sometimes the fates have other plans for us... When my mother bonded with your father, I felt the call to hatch."*

"Wait... what does that even mean?"

"I think the Gods picked me for you."

"You think... the Gods... picked me for... you?" I said it out loud because I could barely process it, but also for Zane to hear.

"Why do you think that?" He asked her.

"Why else would I have hatched early? Silver dragons usually don't hatch for twenty years. Then, when you were born, I knew. I was only eight, but I

felt something. You were born at Lakish Outpost, and I was at the Eclipsera Vale."

"What did she say?" Zane asked.

I repeated back what she said, and Zane just looked at me, as if he was processing everything she revealed.

"How did you move Vales?"

"Once a hatchling turns two, they can go to other Vales. This usually only happens if their parent isn't at the Vale where they were born. If the parent has a bonded rider, then the young dragon usually moves to the nearest Vale to preserve the relationship. Then once we turn twenty, we all go to Sandorg Vale to learn more about bonding with a rider."

"Where is your father?"

"Wherever my mother is, they are bonded."

"Who is it?"

"You know his name... You haven't put it together?"

"Korvanleglunga—wait, isn't Alex's dragon named that? Gods, I hope not."

"No, well, sort of, his dragon's call name is Korven with an e. My dad goes by Korvanle. Ironically, my dad is his dad's dragon."

"What?" I shouted.

"Why do you think your parents and their parents were always at the same base. C'mon, Auri, you're smarter than that."

"Well, I didn't really know that Fae's had mates, or that dragons had mates. My father didn't tell me shit."

"Even then, you should have put it together before now."

"Probably. I've got a lot going on."

"You need to filter out what's not essential. Details matter."

"Why me?"

"You'd have to ask the Gods that, but I don't think they will answer. Fliers are very intuitive. You egotistical riders think you are the ones picking, but we chose you first. Sometimes we choose when you're born, and sometimes we choose when you step onto Sandorg Soil."

"How do they choose at birth? How do you even know they will be a rider? What if they die before they get to bonding day?"

"So many questions."

"Yes, my mind is inquisitive, and I need to know the hows and the whys."

"Oh, Esme, you opened the wrong door," Zane said, and then he let out a loud laugh.

She swung her head at him, and he banked to the left quickly.

"Well then..." he said.

"You can ask me as many questions as you want. I don't know what happens if they don't choose to be a rider or if they die, because you lived. They don't talk about that. Some fliers choose the same rider, and that can cause friction in the Vales. Kekoa also wanted you, and when you picked me, he opted not to bond at all."

"I didn't know that—"

"You wouldn't."

"Ok. So, I know why you bonded so young. What about the other young dragon, who was younger than you?"

"Well..." Esme chortled, and a laugh came through the bond.

"I don't know what's happening right now," I said, and shot Zane a look.

"Remember that dragon friend you mentioned—"

"Wait—What?"

"I hate only hearing half of this conversation," Zane grumbled.

"Lakung and I... are mated."

My mind spun hard. I was trying to remember what Vindex and Bhatta said about mated dragons. I was too preoccupied with the part involving the mated Fae.

"Did he bond with a rider?"

"Yes."

Gods. Fuck. As if things weren't complicated enough. My brain was spinning in all the ways everything was a mess, and now I was tied to another dragon and rider. My brain was flooded with information as I tried to sort out what mattered.

It made sense that Kim was bonded to Lili's dad's dragon, as we were always at the same base. I don't know why I hadn't put the pieces together.

"Who did he bond with?" I asked her.

"Who and what are we talking about?" Zane asked.

"Apparently, Esme has a dragon mate, who also bonded a rider this year—wait, is that why he bonded so young?"

"Yes... with me wanting to bond you, he bonded early." Esme's tail flicked side to side.

"I think my brain might actually overload. Like it might actually explode with information from the last two days."

I can feel the heat rising in my cheeks, my chest rising and falling faster with each heartbeat. The shadows came to the surface.

"If you shadow explode on my back... well, don't."

"Auri, I know this all feels very overwhelming—"

"You don't say..." I shot back at him.

"Esme, let's land in this clearing ahead, before Auri—"

"I'll be fine."

"Shadows are swirling around your legs."

"I fucking know."

I closed my eyes, and the wind whipped across my cheeks. I inhaled deeply, visualizing my lungs and stomach filling up with air. I slowly exhaled through my mouth. I repeated that four more times. I brought the shadows back within.

"See, I'm fine."

"You are getting better at managing it, but it doesn't mean you're fine."

She always brought me right back to reality.

"Maybe, I'll fly with Zane—"

Before the words fully came out of my mouth, she spun upside down, and I started falling through the air. The cold rushed past my face, and gravity pulled me down quickly. My heart started pounding overtime. Screams erupted from me. Shadows started flaring all around. Finally, his arms locked around me.

"Esme, what the actual fuck?" Zane and I both yelled at the same time.

"Jinx," he whispered in my ear.

"I knew he would catch you..."

"What if he didn't?"

"But he did. You said you wanted to fly with him."

"I was vexing you. You almost put me in an eternity box."

"You're fine, remember?" She chortled and then blew a puff of sulfur breath at us.

"We're landing up here," Zane said.

Moments later, we landed in an open field. Zane gently let me down, my feet steadying on the ground. Zane snapped his wings to his body aggressively. I lifted my arms to look at my hands. They were trembling, shadows swirling all around. I looked around the clearing. We were alone. It was peaceful here, quiet. You could hear the winter birds chirping in the distance, the wind whipping against the pine trees, and the faint sound of water.

"I really can't believe you dropped me like that," I said, staring at her with narrow eyes.

"I can," Zane said.

Esme didn't respond, just stared at both of us with a glare. Then she lifted her head to the sky and let out a roar. It vibrated the ground we stood on and sent immediate pain to my eardrums.

"I think you—we made her mad," Zane said down the bond.

"Do you need some time to throw your tantrum?" I asked her.

"No, I'm done now," she said.

"Where are we?" I asked both of them.

"In between the Ashen Vale and—"

"Winterhand Stronghold," I said, finishing his sentence.

"Yeah..." he said.

"Sorry, I can't actually take you to the Vale."

"Yeah, I prefer not to become flier food."

"This is where I learned how to fly. Every Ashen Vale hatchling learns here. It is quiet and remote here."

I looked around. Off in the distance, you could see the sea, then if you turned back toward Ashwynd, the mountains staggered through, all covered in snow. It was truly breathtaking. I felt peace settle within. Nature had always been a force of calm for me, whether it was the night sky filled with the moon and stars or the peaceful woods.

Wingbeats snapped through the air, getting louder each second. All peace scattered away. My head turned to the south, trying to see what was flying our way.

"Oh yeah... Did I forget to mention that Lakung and his rider were going to meet us?"

"By all the fucked stars."

"Let me guess—her mate and their rider?"

I huffed a breath. "Yep."

CHAPTER 9

The grey dragon came into view, his rider clinging on tightly. His wingbeats grew louder as he got closer. The wind from his flaps rushed against my cheeks. I wondered who bonded him. I wished I had paid more attention to the other dragons and Riders during the last week of classes. Things were so chaotic following bonding day, with bodies dropping.

Lakung landed hard, sending snow flying everywhere. I couldn't see anything through the snowstorm he created.

"He's so dramatic," Esme said, blinking.

"Says you, who did a loud war cry earlier…" I told her.

The snow settled, and Lakung and his rider came into view. I finally saw his face.

Fuck. My. Life.

He was in my basic platoon, although not in the same squad, but he was next to my bunk. I barely talked to him after he made that balderdash comment on the second night of basic training. I didn't even remember his name.

"You look like you would be fun in bed," he said, nodding his head my way.

"He said what?" Esme grumbled down the bond.

"Yeah… he said that."

She grumbled, then let out a chortling sound.

"What's happening? I feel like I'm missing something," Zane said.

"Umm… Hmm… Well—"

"Spit it out, Auri."

"He may have made a really balderdash comment about me looking fun in bed, while we were in basic—"

Zane's wings snapped open hard. Anger surged through the bond. The Rider stared at both of us, eyes flashing between us. His shimmer was glimmering on his hands, and what little bit of his chest was visible under his neck. He felt threatened.

"His shimmer activated, I don't think he meant—"

"Oh, I'm sure he meant what he said. I mean, why wouldn't he? You're gorgeous."

"Look, I realize that I probably didn't leave a good first impression, but I also didn't think we would be in the same branch and certainly not have dragons that are bonded."

Esme chuffed a little puff of flame at him, and his entire body went rigid. Lakung chortled and dropped his head lower to her. Interesting.

"This isn't how I expected this to go." She told me.

"Anyway, I'm sorry. Let's start over. I'm Knoxx."

"I'm Auri and my—"

"Zane, her mate," he said with a coldness that could slice a bone.

My head whipped to him, eyes opened wide, locked onto him.

"Nice to meet you both."

"You just revealed we are mates," I said down the bond.

"His dragon is mated to yours. He will learn if he doesn't already."

"Lakung just informed me that it was classified information, and Esme will burn me alive if I reveal it."

"Precisely," Zane said.

"Well, anyway. It was nice meeting you. Zane and Esme are overly protective, and we all need to get along because we will all be around each other for Gods knows how long," I said, barely taking a breath.

"I have nothing but respect for either of you."

"Good, it would be shameful for me to have to end you."

"Fuck the stars," I mumbled.

Knoxx laughed. "No offense, but I am more scared of *her* than you." He nodded towards me. "I was in the courtyard that day. She didn't hesitate when she sliced that guy's Achilles."

"What wing are you in?"

"Eagle Wing, Fire Platoon, First Squad," he said.

"Feather Wing, Electric Platoon, First Squad," I told him.

"Where are you staying for break?" Zane asked, his voice wasn't as cold.

"A small village outside of Winterhand."

"Well, we are in Ashwynd—"

"I figured by the—" he said, then nodded towards his wings.

"Yeah... speaking of which, Auri and I will need to leave. We have a busy evening ahead of us that we need to prepare for. It was supposed to be a quiet flight to unwind—Esme clearly didn't understand the task at hand."

"Do you want me to fly you back or—"

"No, I don't. You dropped me out of the sky *on purpose*, or did you forget?"

"I was hoping you would."

"No."

"Enjoy the ceremony, don't explode into shadows. I can be there quickly if you get cold feet."

"Thanks... but I'll be fine," I told her. I turned toward Knoxx. "It was nice to meet you formally."

Zane nodded at him, then moved behind me and wrapped his arms around me. It flashed dark, then small flashes of light, and then dark again. It was cool, but not outside cold and not indoor warmth. The air was musty, and pressure filled my ears. My eyes flickered open. We weren't in the palace. It was dark with streams of light filtered through an opening. Zane's arms were still wrapped tightly around me.

"Where are we?"

"In a cave that overlooks Ashwynd. Few people know it exists. I used to come here and hide when I was younger."

"It's dark in here..."

I let the power come into my hands, and I snapped my fingers, sending little light orbs floating around the room.

"You're getting better."

"I am."

He spun me around, and our eyes met. Electricity coursed from my head to my toes. He grabbed the back of my neck, pulled me in, and kissed me feverishly. Our tongues glided one over the other. The hair on my arms stood up, then my arms filled with goosebumps. He pulled back, resting his forehead against mine.

"I loved you years ago, I loved you months ago, and I love you now. I will *annihilate* the entire province and kill anyone in my way if something happens to you."

My heart dropped into my stomach. "Why do you say that?"

"Because... you should know how I feel."

"I love you, too. I don't know if I could obliterate an entire province, but I would try."

He laughed. "I think you would be more successful than I."

He didn't let me respond before his mouth crashed into mine again. Demanding and passionate. Our lips pressed into each other, and he held me as close and tight as he could. In that moment, nothing mattered but him and our love.

He broke the kiss and stepped back. He stared at me, then he dropped his gaze to my lips, and then continued down my body. My cheeks immediately felt flushed. The way he looked at me, the way he devoured me with his eyes. They said everything he didn't have to say. My stomach turned. No one ever looked at me the way he did, not even Alex. He looked at me like I was a God that he worshipped.

"Gods, I want you every second of the day," he said, low, eyes fixated on me.

"The feeling's mutual—"

"But we need to get ready—"

"Then why stop here?" I asked.

"This place has always been the calm in the storm..." He let me go, then turned to face one of the rocky walls. He reached out and ran his hand alongside the wall. His hand changed for a very brief second, as if it glowed with it.

"What is this place? What was that?"

"This place has old, ancient magic in the walls. The cavern runs miles deep."

He moved back to me and pulled me into a tight embrace.

"Let's go, my Anam Cara," he whispered.

"Let's."

We roved right into his bedroom chambers. On the bed sat our evening wear for the ceremony. My stomach tingled, my heart hitched a little faster. I was excited for this, but at the same time, I had no clue what I was doing. They may have told me what the ceremony entailed, but it felt like it was much more than was said.

"It's not like you're going to shift into a wolf," Esme purred down the bond.

"I sure the fuck hope not." I shot back at her. I hadn't really considered shifting, given I was two years past the typical age, but what if I did?

"Nothing would change... well," she said, then her laughter rolled through the bond, *"I digress—you would in fact change."*

"Gods above, fucking seriously."

"I meant, you would still be my rider, my little wolf shadow. You and Zane would still be mated, and whatever else you do."

"Thanks, I guess."

CHAPTER 10

Seventeen hundred came quickly. Zane and I showered and dressed in the stunning clothes that his mother set out for us to wear. The lace on my dress was the perfect off-white cream, flowing elegantly to my ankles. Zane was dapper in his black leather pants and tailcoat.

One of the attendants knocked on our door to retrieve us, letting us know that we would see the priestess alone before the ceremony began. We followed her through the wing and down more halls. We briefly walked outside and into another part of the palace before reaching the temple. Zane wasn't kidding. There were giant, beautiful black obsidian statues alongside the hall. At the end of the hall, there were floor-to-ceiling double doors.

As we approached the doors, the two knights standing on each side pushed the door open. The attendant stepped aside and motioned for us to enter.

"Your family will wait out here until the priestess allows them to enter for the ceremony. She is waiting at the dais," she told us.

Zane gave her a nod and held my hand tight as we walked through the doors. Once through, the knights closed them behind us. The priestess stood on the dais at the front of the temple. She wore a floor-length light blue gown with a hood that was over her head. Almost all priestesses wore the same clothing. When they weren't in a temple, they often wore a sheer white veil under their hoods as well.

With each step down the aisle, my stomach turned a little more. My palms felt hot and wet. My heart was beating a little faster. I wanted this, but my nerves were starting to get the best of me.

"Welcome, Auriella and Roarke," she said.

I gave her a curtsy, while Zane knelt before her for a brief moment. Every child learned etiquette when in the presence of a priestess, and you didn't want to make any of them mad. They could and would hex you.

Sage filled the air, candles were lit all around the dais, and fixed candelabras with burning candles were attached to the walls. It was dim, even with all the burning candles.

"I hear today is a special day for you two," she said.

"Yes, ma'am. We want to get our mating bond confirmed," Zane told her.

"That is what I heard. Do you know how this works?"

"Neither of us knows much," he said.

"As it should be," she stated.

I raised an eyebrow at that. Then why ask anyway, as a test?

"I'd like to start with, I am Priestess Analyia."

"Nice to meet you," we both said in unison.

She laughed. "Already like a bonded couple. The reason I see you both privately first is to do a reading on you. I like to keep that a private moment. After that, we will invite your family and start the actual ceremony. Are you both prepared to wear a bond mark?"

"Yes," Zane said, and I nodded in agreement.

"Perfect." She reached next to her, where a small table sat with two small glasses filled with an emerald-blue liquid. She grabbed both of them, one in each hand.

"You will turn to face each other. You will hold each other's left wrist. Then you will interlock your right arms and drink the tincture at the same time while holding each other's gaze. Understand?"

"Yes," we both said together.

She handed both of us a glass. "You will feel tingly first and then very euphoric."

Zane and I stared at each other, arms locked together. We brought the glass to our lips in sync, and then we both lifted and swallowed. Tingles took over from the top of my head and moved all the way to my toes. Zane gave me a big smile, eyes still locked onto mine. His eyes slowly shifted from pale blue to a deeper indigo. My arms felt weightless, my heartbeat sped up, and everything looked brighter. I smiled back, my dimples appearing.

"I love you," he said down the bond, before giggling like a little boy.

"I think we are drunk," I told him.

"It's normal to feel drunk," she said. Zane and I both broke eye contact and stared at her. For a brief moment, I forgot she was there.

"Did you hear what we said to each other?" I whispered to her.

"No, I guess I should have known that you all have consummated the bond already."

Zane started laughing loudly, freely, contagiously. I couldn't stop myself and burst into laughter with him.

"I will start the process of reading you both. You will need to let go of each other's arms, and we will all hold hands, creating a circle."

"I hope she doesn't want more than holding hands," Zane giggled out.

My eyes widened at him before laughing again. We let go of each other and moved to face her. She stepped down off the dais and reached her hands out to us. She grabbed both of our hands.

She gasped loudly, dropped the hold, and took a step back. "Oh, my Gods."

A pulse of air rippled through the temple. The flames flickered sideways. Zane and I both turned our heads towards each other, then back to her. The euphoric feeling started to fade quickly.

"Um... are you okay?" I asked.

"I... I... Um, yeah, I'm okay. I just... just don't know what I saw."

"That sounds ominous," Zane said.

"Let's try again," she said.

She stepped forward and held out her hands. Zane and I looked at each other with a sense of hesitancy before giving her our hands. Every bit of euphoria was gone. Her hands locked onto ours. Her body straightened, her head thrown back, and her hood slipped off. Her entire body trembled.

Zane and I stood there frozen, staring at her. His emotions were overwhelming, fear and anxiety. They poured through our bond, like the shields that I had built to dampen them were gone.

After several moments, and what felt like an eternity, she lifted her head and let go of our hands. She reached back and pulled her hood onto her head. Nothing came out of her mouth. Her eyes were wide, almost devoid of color. She turned away from us and walked away. She opened a door and disappeared, leaving us both standing there.

"Um, is this supposed to happen?" I asked Zane.

"I don't... maybe... I'm not actually sure," Zane mumbled.

My face spun to look at him. I rarely heard him stumble over his words. His face was painted in concern. We both stood there in silence. I didn't know what to do. I had never done this before. I could feel myself breathing a little faster, and my fingers started to rub against each other rapidly. I looked down to see the shadows rapidly swirling around my feet.

"Esme... I don't know what's happening?" I pleaded down the bond.

"Everything is happening as it should."

"What the seven fucks does that mean?"

"Shh, my little shadow, calm your nerves."

I wanted to blow a big puff of flames at her. She knew something, but she wouldn't tell me.

CHAPTER 11

Zane

I told her I didn't know if it was normal, but I *knew* it wasn't.

My mind raced wildly. The floor felt cold beneath me. I didn't know what the fuck was happening. When the priestess touched us the first time, I felt her touch my magic. I felt my magic grab at her. Was that why she dropped our hands like they were poison? Every bit of shielding that I had dropped after drinking the tincture. Terror filled me.

Would she know what kind of magic I possess? Auri was sure to feel the terror that was consuming me. I tried to rebuild my mountains, but they wouldn't fucking build. Auri's shadows were pulling at me, and every bit of my self-control was being tested. The urge was stronger than the urge to take her every night in bed.

Not only were my emotions pouring out of me, but Auri's were pouring into me. She, too, was terrified, and her anxiety was building. However, I didn't need to feel her anxiety. She was rubbing the tips of her fingers against each other, her breathing was heavier, her chest beating harder, and her cheeks were getting pinker.

The door opened, and the priestess returned, but she wasn't alone. Another priestess accompanied her. They both stared at us, eyes narrowed, and faces unreadable.

"What's happening?" Auri pleaded down the bond.

"I'm not sure, but whatever happens, I'm here." I wanted to do anything to comfort her. To take her fear away, if it was overwhelming me, I knew it was crumbling her.

"Sorry about that. I didn't mean to leave abruptly."

Auri looked over at me and then back at them. We both stared at them, neither of us speaking. Too stunned to say anything.

"I am Priestess Nerissa. Analyia asked me to help. She saw some things that she isn't sure how to interpret."

"We don't have to retake the tincture, right? Because I am no longer euphoric," Auri asked her.

"No, No. I will join hands with both of you as she did."

I looked at her, trying to read her. Everything in me was telling me something wasn't right. Nothing felt right.

Before I had any time to protest or think further about it, she grabbed both of our hands. Her eyes closed, flickering back and forth under her eyelids. Her arms stretched out, slightly twitching. Her head swayed forward and back. My stomach turned, bile rising in my throat. What the fuck were they seeing?

She finally opened her eyes, then stared at Auri. Her head tilted to the side, eyes narrowed. Auri's fear poured through our bond. The shadows that were swirling at her feet started to swirl up her body.

"You're staring at her like she's prey, and unless you want those shadows to pick you up, I'd stop," I said to her, breaking the silence.

"They won't harm me," she said, her gaze still on Auri.

The shadows continued climbing up Auri's body, almost engulfing her in blackness. The priestess finally blinked her eyes and straightened her head, then turned her gaze towards me.

"Do you know the God I worship, Roarke?"

"We asked for a Priestess of Freya—"

"Analyia is, but I am a Priestess of Marzana."

My stomach dropped. The Goddess of Death. I looked at Auri. Her face was pale, her eyes wide, and only a small rim of green was left. Her mouth was agape, but nothing came out. Shadows moved around her, dancing in a way I hadn't seen before. I turned back to the priestess. I was done playing games. I wanted truth, not riddles wrapped in words.

"What does that mean?" I said coldly.

"Nothing really, I just honor death a little more than love. I feel more connected to Marzana than—"

"No, that's not what I mean. What does all of this mean? Why did two of you have to read us? Why did Analyia look like she actually saw Marzana? Why do both of you look like you brushed death?"

"I saw great power between you two, I saw a vision that showed you two nearly ending the world—" She twitched. "—I saw exchanged power."

She knew what kind of magic I had, what kind of power I possessed. She didn't say it, but the twitch told me enough. Auri stood stunned, staring at her.

"I also saw the kind of love that can bring death to anyone who threatens it, and that can be either a good or bad thing."

"It will be good..." Auri mumbled. Hearing her voice reassured me she was okay, even if it was faint and cold.

"The most concerning part was that I couldn't read Auriella very well. What I saw came mostly from you, Roarke."

"What does that mean? My dad said the priestess wasn't able to read me well as a baby, either," Auri said.

"I'm not really sure. I haven't encountered anyone whom I haven't been able to read. I did get small visions. I could see the mating bond clearly. I could see the bond you have with a dragon. I got swift glimpses of wolves, darkness, lots of purple aura that I couldn't make out."

"Are you trying to say I am going to shift?" Auri blurted out.

"I simply don't know. You are two years past the typical age. Very unlikely, but not improbable. You are half Werewolf—"

"No, that's not correct. Only a quarter." Auri cut her off. My eyes widened slightly. Not many did that to a priestess.

"Some things were obvious, and one of those was that you *are* half Werewolf, from the Lupine and Dunkel pack. Then you are a quarter Cavendish and a quarter Faucher. How do you not know this, child?"

Auri gasped. The entire room was silent, except for the flames flickering on top of the candles. Auri's shadows froze in place.

"That's not possible, there aren't any Faucher Witches left..." I said, without thinking. My mind was warping against itself. If she had the bloodline of the two most powerful covens to exist on this continent, if anyone knew, they would come for her.

"Clearly not, I am looking at one. She is alive. Do I have to remind you that Priestesses are a form of sorcerers? We *know* Witch bloodline the best. What I can't see is which parent gave her what. I would assume one parent was a Witch and one was a—"

"No... my dad is half Werewolf and half Cavendish," Auri said, her eyes fixated on the floor. The shadows calmed but remained swirling around her.

"Are you sure?" Nerissa said.

"I'm not really sure of anything, but my dad seemed pretty sure of his heritage."

"And your mom?"

"She's not here anymore. He said she never knew where she came from—"

"Weren't you blessed as a babe?"

"Yes, or so they said."

"Your mom knew. Any priestess would pick up on the Faucher. It's—well, it's not really important."

Analyia stepped up next to Nerissa, way more composed, and had regained her color. "What is strange is that both of your parents were half Werewolf and half Witch—Witches from the oldest and strongest covens, no less."

"Does any of that affect what we are here to do?" I broke in. I knew Auri was getting more overwhelmed by the second with the history lesson.

"No, we've both seen the mating bond. We can move forward with the ceremonial part whenever both of you are ready. Since I am an older, more experienced priestess, I will finish the ceremony if you both are okay with that?" Nerissa said.

"Blessed by Marzana?" Auri shot out.

"I know I am special, but I am no Marzana. I am just a priestess."

"I guess... It's okay." Auri said.

"Before we let your family in, do either of you have any questions?"

Auri shook her head no.

"What happened here won't be repeated or shared, correct?" I asked. Every part of me wanted to keep her safe, keep us safe.

"No." They both said at the same time.

"Good."

CHAPTER 12

I stood in front of the dais, numb. Words barely escaping past my lips. Everything that could go wrong went wrong. One priestess turned into two. One of them worshipped death. Did I represent death? Gods. I wanted to scream at the top of my lungs, a battle cry—loud and piercing.

The walls I built within were gone. I knew Zane felt every emotion I felt, just as his were overwhelming every ounce of me. Esme was eerily quiet. I wasn't even sure I was processing everything I was told. It felt like every single day was chaos. It was too much. Too fast. I wanted to run and never look back.

The opening of the double doors startled me, breaking me out of the self-destructive trance that was occurring. His parents and my father walked in first, and I gave them a half smile. I was sure my father saw right through it. His siblings trailed behind them. They all walked to the front rows and took a seat.

Lizzy looked all around, taking everything in, beaming with smiles. Aeliana was locked onto Zane. She, too, had a wry smile. Our parents sat together on one bench, and the siblings sat on the other side of the aisle.

"The ceremony will begin," Nerissa announced.

She stood in front of Zane and me. She reached towards us, and we joined hands. She slightly trembled at the initial touch, then locked eyes with both of us.

"Alligo Auriellam Blackcreek ad Roarke Braegon secundo," she chanted.

Warmth spread from her—and from Zane's—into my hands. My skin tingled all over.

Analyia stepped up next to her, two long red ropes in her hands. Nerissa dropped our hands and grabbed them. She wrapped her hands around the ends of both and brought them to her mouth. Her eyes closed, and a burst of flames popped through her hands. She slowly opened her palms, showing the two ropes burned and joined at one end.

"I will say a chant, and then you two will create a knot. We will do that seven times, making a total of seven knots," Nerissa said.

We both nodded and took the rope from her.

"*Per nodum unius, amor vester incipiet.*"

We tied the first knot, binding our bond.

"*Nodo duorum, corda vestra unum fiunt.*"

We tied another, our hearts becoming one.

"*Nodo trium, animi vestri iunguntur.*"

Our spirits joined.

"*Per nodum quattuor, non amplius separati.*"

Apart no more.

"*Per nodum quinarii, vires vivificantur.*"

Powers awoken.

"*Per nodum sex, inscriptiones adfigentur.*"

Tattoos affixed.

"*Per nodum septem, benedictum a caelis et diis septem.*"

Blessed by the heavens and seven Gods.

Lightning cracked outside, and I jumped. Zane held my hands tightly.

"The Gods approve," Nerissa said, "*vinculis tuis vincti erunt, per totam vitam. Ignis.*"

The rope we held burst into flames, and Zane and I quickly let go. The ashes floated to the floor, no longer flaming.

"*Dii hos duos benedicant. Dii hos duos in perpetuum signent. Signum Vinculi. Signum Vinculi. Signum Vinculi.*"

My right forearm seared in pain, like boiling water pouring on my arm. I screamed out in pain.

Stars flashed through my vision, and my stomach twisted on itself. My head throbbed with my heartbeat. I closed my eyes and took a breath in.

Focus on the breath, not the pain. Focus on the breath, not the pain. I breathed in and out, slow and steady. The pain faded away slowly. I opened my eyes, and Zane met my gaze. There wasn't any fear, just awe.

I dropped my head to look at my forearm, where the pain originated.

Holy shit. There was nothing subtle about it. Our bond mark would be visible to all. One of our parents gasped, maybe all three.

"Interesting," Analyia said.

I shot her a glare and narrowed my eyes at her.

"Sorry. It's just... well—"

"Most bond marks are small, sometimes hidden. The Gods really wanted everyone to know about your bond, about your heritage," Nerissa said, finishing what Analyia was trying to get out.

"Um... yeah, you don't say," I said.

Zane stared at my arm, then back at his. His eyes were wide, lips tightly closed. Our bond marks were identical.

I looked down and rubbed my forearm.

There was a grey wolf with large black wings behind it. Above the howling wolf, there was a crescent moon with five tiny dots going down the inside of it—like my birthmark. I couldn't process it all. It spanned my entire inner forearm. It looked smaller on Zane's much longer arms, but still the same.

I lifted my head, and Zane's eyes followed me. Our eyes locked, and he gave me a gentle smile. My heart instantly melted. Despite everything, he still looked at me like I was the only soul that lit the fire in him. Everything around us faded. My entire body quivered. In that moment, nobody else existed in that room. It was just him and me.

"I loved you then, and I will love you every day until I no longer breathe," he said down the bond.

"I love you too, until we no longer breathe."

He reached up with both of his hands, grabbed my face, and pulled me in. He kissed me, deep and demanding. My heart pounded faster.

Then there was a cough.

Someone coughed.

We weren't alone.

Gods.

I pulled back and dropped my eyes, too embarrassed to look at any of our family.

"I couldn't care less what they think," he said.

"This concludes our ceremony. I have confirmed and bonded Auriella Reyna Blackcreek and Roarke Zane Braegon the Second. Their bondmark further marks them as bonded by the Gods."

Our parents and his siblings all rose and gathered around us quickly. His mom pulled both of us into her arms. Her cheeks had little streams of tears. As soon as she let us go, my father pulled me into his embrace.

He held me tight and close. I missed these hugs. It had been so long since he held me this way.

"We need to talk," I whispered. I didn't want our embrace to end, but I needed to say that. I needed to discuss with him what the priestesses discovered. I needed to see if he was hiding more from me. I was tired of being surprised by revelations in my life. I was tired of being shielded against things I needed to know.

He kissed the top of my head. "After dinner. I'm leaving tomorrow," he whispered.

"While you're having daddy dearest time, I am having mommy dearest time," Esme said, with evident annoyance in her voice.

"Maybe you'll get more answers than I."

She rumbled through the bond, or maybe it was a laugh.

"Let's all go enjoy dinner—there is a feast waiting for us," Zane's mom said.

"Yes. General Blackcreek will be joining, and you all will mind your manners," his father said.

Adrian let out a full belly laugh, then Arkin followed in. His father snapped his head in their direction, with those unyielding eyes. They both went instantly silent. His father grumbled under his breath. I looked at Zane, who winked at me. Gods bless this dinner. Hopefully, it went better than the previous one.

We all went into the large dining room. His mother wasn't kidding—there was a feast prepared for us. The dining table was filled with every shape of bread there was—boules, baguettes, and loaves. Two platters of every cheese possible, one at each side of the table. There were bowls of apples, pears, and oranges. There were bottles of wine staged down the middle of the table. It smelled absolutely delicious—my stomach grumbled in response.

Zane's father sat at the head of the table. He motioned for my father to sit next to him on the left. His mother took the seat to his right. I sat next to my father, and then Zane sat to my left. Aeliana sat next to their mother and across from me. Thea was next to her, then Helena and Lizzy. Arkin sat next to Zane, and then Adrian next to him.

Dinner was quieter, more restrained than the night before. I wasn't complaining. I needed a little peace after the past several days.

My father told us that he would be going to Fort Kalona for his next assignment, that it was his choice. My heart skipped a little beat. Kalona was in Veskonia, which was also known as Shapeshifter territory. What was he doing? I was sure there was some political reason he wasn't going to share with us.

Zane's hand slid onto my thigh and gripped it, reminding me he was here. Reminding me that he could feel what I felt. He always had a way to ground me and calm me with a simple touch.After we were served a copious amount of meats, potatoes, and desserts, everyone slowly left the table. I told my dad I would give him some time to clean up before I came to talk with him about the ceremony. Zane walked me around the palace and showed me more places. He took me into one of the largest home libraries I had seen. It was a cozy, bookshelf-filled room with books lining the walls. There were rocking chairs and lounge seats to get comfy in. Moving from base to base meant we simply did not have luxuries like libraries in our homes.

We headed back towards the guest wing. I needed to ask my dad some questions without the audience, and before he headed out the next day.

Before I even knocked, he opened the door and motioned for us to come in.

"I'm assuming the ceremony brought on more—"

"Questions? Like how you failed to mention that my mother is also a Shapeshifter and half-Witch?" I cut him off. I didn't mean to be blunt, but quite frankly, I was sick of the games.

His eyes went wide, his mouth agape. His face said everything—he didn't know.

"They... they said that?" He rubbed his forehead, like he was trying to see if this was real life.

"Yeah... yeah, they did."

"I... didn't know..." he said. He took a step back slowly and sat down in the chair. He was usually calm and composed. Even when I nearly strangled him, he kept his composure.

"They said that mom had to have known—"

"She said she knew nothing of her heritage," he said.

"They said when I was blessed, the priestess would have known."

I took a seat next to him. Everything in his face worried me.

"Your mom spoke to the priestess prior to us taking you there, but... I don't know. She told me she just wanted to know what the process was like. She... must have... Gods... why didn't she tell me? My Gods, you might actually shift. Fuck me... Gods," he said, voice cracking.

I had never heard my dad stumble and babble his words like this. He was holding back tears of betrayal. His eyes reminded me of the days following my mother's death.

"What do you know of the Faucher Witches?" Zane asked.

He lifted his head, and his eyes widened at Zane. "You're not... No. You can't be fucking serious right now?"

"I wish I were joking, sir. I, too, was in shock when they revealed that she was a quarter Faucher."

"What am I missing here?" I asked. The name Faucher meant nothing to me, but clearly, both of them knew something.

My dad's head dropped into his hands, and he started rubbing his face. "The Faucher coven was some of the most cunning, devious Witches. They were brilliant, and most of them had unbelievable power. Most of them dabbled in very dark magic, and there was a movement to eliminate them."

"Let me guess... The Cavendish Witches?" I asked.

He looked up at me and nodded his head.

"This happened when... oh my Gods—"

"Around the time you and mom were born?"

"It happened when I was months old, I don't know the exact time. Did they happen to say which pack she came from? Or which of her parents was which?"

"Didn't say which was which... she did say it was the Dunkel pack."

"I sometimes think the Gods have the darkest of humors..."

"I'm going to go out on a limb here and say the Dunkel and Lupine pack didn't get along," I said.

"Yeah... something like that," my dad said.

"I am guessing that her parents fled and left her to try to protect her. She was found in a village in Northern Eastvwyth, which is clear across the continent from Witch Territory. The Dunkel pack still exists."

"I don't know anything about them," Zane said.

"There aren't as many these days. It's an elusive, quiet pack. They are in the mountains of Southwest Veskonia."

"Oh..." I didn't know what to say. Were her parents still alive?

"I'm sure your father brought this up, but I don't think you two should return to Sandorg?"

"We can't just run away. I'm bonded to a dragon, if you forgot—"

"I didn't. I can have you taught privately."

"We are returning."

"Okay. I'm not going to pull command, but if things change and anyone figures any of this out. I will not hesitate to have you discharged—"

"I can handle myself—"

"You were kidnapped because you are the niece of the Lupine Alpha—"

"Say what?" I shot out.

"Yes, my brother is the Alpha. It was my destiny, but I was... broken."

"I thought you said it was because of the experiments—"

"Both can be true. Look, Auriella, you are my purpose in life. You have been my purpose. I may have been distant the last several years while trying to navigate life without your mother, but I continued to live *for you*. I have done unspeakable things to protect you, and I will continue to do unspeakable things without remorse. I have eyes and ears at the college, and I will not hesitate to have you both removed."

"Understood," I said. I was staring at the floor. What he said brought tears to my eyes. I *knew* he loved me, but in the last few years, he felt cold and not himself. Hearing him say his devotion to me was bittersweet. I needed to hear that. I was trying not to cry in front of him, in front of Zane, but I felt the tear roll down my face.

"It is getting late, and we all need some rest over the last few days," my dad said.

I stood up because he was right. I was exhausted, and my eyes were heavy. My shoulders were tight, and pain was radiating from my head down my back.

He pulled me into a tight hug. "I love you, my sweet girl, never forget that. If you need anything, Esme knows how to get messages to Kim. Please, for the love of the Gods, stay safe," he said, barely above a whisper.

"I will take care of her, sir," Zane said.

My dad let go of me, looked between us, and let out a loud exhale. "Well, I hope so, because your lives are united now. So, I'm gonna need you also not to die."

Zane and I strolled back to his bedchambers in silence. It had been a really long day filled with information. Part of me was worried. I was worse than he bargained for. I wasn't *just* a dragon rider. I was a Shapeshifter *and* a Witch. It couldn't get any more complicated.

CHAPTER 13

The days following the ceremony were calm, far less chaotic than the first two days. We spent most of our days working on my magic, controlling and managing it. Zane's father brought in someone to help me practice controlling and manipulating the shadows. I was sure my father had a part in that. Finley was a Witch from the Cavendish clan, sworn to secrecy.

When I wasn't practicing my magic, Zane and I explored the city. We started and ended the day tangled up in each other and the sheets. Both of us were using it as a distraction from everything else that was happening.

The third of January came quickly, and we headed back to Sandorg. All Wing Commanders, Executive Officers, Platoon Leaders, and Riders' First Year Flight guides were required to return on the third. The rest of the cadets and other leadership would return on the fifth.

The flight back consisted of Remus, Nikolai, Zane, and me. Like our flight to Ashwynd, we met up with the others who flew here, and planned to leave thirty minutes before them. The flight back went smoothly, with no incidents.

As soon as Sandorg came into view, my stomach turned upside down on itself. My hands trembled underneath my flight gloves. Those first two days in Ashwynd tested every part of me. Seeing the college reminded me of the bullshit we were about to walk into. Someone was murdering cadets and hanging them up for sport.

"Remember what your father said before he left," Esme purred along the bond.

"He said a lot..."

"That's fair. I was referring to who to trust."

"Yes, Professor Pascal, Melamora, and Vindex. No one else. I'm not going to forget that."

"We are about to land, and flier chatter says there is chaos on the ground. Control your anxiety—keeping your ability a secret for as long as possible is paramount."

"Yes... Mom," I teased her.

She responded by doing a barrel roll in the sky, something I had been getting accustomed to when I got sassy back with her. We landed in the flight field. There were dragons, phoenixes, and griffins scattered in the field, but no Riders.

"Everyone is in the courtyard... There are bodies scattered about," Esme said, flatly.

My heart started pounding in my chest, my cheeks felt like fire, and my lunch was trying to exit my throat.

"Control it," she said, *"or I will sever your ability to channel it, until you can."*

She hadn't threatened me with that, nor had she done it yet, but she was right—I needed to control it. I took a breath and shut it down. I slid down her leg, my feet hitting solid ground. My legs wobbled beneath me. Nine hours in the saddle still wrecked my legs.

Zane was there instantly, standing in front of me. His hands gripped my arms, staring at me with his fierce eyes. He pulled me into an embrace, holding me tightly.

"No matter what we are walking into, you and I are one."

"Yesterday, today, tomorrow, and forever," I said back.

He let go and grabbed my hand, and we walked toward the chaos. It seemed everyone was talking all at once, nothing comprehensible, as we made it through the outdoor arena and started to walk into the courtyard. Nausea washed over me.

Seven bodies hung around the courtyard walls. I turned in a circle, looking at each one. They were displayed like before, flayed open and left for us to witness. Voices started to crash in around me.

"How did this happen?"

"Who are they?"

"She was in our wing."

"He was in our clan."

"I thought everyone was gone."

I spun to look at the body that hung above Dining Hall Two. It was Asmoth. Shit. The asshole who attacked me.

Looking around, it seemed like it was a cadet from each branch. No branch was off-limits. My mind started to spin with questions, the same ones that everyone was asking. We were all gone, and my dad cleared everyone who was coming back early.

More wingbeats filled the air, getting closer to the courtyard, not landing in the flight field. I lifted my head and looked to the sky. There were dragons, phoenixes, griffins, and Drusearons incoming. Kim landed on the courtyard ledge that separated the courtyard from the arena. My father sat on her back, straight and poised. She lifted her head back and let out a loud screech. The ground vibrated beneath us, and most of us covered our ears.

She lifted off the wall, dipped down into the arena, then fluttered back up—without my father this time. Pascal dropped into the courtyard, quickly masking his wings.

His eyes were wide, darting around the courtyard. Shocked, unsure of what to do or say. Seven more cadets were dead. My father ran in from the arena, stopping in the middle of the courtyard, looking around. His eyes wide, he too was in shock. After he looked at each of the slain cadets, he turned and locked eyes with Zane and me. He took in a large inhale and blew out a large breath through his lips. I knew what he was thinking. I wasn't running. I wasn't going to hide.

One of the Witch professors was walking from body to body, closely looking at what happened to them. She then walked over to my father.

"They have been dead for weeks... probably never made it home," she said low, but not low enough.

"I thought second lieutenants were on overwatch?" he asked her.

"They were..."

"Alright, cadets, listen up. Get settled into your chambers. All cadets present will meet in the stadium classroom at seventeen hundred, before dinner." My father announced, with the voice of discipline.

Zane's hand was still holding mine tightly. He pulled me, snapping me out of the trance I fell into for a moment. I followed him as we walked through the door to the Riders' wing. We climbed the stairs up to the second floor, he pushed my door open, and pulled me into my room.

He let go of my hand and did a quick scan. I set my bag down in the room and moved to the window to look out into the field. Fliers could be seen in the distance, heading towards the flight field. I looked down and saw a folded piece of paper sitting on my desk. I cocked my head to the side. I don't remember that being there when I left.

"What is it?" Zane asked.

"I don't remember leaving anything on my desk..."

Before I could grab it, he reached down and took it. He opened it up. His eyebrows furrowed, eyes narrowed, and lips pressed into a thin line.

"Well, don't leave me hanging?"

Instead of reading it aloud, he handed it to me. One line. My shadows started to swirl around my ankles. I had control, but they reacted. *I do it for you. Everything is for you.*

Who wrote this? What does this mean? How did they get into my room? Why did they leave this for me? Question after question poured into my mind.

"Do you remember what we practiced about warding in Ashwynd?" Zane said.

"Yeah, you and Finley shoved warding down my throat for days."

"Good. Let's check your wards. Someone put that in here."

I walked to my door and held my hand up to the door. The power underneath my fingertips pulsed. I closed my eyes and visualized the shield around the room. It was violet with streaks of indigo. Just as they taught me, I visualized who could enter my room without me—only Zane. I visualized myself pulling people in.

The ward hadn't been altered. It was intact. I brought my hand down and opened my eyes. Zane stared at me, concern painted on his face.

"What did you see?"

"Nothing, the ward is just how it should be, intact and not meddled with."

"Hmm... that's what I saw as well. It doesn't really explain how someone got that in here, though."

"Going back to Ashwynd sounds like an excellent idea right now."

"Way less chaos than this place. Let's keep this note a secret. We don't need to freak anyone out any more than they are," he said.

I nodded. He was right. Everyone was already walking on eggshells around here. He turned toward me and pulled me into him, holding me tightly again. I've learned that hugging was as much for him as it was for me. He pulled back, moved his hand to grip my throat before pushing my body against the door, kissing me feverishly.

"I could stay in here and devour you and pretend whatever fuckery is happening out there doesn't exist."

He nipped my bottom lip before sucking on it. Gods, every time he kissed me, I wanted to climb on top and fuck him wildly. He pushed my flight coat off my shoulders, letting it drop to the floor. I pulled at his, and he let it fall behind him. He pushed me against the door and started kissing down my neck, whilst still gripping my throat.

Someone knocked on the door, vibrating it behind me. My entire body jumped before it froze in place. The knock rattled through the door, breaking our haze with each other. Zane pushed back off of me, eyes wide.

"Auri!" a familiar voice yelled.

"Lili," Zane whispered, "you'd better let her in before she starts a search party."

"I know you're here, I saw your dad," Lili yelled.

Zane reached down and grabbed both of our flight coats off the ground, then I turned around and opened the door.

"Oh? Did I? Am I interrupting something?"

I blinked my eyes at her. She knew damn well she was. I reached out and grabbed her wrist and pulled her through the ward and into my chambers. She grabbed me into a hug, holding me tight.

"I'm so glad you're okay."

"Why wouldn't I be?"

"I don't know... A murderer is running around."

"I'm fine," I told her.

"I'm just happy to see you."

"How was the flight from Zion?" I asked her.

"Yeah, everything went well. Alex and I made it home safely. My father was out most of the time, but my mother took leave to spend time with us."

"Did you know that Kim is bonded to your father's dragon—Korvanle?"

"I never confirmed it directly, but I suspected, yes. Why else would we always move from base to base together?"

"I guess I hadn't put two and two together—"

"You would have as you learn more about flier relations, which is something that happens after winter break."

"They told us that fliers can have mates."

"Yeah, but now that you are actually bonded, the discussion of bonded fliers arises because when we are doing training exercises where we may leave the college, pairing the mated dragons is crucial. Sometimes, Riders change wings to better accommodate."

"Gods, I hope not."

"You should be fine, Esme is a little young—"

"She's bonded," I cut her off before she could finish.

"Oh." Her eyes dropped to the ground. "Well, I will use whatever pull I can to keep you in my platoon. That Rider can join us."

"Is the courtyard a mess still?" Zane cut in.

"Yeah, the bodies weren't there anymore, but it is still chaos down there. Everyone will be greeted before they enter the courtyard and given instructions before being turned around and instructed to go through the Watch Tower One or Four."

"What is this?" Lili screeched before grabbing my left arm and inspecting my newly branded bondmark. Her eyes were wide. Nothing came out of my mouth. I knew anytime I would be in only a tee, someone would notice it. Her gaze drifted over to Zane and looked down at his arm, where his matching bondmark stayed.

"Is this what I think it is?" she asked.

"If you think it's a bond mark, then yes," Zane said.

"Oh... umm. Wow. I have never seen one in person, and wow, those are quite the marks."

"Yeah..." I added, really unsure of what to say.

"Apparently, the Gods really wanted to bless us," Zane added, then laughed.

Even surrounded by Lili and Zane, the words on the letter played back into my head. Was it from the murderer? Were they killing for me? Gods, I hope not.

CHAPTER 14

All the cadets who returned early shuffled into the stadium classroom, sitting in our respective sections for our branch. The riders made up the largest group present, with the extra twelve First Year Flight Guides.

"Thank you for your early return," my father stated in his usual flat, authoritarian tone. "Let's get down to business."

Major General Kamban stood next to my father, his shoulders back in the perfect posture. "Part of the protocol, every cadet and professor left. Second lieutenants manned the watch towers, as well as some experienced Riders and Drusearon flyers. As you know, despite our efforts, there were seven cadets on display. One from each branch. We don't know how someone got through patrol."

Murmurs started rising from the crowd. My father raised his hand into the air, and the room fell silent.

"As we discussed before your departure, I will be silently checking every cadet as they return. As a reminder, what you have learned is classified information. Sharing that information will result in your death. All the generals and I will be discussing further plans to make everything work seamlessly on Monday. As of right now, all cadets will be directed to enter through Watch Tower 5, one by one. It will be a long day, though cadets will be staggered throughout the day, instead of all at once. You will receive your duty assignment tomorrow from your Wing Commanders. All Wing Commanders and Executive Officers—we will be discussing further plans tomorrow at zero-nine hundred in the administration meeting room," my father stated.

"Are there any questions?" Kamban asked.

Hands shot up in the air all over the room.

He pointed to one of the cadets in the Infantry section. "How long were those cadets dead?"

"We don't know. We estimated they had been dead for a couple of weeks, as they were almost frozen," Kamban answered, then pointed to a rider.

"How did they kill a rider mid-flight and bring them here?"

"We don't know if that's what happened, nor the when," my father answered. "I know that you all have a lot of questions surrounding their deaths; however, we learned of these deaths at the same time most of you did. Are there any questions not related to the slain cadets?"

Most of the cadets dropped their hands; a few remained up. My dad pointed to one of the Shapeshifters.

"What is the status of the war with the Rudemont?" he asked.

"Ongoing, there have been several more attacks on our coastal bases. This will be a more extended discussion with Professors Melamora, Pascal, and Fogg when all cadets are back," my father said, then pointed to a Drusearon sitting behind Zane.

"Will third or fourth years be called into service?" she asked.

A few cadets shifted in their seats, and some grumbled.

"At this moment, no. This could change. In years past, fourth-years would be called before third-years. However, an exceptionally skilled or powerful third-year could be put into service."

I knew that. I didn't want to hear it, though. The thought of Zane, Lili, or Alex being called into service made my stomach knot.

"We are pairing everyone up with a buddy. It will be someone whose bedchambers are near yours. If you go to the dining hall, they will too. If there are any odd numbers, then there will be a buddy pair of three. There will be a pair of first or second lieutenants stationed in each hall. This will ensure each cadet isn't vulnerable. Each Wing Commander will be paired with their Executive Officer, and those two will assign all other partners in their wing before we leave this room," Kamban said.

"After you are paired, you should eat dinner and stay in your chambers. If your room isn't warded, get it done. If you don't know how, reach out to your Wing Commander," my father said. Then he turned, stepped off the dais, and headed out the first-floor door.

I got paired up with Laderra, the Flight Guide for the Fire Platoon in Feather Wing. Her room was two doors down from mine. After we all received our buddies, we all shuffled down and out of the first-floor door, into the courtyard, and into our assigned dining halls. Feather Wing gathered at tables near each other. Chatter in the dining halls wasn't the typical cheerful banter. It was charged with worry. Nobody laughed—all conversations were serious.

Zane sat next to Remus—his face said everything he was thinking. He was worried about what would happen over the next few days, as we prepared for the cadets to come back. Concerned about his wing, worried about me, worried about possibly being pulled into service early. Everything was weighing on him.

After we finished our meal, our wing walked back to our chambers as a large group. While we were assigned another cadet to buddy with, Nikolai made it clear he wanted us to try to remain as a larger group whenever possible. He planned that we would go to the second-floor rooms, and then once we were inside, the rest of them would move to the first floor. He wanted all of us in the hall at zero-seven hundred to go to breakfast together.

By the time we made it back to our chambers, the day's tension clung to me. The bodies. The note. I walked to the desk and lifted the letter that lay there folded up. I opened it up and reread it. What did it mean? What were they protecting me from?

"What do you think it means?" Zane asked. I screeched and jumped all at one time, turned to face him, dropping the letter on the floor.

"Fuck my shadows, Zane," I yelled out. He scared the living shit out of me. My heart was beating double the normal rate.

"I mean... I am always happy to fuck you every day, all day."

"I thought we talked about warnings before you just rove in here."

"Surprise?"

"Did you come... to fuck me all wild?"

"I always want to do that, and if that happens, it happens, but I came because I haven't slept without you in my arms in weeks, and I'm not gonna start now." He looked around the room, grinning. "But... we are gonna need to go to my much larger bed."

He moved closer, closing the gap between us. He reached out and pulled me into his arms. Lights flashed, cold then warm air brushed over my face. We were in his room.

"I never missed my room at home, until you filled the space, and now I just want to take you back home and lock ourselves into the room."

"Your room here is decent-sized."

"Yeah, but I am not worried about a psycho killing people, and my bed is much larger at home."

He was still holding onto me, staring into my eyes. He lowered his head, placing his lips on my forehead and keeping them there. We breathed in sync with each other for a few heartbeats. He locked his fingers into my hair and pulled me into him, our tongues locking together. He broke away and stared at me, his arms still wrapped around me.

"We could go back there," he said.

"You sound like my dad," I said, "not exactly a turn on."

"Hmm... then how about I taste every part of you. Lick you up and down, suck on that little spot that makes you squirm," he said, smiling, letting his little dimples show through.

"Much better... maybe I could taste—"

"Not tonight," he said.

He reached down, gripping my ass, and pulled me up into his arms. He kissed me passionately with demand. His lips were soft and full, and wetness spread between my thighs. He lowered my legs down, then gripped his hand around my throat, lifting my head slightly. He bit my lip, pulling on it. My entire body craved his, my stomach tingled, my nipples ached for his touch.

He reached down and pulled my long sleeve up and over my head. I reached down and removed his shirt. He quickly removed the rest of my clothing and threw it to the side. He moved me to the bed, gently laying me down. Then removed his clothing slowly, teasing like always. I pulled my knees up and spread my legs to the side, reached down and took one finger, dragging it up one side and then down the other side, before putting it inside. Gods, I was wet. Tingles filled the area, and warmth rushed to the area. No longer feeling cold. I threw my head back and let out a moan.

He moved to get his boots and breeches off faster. He gripped my thighs and pulled me to the edge of the bed, and knelt. He flattened his tongue, placing it at the bottom, and lifted his head, dragging his tongue all the way up me. Fuck me. I reached down and grabbed a handful of his hair. He let out a moan.

He did it a few more times, getting wetter with each pass. Gods, he knew how to devour me just right. He lifted his head, stopping at my clit, he drew me in, and started sucking on my clit. He moved his middle and ring fingers into me. I threw my head back and let out a moan. He pulsed his fingers inside me while sucking my clit.

My entire body rushed with warmth. I could feel myself teetering on the edge. My vision blurred. My toes curled tightly. Every grunt he made, I came closer. He sucked on me harder, and lightning coursed through my body. He moved his fingers within me faster.

I erupted. Electricity shot through from my head to my curled toes. I moaned loudly and uncontrollably. Shadows swirled around my hands. Reminding me they were there. His fingers were soaked, his warm, full lips still gently sucking on me. He slowed, but still moved within me.

"I love when you squirt in my mouth and all over my hand."

I let out another moan, trying to steady my ragged breath. In my nose and out of my mouth, I reminded myself.

He pulled his fingers out and slowly climbed up my body, kissing along my hips, then to my stomach. He moved to my nipple, he swirled his tongue in circles around it, and then moved to the other one.

"Can't make the other one jealous."

I let out a little laugh. He was impossible. He moved up to my neck, gripping my throat before kissing me.

"Let's try something new."

I nodded my head. Experimenting with him left me wanting more and more, left me wanting to try something new each time.

"You're gonna sit on me backwards, and then lie back," he said down the bond.

"Mmm, that sounds nice."

He moved to lie down on the bed. I rolled over and climbed over to him. I straddled him backwards, lowering myself onto his cock.

I gasped. He let out a loud moan. I stayed there for a couple of heartbeats, taking in that feeling. He pulled me back gently, my back pressed against his chest. I reached my hands up and gripped him. He reached down with one hand, putting his finger on my clit. His other hand grabbed my tit. He moved under me. Oh Gods. He was hitting every good spot inside of me. He thrusted under me, thumb pressed into my clit, and his other hand gripped my nipple.

"Grab my hair, and fuck me harder, Zane."

He let go of my nipple and reached up and grabbed a handful of my hair. He thrusted his hips harder beneath me. I reached up and fisted a handful of his hair, pushing my knees into the bed. He moved in me faster. His breath was ragged against my neck.

"You're so fucking slick, Auri."

He bit my neck. Gods. I was going to cum all over again, all control gone.

"You're about to be dripping with my cum." He thrusted harder and deeper. My vision blurred again, my stomach tingled, my whole body flushed with heat. He moaned deep and guttural. Shadows engulfed both of us—turning everything pitch black. I screamed out a moan.

"Fuckkkkkk, fuckkkk me," he moaned. His thrusting slowed down, but still moved deep within me. Every thrust made my body quake. The shadows slowly dissipated within me.

Zane reached his arms around, holding me tight.

"I love you, my sweet Anam Cara," he whispered into my ear.

"I love you too, Roarke," I said down the bond. He let out a low laugh.

"I hope your humor never dies."

I rolled off of him and onto my side to face him. He grabbed my hips and pulled me as close as he could. He moved his hand up to cradle my cheek.

"You're so gorgeous. I'm happy I didn't have to wait any longer to have you a part of my life."

"You were the best unexpected thing to happen to me."

"Sleep, my sweet love, tomorrow is another long day."

CHAPTER 15

Zane

Lying in this bed holding Auri made everything inside me feel at peace. I knew that shit was happening outside of our chambers—the continent was falling apart. I didn't care about any of it. I cared about her. That's it. Nothing else. Nothing more. I knew my infatuation with her would end me, and I didn't care.

My powers felt like they were on the verge of losing all control. Every time she lost control of her shadows, I had to lock every urge inside of me. My magic called her magic. It wanted it. I didn't want it. The primal part of me tasted it twice—and ever since, it craved more. I needed to tell her. I wanted to tell her, but I was terrified of how she would respond. I didn't know why because she had never shown me a sign she would push me away, but the tiny doubt was seeded deep within me.

The thought of taking her and running off to the mountains crossed my mind, but I knew her father would burn the world down looking for her. Before we went home, I hated that man. That changed. I saw his true side, the one he doesn't let many see. The soft side. The protective father who would end a life without hesitation. No doubt that would be me one day.

I roved Auri back to her chambers before anyone realized she hadn't slept in hers. After breakfast, all Wing Commanders and Executive Officers were required to attend the meeting to discuss our plans for the cadets' return tomorrow.

We all piled into the administration room. Her father and Kamban sat at the head table. Professors filled the chairs, and cadets lined the walls. Remus stood to my left, and Nikolai took my right. No matter what, I knew I could rely on either of them.

"Attention," Auri's father commanded, "we want to get this over with as swiftly as possible and get everyone onto their tasks."

"Most cadets will return via train in Chalahana, but the Riders will land in the flight field first. Drusearons will fly in all over. All cadets will come through Watch Tower 5, regardless of their branch. The first train is expected to arrive at zero-seven hundred. I want every cadet who is on the premises to be on patrol by zero-six thirty. All Drusearons here will be in the air, intercepting any cadet. You will make sure they land in the admin field," Kamban said.

He paced around the room, taking everyone in. "I want all the Riders to be doing overwatch, stepping in to help the Drusearons. Historians will be in front of the Bravo side, Healers in front of the Alpha side, Infantry outside of the arena, Shapeshifters on the west side of the admin building, and Sorcerers on the north side. Lieutenants will cover all other gaps. Any questions?"

No one spoke. Instructions were straightforward.

Her father stood, arms crossed. "I want every door to be covered. Your job as Wing Commanders and Executive Officers is to assign the cadets who have been cleared, keeping your assigned area clear. I want every one of you to go over the protocols. Once a cadet is cleared, they will be ordered to the stadium classroom."

"All cadets are dismissed," Kamban said.

We all moved out of the room quickly.

"That's a nice... um... mark there, Zane," Nikolai said almost under his breath.

"It's nothing," I said, and I pulled my forearm next to my body.

"Hmm... nothing? I might have seen something very similar on Blackcreek," he said. He stopped and turned to face me.

"It really is nothing..."

"As her Wing Commander, it isn't nothing, if it's what I think it is. As your friend, congrats on finally finding the girl that was plastered over your palace."

"Our parents were present, so the General is aware, and thank you. She is... the greatest gift to ever happen to me."

"If you haven't informed Remus, you need to. We will need to coordinate assignments," he said, before he turned around and carried forward.

"Inform me of what?" Remus asked as he walked up behind me.

"When there are fewer ears," I said, nodding towards the other cadets. He nodded.

Since he was my assigned buddy, we walked back towards our wing.

"Want to hit the sparring gym?" I asked him. I needed to get some of the pent-up energy out.

"Sure, it's not like you can go without me, and you look like you need it."

Like many of the other branches, we also had a small sparring gym in our wing. Ours was on the second floor. It smelled like sweat and leather mixed. No one else was there. Most of the cadets hid in their chambers.

We both stripped off our tees and stepped onto the foam mat in the middle of the small gym. As soon as we tapped knuckles, I started throwing punches fast and furious. He blocked and threw them back just as quickly.

"Auriella and I are mated, both wearing bondmarks," I said, through my fast-paced breathing.

Remus stopped, dropped his arms, eyes wide at me. I threw a punch, hitting his chest, but he didn't move. He stayed staring at me.

"Are you for real?" he cracked out.

"When have you known me to joke about something like this?"

"Fuck, Zane."

"Arms up," I said, before I threw another punch. He delivered a brutal kick to my calf, making me stumble back a couple of steps. "Whatever you have to say, get it over with."

"It really fucking complicates things," he barked.

"How?"

"I just thought she was someone occupying your time, not... well, whatever this is now."

"You don't remember seeing a painted picture of a female in my room?" I cocked my head sideways at him. Slightly confused by his reaction.

He closed his eyes, dropped his head, and took a few steps off the mat. "I never put two and two together, and I never knew what that painting meant."

"We hadn't really planned to tell anyone. However, the Gods really fucked that up and blessed us with large tattoos on our arms," I said, flipping my arm out for him to see.

"I saw the new markings, but didn't realize what they were. You know, third-years start doing field assignments after the winter solstice. That really complicates things. I am happy for you. You have something we all dream of."

"Thanks, now back at it." I motioned for him to come at me.

He threw a right-right-left-right combo, and that last one got me in my chin, making my head spin to the side. I needed that. I wanted that pain. He lit that fire inside of me, and I moved forward, unleashing myself. Remus and I sparred since we were children. We both knew what the other needed. He knew I liked the pain—it was the perfect outlet when shit went south.

We sparred for over an hour before both of us took our sweat-drenched selves to our chambers for a shower. Afterwards, we went to our Platoon Leaders to give them their orders for the following day. Between the Riders and us, air patrol should be well covered. We planned to perch on the top of the towers when we needed breaks.

I hoped that the murderer would be found, the hysteria would fade, and we would go back to some normalcy. Well, as normal as it could get, considering there was a war brewing. During the second semester, third and fourth-year cadets were often sent on short-term assignments to different bases.

What Remus said flashed back in my head about it causing complications. I hadn't really thought of it or considered it. Mates couldn't be separated over a long distance for more than three days before their powers started to weaken. By day seven, their power was almost nonexistent, and they were weakened.

Field assignments often lasted two to three weeks. I couldn't expect her to leave the safety of the college to come to me, and I also couldn't skip assignments. The goal was that cadets visit the majority of the bases before they graduated. This would limit me to only going to nearby ones.

The thought of leaving her made my heart race. If something happened to her while I was away, I would never forgive myself. Even if I survived losing her, I would choose not to. It was pathetic, but it was the most honest I had been with myself.

"What are you doing?" I said down our bond.

"Reading a book in my room," she said.

"What's your assignment tomorrow?"

"Esme and I are to make rounds around the college. The fliers will communicate the orders... I'm just a pawn sitting on top of her."

"I think the bigger concern is the non-Riders on foot trying to skip the line."

"Yeah... Esme said she would just blast them." Then she laughed.

"I'm coming in."

I roved into her chambers. She sat in her high-backed chair reading, legs on the footstool, book in her hands. Her hair was down, not braided or in a bun. Something about that view made me ravenous. I used to have control, and yet I had none with her. She was my vice, and I wanted to be greedy with her.

"Remus and Nikolai are both aware of..." I flipped my arm over, motioning to the bond mark.

"Oh?"

"Nikolai noticed it first, and happened to see yours as well, and put two and two together."

"It's not like we can hide our marks forever. They are cumbersome, and long sleeves will only work for so long."

"Yeah, especially when I don't wear them often anyway," I said.

I sighed, and she cocked her head at me, but didn't say anything.

"Do you know that third and fourth-years go on assignments during the second semester?"

"I didn't. Well, I did, I just forgot," she said, then sighed.

I sat down on the edge of her bed. I knew from other conversations that she worried about the future, our future. She often asked about it, and I tried to calm her fears, but here we were. She closed the book and put it on the table next to her.

"I don't know what that means for us, for me, but Remus brought it up. The inland bases shouldn't be a huge deal, I can rove back for a few hours each night. During those assignments, we can be called out—"

"Any hour of the night. I'm not familiar with how our bond and powers work." She was rubbing her fingertips on the palms of her hand, and her knee bounced side to side faster.

"It won't happen for a few weeks, and with the whole murder thing, it may be postponed. We don't have to worry—"

"How long can we be apart?"

"Seven days, max. After three days, both of our powers will start to diminish."

"We really are tied together forever, huh?"

"Yeah, we are... and I wouldn't have it any other way. Even if my powers didn't diminish, I don't want to spend a single day without seeing you."

She looked over at me, our eyes locked onto each other. "I guess I will be joining you—"

"No."

"No?" she repeated back, her eyebrow raised at me.

"I don't want you in any danger—"

"I grew up on these bases, Zane. I will be fine."

"You need to be here—"

"For what?"

"There is plenty for you to learn."

"I grew up on military bases. I know everything I need to know. I have my dragon, and I know how to ride her."

"You need to learn and master your magic—"

"The magic that I am not supposed to let anyone know about?" Her voice was cracking, and her eyes started watering.

"Auri..." Watching her start to break, broke a part of me inside I didn't think could break. I stood up and moved to her and knelt before her.

"You know you can't control what I do, right?" She mustered out.

"I'm not trying to control you, but I will beg you to please not follow me into danger. You may have grown up on the bases, but some of our coastal bases are in hostile status."

"I'm trained, I'm not a weak, pathetic female. I was born for this," she said, very faint shadows swirled around her ankles, touching me every few swirls.

Her magic was formidable. I reached my hand out and touched them. I closed my eyes, my entire arm tingled, and my chest tightened. Her magic wanted me, and I wanted it. Fuck Zane. Fucking control it. I snapped my eyes open and drew my hand away. She was still staring at her lap, unaware.

"I've never thought you were weak. You're incredible, but my own fear controls me. I refuse to live in this world without you. I'll set it on fire, then myself." As soon as it came out, I wanted to take it back. I didn't want her to know those darker thoughts I had.

I grabbed her in my arms, pulling us to a stand. I grabbed the back of her head and kissed her the way that made her delicate little moans. I couldn't control her, but I could own this moment. Own her in the bed, command her in all the sinful ways she wanted. The only control I had over her was when she was screaming my name and filling my mouth with her sweet nectar.

Tonight, she would be safe in my arms, but I could feel it. Her shadows weren't the only thing stirring in the dark.

CHAPTER 16

The bells tolled early—we were expected to be finished eating by zero-six hundred, and in our assigned patrol areas by zero-six thirty. Zane fell asleep in my chambers last night. There was something bittersweet about my smaller bed. Sure, it was narrow, but it meant we stayed close all night.

What he professed to me weighed heavily on my mind. He didn't want to exist if I didn't, and I wasn't sure how I felt about that. He didn't let me speak, instead devouring me. I knew both of us used intimacy to avoid tough conversations, but sometimes I just wanted to overtalk things.

I wasn't sure I shared his sentiments. I knew I didn't want to exist without him, but I wasn't sure if I would go as far as he did. He left before the bells tolled, back to his chambers.

Our wing walked to the dining facility together and then went to the flight field together. Our fliers waited for us. Laderra was bonded to a gorgeous phoenix. She and I would remain together as we flew overhead. When our dragons needed a break, they would let the other fliers know. No more than four of us were allowed to take a break at a time, each lasting no longer than thirty minutes.

We launched into the air and began our endless circles.

"You just sit up there and sit pretty," Esme purred.

"The only good thing about this is that—you and I get uninterrupted talk time."

"Oh, goody, I like to spill secrets. That's probably why they don't like us youngins to bond," Esme let out a loud rumble.

"What if I didn't choose you?"

"Right to the point."

"It's a question that has been burning in my head."

"I don't know. I just knew you would pick me, but if you had picked Kekoa, maybe I would have challenged him before you left the forest with him."

"Does that happen?"

"It has—many, many moons ago."

"Other than my dad and me, have there been any other Shapeshifters that have bonded with a flier?"

"I really don't know."

"Melamora said that fliers wouldn't entertain a bond with a Shapeshifter—"

"Hmm... last I knew, she was a Witch and didn't speak for the fliers..."

"That didn't really answer it," I pressed on.

"Well... I am bonded to you and my mother to your father—"

"But we don't shift?"

"Still undetermined."

"I don't want to be a wolf, Esme. I am where I want to be."

"Hmm..." She lifted her wings, and I prepared for her to do a barrel roll.

"Predictable," I told her.

"Hey, down below. There is a pair of cadets coming through the corner of the Alpha and Bravo side. Zane and Remus are near there, let him know," Esme said down the bond.

"Hey, Esme spotted two cadets coming out of the woods, corner of Alpha and Bravo," I told him.

"Got it. Thanks, babe," he said down the bond.

Esme and I continued flying around for hours. We took a short break for me to use the bathroom, grab a bite to eat, and she did whatever it is dragons do. We continued flying endless circles. We redirected at least fifty cadets who traveled on foot or flew in. Kim occasionally did some flyovers, but mostly stayed perched on the ledge of Watch Tower Five.

We all watched the sunset from the sky. It grew dark and was getting colder by the minute when the bells finally tolled. Our signal that our overwatch was over, and we were expected to report to the stadium classroom.

The Riders and Drusearons all landed in the flight field and walked as a group towards the ground floor door to enter the stadium classroom. My father, Kamban, Pascal, Melamora, Fogg, and two others I hadn't seen before. It took several minutes for all the cadets who were doing overwatch to arrive and get seated.

"Welcome back, cadets," Melamora said, standing confidently.

"First, I want to say thank you to our leadership cadets who braved the cold and helped with the efforts of checking every cadet back in," my father said, "there are currently sixty-seven students who are unaccounted for. We will be attempting to locate them."

His head dropped to the floor, and worry spread across his face. He paced in a circle around the dais. "Unfortunately, we haven't narrowed down who has been murdering cadets."

"Same rules before you left, with the addition that everyone will be paired with either a partner or two. You will stay with that person no matter what. More lieutenants will be positioned throughout the campus and in each hallway. Every single cadet here is being trained to be a soldier, start acting like one, and watch your backs," Kamban ordered.

"Standing on this dais with me are Colonel Foret and Lieutenant General Benning. They will be remaining here until the situation is under control," my father said, "Wing Commanders and Executive Officers will be assigning your partners before you leave this room. Then they will dismiss you."

My father, Kamban, Foret, and Benning stepped down and left. Nikolai, Casey, and Arya got up and walked to the front of our section.

"We will have everyone separate by their assigned wing. All leadership that has already been paired is free to leave. Classes resume tomorrow morning. Feather Wing cadets come down to the first couple of rows," Nikolai said.

Laderra and I looked at each other. We both stood up and quickly got out of the room.

"Let's get dinner before we go to our chambers, and before the rest of the cadets crowd the dining facility," Laderra said.

"Sounds good," I told her.

We both got a tray of food and ate quickly. It was clear that both of us wanted to get out of there before every other cadet came rushing in for dinner. We headed back in and went to the second floor.

Laderra stopped in her tracks. I walked into her, making me stumble. A strange smell hit my nose. My head lifted to where Laderra was staring. My dinner surged up, splattered onto the floor. Laderra's arms trembled.

Nellie Pitino and the Lieutenant who had been watching over our hall. Both of them were strung up, arms and legs spread wide. There was a slit across their necks, blood down the front of them. My eyes fixated on them, unable to move. I gripped Laderra's arm. She was frozen in place. My magic boiled. Shadows wanting to erupt.

"I've let Inna know, Nikolai is coming. Control your powers, Auri," Esme said.

Hearing her voice snapped me back to reality. I turned my head to Laderra, who had tears streaming down her face. Hands shaking violently.

"Laderra, look at me," I said. I moved in front of her, grabbing the sides of her arms. "You're okay, I'm here with you. Take a breath."

Within moments, the hall filled with cadet leadership and officers, including my father. He looked at the bodies strung on the wall before he grabbed my shoulders. I turned toward him, and he pulled me in close.

"Please, go home with Zane," he whispered to me.

I looked up at him and shook my head. He pulled me in tighter, holding for a few more seconds, before he let me go and walked towards the bodies.

"I'm on my way... I had to get these cadets straightened out," Zane said.

"I'm fine."

"Your favorite line..."

"If you're not an officer, get into your chambers. Now," my father barked.

Laderra walked into hers, and I walked into mine. I slumped onto the floor in front of my bed and wrapped my arms around my legs. Most of these cadets who had died hated me or caused me harm. The note said they did it for me. Did they mean these murders? I didn't want anyone killing on my behalf.

I dropped my head onto my knees, and shadows spread out from within, swirling around me. Tears slowly rolled down my face.

"Incoming," Zane said, and then roved into the room. "Oh, Auri. This is not on you." He knelt next to me—shadows spread out from me to him.

"It feels like it. Some of these cadets have caused me harm. Then there's the note—it seems like someone is killing for *me.*"

"You are not responsible for what other people do."

"If they are doing it on my behalf..."

"You can't think that way—"

"My dad pretty much begged me to go home with you..."

"Oh."

He sat down next to me. He grabbed my hand and interlocked our fingers. We sat in silence on the floor in front of my bed, no words shared. What was I supposed to say? Nothing he could say would make any of this better or go away.

A knock on the door brought both of us out of a trance. I snapped my head to Zane. Fuck. He wasn't supposed to be in here. He looked at me with his eyes wide.

I stood up and went to the door. "Who is it?"

"Your father."

Fuck. He would surely scold us for not following the rules.

I opened the door and stared at him. He went to enter before bouncing back. "Effective shield, above your level, I presume, Zane?" he said.

"Yeah, he's an overprotective mother hen." I reached my arm out, grabbed him, and pulled him into the room. He pushed the door behind me.

"I see you still struggle following the rules," he said, motioning behind me to Zane.

"To be fair, sir, I'm the one who breaks the rules," Zane said.

My father walked over to my chair and took a seat.

"Zane, is there any way I can talk you into persuading Auri out of this place?"

"No," both of us said.

"I'm not surprised, and honestly fuck the rules."

If my eyes could have fallen out of my head, they would have. Zane's eyes were also wide open, and both of us were staring at my father. I'm not sure what was more shocking, the part of him saying to disregard the rules or dropping a curse word.

"Good Gods, you both act like I am so prim and perfect. C'mon, Auri, you curse like a sailor. The only reason you hadn't heard me curse in several years is that I became mindful of it while you were around, due to your growing mouth."

A little giggle escaped from my mouth. I thought back to when I was younger and remembered him cursing quite a bit.

"Either way, I don't care if I break every rule to keep her safe, so you unofficially have my permission to continue breaking this rule."

"Understood, sir. I have no intentions of letting harm come to her," Zane said.

"Good Gods, first off, I am right here. Secondly, I can handle my own." They both just looked at me. I summoned my shadows to my hands, let them envelope my hands. I flung my right hand toward the ground and visualized them lifting me in the air, and I slowly lifted off the ground. I turned my left hand over, holding it out towards my father, and the shadows shot towards him. He gasped, and I smiled. I wanted him lifted off the ground, no harm to him. They followed my command and slowly lifted him off the ground.

"I got it, Auri. You are... quite something," my father said.

I pulled my shadows back and let him drop the three feet to the ground. He narrowed his eyes at me.

"You see, I have been practicing," I told him. Zane smiled.

"That you have, but it still doesn't mean I'm not worried. The reason I came in here was to tell you that we didn't find anyone, but clearly they are here."

"Yeah… what are we gonna do?" I asked him.

"*You* are gonna do nothing," he said, tone flat.

"Well then, you should know… I had a letter waiting for me when I arrived back—"

"What?" His voice dropped.

"I can't say with certainty this has to do with me… but the letter stated they are doing it for me."

"Doing what?"

"It didn't say," Zane said.

"That's… ominous," he said, "and doesn't ease my concern at all."

"Mine either," Zane added.

"Well, I'm not leaving campus until things are resolved and we find out who is doing this," my father said.

"Fun," I said.

"Don't expect special treatment outside of this room," my father quipped.

"I know, Dad," I said. It had always been that way, cold and distant when others were around. When he hugged me in the hall earlier, it was one of the few times he broke character around others.

My dad left us, but not before he tried to plead with us to pack up and head out. Zane and I both insisted we would be fine and were watching out for each other.

CHAPTER 17

Zane stayed with me until the early morning, before he returned to his chambers. No other orders came that evening. Laderra and I walked to breakfast together, neither of us saying much. We both saw way too much over the last several weeks. It was a realization that we weren't safe anymore.

Chatter around the dining facility was normal, like there wasn't a cadet and an officer strung up. Maybe they hadn't known. Only Laderra and I were in the hall, and leadership showed up quickly. We sat at the table with the rest of the first-year cadets in our squad, neither saying much.

Afterwards, my squad walked to the stadium classroom together. I sat with the other flight guides, who sat higher than the regular cadets but lower than the upper cadet leadership. Groups staggered in after they finished eating, and the seats filled up.

Melamora, Pascal, and Fogg entered as they usually did, but my father and Kamban were behind them. Both of them stood with their arms crossed, eyebrows narrowed, lips pursed.

"Good morning," Melamora said, with a smile. Her smile felt so out of place.

"Unfortunately, it looks like there is still a security concern. We will not cower, but we will all be vigilant. No cadets should be moving around campus without their assigned buddy, regardless of whether you are a Wing Commander. There will be no extra activities allowed. You will go to the dining facility when assigned to you and attend your lectures. If you're not doing those, you should be in your chambers. Every single cadet should have a ward on their room. If you don't know how, reach out to your leadership. The ward placed should only allow you—and your roommates, if you have them in," Kamban said.

"These policies are in place until further notice. I will be remaining on the campus, and you may see me in your lectures," my father said.

"Thank you, General," Melamora said, giving a nod at him.

"You should have received your new schedules this morning. Usually, third-years start rotations at various bases. That has been postponed, as well as fourth-year rotations," Pascal said.

Cadets all around grumbled and shifted.

Fogg held up his hand. "I know it's not the news you may have wanted to hear. We will be doing our best as your professors to get you back to field assignments."

"One of the reasons that rotations have been postponed is due to the increase in attacks on our coastal forts. Some of you may have witnessed some of these attacks while on leave," Pascal said.

More cadets shifted in their seats. I shot Zane a look. We were in the palace the majority of the time, but I knew more attacks were happening. Zane's father kept him up to date as he received information.

"Does anyone who went to Camp Echo want to share any firsthand experiences?" Melamora asked. A few cadets raised their hands, and she motioned to a third-year Infantry cadet.

"Both of my parents are Infantry cadets. A few days after I arrived home, the alarm bells went off, letting the base know we were under attack. My parents didn't let me go out, and thankfully, they returned. They said that there were... well... Nosferatu running around. They were trying to drain the blood of the town..." The cadet stared into his lap, terror spanned across his face.

A couple of cadets gasped. I couldn't pinpoint which section it came from.

"Unfortunately, that is what the reports are saying, that the Nosferatus are back and are invading our lands," Melamora said.

"Why don't we stop fighting them and let them live here. It's not like we are human either, and we are capable of—"

"No. They are blood thirsty, often killing for sport," my father said, cutting the cadet off.

"They aren't always like that?" the cadet shot back.

My dad cocked his head to the side and took a step toward the healer's section. "Why are you so pressed on this, cadet?"

"No reason, I've just heard that they aren't all killing for sport. They aren't all bad."

"And where did you *hear* this?" my father scolded.

"Just some scuttlebutt when I was home."

"Hmm. Okay," my dad said, before turning to Melamora. "Continue."

Melamora looked around the room, pacing back and forth. "Any other stories?" A cadet in the Shapeshifters raised their hand, and she pointed towards them.

"My family lives north of Kalona, close enough to hear the lockdown sirens. My father is still in service... well, he was..." he said, his voice got shaky. It was hard to tell from here, but I think he may have started to cry.

"I'm sorry for your loss, cadet," Pascal said.

"He left to defend our borders... and he never came home."

The room fell silent. One of the cadets sitting next to him patted him on the shoulder.

"He will be honored and remembered for his service," my father said.

My dad was going to go to Kalona next. Usually, generals didn't go to coastal bases due to the higher threats that come with coastal bases. I still hadn't figured out why he was going there. Was it something he wanted, or was it something the King was ordering?

I started thinking about Lili's parents and wondering where they were staying currently. Were they going to be coming to the college to stay? How long would Kim be able to be away from Korvanle?

"We can be away from our mates without issues. We just tend to get cranky after a while, as normal couples do," Esme said.

"So, only bonded mates have repercussions for separations."

"Yeah... there is nothing normal about bonded mates," she said, then laughter rolled down the bond. *"To answer your inner questions, my father and Lili's father are at Fort Daysn until they go to Fort Kalona."*

"Lili's mother?"

"She and her flier are there too."

My mom had put in one of her letters that I could trust Lili's mom. It left me wondering what she knew, or if she knew more than what my father had told me.

The class continued discussing various attacks all over our continent. By the end of the class, everything seemed solemn. There weren't quiet side conversations anymore. We all stared at our professors. Through the discussions, it was pretty clear that war was already here. While Sandorg sat in the middle of the continent, it was an intentional design. We had our own threats and deaths happening right on our campus. No matter where one went, they probably weren't safe.

"That is very gloom and doom," Esme said.

"You're probably right. I need to think of some positives, but in this moment I don't have any."

***

My second class was sparring, which included Riders, Healers, and Drusearons. When they reorganized lectures for this semester, the intermingling between branches was changed to only include the wing one belonged to. This meant I would likely only spar with other Riders or Drusearons, since most Healers opted out of sparring.

We all piled into the Gile's sparring gym. It was full of Electric Platoon cadets and a large group of Drusearons. In the corner, a small group of Healers.

"Welcome back, cadets. We were able to get a group of Healers to join us. I expect that if any of you match them, please be mindful that they don't normally spar. We also have temporarily suspended all call outs, nor is there any lethal blows allowed during sparring," Gile said.

He looked around the room. "Alright, let's begin. I'll start calling out names and mats. Stoot and Aamir—mat one. Blackcreek and Imera—mat two..."

My head shot ahead of the room, that name sounded familiar. I walked to mat two while still looking around. My head was spinning trying to figure out where I knew that name—

She walked to the mat wearing a baby blue tunic. It was Dafne. My stomach knotted. I hadn't seen her since we were twelve. She was absolutely awful to me. She made fun of my freckles, my height, and often called me dumb.

"Your dad isn't here to protect you—"

"I don't need protection from you. It's the other way around, and my dad is here," I cut her off.

I stepped onto the mat and bounced onto my toes. Did I really need to be gentle like Gile said? This bitch bullied me for years. I never fought back, afraid she might actually win. In the last eight years, I became stronger and had power simmering within me. It rose within me as everything she did to me as a child played back into my head.

I threw out a weak punch right towards her, but she dipped back out of the way.

"That's all you got, shorty?"

I raised my eyebrow. Now she was fucking taunting me.

I threw another right, as she threw one. I then put my entire weight forward and threw a left. It made contact and hit her nose hard. Blood started pouring on the floor. I reached up and grabbed a handful of her loose hair—rookie mistake. I pulled her forward and jumped onto her back. I locked my right arm under her chin and locked it into place with my left arm. We collapsed onto the floor, me under her. She was thrashing, and I squeezed tighter.

"Tap," I demanded.

"No," she barely wheezed out.

"Then it's time for you to take a little nap," I whispered into her ear. I tightened my arm under her neck, restricting her airway. I could feel her struggling to breathe under my arm. I didn't give a fuck.

"Blackcreek," Gile screeched.

I let go of my grip and let her fall to the side. "She's fine. Just taking a little nap." I flashed him a smile, then stepped off the mat.

"Oh, my little shadow, I love to see that side of you," Esme purred.

I lost control for a moment, but I didn't kill anyone. I just subdued her. This time.

CHAPTER 18

"This is crazy, I thought they were trying to reduce our deaths," Micah said.

All of Feather Wing First Flights were standing in the flight field with our fliers. Professor Hildegard went over what flight lessons would be like for the next several weeks. The first lesson would include our fliers locking a long rope in their talons, flying over low, we would jump on, and then climb up the rope mid-flight and mount our flier.

It was nice to hear Micah's banter again, even if he wasn't wrong. This was ridiculous. We went in our squad groups, our fliers launched into the air, gripping the seven-inch-thick ropes. Fire Platoon went first. One by one, fliers launched, and then they would lower just enough, the rope hovering three feet above the ground.

Laderra was up first in that group. Her phoenix dipped down into the field, and Laderra took off into a run, just as her phoenix flew beside her. She reached out and gripped the rope. Her phoenix rose into the sky slowly, as Laderra climbed the rope. My stomach was in knots watching it happen for the first time. One slip and she could fall. She had twenty feet to climb.

Before she was halfway up, Robert's dragon swooped down, ready for Robert to run towards the rope. He reached out to grab the rope, but before he could grip it, it slipped out of his grasp, and he fell forward. He yelled out some colorful words.

"Ludewuggin, get up. It happens to all of us. That's why we practice. She will wrap around and try again," Hildegard said.

"Yes, sir," Robert said. He stood up, brushed his pants off. He looked back over his shoulder, but none of us laughed, none of us snickered. If there was one thing we learned in flight lessons before we left, any of us could falter.

His grey dragon banked hard in the sky and came back around to try another pickup. Laderra had made it up the rope and was on her phoenix's back. This time, Robert gripped the rope effortlessly and climbed much quicker than Laderra. The fire platoon did three rounds climbing up their ropes. Nobody fell from the sky, thankfully.

Our small group was up next—Sadie, Akira, Micah, Lorenzo, and me. Flight Guides were to go first in each group, which meant me. My stomach was still knotted from watching the group before us go.

"We will be fine, we will show everyone how graceful we work together," Esme purred.

"Graceful... ha ha ha," I said to her.

I heard her wing beats approaching. The more I heard them, the more I knew them like the sound of my beating heart. She held the long rope in her talons, then she dipped lower. I took off running in the field, and she flew in closer. As the rope got next to me, I reached out and grabbed it, pulling it close to me. I held on, and she started lifting.

Don't fall. Don't fall. Don't fall.

I chanted in my head over and over, as I gripped the rope with my arms and my legs and started pulling myself up the rope. I could hear other wingbeats, and I closed my eyes for a brief moment and tuned them out. The only important thing was climbing this rope without falling. I didn't know what would happen if we did fall. Would someone swoop in?

"I'd drop the rope and grab you, silly," Esme said, then laughed.

"Good to know. Well, let's not test that out."

"Yes, please don't. I don't want to be the first to have my rider fall. The embarrassment."

"Do you always care what others think?" I asked her.

"Not normally, but our elders did protest Lakung and me from bonding, and I want to prove to them I am better than they are."

I laughed, gripped my hands tighter, and kept climbing. We both had something to prove. I surely didn't want to embarrass her because she usually made me pay with her crazy maneuvers.

"I'm glad you know the price of embarrassing me."

I finally climbed the rope to her talon, and I gripped onto her leg. Now the task of climbing up her, while in mid-flight.

"Do you always overthink things?"

Before I could even respond to her, she let the rope fall, jerked her leg, I slid down into her talons, and she threw me up and to the side, and dipped under me. I slid into the saddle perfectly. I also felt like throwing up.

"Over the side if you do…"

I took a huge breath in, calming my stirring stomach. The shadows responded and started swirling around my feet. I closed my eyes and willed them within. No one needed to see them yet.

"Do you think you could give me a warning before you do that again?" I asked her before reaching forward and rubbing her neck.

"How else did you think that was supposed to go?" She asked.

"Well, I couldn't see anyone actually mount."

"Now, let's do it again," she purred.

***

Our flight all climbed the rope and mounted. One of the Fire Platoon cadets slipped and fell, but before he could hit the ground, his griffin swooped down and caught him. Our wing stayed together and went to our next class with Professor Vindex. We were down to nineteen of us.

"Welcome back. When we all left here, we were talking about your powers manifesting. If your power manifested while you were gone, please move to the back of the room."

The majority of us stood up and moved to the back. We hadn't really talked about it since we had been back. Everything was chaos from the moment we stepped into Sandorg, there wasn't time to celebrate and be excited by what powers the Gods had gifted us—well, them. I'm pretty sure they cursed me.

"And then there were four. All of you don't come from magical Fae, so no surprise. Your power will be emerging soon. For now, you can sit back and watch the show."

"The show?" Robert asked.

"Yes, now we get to play with magic. I want everyone to make a circle around the room, standing side by side.

We all moved, standing side by side, including the four who hadn't manifested yet.

"We are going to go around, and you will tell or show your power. Do not explode the room if you don't have control over it yet."

"What if our powers are classified?" Thora asked.

He cocked his head a little bit at her. "You will say that it's classified, and everyone who has a classified ability will stay with me after class for a few minutes."

I wasn't actually sure if mine was classified or not. My dad didn't say, did he? Wait, what did he say? If I told the class, and it was classified–Gods, that would be a nightmare. If it wasn't actually classified, and I said it would, I would look silly. I wish I had asked my dad this, or he told me.

"Before you derail... I have taken the leisure to ask my mother, who asked your father... and it is classified. Please do not spill your ability to the entire class."

Vindex closed his eyes and spun around with his finger pointed out. He was pointing at Akira. I was standing on the right of her, which meant I would be close to last to say mine.

"You first, and then we will move clockwise around the room. Remember, please do not demonstrate your power if you might lose control of it."

She held her hand out, held one finger up, and started twirling it. Air rushed around her.

"Wind wielder. Nice," Vindex said, "next."

Sadie was standing to the left of her. She held her index finger up, and a little flame popped up on the tip. She leaned forward and blew it out.

"Hmm. Nice control."

Lorenzo looked over at Sadie. "Can you do that again?"

She gave a little nervous giggle and brought a little flame to the tip of her finger. He reached out and touched her flame, turning it into ice.

"You have clearly been practicing," Vindex said. He looked at Thora, who was next. "I presume classified?"

"Indeed, that was why I asked," Thora said.

As we moved around the room, three others said classified, making five of us in our wing with classified abilities. Among us, there were two fire, two ice, two water, one wind, one Mender, one astral projector, and one metal. After we all said our abilities or didn't. Vindex had mini duels with their powers. It was interesting to watch my fellow cadets use their powers, even if it wasn't in explosive ways.

"Everyone who doesn't have a classified ability or doesn't have one at all, you're dismissed."

As most of the cadets left, they looked back, staring at the five of us remaining in the room. The five of us looked around, at each other.

"Wow, I can't believe there are five of you—"

The door opened, breaking our attention. All of our gazes went to the door.

My father.

Of course, he would be here.

"Welcome to the club of classifieds. What you learn in here will remain classified—it isn't scuttlebutt. You may see powers in this room that may terrify you," he said. He locked eyes with me before looking at the rest. "Don't fear what you don't know. Just because you are learning classified abilities doesn't mean you are granted to know everyone else's," my father said.

"All first-year cadets who have classified abilities will have an additional lecture time with me at the end of the day. You all will need to be able to practice," Vindex said, "now you all didn't really get to participate in show and tell, but now you can."

Vindex pointed at Micah, who was sitting next to me. Before I could even fully blink or process it, he was across the room.

"Teleporter. Always a favorite. How far have you gone?" Vindex said.

"Just across a room, not far. It only manifested a couple of days before getting here," Micah said.

Vindex pointed at Thora. She didn't say anything, just gave him a hard stare. He cocked his head at her and raised an eyebrow.

"My dear counterpart, I keep my brain locked tight. Try that little trick on one of your classmates, and hopefully they have practiced their shielding," Vindex said.

She looked around the room. "I only learned of my power by accident when I wanted to yell at my mom and accidentally did so."

My dad let out a laugh. "Knowing your mom, how'd that go for you?"

"Well, she was shocked, then she was mad for what I said, then she laughed that she had let her shield down in the house, and I screamed into her head."

"Telepathic relays can be very beneficial. However, you have to learn to break down shields to push your messages out. Vindex will love to mentor you, I'm sure," my dad told her.

"Oh yes, it has been far too long since we have had another relay." Then he turned and pointed at Christoph Saltz, who was in the Fire Platoon, First Squad.

"I actually haven't quite figured mine completely out. I just know that when I got here, I reached out to Vindex, who explained that I was having precognition. It has only been little things like someone walking through the door, I see it happen a minute before they do it."

We all stared at him. That could be a monumentally powerful ability, if he learned how to hone it.

Vindex then pointed at me. It was my time to shine. I wasn't sure how everyone was going to respond. Part of me didn't want to share, and part of me wanted to show the whole world. What if they reacted worse than my father's? I closed my eyes and inhaled a deep breath.

I opened my eyes and let the shadows free. I visualized them lifting me off the ground, and they did as I willed them to. I spun in a couple of circles before I lowered myself slowly. I lifted my head and looked at my fellow cadets. Every one of them stood with their mouths agape, including Vindex. My dad, however, stood proud.

"Sir—oh my Gods—why didn't you tell me?" Vindex said, staring at my father.

My father let out a little giggle. "I wanted you to be as shocked as I was—"

"Well, you succeeded that, sir."

"What the hell was that?" Micah shot out, finally breaking the stunned silence of the cadets.

"That, Cadet Riggins, is what we call a shadow summoner."

"I mean, I can see *that*, but why haven't we ever heard of that?" Micah asked.

"Because... because we haven't seen one in a really long time," Vindex said.

"Five hundred and thirteen years," my father said.

"Wow," Micah and Thora said.

Vindex pointed to the last cadet, Crispin. "We didn't forget about you."

"I'm also figuring mine out, but I'm pretty sure I am reading memories, or I hope it's just memories," Crispin said. He was staring at the floor.

"No need to worry about something the Gods have gifted you," my father said.

"Unless I am reading minds... and then... the rumors say I'll be killed," Crispin said.

"Memory reading is like reading minds, and I can assure you that they are alive and well," my father said confidently.

Vindex walked in closer to my father and whispered, "Sir, we have fourteen classified abilities that have manifested among the first-years."

It didn't seem like any of the other cadets heard him, but *I did.* What did that mean? Was that not enough? Too many? I didn't want to ask right now because I wasn't sure if I was even supposed to hear that.

My father nodded at him before looking our way. "Now, you all have learned something about each other today. What you saw here isn't for you to tell your best friend, or the person who occupies your bed tonight. While every ability here is classified, Cadet Blackcreek's ability is unique. I will implore the punishment by death if it is leaked."

I instantly felt the tension. If I weren't already disliked, they would really hate me.

"Starting tomorrow, all first-year classified cadets will meet in here. We will work on your abilities. We will also be pairing each cadet up with a mentor who can help you master your ability... except maybe you," Vindex said, as he stared at me.

Great. Fan-Fucking-Tastic. I was going to be left to figure this out on my own. I let my head drop and stared at the ground.

"I will be with you. We will figure this out, together," Esme said.

"You all are released to the dining facility," Vindex said.

"Auri, can you stay back, please?" my dad whispered. My eyes darted to others, but no one else heard him.

I stopped in my tracks, and the other cadets walked out. Vindex shut the door.

"Do I really not get a ment—"

"I'm working on it, Auri," my dad said. He stepped closer and placed his hand on my shoulder.

"Your dad, and I will do as much research as we can, so we can best help you."

"What did you mean, there are fourteen of us?" I asked them.

Vindex shifted on his feet. "That's not your—"

"It is higher than we usually have. I'm surprised you heard that," my dad said, cutting him off.

"Not holding anything back from her, eh?"

"No. I've held way too much already and hurt her."

"Fair. History tells us that when we have an influx of powerful abilities, including classified, there is something big coming. Magic is all about balance, and the Gods know," Vindex said.

"Oh... how many were there last year?"

Vindex shot a look at my dad, and he nodded at him. "Four."

"Oh, wow," I said.

CHAPTER 19

As I joined the rest of our wing for lunch, there was a sense of quietness when I sat down. I don't know why it would be a surprise for the general's daughter to have a classified ability as well. It wasn't a surprise that Thora manifested a classified one, either, with her having a parent who had one. It wasn't a secret that when your parents had very powerful magic, it was likely for you also to be gifted something extraordinary.

Even then, some of the cadets in my wing gave me a look. It was a look mixed with wariness and envy. I couldn't focus on them. They weren't worth the energy that I needed to put elsewhere. I couldn't care about what the other cadets thought. I focused on eating my lunch instead. It wasn't my problem. There were other, greater things that I needed to focus on.

I got up and carried my tray to the return window. A rider cadet walking in the opposite direction bumped into my shoulder, making me stumble back. Their shimmer was of flaming embers—a phoenix rider—dull but still there.

"Excuse me?" I said to her.

"Don't be in my way—" she said.

"I wasn't."

"You're always in the way."

"Look, I am not the fucking one. Nor am I in the mood."

"Whatever little daddy's bitch—"

Before she could get the words out of her mouth, my fist connected with her cheek and nose. My shimmer flared on my arms, hardening. She grabbed her face, and blood poured from her nose. Two dining attendants and the three officers in the dining facility ran to us. The five of them stood between us, and she tried to surge towards me.

I turned around and made my way around her and out of the dining hall. Everyone had stopped eating and was staring at the situation. Staring at me. I didn't care. I was done taking bullshit from people, and I wanted people to see. To stop underestimating me. I waited outside the door for Laderra to join me.

All first years in our wing had Professor Quillet after lunch. I don't know what kind of obstacle courses we would be doing now, but I knew it would suck. We all walked in pairs onto the flight field on the Flugblatt Forest side, none of us in any hurry. Quillet stood there, hands on his hips, annoyance on his face. His red dragon stood behind him, towering over him.

"Obstacle training will look a little different. As riders, you will be doing aerial training, mostly. Hildegard and I will be together some days, and other days we will be solo.""What does aerial training look like exactly?" Micah asked.

"Fun," Hildegard said, startling most of us, as he walked from behind us.

"I don't think our idea of fun is the same as yours, sir," Micah said.

Both Hildegard and Quillet gave a soft laugh in unison.

I swallowed. Their little laugh didn't feel comforting at all.

"We will be playing Barlaufen," Quillet said.

"What is that exactly?" Lorenzo asked.

"I'm glad you asked," Hildegard said.

"You will be split into teams of three. There are nineteen of you, so two teams of six and one team of seven. Each team will have a color assigned. Each team will pick two of its members to be defenders of magical orbs that have been stationed in the outer woods and mountains. The other team members will be on offense, and your goal is to locate and try to capture the other team's orbs," Quillet said.

"This is a game, and we are not enemies out here. You can use magic, but no fatal hits. And... uh... oh yeah, each rider will be blindfolded," Hildegard said.

The audible grumbling was heard all around.

"You must learn to communicate effectively with your flier and with your teammates through their fliers. The Eagle and Dragon Wing will also be practicing. On January Thirty-First, all first and second flights in all three wings will be competing. It is something the Riders branch really looks forward to," Quillet said.

"Is there a prize for the winning Wing?" Erik asked.

"Yes, to be announced that day," Quillet answered.

"Any other questions?" Hildegard said.

We all looked around at both professors and each other. No one spoke.

"Perfect," Hildegard said.

"Purple Orb Team or The Wonderful Seven: Sadie Devins, Auriella Blackcreek, Thora Stoot, Lenora Vidacovik, Torvi Stang, Jameson Leon, and Crispin Onstad. I will be overseeing your team," Quillet said.

"Green Orb Team or whatever fancy name y'all want to come up with: Laderra Holmes, Lorenzo Carnethon, Michalova Sulivar, Gregor Stoss, Akira Faraday, and Dirk Hanik. I will be the team captain," Hildegard said.

"Then who is our team captain?

"That would be me." As soon as I heard the voice, I knew who it was. My father.

"Dad? I mean... General Blackcreek."

"This is one of my favorite traditional games we do. Since I am here, might as well make myself useful," my dad said. He turned to the other six cadets. "Looks like I got the number one class clown."

"Your team," Hildegard said, motioning to the group, "Orange Orb Team: Vida Aamir, Micah Riggins, Erik Zufall, Robert Ludewuggin, Christoph Saltz, and Aeltharion Gaglonda."

"Now that we have our groups, there are three colored orbs hidden around the college. Your team's mission is to find your own color orb and guard it, while also trying to either take or break the other team's orb. Remember the cardinal rules—don't add to the population and don't subtract from the population," Quillet said.

Laughter filled the flight field.

Hildegard walked around and handed out flight goggles that were blacked out. This wasn't going to be fun. I hated not being able to see.

"Alright, we have less than an hour of play time. Let's make this fun, we all need a little of that as of lately," Quillet said, "my wonderful seven, put your goggles on, and let's get in the air. My dragon, Reardin, will be relaying information to your fliers, and no, I don't know where our orb or their orbs are. Someone else hid those."

Within seconds, fliers started approaching with something hanging—ropes—from their talons.

Oh, what the fuck?

"Goggles ON!" Quillet yelled out.

I was supposed to grab it and climb it blindfolded. Fuck.

"Have some faith in me, will you?" she purred along.

"I don't have any faith right now. I can't see. Now, I am supposed to climb a rope blind."

"You practiced this maneuver this morning. Trust your flier," Hildegard barked out.

"I'll be over you in five seconds, when I say now, reach your arms out and climb. Five, Four, Three, Two... NOW!"

My arms reached out, and I felt the rope within my fingers. I grasped tightly and started to pull myself up the rope.

"About five more feet."

I kept pulling myself up. My hands gripped the rope as tightly as I could. I knew she would catch me if I fell, but part of me worried that she wouldn't make it on time. My heart was beating in my chest as fast as it could. My breaths had become labored, partly from the fast-approaching anxiety and partly from exerting myself.

"Alright, pull yourself up past my talon, just as we did this morning, and no, I won't let you fall. Also, our parents are out here. We have to make it look like we were made for this, because we are."

I pulled up onto her leg, clinging to her. Her talon opened beneath me. Within seconds, she flung me up in the air and swooped under me, and I was in her saddle.

"First, what happened to one?" I asked her.

"I underestimated how quickly I was approaching."

"Second, what is my—our—purpose out here. We are blindfolded on top of fliers that seem to be doing everything."

"You, my little shadow, have the magic I don't."

"Speaking of magic, I thought Silver dragons could blow ice."

"Yeah, they can... I can't yet."

Something in her tone told me to drop it—there was sadness in it.

"Where do we go, now?"

"Reardin said we are gonna meet on the top of Pass of Bête Noire," she told me.

"Great, the pass that almost killed me."

"Us fliers will be looking for the purple orb, in the meantime."

Flying without being able to see was disconcerting. The cold winter air brushed against my cheeks, and even with my thick flight coat, the air chilled me.

"Landing."

I felt a slight descent and then the jolt of us touching down on the mountain top.

"All riders are to keep their goggles on and can remain on their fliers," she told me.

"Our first objective is to find our orb. Once we do that, Thora and Jameson will play defense. You may not have been able to see anything, but tap into your other senses. Some of you may be able to feel magic better than others. This is a good way to test that. As a professor, I am not allowed to really help or spill secrets," Quillet said.

"Then what are you here for?" Crispin said.

"Referee. Mediator. Whatever you want to call it. Let's find our orb and destroy theirs," Quillet said.

Esme's muscles bunched below me, and we lifted into the air. I couldn't see anything. I closed my eyes. Somehow, having them closed felt less like looking into a black hole. A little less disorienting. I focused on my senses. Concentrated on the feel of magic. When I walked through wards, when my dad would read my mind, there was a sense of tingling. The outer part of my right arm tingled.

"*Turn right,*" I told Esme.

"*Yes, boss,*" she purred back.

We banked to the right. I took a deep breath in, and tingles hit my entire front.

"*Where are we?*" I asked.

"*The mountains between Fort Daysn and us.*"

"*Do you see anything?*"

"*I see Michalova and Eryn.*"

"*Dip and try to stay hidden.*"

"*Or I could rise, and blend with the bright sky.*"

"*That could work.*"

We rose in the sky, the air getting thinner.

"*Did you know that silver dragons have some of the keenest eyesight?*" she purred.

"*Yes, we learned that. Now, I presume you are saying this means you have spotted something.*"

"*Yes. Something a little green and magical.*"

"*Michalova is on the green team... they might have already found theirs and are guarding it. Go high, and come from the other side.*"

We rose higher in the sky, and I took deep, slow breaths. My lungs burned a little from the higher altitude. We banked hard to the right. I focused on the magic I was feeling. We were getting closer.

"*Did you let the others know we have found the green one?*" I asked her.

"*Yes. Quillet has ordered Lenora to come to us. No luck on our orb—never mind, they think they may have found ours. We are too high for me to see the green orb, but I believe it is below us. We will do a quick descent.*"

The quick descent caused popping in both of my ears. I swallowed hard, trying to will the pressure to lessen in them. Tingles crept all over my arms and legs. We were getting closer to the magical orb.

"*We are getting closer.*"

"It is right below us, and you were right, Michalova is guarding it. Laderra as well. If I drop lower, they will hear me," she said.

"How do we get it?"

"Magic—"

"If I use my shadows, they will know." I cut her off. *"Not if they even know what it is,"* she purred. *"They are right below us, straight down. You can do it."*

I swallowed. If I got caught doing this, I could get in trouble, but they did want us to practice using our powers. I lifted my arms and let the shadows free. Air swirled around my arms.

"Directly below us, right."

"Yes. You have to be quick."

I took the deepest breath in. I could not fuck this up. The shadows dropped off my arms and fell below me. Light flashed beneath my closed eyes. I could see Michalova on top of his black-gold griffin—Eryn. Next to him was the three-foot green orb, glowing brightly. On the other side of him was Laderra sitting atop her phoenix.

I was seeing through the shadows.

Oh, my fucking Gods. Shock hit me. This was super cool, but this was not the time to be excited. I was one with the shadows. They were a part of me, but not me. I needed to get this done before they realized the shadows hovering above them.

I dropped them fast and wrapped my shadows around the orb and lifted them back up. Michalova shot his head to the side, eyes wide.

"Fuck!" he yelled.

"Quicker!" she scolded.

Esme started rising higher. I was pulling the shadows to me as fast as I could. I drew my shadows to me, orb into my hands. I pulled it into my chest and held it tightly.

"Kill the magic, and drop it. We have to go!"

I held the orb, focused on my magic within it. It exploded in my hands and fell wayside. We rose high so quickly, and pressure filled my ears. I raised my hands, poking my fingers into my ears.

"What the hell was *that?*" Michalova shouted below us.

"I don't fucking know!" Laderra shouted back.

I held the giggle in that I wanted to let it roll out.

"Our orb is under attack by the orange team, and no one has located theirs yet."

"Where is our orb?"

"Flugblatt forest."

"And this one was near Fort Daysn... the other one is probably on the Northwest side of the college by the river. Go—"

"Going now."

We were still high in the sky, and Esme's wings were beating as fast as she could.

"Did you let the others know?"

"Yes. Sadie and Torvi are headed that way as well."

My hands and toes started tingling. We were getting closer.

"Do you see anything? I can feel it." I told her.

"We are too high in the sky. Let me know when you feel it closer, and I'll drop lower."

Within a few more wingbeats, I could feel the tingling taking over my entire body.

"Drop."

We descended a little lower, and I could feel us getting a little closer.

"There," she purred.

"Like I can see anything."

"You did do a little magical trick earlier that let you see everything..."

"Yes, that I should only do sparingly."

"Well, what you can't see is that Micah, Christoph, and Erik are surrounding the—"

"Fuck Esme. Micah can teleport, and Christoph will see us coming before I can grab it."

"You will have to be quick. Sadie and Torvi are a distraction."

"Tell their fliers then."

"Done."

We moved in slowly. I heard approaching wingbeats—softly.

"They are approaching," I told her.

"You can hear them?"

"Yeah, you can't?"

"Um... no."

"They said we need to be quick to figure this out, because the other team is putting up a good fight. Apparently, Vida is pretty good at her telekinesis."

Within minutes, the wingbeats grew louder, and the air rushed past me as they moved past us. We lowered slowly. They were the distraction, we were the secret threat. I could hear the chaos below us. I inhaled and willed the shadows out. I lowered them below us, focused on seeing through them. The mountains below us came into view. Micah was on his phoenix—Sera—launching after Sadie.

"Try to move over, directly over the orb, like below."

Christoph sat atop his black dragon. How could I outwit his precognition? How did one do that? Better shields? I focused on my shields, building them block by block.

"Oh, love, I can feel the block. Leave a little space for me," Zane said down the bond. My stomach twitched, the bondmark on my arm tingled.

"Sorry, I'm a little busy, and you are the distraction they needed," I told him, a line he once used on me.

I fortified my shields, blocking him out. It would only be for a few minutes. Torvi and her grey dragon dipped lower. Christoph and his dragon lifted off the ground, his head swiveling around watching Torvi. This was our window. Esme floated over some. We were still high enough. They hadn't noticed us below. I dropped my shadows quickly towards the orange glowing orb.

Just as my shadows wrapped around the orange orb, Christoph jerked his head back to the orb. He tilted his head.

"Auriella. What a cheat," he said. Then he grabbed the orb, holding it against his body tightly.

The shadows followed, wrapping around the orb in his arms. It tightened around it. If I could squeeze it and explode it, then we would win.

"Control your shadows. There are others who shouldn't see them present."

"They are blindfolded, and it's just wisps of black."

"That seems to be getting darker and angrier."

I needed to focus. Don't let them control me. I controlled them. I tightened them around the orb.

"We won! Let go!" Christoph yelled out.

"Is he serious?" I asked.

"Yes, word came across that they destroyed our orb first."

Fuck.

I tightened around the orb. A loud explosion sounded below us. I pulled my shadows back within.

"Let's go before anyone is the wiser."

"Pretty sure everyone is now wise, Auriella."

She said my entire name. I clenched my jaw, and my eye twitched. She had never scolded me before. Was that a scold?

"Something like that," she said, annoyance lacing her tone.

We flew to the flight field.

"Your father is aware of your little shadow explosion."

"Great..."

CHAPTER 20

Zane

I roved into Auri's room after dinner, and then I roved her back into my room. We no longer had the luxury of wandering the walls or sparring in the gym in the evening for fun. Luckily for me, I had Auri to keep me busy during the evening hours. I had become quite fond of cuddling her each night. Selfishly, I didn't want to give that up.

As soon as we were back in my room, she stared up at me, eyes that begged me to take her and make her scream. It was the look that always made me come undone. I could instantly feel my dick twitching.

I grabbed the back of her head, gripping her neck, pulling her into me—kissing her deeply and intently. Every time I was alone with her, part of me didn't trust myself. I held back from what I wanted to do. I wanted to lose control with her, but I knew I couldn't. I didn't know what I was actually capable of.

I ripped her clothes off, savagely. Her breasts fit perfectly in my hands. I gripped both of them. I stepped back and knelt some. I teased her nipple with my tongue, flicking my tongue over it, slowly. Her head dropped back, and she let out a soft moan.

My dick pulsed in my pants against my thigh, dripping. The anticipation of her made me want to throw her on the bed and fuck her wildly, but making her have an orgasm slowed me down. I wanted her to enjoy every single time I fucked her. I wanted her to see stars.

I led her back to the bed and lay her down gently. I dropped my pants and threw my tee off. I wanted to play and touch every part of her, making her squirm. I trailed my finger down her body, stopping to circle her nipple, and then continued down her stomach. Once my finger made it to her clit, I rubbed it in a half circle just above it, moving it slowly, applying just a little pressure. She let out a little moan of approval.

I moved my finger down and into her, letting her get my finger all wet, before pulling it out and dragging it up one side. Feeling her warmth and wetness made my dick twitch more. Her breathing had started to become more ragged, in between little moans that came out of her lips. I moved off the bed, dragged her to the edge of the bed, and knelt. I wanted to taste her. She tasted like the sweetest strawberries. I gently moved my tongue from the bottom to the top.

She let out a loud gasp followed by a moan. I continued tasting every part of her. I moved to put two fingers in. So fucking slippery. Warmth rushed through me. I had to control it. Her taste alone could make me cum. I wanted more than that, though. I wanted to make her cum with my tongue and my dick. I was greedy in that way.

I moved my fingers in and out of her so very slowly. I moved my lips to her clit and drew it in, sucking on it slowly. I felt her grab a handful of my hair, holding me tightly. It was her way of controlling me, slowing me down when I got a little carried away with my tongue. My face flushed with warmth. My heart beat a little faster.

"Gods. Fuck. I'm... about..."

She screamed, gasping in between. I moved my pace faster.

"Let it go, let it all go," I told her in her mind, my mouth occupied.

She moaned louder, air gasping from her lungs. I wanted to explode just from listening to her. I slowed down, let her jolt as I passed my tongue over her clit. Her breathing became less frantic, her grip on my hair lessened. I pulled my fingers out of her. Pulled back from her, locked eyes with her before sticking my fingers in my mouth, tasting her all over again.

"Mmm... strawberries," I growled to her.

She let out a little giggle. "Come here."

She reached her arm out towards me. Once my hand made hers, she pulled me onto the bed next to her. She pushed my chest down, and I fell flat on the bed. She moved to straddle me, she lay on me, our bare chests pressed together.

She moved her arm down and guided me. She held her hips up, just holding the tip inside her. She lowered her hips just enough to bring me inside her a little more. Gods. She fucking loved teasing me. Bringing me to the edge and holding me hostage there.

She lowered her hips and sat up, bringing me deep inside. Oh, my fucking Gods. Tingles filled my lower stomach. I needed to last just a little longer. I wanted her to cum again, with me this time. I gripped her hips, slowing her down. I reached up and grabbed the back of her neck, bringing her to me.

"You're going to make me cum if you keep at this," I whispered to her, before crashing my lips into hers. I drew her tongue into my mouth, sucking on it. I pulled back and gasped for air. That too was a sure-fire way that made me cum.

She ground herself against me, the tip hitting the right spot inside her. I wanted to grip her hips and move her faster. Watch her breasts bounce as she rode me. She had started to breathe heavier, her heart beating beneath her chest was thumping faster. She gripped my chest tighter. She was getting closer and closer. Her head threw back. She moved her hips faster, grinding herself on me. She tightened her grip on my chest.

I was seconds from exploding in her. She tightened on me, and moans started spilling from her mouth. Bright stars flash through my vision. The buildup pressure exploded, and the relief was euphoric. Toes curled. Chest beat faster. Grunts spilled out. I pulsed inside her. I gripped her hips, taking control, moving her on top of me. Every movement sent jolts through me.

Shadows rolled out of her—magic seeped out. Touching me. Teasing me. I wanted to take it and play with it. If I played with it, control would be lost.

She rolled off of me and lay her head onto my chest. Our breathing slowed down as they became in sync with each other. I rubbed my hand up and down her back. It felt like everything was perfect in that moment. I never wanted it to end. Every morning, we woke, and new chaos happened within the campus.

"How was your day?" she asked, finally breaking the silence.

"Oh, the usual. Third years are usually leaving, so now we are mostly twiddling our thumbs and helping the first years."

"I don't want to think about you leaving me for any period of time."

"I know... how was the great scavenger hunt?"

"Barlaufen is always fun to play. We played a younger version growing up on various bases," she said. I loved hearing the excitement in her voice.

"I may have heard there was a little shadow explosion out there?"

"Who... who told you that?"

"I have my ways. So... did you?"

"I may or may not have used my shadows. It got us second place, but they got our orb before I blew up the other one. I got angry and still exploded it. Oops."

"Oops." I let out a laugh. I shouldn't encourage her.

"My dad reamed my ass for it too."

"Oof."

"Yeah, oof. My lack of control did not amuse him."

"He'll get over it."

"I think part of him was proud, but he couldn't show it. Tomorrow, we start our private classified training. Have you heard anything about how there is a historical amount of classified riders?"

"What do you mean?"

"There are apparently fourteen of us who have a classified ability. Last year, there were only four. My father and Vindex seemed to be quite worried about it."

"That is... concerning."

"Do you know what it means?"

"No... I wish I did."

"Something amazing happened with my powers today..."

"Oh?"

"I could see through them, as if they were an extension of me. I had blacked out goggles, yet I could see through the shadows."

"Wow... that's quite amazing."

"Yeah..."

Her power was greater than I had thought it to be, and it was growing every day. She was unaware that the magic seeped off of her, but I also didn't know if it was because I was hypersensitive to magic or if anyone else felt it while around her.

It was becoming more complicated by the day to control myself around her. I started questioning fate and the Gods. Why did the Gods destine us? A shadow summoner and a siphon manipulator. Why were we the greatest power to be seen? Was I meant to use her power? I wasn't like a normal siphoner. I didn't drain someone of their magic. I siphoned it and then was able to mimic their magic. It was great, honestly, and it was a curse.

The person felt it when I siphoned from them, but didn't know what it was exactly. I learned quickly that I wasn't really able to use it, but I wanted to every single day. The first year here was the hardest year of learning how to control the urges. Cadets were seeping in uncontrolled power, and I felt it everywhere. The air was thick with a metallic taste. I learned to build my mental blocks. To tune it out. Since Auri manifested, my urges have been tested every day. Her magic felt different from the other cadets—stronger. She wasn't even aware of how powerful her magic manifested over the last couple of weeks—but I was.

"Do you want children?" she asked.

My eyes widened. I hadn't expected that.

"I... I... don't know. I think so. Maybe. One day."

She giggled—so soft, so pure.

"I don't know either. We hadn't really talked about it."

"Fae children don't come as easily as human children, but I think I would like one—one day," I told her. It was the truth. I wasn't sure that I wanted as many as my parents, but I always thought I would have one when the time was right.

"I would want two..."

"I think we can make that work... in a long while, right?"

"Oh, yes. Many years from now."

"Deal. Why two?"

"I grew up lonely. I always wanted a sibling. Sure, I had Lili and Alex, but it wasn't the same."

"And I grew up with more than I could handle." Deep laughter rolled out from me. I did love my siblings, but they were very overwhelming at times.

"I love you, Zane." Her voice was heavy, on the brink of falling asleep, as her head rested on my chest, her body pressed against mine. Our heartbeats beat in sync.

"I love you, Auri."

CHAPTER 21

Zane was gone by the time my eyes fluttered open. It was the middle of the week, and it had already felt like it was too long. Every day was exhausting, and the last several days felt like we were in prison. Laderra knocked on my door for our walk together to the dining hall. We both walked in silence, as we usually had, both of us not being chipper morning people. We walked to the staircase and down one level to the first floor before exiting into the courtyard. I stopped dead in my tracks. Laderra, who had held the door open, letting me pass through first, ran into my back.

A large gasp escaped from my mouth before my hand flew over my mouth.

"Oh, my Gods," Laderra gasped out.

My eyes were fixated on the two bodies—the bodies of cadets I knew. Dafne and the Phoenix Rider from the dining room. Dafne was strung to the side of the dining facility above us—in only her underwear. Her arms and legs splayed wide, held by black ropes. Her head hung forward, black hair falling all over her face. Her light brown eyes were unnaturally wide open and staring towards us on the ground, as if she was alive—but wasn't. Both sides of her lips were sliced open, blood seeping out of her mouth and the wounds. Her chest was gaped open, like a flayed fish.

I could hear cadets surrounding us, but I couldn't peel my eyes away. The Phoenix Rider was displayed the same way, but my eyes were fixated on Dafne. She had bullied me while in school. Part of me didn't care that she was splayed up there dead, but the other part made my stomach queasy.

"Back up! Back up!" a professor yelled.

"Continue to your schedules," a familiar voice barked.

I turned, and my dad quickly approached us–the bodies. His face was void of emotions, like he usually was, but there was something about him that screamed that this was starting to affect him.

Cadets whispered all around. I could hear bits and pieces from all over filtering in.

"Stay away from Blackcreek."

"Didn't both of them antagonize Blackcreek yesterday?"

"She's probably killing them, and her father is letting her."

I finally broke my gaze and turned my head to look at the cadets whispering. My eyebrows drew in, narrowing my eyes, and I stared at who I thought was whispering. Their eyes widened. I cocked my head to the side at them.

"I think she heard us," one of them whispered.

I tilted my head to the opposite side, and their eyes got wider. Five of them turned around and headed back into their wing.

"Let's go. Go back to your class or the dining room," Melamora said as she approached.

Laderra grabbed my hand and dragged me towards the dining facility. My appetite was completely gone. I felt like giving my dinner back to the soil as it was. The dining facility was chaotic as we walked in, cadets were all around, most of them weren't eating but standing in circles talking.

"I'm not hungry anymore," I said to Laderra, barely above a whisper.

"Yeah, me either..." she said.

"Can we just go to our current events class?"

She nodded her head, her eyes jumping around the room, looking at the cadets who were staring at us. She did a quick circle around and walked toward the door. I followed right behind her. I wanted to go to my room and lock at myself in there, but I knew I couldn't do that. Not only would Laderra protest, but I am sure Zane would drag me out.

"You aren't wrong, little shadow," Esme purred down the bond.

"I know... do you know more than you are letting on?"

"What? Know what exactly?"

"Whose behind the murders?"

She grumbled, *"No. I would tell you that, if I knew that."*

"Then what do you know?"

"Oh, my little shadow, I know so much."

That made my stomach twist.

"Then say it," I pushed back. *"Because people are hanging from walls, and everyone thinks I'm next—or worse, that I'm the reason."*

"You'll be just fine."

I huffed out a breath. *"That's not comforting."*

We rounded the corner toward the lecture hall. Cadets clustered near the entrance, their conversations dropping into murmurs the moment they saw me. I felt it then—that subtle shift. They were looking at me differently.

"You're being measured," she said.

"I don't like it."

"You're not meant to."

"I'll meet you inside," Laderra said quietly, already scanning the crowd. I nodded and stepped forward alone.

The lecture hall doors were open, light spilling out into the hall. I crossed the threshold, and the room changed. Everything looked the same, the tiered seating, dais in the middle, but the atmosphere was different. Conversations hushed as I moved down the aisle.

I took my seat, shoulders squared, chin lifted. If they were going to stare, I wasn't going to give them the satisfaction of shrinking. The professors entered moments later. Melamora first, her expression calm but tight around the eyes. Pascal followed, jaw clenched, his usual warmth absent. Fogg brought up the rear, gaze sharp as it swept the room.

Then my father, and the room went silent.

He didn't look at me as he took his place near the dais. He didn't look at anyone. His presence alone was enough to pull every spine straighter, every whisper into nothing.

"We'll begin." Melamora cleared her throat. "Two additional deaths occurred this morning."

A ripple moved through the room. There were gasps, sharp inhales, and someone choked back a sob.

"These deaths are under active investigation," Pascal said, "as before, speculation will not be tolerated."

"Then tell us something," someone muttered.

I felt my shadows stir, reacting to the spike of emotion around me. I pressed my fingers into the seat, grounding myself.

Melamora paced slowly around the dais. "We don't believe they are random."

My pulse kicked up.

"They are targeted," she went on. "Which means patterns matter."

I could feel eyes shifting. Not just on the professors—on each other. On me.

A hand shot up—a healer, second-year. I recognized him only because he'd been staring at me since I walked in. "So, you're saying this is personal?"

My father spoke before anyone else could. "We are looking at all possibilities."

The healer swallowed but didn't back down. "Then maybe we should be looking at who benefits."

The room held its breath. A mouse could be heard skittering on the ground.

Melamora shut the conversation down before it could spiral. "That's enough."

The damage was already done. I didn't need to look around to know what they were thinking. I could feel it pressing in on me, the unspoken conclusion forming like a bruise.

As class continued, I barely absorbed the words. My focus narrowed inward, sensing every flicker of magic, every shift in the room. Every sideways glance that came my way. Every so often, I would try to focus on what the professors were talking about before my mind drifted off again. The war was escalating on the coast, and Nosferatu sightings were getting worse.

"Dismissed," Pascal said. My head shot up, and I looked around. How had an hour already passed by?

Fuck.

I hope I didn't miss anything important.

As the cadets around me stood up and shuffled out of the stadium classroom, I sat in my seat, my eyes locked onto something not important—

"Hey." My entire body jumped, my head jerked up to Zane.

"Sorry, I didn't mean to startle—"

"No. No. It's okay," I cut him off.

"A penny for your thoughts?" he asked.

"Everyone is staring at me. Whispering around me. These deaths have something to do with me, and they think it's me."

"You and I both know it's not you, first off. They aren't completely wrong, you are central to whatever the hell is happening around here—"

"You think I am at fault?"

"No, No. That's not what I meant. I just meant—"

"Someone is killing on my behalf, and it is my fault."

I stood up and stared at him—his eyes were filled with sorrow. I knew he didn't mean it like that, but nothing inside of me felt rational.

"You are not responsible for anyone dying. It's not on you," he said after what felt like way too long, but was only seconds.

"It feels like I—"

"Cadet Blackcreek," my father's voice cut in.

"Yes, sir," I said, turning toward him.

"I know you aren't responsible, but it seems like there are a lot of speculations going around, and I have heard your name... and mine being whispered. You're being asked to leave—"

"WHAT?"

"It's not permanent," he said, his voice not wavering.

"I don't want to leave, I told you," I pleaded with him.

"Sir—" Zane started.

"You aren't being permitted to leave—"

"No," I said.

"It's not up for discussion. This is above my head. You are going to go to our home at Zion's Outpost."

"We—Zane and I—can't be separated. You know this."

"Zion's outpost isn't far, and he will be granted to come to you every weekend until this is resolved," my father said.

"This isn't fair. This has nothing to do with—"

"Now, we all know that isn't true."

"But I am not doing anything."

"Auri, I really wish it didn't have to be this way, but it does—"

"You never wanted me here anyway." My eyes dropped to the floor. Defeat took over every feeling I had. I wasn't winning this. I wasn't negotiating this. I was leaving here. Without Zane. The worst possible scenario was unfolding. Was this what they wanted?

I turned away and walked down the stairs. I didn't want to be a part of this conversation anymore.

"We leave this evening," he shouted at me as I walked away.

I went straight to my dorm. What was the point in even going to lectures? I would be missing them anyway, not to mention everyone had started to stare more. Coming here and being the general's daughter had already put a target on my back for anyone who had figured that out.

"You can go to class..." I insisted to Zane.

"I won't leave you alone, and right now you are upset and really shouldn't be left alone."

"I'll be fine."

My feet hit the floor more heavily with each step, and my sighs grew louder as we neared my room.

"Hmm... Yeah, okay. Yep, fine you are."

I ignored him. I didn't have anything left in me to argue.

I opened the door to my bed chamber and came abruptly to a stop. Zane slammed into my back. He quickly grabbed me, shuffled me behind him, and drew a dagger in both hands.

"No need," the female said.

"Who the fuck are you and why and how the fuck are you in a warded room?" Zane said. His voice was fierce and threatening.

"I am no harm to Auriella... well, I am if something happens to *me*," she said.

"Who. Are. You?" He insisted.

"I'm her sister," she said.

CHAPTER 22

My mouth dropped open. What the fuck did she just say? Zane's eyebrows furrowed at her, but nothing came out of his mouth either. He stared intently, like he was trying to see through her.

"Cat got your tongues?" she finally broke the silence.

"My... sister? Ain't no fucking way. I am the only one."

"That is what you have been told, but here I stand."

I stared at her, not really sure what to even say. As I stared at her, it was like I was looking at my mom. My eyes widened. She was the same height as my mom, a little shorter than me. She had long, dark brown hair with blue eyes that looked like they were copied from my mom's. She had the smooth, perfect skin my mother had, with higher cheekbones. Once I saw it, all I could see was *my mom.*

"How?" I managed to squeak out.

"Not possible," Zane said, finally breaking his silence.

"She looks just like her..." I mumbled.

"I... actually... don't... we have only met a couple times," she barely got out.

"I don't understand," I said.

"Me either," Zane said.

"Our mother placed me for adoption when she was nineteen—"

"Why?" I shot out. My brain was struggling to process everything that was happening, what was being said.

"Do you think she's telling the truth?" Esme said our bond.

"I don't know... I don't even know what to think of any of this."

"Hear her out..." Esme said softly.

"If you are asking why she left me... I don't know."

My eyes dropped to the floor. The sadness in her voice when she said that made me realize that this wasn't just about me—

"My name is Genevieve—"

"Did you *kill all* of those cadets?" I cut her off. I needed to know. I couldn't dance around this anymore.

"Yes. Their lives weren't worth it, and they were a danger to you."

Zane moved across the room in an instant, flashing through time. His dagger pressed against her neck. I stood frozen, unsure if I should stop him. She just admitted to killing cadets—seventeen of them.

"I... I... wouldn't do that. Our lives are tied together," she muttered.

"What the hell does that mean?" he asked, pressing her against the wall.

"It's not important—"

"It fucking is," Zane said, cutting her off.

"I die... she dies. That's all you need to know."

"What?!" I yelled out.

"I said what I said. I needed insurance to make sure I wasn't killed."

Zane lowered his dagger and took a few steps back—in the blink of an eye, he flew into my dorm wall. Genevieve's hand was held out in front of her. She was a Witch.

"You will not touch me without my permission," she seethed.

"You put Auri in danger—" Zane yelled back.

"Auriella can handle herself."

"Then why kill all these people to protect her?"

"Hmm, they said nasty things and wanted to cause harm."

"They are children compared to you," he said.

"I will do *anything* to protect her."

"Why?" I asked her.

"Because you are my sister and you are a Witch that belongs to my clan."

"You don't know—"

"I was ten when you were born. She came and told me—I was angry and pissed that Lucille left me, yet had another child. Over the next seven years, I worked through a lot of my emotions and realized *you* weren't the enemy.

You didn't do anything to me. I have been following you and watching you grow up."

A loud bang on the door startled all three of us.

"Auriella," my father yelled from the other side.

Fuck. Could this get any fucking worse? Did he know?

"Hold on, Dad," I yelled to him. "Does he know about you?" I whispered.

"I don't know," she said.

"I guess he is about to find out if not..." Zane said.

I walked to the door and opened it. The creases on his forehead looked more prominent, and his eyes flared. His knuckles were clenched at his sides.

"You know I don't want you—" His eyes shifted to Genevieve, and widened even more than they were. His mouth hung open, and I clearly got his shocked face.

"Lucille... oh my Gods," he said, his voice breaking.

"I'm not... Lucille... I'm not her, sir," she managed to get out.

"I... I... I... know, but you look like *her*. Who are *you*?" he said, finally getting his voice back.

"I'm her daughter," she said, eyes focused on the ground.

"Impossible. Auri is her only child."

She lifted her head to meet his eyes. "That she raised."

"Why should I believe you?"

"Are you familiar with her birthmark?"

"Of course, it was unique."

She lifted her shirt, cupping her breast, and revealed a mark on her left side, below her armpit. A pawprint with seven small dots above it.

"That just proves that you are related, which is obvious by the resemblance."

"Listen. I know who you are and what your powers are. Touch me and see the memory of my birth," she told him. Her voice became fierce, reminding me of my—our—mother when she got angry.

Without hesitation, my dad reached out for her. Zane quickly grabbed his arm, stopping him from touching her. My dad's head shot towards Zane and cocked it to the side.

"I don't know what she has done, but don't harm her, she claims, if something happens to her, something will happen to Auri," Zane said, before staring at her intently.

"Thanks, boy, but I was just going to read her memory. If she is indeed Lucille's daughter, killing her is the last thing—"

"Yeah... until you find out she is the cadet slayer—" Zane seethed.

"What?" my father shouted. "Shit," he muttered.

He reached out and grabbed her hand, his eyes closed, head tilted back. As I studied him, his eyes moved rapidly under his eyelids, and his face twitched. He looked as though he was in turmoil.

"Are you hurting him?" I blurted out.

Neither of them spoke—both of their eyes were closed, head tilted back. My dad's chest started rising and falling faster. My pulse started racing, and my hands began sweating. I wasn't sure if I should pull him away from her. Tears streamed down his cheeks, and my chest got tighter. I knew he was probably watching—

They both gasped, and my father let go, his head jolted forward, eyes wide, staring at Genevieve. His cheek was dampened with tears. My eyes moved to look at her, and tears were steadily streaming down her face. She stayed fixated on the ground, arms hanging to her side, hands trembling.

"It's..." my dad said before inhaling a deep breath, "true."

"Why did you make me see that?" Genevieve gasped out.

"Because if I had to watch it, you deserved to see what really happened at your birth. Implicit memories can't be accessed without assistance, and I can reach them."

"She didn't want to give me up... why... why hadn't she told me?" she said, through cries.

"I wish she were here to tell you, to tell us," he told her.

Genevieve rubbed her face. She took a few steps back and sat in my high-back chair.

"I'm sorry. This meet and greet has turned out to be more than I anticipated..." More tears fell down her cheeks. The more I stared at her, the more it felt like I was staring at my mom.

"Mama, why are you sad?" I asked her.

"Oh, Hunny, sometimes adults have days that make us sad."

"Why does April Fourteen make you sad, mama?"

"It reminds me of someone from when I was younger."

"Who?" I reached up and wiped her right cheek.

"A beautiful little girl with brown hair and blue eyes. She was happy, and I had to say goodbye way too soon."

The memory flooded back into my head. I was five or so, and we had been sitting on the porch in the rocking chair. Tears streamed down her face and dripped onto my shoulder, alarming me.

"Your birthday is the fourteenth of April?"

"Yeah... how did you know?" She looked up at me, confusion on her face.

"I just had a flashback, and it was that day. She was crying, and she told me it was because it reminded her of a little girl with brown hair and blue eyes, one that she had to say goodbye to," I told her.

"I know you all have a lot of questions, as do I, but it's time for me to go—"

"You are *not* free to go. You have murdered cadets. I can't let that slide and continue," my father said.

"Except that I am not a student here, nor am I in the military anymore. The rules around here don't apply to me."

"You can't just go around killing people," I said to her.

"There are people all over this continent killing people for fun, for experiments—" she cocked her head at my dad, "for revenge, and yet they are never questioned, never detained, and neither will I."

My father inhaled a deep breath. "Killing cadets isn't acceptable—"

"They threatened the only purpose for which I exist," she yelled. She rubbed her thumb and finger together, and in an instant, she was gone.

"Well, that was a neat little party trick," Zane said, while rubbing his head.

"I would vanquish anyone who actually threatens..." Esme purred.

"I think she might be a little delusional," I told her.

"Her perception is that they were threats, and maybe they were."

"What the hell are we going to do now?" I asked, looking at my father, then at Zane.

Neither of them spoke, just stared at the spot where Genevieve stood.

"Or we can just stand here..." I said

My father let out a rumble. "You're still leaving."

"Why? We know who has killed the cadets, and spoiler alert: it wasn't me."

"Always the comical when the world is falling apart," my father said.

"Someone has to be," I said, then let out a small chuckle.

"I will go speak with King Fen and Duke Soldat. Ultimately, it is up to them what happens—"

"You can't tell them about Genevieve," I pleaded with him.

"I do actually. She is right, military laws don't bind her, but Duke Soldat isn't... well, let's just say his moral compass sits a little crooked. Regardless, I still think you should leave here—"

"I am clearly not in danger, Father."

"Maybe not from her, but from others who are blaming you, and quite frankly, you are a danger to them. They bump into you wrong, and she perceives them as danger and takes care of it."

"Whatever. I don't want to leave. I need to hone my magic and flying."

"I'll be back," he said, before I could say bye—the door opened and closed. I never realized before how fast he moved.

"How are you doing, my love?" Zane asked, before grabbing me into his arms and holding me.

"If I told you I was fine, you would know I was lying. I'm processing. I'm in shock. I'm pissed."

"As you should be, I couldn't imagine. You have had one hell of a year, and it has just begun."

Zane held me tight, not letting me go. His lips pressed into the top of my head. Our breathing started to sync—I hadn't realized I was breathing rapidly until my breathing slowed and moved into Zane's pattern. His hand rubbed up and down my back. My shoulders relaxed, letting go of the tension I was holding. I inhaled a deep breath and visualized releasing the stress out of my neck and shoulders.

"I don't know what I am doing anymore," I whispered to him.

"It's okay to feel lost sometimes. That's when you lean on the people who are here for you—me or Lili."

"Why are we even here?" I blurted out. I felt him suck in a breath between us and let it out slowly.

"Because we committed to joining the military?"

"But why? We didn't have to. I am hated here, clearly."

"Maybe this is where we were meant to meet?"

"I think we would have met no matter what."

"You couldn't have been a dragon rider without coming here."

"True, but apparently I am a Witch..."

"Not trying to butt in, but you need me. Don't forget it," Esme said.

"Yeah. Yeah, mom."

CHAPTER 23

I waited in my room for hours with Zane until my father came knocking on my door again. We sat for hours talking about the last several months, about what both of us wanted. While I knew I wanted to be a dragon Rider, and I really hadn't wanted to give up Esme, as she had become a part of me, it was clear I wouldn't be able to remain in the military for life, nor could he. Through all of this, we just wanted each other. We wanted a simple life, one without being targeted, one where our lives weren't constantly on the line, and most importantly, one where we weren't controlled.

"Duke Soldat doesn't want you to remain at the campus; however, King Fen overruled him and has granted you to stay for now."

"I feel like there is a catch coming?" I said to my father.

"They want Genevieve dead."

"That's not surprising, and what did you say?"

"Hmm, it doesn't really matter what *I* say. The King has the final say for now."

"Okay? And what about the whole if something happens to her, something will happen to me?"

"Ah, yes, that is where things changed. We are pretty sure she used a linking spell... which is interesting—"

"Why is it interesting?" I cut him off.

"Well, the linking spell is a type of spell that only a particular clan of Witches can do."

"And?"

"As far as we knew, the last living member died over five hundred years ago."

"Hmm, funny that's almost exactly what was said about the Faucher Witches."

"Yes, but the Sarradet Witches weren't outlawed or killed off. Among the Witches, they were powerful but reasonable. They had access to magic that, for whatever reason, the fates didn't give to the other Witch lines. There were always some conspiracy theories that said they weren't really gone, but chatter about that died off hundreds of years ago when none of them surfaced until today."

"I don't think I ever learned about them," Zane said.

"Not surprising, they didn't do anything super diabolical, like the Fauchers," my dad cocked an eyebrow at me.

"Maybe, that's where her diabolical side comes from," I said, then a loud rumble laugh flowed out of my mouth.

Zane let out a chuckle. I knew that I wasn't the funniest person, but having him laugh at my corny jokes made me happy.

"I make corny jokes all the time," Esme said down the bond.

"And I laugh at you," I told her.

"So, then what is the plan here?" I asked my father.

"Well, obviously, killing her means killing you, if we are correct, and it is a linking spell. Once I shared about the possible linkage, they decided it was in their best interest not to demand her execution."

"Hmm, I'm sure it had nothing to do with my life and all to do with her suspected heritage."

"I'm sure that is why, but no matter. As far as you are concerned, you can return to classes. I will be attempting to find her to reason with her and let her know she is banned from Sandorg College premises, and you are safe. Not only are there several professors here who are keeping an eye on you, but you have a very protective mate *and* dragon."

"So, that's it? We just carry on like there weren't seventeen cadets that she mangled, tortured, and hung up as trophies?"

"Yes. Neither of you should speak on this."

"Are you fucking serious?" Zane blurted out.

"Yes, I am. What else would you like us to do right now? Announce that it was a half-sister of Auriella, and they were seeking vengeance on her. Oh yeah, and we are allowing her to continue living."

"I guess when you put it like that," Zane said.

"Exactly. We will be announcing tomorrow morning during current events that the murderer has been caught and dealt with. It seems it was a deranged Witch practicing black magic, and she has been dealt with. All professors will be told this version as well."

"Wow. Everything you just said makes me question everything else we have been told," I said.

"Same," Zane said coldly.

"I don't like to deceive, but this is about protecting you and protecting your mother's secret. Two things I will die to protect."

"Ha. Earlier, you said I had a very protective mate and dragon. You forgot to say a hovering protective father."

"Hmm, because you don't need me, my little Reyna. Do you know why we chose that middle name? It means a wise queen, and my dear, you have the power to be any queen. *You* don't need my protection, you don't need his or Esme's either."

"Then why do you want me to leave here?"

"No matter how strong you are, there is always someone stronger, especially when they band together, most importantly, the fear of the unknown."

"Funny, weren't you the one who always told me, *'Don't let fear control you, it gives ammo to someone to manipulate and control you.'* Don't let your greatest weakness be me, Dad."

"One day, many, many years from now, when you become a parent, you will understand that it is the greatest gift to be given, and yes, your greatest weakness. Please, Auri, keep your head low and fewer eyes on you. You have been excused for the remainder of the day due to some sort of stomach illness," he said, "do come to class tomorrow, though."

"Thanks, Dad."

He stepped forward and pulled me into a hug. "I love you, Auri."

"Love you too, Dad."

***

We spent the remainder of the evening in my room. I had wondered what, or if, my dad said, why Zane would be missing lectures today. The thought of the campus going back to normal was a bit of relief, but part of me was still reserved and worried that it wasn't ever going to go back to normal, truly. What was normal? I had so many questions running through my brain that sometimes it felt overwhelming trying to quiet them down.

Zane attempted to distract—well, he did distract me graciously with his tongue and body, but as soon as I regained my breathing, the rampant thoughts came back. He didn't know the answers to any of the questions. Were we really going to go back to our lectures as if nothing happened?

Laderra brought me soup and a biscuit from the dining facility for me to enjoy in my room. She was no wiser, believing that I was sick. She quickly dropped the food and left me. Granted, I wasn't actually ill, but the soup was delicious, with strong hints of garlic and onion. Something that many cooks believed would cure any illness if you had enough of it. There was a small cup of honey garlic for the biscuit as well. All of it was savory, which was fitting because sometimes the food at the dining facility wasn't.

I curled up into Zane's arms on the bed. I had the curtains pulled back, revealing the night sky. Stars glittered in the sky atop the mountain.

"Why do you think my mom placed Genevieve for adoption?"

"Some families are strongly against having children outside of marriage, while most look the other way or don't care about premarital sex. They do care about the proof of premarital sex. It may not have been her choice exactly."

"Why not disappear in the night before the baby comes? She didn't have to tell me much, but I knew it bothered her about not knowing her *own* parents."

"I wish I knew the answers to the questions that are running through that pretty little—"

Knock. Knock. Knock.

We both turned our heads to look at each other, narrowing our eyes at each other. Neither of us was expecting guests in the late evening, nor should there be anyone moving around campus, with the lockdown not being lifted until tomorrow. I moved off the bed and walked to the door.

"Yeah?" I called from behind.

"Genevieve," the female voice said. One word. My eyes widened, and I quickly opened the door. She stood there quietly staring at me. I reached for her hand and pulled her in. Not that she needed to be pulled into my warded room, she seemed to break through my wards many times before.

"What are you doing here?" I seethed.

"Oh, hi sister, nice to see you too."

"We met and saw each other this morning," I told her.

"Yes, yes, we did, but we didn't really get to finish our conversation, now did we?"

"Was there more that needed to be said?"

"Now, now, now, you know that there are many questions we both seek to know," she said.

"Hmm, yes, but it is late, and quite frankly, I am overwhelmed by today's discoveries."

"I am sorry to have dropped all of this on you. I hadn't expected you in your room earlier, and I was just going to write you a note, but honestly, it was time—"

"Time for what?" I cut her off.

"For us to meet. To clear the air."

"We met. Now listen, I really, really need you to stop killing people on my behalf. I don't need *your* protection. Not only am I quite powerful—"

"You are nothing to what you can be, to what I am—"

Before I could control it, shadows exploded out of me, they wrapped around her neck and lifted her into the air. Zane shot to his feet and was behind me in a single breath.

"Auri, that's not very nice," he told me through our bond.

"I don't like to be threatened, and she should see me, see who I really am," I told him.

"Not very hospitable," he growled.

"She murdered cadets..."

She stared at me, eyes wide, shock painted her face. She lifted her hand and swiped it to the right. I flew into the wall, but my shadows felt the threat and held tighter.

"Stop!" she yelled.

"Or what?"

"Because... this... violence... isn't... needed..." she gasped out.

I tilted my head to the side and then lowered her to the ground before pulling my shadows back to me. I let them stay encircling my feet, ready to defend me and come to my aid.

She gasped in, then rubbed her neck, before standing straight up. She stared at me, eyes wide, blinking every few seconds.

She clicked her tongue three times at me. "That was... unexpected."

"Oh, you didn't know that I wielded shadows?"

"Do I look like I know? No, I didn't."

"Well, as you can see, I don't need protection."

"I can see that, yes."

"My father is searching for you. The Duke of Woxweth has banned you from the college premises. You're lucky they aren't ordering your death."

"Let me guess, it's only because we are linked together, which also means they probably figured out the Sarradet Witch connection," she said, twirling her finger in her hair.

"It's neither here nor there for the reasons—"

"Except that it does matter—fuck—me exposing my clan is... well, there will be consequences. That's not your problem. Listen, I lost my way, and I may have overreacted—"

"You. May. Have. Overreacted. You killed seventeen cade—"

"Hmm... and Twenty-two in total... Oops."

My heart dropped into my stomach, and my entire chest was hard to breathe, like a vice grip clenching me tight. My stomach burned like fire.

"Twenty-two?"

"Yeah... Other threats. Don't worry about them. We have other things we need to discuss."

"I'll listen to whatever it is that you have to say, but you have to answer my questions," I said. There were things I needed to know—had to know. With her being banned, I may not see her again for a while.

"Deal. You get five questions. You'd better make each one of them count. You can go first."

"Why did you kill them in the manner that you did? How were they a threat to me?"

"That's two questions. Sometimes things need to become statements, and the best way to make a statement is by shocking people and putting fear into them. Anyone who makes verbal threats, whether directly or indirectly, to you. Take Asmoth, he attacked you and then called you to a challenge. Dafne was bragging to her friends about how she would catch you off guard. Some of them were unfortunate obstacles that interrupted me."

"When and why did you link us?" I asked.

"You really like combining questions, huh? I have been staying in Chalahana and coming here to keep a watch on you when I could. I stopped in after you were kidnapped. It was clear you were a bigger target than I had thought. I linked us then. The details of how aren't important right now. This was an alarm system for me—when someone caused you harm, I would know. One more question, Auriella."

"What made you reveal yourself now?"

"I wasn't planning on actually revealing myself, but you came back to your room early. When I overheard that you would be punished for what I did, I knew I wasn't going about it the right way. I was going to leave you a note, but when you walked in, I couldn't help myself. I needed actually to talk to you, to know you better."

"Where are the Sarradet Witches?"

She shook her head at me. "Even if you hadn't already asked your five questions, that one isn't just my secret to reveal."

"Now your turn."

"The best part about allowing someone to ask their questions first is that they used their questions to ask the very things one would share anyway," she said, before letting out a laugh.

I pursed my lips at her and raised my right eyebrow at her.

"I like to move around, I leave my village in the night and don't come home for weeks, sometimes months at a time. My family is used to this by now. They think I like to travel and explore the continent. What they don't know is that I have been watching my little sister grow. I have been gone more of the last year than I have been there. I need to go back home and probably for a while—" she dropped her head and stared at the ground. Something told me there was something much more than she was telling. "—I hadn't planned to leave yet—"

"What aren't you saying?" I blurted out.

"I was betrothed to be married when I was twenty-five. He didn't care that I traveled around, and thankfully, he never asked questions. We played a good married couple, and are intimate when I am home. Honestly, he is a good guy, and there is some love there."

"Why are you telling me this?" I asked her.

"There is a point to this... I never knew if I actually wanted children, learned when I would be fertile, and avoided him when I was. You see, the abandonment I have struggled with has loomed over me for years, unsure of what kind of mother I could be when I hadn't worked through my childhood—"

"Is she saying what I think she is saying?" Zane said in my mind.

"I think that's where this is going. How many times do you think she will let me interrupt her before she snaps?" I asked him back.

"My turn..."

"Are you trying to say you're pregnant?" Zane cut her off.

"Yes. Maybe. I don't know. I haven't gone to a healer, and if I go to any priestess, then they would figure out my heritage. I need to go home, and if

I am, I may not see you for a while. I actually wanted to meet you. For you to know that I did this for you, and you may not really understand why, and maybe I don't either. I know that I am not sane, but everything I did, I did it for you. I have loved you as soon as I knew about you, I feel connected to you, more than even our mother. I don't know how to explain it. I know this all is confusing and doesn't make sense..."

Both Zane and I stared at her, unsure of what we should say. This didn't sound like something she wanted a congratulations for or a sorry. She was clearly in a state of turmoil over the situation, and I wasn't even sure what to say. I wasn't even sure what to think.

"Did I actually make you speechless?" she asked.

"Uh, yeah. I don't know what to make of this or feel about any of this. I'm also unsure of how to respond to this pregnancy announcement, and I also feel bad that I just choked you while in such a state..."

"Are you familiar with astral projections?"

"Yes."

"Good, once I get settled. I will astral project at nineteen hundred on Friday nights. If you are here, you're here, and we can chat. If you aren't, then I will assume you are busy or don't want to talk. If you could, though, leave me a note if you don't want to talk or aren't available."

"Got it. Don't want you to go on any more murder sprees looking for me."

"And I will," she said, deadpan.

"Is she serious?" Zane asked me.

"I hope not."

"Please let your father know, I am sorry that we didn't get to chat, but that he doesn't have to worry about me anymore. He also needs to locate Oscar Trahan."

"Who's that?"

"Someone that can help you hone those shadows..."

"Where are we supposed to find him?"

"Somewhere in the mountains, that's all I know. Zane's father might know more. I have to go."

"Um. Okay?"

"Please, Auri, take care of yourself. Trust no one."

"Be safe on your journey back to... where'd you say you lived again?"

"Oh, clever girl, I didn't. Bye."

Before I could say anything more, as she had done before, she was gone in an instant.

CHAPTER 24

Everyone was on edge during breakfast. It was clear that the murder of the recent cadets made everyone feel on edge. Several cadets stared at me and whispered amongst each other. I tuned it out to the best I could. The reality was I was to blame for these murders—it was my fault. I may not have killed them, and I may not have strung them up, but they were killed because Genevieve perceived them as threats to me.

Laderra was quieter than usual, which meant she had said almost nothing during our walk to the dining facility and during breakfast. As we walked to the indoor stadium classroom, we moved to our seats. The professors hadn't arrived there yet, and there were fewer lieutenants. I wondered if anyone else noticed the lessened presence, or if it was only because I knew that the threat was gone.

Over the next thirty minutes, the room filled with cadets as it did every morning, Monday through Friday. All three professors and my father walked onto the dais, and the professors looked more at ease than they had in the last month. My father was stoic as he always had been. He raised his hand high, fingers splayed, and the lecture room instantly quieted.

"Good morning, cadets. I am pleased to announce that all lockdown procedures have been lifted—"

"Does that mean the murderer has been caught?" an Infantry cadet shouted out.

"Please do not interrupt me," my father said.

"Sorry," the cadet muttered.

"To answer your outburst, yes. The murderer has been caught. It was not a cadet, and the matter has been dealt with," my dad said.

"I know that the past month has been gruesome and filled with anxiety, but we are relieved to tell you that everyone here is safe. Over the next few weeks, our second lieutenants will be slowly going back to their bases," Pascal said.

"I am the happiest to tell you that we will be celebrating! Classes will resume to normal today, but there will be no classes tomorrow, and we will be having our Winter Solstice Celebration tomorrow. It isn't mandatory, of course, but we do hope for any of you to join us in celebration," Melamora said.

"Are there any questions regarding this announcement?" Fogg said.

"What was their motive?" one yelled out.

"Were they executed?" another shouted.

"Are they connected to anyone currently here?" another asked.

My dad held his hand up as the questions started to overlap one another.

"Maybe asking for questions following such an announcement on our part wasn't smart," my father said and shot Fogg a look. He rolled his shoulders back. "There is no direct motive that was revealed. Details regarding who and how they were handled are classified. What I can say is that everyone here is now safe."

Grumbling was heard throughout the lecture hall. It was clear they wanted more answers, ones that my father was not going to give to them.

"We do have other topics we need to discuss," Pascal said, then gave my father a nod. My father took a step back, letting Pascal, Melamora, and Fogg take the lead. I needed to catch my father before he took off. I needed to relay information from Geneveive.

"While things seem to be moving in a positive direction here in the college, the war on the coastlines is growing. More and more reports have been coming in, and the attacks at our coastal bases are very concerning. If you were the general of the military, what information would you want from your base commanders?" Pascal asked.

"How many infiltrated?" an Infantry cadet asked.

Pascal nodded.

"How many were killed in action?" a Drusearon warrior said.

All three of them nodded.

"How many enemies survived, and were they questioned?"

"Good, think deeper," Pascal said.

"Were the attacks consistent across the bases?" I asked.

Melamora nodded.

"How are we changing our defenses to prevent better attacks?" a third-year Shapeshifter asked.

"That is a great question, but this is what the general would be strategizing," Melamora said.

"Is there any difference between the newest attacks and the previous ones?" a Witch cadet asked.

"Great. All of these are great questions that a general may want to know, wouldn't you say, General?" Pascal said, while turning to look at my father.

"I agree. As I have received correspondence from the bases that have been attacked, it has included just the information that you all have asked for. If any of you shall be a base commander one day, these are the questions you will need to know to pass the information on," my father said.

"Now I will share with you what has been disclosed to us to share," Melamora said, "at this time, Fort Kalona, Camp Echo, Whisper Outpost, Lakish Outpost, and Night Side Outpost have had multiple attacks over the recent months. Since the first of January, there have been three attacks. In those three attacks, we have lost eighteen warriors. All attacks have been reported as similar. A ship coming to the coast, that appears empty, while being investigated at sea, an attack from Nosferatu happens on land. All of these attacks happened at night. While we have successfully eliminated most of them, a few of them have escaped onto our lands. They have not been located."

Gasps filled the air.

"This isn't the first time, and while it may seem concerning, we also have not had any mysterious attacks that have led us to believe they are here attacking Fae, but we also don't know where they are or why," Pascal said.

"Are we in danger here, again?" a Witch cadet asked.

"We do not believe so, which is why not every lieutenant is leaving. We also have recruited a group of quite powerful Witches to construct a ward over the campus grounds that will not allow a Nosferatu through," my father said.

"I wonder if he is one of those powerful Witches," I told Zane.

"Probably, he isn't gonna say that though. You don't sound worried about this news?"

"Naw, as recently pointed out to me, I have these crazy protective stalkers, not to mention my own powers," I said with confidence.

He laughed down the bond. *"Funny girl."*

Current events class carried on with other details. They announced that third-years would be starting their rotations in the following weeks, as they finalize details. The announcement of that made my chest burn. I knew that meant Zane would leave me. I knew it was silly and I knew I was being irrational and clingy, but the thought of being separated from him felt like a piece of my heart was getting ripped out.

They would also be going back to lecture integrations, and new schedules would be released on Monday to reflect that. By the end of the lecture, half the cadets were back to their usual chipper selves. The rest were like me, looking like someone was trying to take parts of our souls.

I lingered behind as the rest of the cadets left to head to their next lecture. I wanted to make sure my dad knew I spoke with Genevieve again. Watching some of the cadets bounce out of the lecture hall, as if every worry of theirs disappeared in a matter of minutes. Were they not listening to what was shared after? Our continent was going to war with Rudemont. It was coming, and it was on our doorsteps. Maybe their parents weren't still active, or perhaps they didn't have family members who were upperclassmen.

I knew what the implications of a war like this could mean. It could mean my father being on the front lines, and Zane being pulled into service early. I wondered if they knew what it truly meant, or if they were just naive. As the room emptied, my father remained on the dais and noticed I was still in my seat. He cocked his head slightly and headed towards me.

"Cadet Blackcreek, you will be late for your next lecture?"

"I may, but what I need to tell you was more important. With wandering ears, I think maybe we should hug?"

"Understood."

I stood up, moved into the aisle, and pulled him into a hug. I thought about what Genevieve shared with me last night. I felt him within my memories. Within a few minutes, he pulled back, held my arms, and stared at me.

"Get to your lecture, cadet. I will be in and out for the next few weeks, getting everything settled before I leave."

"Yes, sir."

He let go of my arms, and I moved past him and headed to the sparring gym, which was next door to the stadium classroom.

***

I chose to sleep in the following morning, instead of getting up and going to breakfast. I also knew that celebrations meant a free-for-all when it came to food. Lunch foods would start around zero-ten-thirty, and winter activities would fill the courtyard, outdoor stadium, and flight field. Zane left me early this morning to tend to some duties that Remus had assigned to him with some of the Drusearons that needed extra training.

I enjoyed the morning reading in my chair with my curtains open. It looked beautiful out, with the sun shining, but I knew that was a deception—it was cold out.

"I'm coming in," Zane said.

Within seconds, he was standing in my room, and with no surprise, a dress in his arms.

"I could have almost predicted this," I said, then let out a small chuckle.

"Hmm, what's that?"

"You standing here with a dress draped over your arm."

"Ah, yes. I do fancy a beautiful dress."

"Lucky for you, I do enjoy one. Let's see it."

He let the dress drop and held it up, as if he were holding his newborn child. Smile across his beautiful face. A light blue fitted dress with long, loose bell sleeves. It was floor-length, with overlapping slits on each side. The perfect kind where one may not know they are there unless they see me walking or I am pulling a dagger from my outer thigh. I loved that he knew even with my powers, I didn't prefer to be without my daggers.

"You sure do know how to pick a beautiful dress," I told him.

"My favorite part about picking out your dress is envisioning me removing it from your body."

"Oh... do tell?"

"I'd rather show you tonight."

"Hmm, or you could show me now?"

He moved closer to me, cupping my cheek, and placed his thumb on my lip.

"I would very much love that, but I was one of the lucky ones assigned to assist with setup for today's celebrations. I won't be free until seventeen-hundred."

"Then tonight."

"Tonight."

He stroked his thumb down my lip in the most teasing way. He leaned in and kissed me, drawing my lip into his. I pulled away and pushed him back.

"Enough, or you will be late," I said.

He laughed and then roved out.

I placed dress on my bed and headed to Lili's room. We hadn't seen each other much and hadn't really gotten to catch up with everything that had been going on.

I knocked four times and waited. I could hear shuffling in the room, yet she hadn't yelled out anything.

"Lili?" I finally said.

"Oh... um, hold on."

It hit me that she had company in her room with her, and I had interrupted her. The door swung open, and I stood staring at her male companion. Gods.

"Auriella Blackcreek," Knoxx said.

"Knoxx Quinnly," I said back.

"And of course you two know each other..." Lili said.

"That we do," I said, while keeping my eyes locked on his.

"Oh, please don't tell me y'all have hooked up?" Lili said.

"No!" we both said at the same time, while jerking our heads to her.

"Wouldn't that be awkward?" Esme laughed down the bond.

"This whole encounter is awkward. I am sure you and Lakung are laughing together."

"Oh, we are and doing much, much more."

"Gods, I really don't want to know about your dragon sex. Thanks, though."

"Why not? I can feel your emotions and know when you are doing it."

"Oh, my fucking Gods. I am gonna perish with embarrassment."

"I am gonna go get... um... cleaned up and changed," Knoxx said.

I let out a laugh, not because it was funny, but because this whole thing was cringeworthy.

Once he walked out, Lili reached out and pulled me into her room.

"Glad to see you shielded the room," I told her.

"Yeah, well, it was mandatory and I kind of like living," she said.

Before I could say anything else, she pulled me into a hug and squeezed me tight. I wasn't big on hugging, but she was. I embraced her back, for I knew that she wouldn't let go otherwise.

"Are you okay?" she finally said.

"I am doing better today."

"I never thought you had anything to do with it."

I wanted to tell her everything. She was my best friend, and she was more like a sister to me than the sister who showed up in my room yesterday, but I knew I couldn't.

"So, how do you know Knoxx?" she asked, the question I knew she was burning to ask me.

"Ahh... yeah... we will forever be connected."

"What does that mean?" She narrowed her eyes at me.

"Think about it, why did our parents always move together?"

She squinted her eyes closed and clenched her jaw. "Your dragons are bonded."

"That they are, something I discovered while on leave."

"Well... shit."

"I don't know anything else about him. Is this thing between you two getting serious?"

"Oh, I don't know. I am two years ahead of him, and I will be ushering off in a few weeks anyhow."

"You got it bad, though."

"I do indeed," she said, shrugging her shoulders.

"How are you feeling about leaving?"

"Honestly? I am nervous. During leadership meetings, the discussions of what is happening on the coastlines are discussed in more detail. Initially, they weren't going to do rotations because of that. Now, they decided to move forward with them and keep them at the inland bases."

"I'm also a nervous mess. We both know how the military works. We have been around it our entire lives. I am worried about you, Zane, Alex, and my dad," I told her.

"I am also worried about my parents. They will be going to Fort Kalona with your father. I'm sure you know that base can be hostile."

"Yeah... I know."

"What else is on your mind?"

"There is a lot, but I... can't share."

"Oh."

"I hate keeping secrets from you, and it is tearing me apart."

"You manifested a classified ability, huh?"

"Yes."

"I'm not surprised, given that your dad has one."

"Aside from that, there are some things that aren't exactly classified, but they um... well...you can't tell anyone, not even Knoxx."

"That sounds ominous."

"I'm about to shock your core, so buckle up, Lil."

"On that note, I'm just gonna go ahead and sit down."

"Yeah, you probably should. My father *is* actually half wolf and half Witch, well, my mother was too," I said, my eyes locked onto the floor. I knew her hand covered her mouth from the half gasp I heard.

"You *are* a wolf *and* a Witch?" she said.

"Yeah... apparently."

"You gonna shift into a wolf or something?"

"Well... I am over the age where one typically shifts for the first time, so hopefully I am safe, but apparently, it is pretty rare for a child born to a full Werewolf not to shift. My father never shifted..."

It hit me like a sack of potatoes in my stomach. Did my mother ever shift? Was this something she hid? What did she actually know about her ancestry? In that moment, questions about her flooded into my head. Why join the Healers if she could have joined as a Witch? Or if she had shifted, why not the Shapeshifters?

"Auri? You went somewhere other than here?" she asked, breaking my concentration.

I shook my head a little bit. "Sorry, it hit me how much I didn't know about my mother. How many questions I truly had about her. Let's just say that after I left here, my world has truly turned upside down with family secrets coming out left and right."

"I'm sorry, Auri. If there is anyone who is resilient to see the positive and come on the other side, it's you."

"Thanks. You have always been there for me."

I stayed in her room for hours, catching her up on everything. I told her about my sister, but left out the part about her being responsible for killing the cadets. Catching up with her, crying and laughing, was precisely what I needed after the past several months.

I headed back to my room to get ready for the evening festivities. I opted to skip most of the day's activities. It probably would have been fun, but I hadn't felt like embracing large groups. The same large groups that had looked at me like I was the *cadet slayer*. Evening festivities would be like other solstice celebrations: eating, drinking, and dancing.

CHAPTER 25

Zane

What I didn't tell Auri was that being assigned to the solstice preparations was punishment for skipping lectures with her. Her father didn't give an excuse for my absence. After Remus informed me of where my first field assignment would be, I knew he was making a statement on not showing me any favoritism. I hadn't told Auriella this morning when I dropped her gown, not wanting to ruin her day.

I was assigned to help turn the flight field into a winter wonderland. The ground was turned into a frozen skating rink, thanks to the help of some Riders with their abilities to manipulate water and ice. A station for Healers and menders was set up on the edge with a tent and heat for any cadets who fell and broke any limbs. Every year, the numbers ranged in the dozens, yet every year, they made an ice rink. Despite broken bones, skating on the ice was quite enjoyable.

Inside the outdoor arena, there was another ice field, where cadets played stick and ball in teams against each other. Professors played as referees, and it was needed. Some cadets played so fiercely that by the end of the night, the entire ice field would be red. It was gruesome and thrilling to watch. Cadets often filled the seating, coming and going as different teams defended their goals.

I played my first year here and decided then it would be the last time. I came out with a broken nose, three broken fingers, and several lacerations. Thankfully, we had menders on site, ready and willing to heal our injuries.

It was no different as cadets played various games around the college grounds. I knew Auri hadn't planned to attend the daytime events, but was planning to be here for dinner and evening festivities. Which was perfect, as I was babysitting other cadets while they skated around. A second-year cadet who got himself into some trouble with one of the professors would be swapping with me.

Time ticked slowly as I watched cadets skate around the rink. A handful of them fell and broke bones, mostly wrists. There were several cadets holding hands and skating together, sharing glimpses of lust. It made me joyful to watch others enjoy company, something I was once envious of in previous years.

As soon as the cadet released me, I headed back to my chambers and quickly changed into a nice, tailored suit that had baby blues to complement Auri's dress. As soon as I was changed, I headed to her room to escort her to the courtyard. She had told me she would wait until I came for her, instead of meeting me there.

As soon as she opened the door, our eyes locked. My heart stuttered, no words left my mouth, but I was sure my eyes were saying everything I couldn't. She was stunning, the dress curved her body perfectly. The neckline dipped down just enough to see a little bit of her breasts, but not enough to show much more. The sleeves were loose and flowing, contrasting with the way the rest of it hugged her curves. The overlapping slits that started at mid-thigh showed just a little bit of her when she walked. Gods, I hoped I made it through this evening without wanting to shred the dress off of her and fucking her in front of everyone.

"Your eyes are saying everything you're not," she said, smiling with her little dimples showing.

"Mmhmm, are they saying I want to rip your clothes off and fuck you anywhere, in front of whoever witnesses?"

"Something like that... never thought you would want other men to see me... in such provocative ways."

I let out a low growl. "Oh, you see, I could actually give no fucks if anyone was to look and see however they want. I *know* you are mine, as I am yours, and they can think whatever they want—they will *never* have you."

"Is that so?" she asked, with that sly grin.

"It is." I leaned in and pulled her into me, pressed my lips onto hers, and held them there for several heartbeats before pulling back.

I knew I couldn't kiss her as passionately as I wanted, or we wouldn't leave this room. She had that hold on me—my vice. I grabbed her hand and pulled her out of her room and down the hall to head to the courtyard.

"I love you, Zane," she said, breaking the silence between us.

"I love you too, Auri, and while I love hearing you tell me that, is everything okay?"

"I... I... just needed to tell you. I feel like with everything happening, I need to say it to you as many times as I think about it."

I stopped, stopping her in the middle of the hall, and turned towards her. I reached my hand up, cupping the back of her neck, my thumb rubbing her cheek.

"Auri, what worries you?"

"Everything. I know you will be leaving soon, and I know that there is more to what is happening at the coast. My family is in chaos, and everything is imploding. I've almost died twice in a year. I'm just worried—I guess—that's all."

"Everything will be okay. I will be okay, and I will burn this continent to the ground before I let anything happen to you," I told her.

I turned and moved down the hall. We needed a distraction—she needed a distraction. Food, drinks, and friends would surely help. Like previous celebrations, the courtyard was transformed into a mystical wonder. Light orbs floated above, casting a light blue light throughout. Icicles floated in between light orbs. Tables lined the outer walls, filled with candies, cookies, fruits, smoked meats, and cheese.

"Let's grab a meal from the dining facility and find a seat. I am sure you are hungry from skipping meals today," I said.

"Starving."

We moved into the dining facility, where they were serving roasted goose, turkey, venison, and oysters. They also had potatoes, bread, and cabbage. Winter celebrations were often filled with hearty meals, meant to be fulfilling and rewarding. Some villages held huge parties for the winter solstice, while some preferred other solstices.

Auri practically gagged when she saw the oysters. She picked roasted goose with a hearty side of potatoes and cabbage. I had thought about getting the oysters, but opted out once I saw her visceral reaction to them. We walked to the table that Alex, Lili, and Elijah were sitting at. All three of them were laughing amongst themselves.

"Hey, love birds!" Alex said. He had accepted our relationship over the previous weeks, but anytime he had seen us show any kind of affection, his eyes said it all.

"Evening," I told them.

"Hey," Auri said. She sat down and started shoveling food into her mouth.

"Have you been starving her, Zane?" Lili asked.

"She has free will," I told her.

I didn't want to say to her that I was worried when she skipped meals, or that I tried to encourage her eat all the time. Some days she ate great, and some days she would skip meals. This was one of her greatest tells in how she was emotionally.

"I love roasted goose. We don't get it enough," Auri said.

"I'm surprised you'd ever eat a goose again," Lili said. Auri shot her a look, something unsaid between the two of them.

"They are indeed yummy," Elijah said, "how are you feeling about our upcoming assignment?"

I swallowed hard. This was not how I wanted her to hear about this.

"I am going to enjoy mine," Lili said.

"Where are you going?" Auri asked.

"Zion Outpost," Lili said.

"We always did love that place," Auri said.

"Our wing is going to the fucking Arctic," Alex said.

"The Northhold Outpost is quite cold at this time. You'll be fine, little baby," Lili teased him.

"And our wing is headed to the tropics," Elijah said.

Auri shot her head towards me and cocked her head to the side. She was silent, but I could tell she was taking everything in.

"I was going to tell you, I promise," I told her in her head.

"Oh, she didn't know... someone is in trouble," Elijah teased me.

"I'm not his keeper, but yes, I didn't know," Auri said, before looking down at her plate, moving food around with her fork.

"I'm sorry, I just wanted us to enjoy the evening first," I told her.

"What post will you be going to, Zane?" Auri said.

The entire table fell silent, the tension thicker by the second. I might as well tell her and get it over with.

"Fort Kalona," I said low.

"Wait, what?" Alex said.

"Holy shit," Lili said.

"Yeah, apparently, we get to go to a base that has been attacked. Yay us!" Elijah said.

Auri had lifted her head and was staring at me, eyes wide.

"I see why you didn't want to tell me..." she said, down our bond.

"Yes, but our stay will be shorter than some of the other assignments."

"Can we pretend this didn't add to your already growing anxiety for the night, and talk about it later?" I asked her.

"I can try. I can't believe they are allowing any cadets to go there. Why is your Wing getting sent to a coastal base? I just have a lot of questions..."

"I don't know the answers to most of them... it will be alright, my Anam Cara."

"Well... how about I get us a round of drinks?" Alex said.

"That sounds exactly like what we need," Lili said.

Within minutes, Alex had returned with five glasses, all filled with Whiskey Sours. I took a big swig and was quite surprised to find it was more whiskey than citrus juice—a quite aged whiskey at that.

"Owwweee, that's stout," Elijah howled.

Auri burst into a coughing fit. "You don't say."

Within thirty minutes, the mood had gotten lighter, and I could tell Auri was more relaxed. Elijah had gotten the next round, and I wasn't sure if he and Alex were in it together to get liquor-heavy drinks, but the drinks he brought back were about the same. Once we finished that drink, we all moved to the area where dancing was set up. The music was upbeat, and Auri and Lili were dancing like they were born for dancing.

She moved effortlessly, and her smile while dancing felt refreshing. I hadn't gotten to see her truly smile in a little while. She has been carrying this heavy weight on her shoulders. Before long, most of her flight had joined her in dancing. Dancing wasn't my most favorable activity, but with a bit of alcohol, it made it easier to let go and dance with Auri and our friends.

I wanted to relax and forget about the troubles that we would soon be facing, but it was in the back of my mind, pressing in. I was worried about our first assignment. The questions that Auri had asked were some of the ones that Remus wondered himself. Why were they sending cadets to a base that been attacked several times in recent months?

The struggle with my own powers was getting worse. When Genevieve had shown up in Auri's room, I could feel her magic throughout the room. It was strong, stronger than what I had felt from any other Witch I met, stronger than Auri's. I never really felt Auri's father's power, but I suspected that he kept his shielded.

The band moved into a slow song, couples gravitated towards each other, and single cadets left the floor quickly. As if the couples were contagious and being on the floor with us would magically lock them into a relationship.

Auri wrapped her arms around my neck, and my hands fell to her hips, gripping them tight and pulling her closer to me. My head was tilted down, lips pressed into her head. My stomach fluttered with excitement. I slowly inhaled, savoring her scent.

"Gods, this makes me want to fuck you," I told her.

"You want to fuck me every time you touch me," she said back.

"You aren't wrong, you control me more than you know."

"Oh, and I have behaved so well and not teased you lately."

"Are you suggesting you might start teasing me?"

"Guess you will have to find out."

"I'd be delighted for you to tease me for the rest of my life."

She let out a giggle, so pure. I instantly felt the butterflies move from my stomach to my dick. I moved my hand from her hip to the small of her back and pulled her closer, our bodies pressing into each other. The band moved back into an upbeat song, and she pulled back away from me.

"That's enough of that before we leave early," she said.

"I'm not opposed to that," I told her, before letting out a small laugh.

"Esme said my dad would be arriving very soon, and he needed to talk with me. It would be very awkward if you are making me scream your name when he starts knocking."

"Instant turn-off."

She let out a loud laugh. "I thought so."

"Can I steal her?" Sadie asked.

"Only for a little bit," I told her, then let Auri entirely go. Sadie grabbed her hand and pulled her into a group with her, Akira, and Thora.

I stepped back, leaned against a table, and watched the four of them dance together. Alex slid in next to me, and within a few seconds, Elijah slid to the other side.

"Sorry about earlier..." Elijah said.

"She was gonna have to find out anyway, just had planned for it to be later this evening," I told him.

"She didn't seem super upset," Elijah said.

Alex burst into laughter, and I felt Elijah jump next to me.

"Or maybe not," Elijah said.

"She's always cool and collected while she processes something that pisses her off, and then she," Alex said, then made an explosive sound and motioned an explosion with his hands.

"Are you saying I am in for an explosion, because I have yet to see one?"

"Maybe. Then again, she's different with you."

Lili slid in next to Alex. "There's a brutal game about to start in the stadium."

Never was I so thankful for her coming over here and changing the subject, avoiding the awkwardness that was coming from that conversation.

"Whose playing?"

"Fairies against fairies," Lili said, then let out the deepest laugh I had ever heard from her.

"We are warriors," Elijah quickly retorted.

"With wings," she giggled some more.

"How drunk are you, sister?" Alex asked.

"Um... well maybe," she said.

"Well, sister, let's go watch the winged warrior fairies beat each other up with a stick over a ball," Alex said, before linking his arm around hers and pulling her towards the stadium.

"Fucking fairies," Elijah muttered.

I let out a laugh. He had always let the little things get under his skin. My eyes drifted to where Alex and Lili were walking through to the stadium. Walking in was Conri. The song was starting to dwindle, and the girls weren't moving as quickly.

"Your father has arrived," I told her. She had almost come to a stop and locked eyes with me. I nodded my head towards him. She turned her head and looked at him. She looked back at me and started walking toward me. Elijah gave me a nod and headed towards the stadium.

"I wonder what he needs to talk to me about," she said.

"I'm sure it has to do with whatever you told him yesterday, he left out of here right away," I told her.

We both stared at him as he walked towards us. He had always been hard to read. His face carried a blank expression—the master poker player.

"Auriella. Braegon."

"Hey, Dad," she said.

"Hello, sir," I told him.

"Let's move to the side, I will do a small sound shield," he told us, and walked to the corner a little further from the crowds. Surely everyone had already seen him arrive and was paying attention to us. He rubbed his thumbs on his middle fingers, moving in a circular motion. I felt the shield go around us. It was barely noticeable, but the noise around us went a little quieter.

"I found Oscar," he said.

"That was quick," we both said in sync. His eyes darted from hers to mine and back to hers again.

"Yes, I went to see Zane's father, who had said he knew of some Trahans in the far northeast corner in a little village, but hadn't recognized the name Oscar," he said.

"How did it go? Why did she want you to meet him?"

"I assume she wanted me to find him because he was once a shadow summoner—"

"He once was?" Auri interrupted.

"Yeah, he is an older Fae, and his dragon died about fifty years ago, which severed his ability. He, too, nearly died, and it took him twenty years to recover from that. He and his dragon were in the mountains hiding for quite a while."

"Oh, how does no one know about him?" she asked.

"Well, he bonded that dragon almost five hundred years ago, and he has spent the last two hundred years making sure he doesn't exist to anyone. His dragon was injured, and both of them were getting older. He left the military long ago and has worked hard at making his existence non-existent. Even I did not know of him."

"Then how did Genevieve?" I asked.

"That is a great question. I would love to ask her myself, but I have had absolutely no leads on her."

"Why did she want you to find him?"

"I presume because you two share an ability, for him to teach you, but he was very adamant that he was not leaving the mountains, nor was he in the mood to teach any young Fae, no matter who you were," Conri said.

"Well, I guess that was a dead end—"

"Not entirely," he said, cutting Auri off. "He has agreed for you to come to the mountains at some point to give you some pointers, but he did say that wielding his shadows was easier. It was the magic that was hard. You needed to accept that the shadows are a part of you, an extension of your body. You can do anything with them as you can conjure. Which, by the way, is a little terrifying."

"I have been doing that. I have an unrelated question, Father," Auri said.

"Sure," he said.

"Why the hell is Zane and his wing going to Fort Kalona?" she shot out, anger laced with her words.

"That wasn't my decision—"

"But you do make the final approvals?"

"Yes, and the argument was a solid one. Not that I owe you an explanation, but his wing in particular has been one of the strongest groups of Drusearons we have seen collectively. They will probably be stationed at a coastal base, and at this rate, possibly early. Most importantly, I agreed because I would be there during their stay."

"I just don't understand why we would send third-years there for their first assignment—"

"You don't have to understand. You're a first-year. I am the General. Do not question me. This conversation is done," he said, then quickly turned and walked away. The sound shield dropped, and the noise rumbled back in.

"Wow," I said.

While I was used to closed conversations when it came to leadership, and the lack of being able to get the reason for something being ordered, but seeing it play out between a parent and child felt different to me. My parents very much didn't like it when we questioned them, but they did explain their reasoning often. The times they didn't, we usually respected it, because we knew that if they didn't explain it, it was because they couldn't.

CHAPTER 26

Zane and I stood there staring at my father's back as he walked back towards the courtyard, after he gave his order. I was used to it. Sometimes he would reason with me, but often he would tell me how it was, and there was no room to negotiate with him.

Zane wrapped an arm around my waist and pulled me back against him. He nuzzled his nose into my neck.

"Don't let him bother you. Don't worry about my assignment, I'm more rugged than you think..."

"I know, I'm just worried. It's my fear of the unknown. It's hearing them talk about blood suckers every morning."

"I'll rip every one of their heads off and more to make my way back to you," he said.

My eyes widened, and nothing escaped my lips. When he talked about his killing for me, I wasn't sure what I should say. Part of me felt warmth in my chest, the other part worried that it might not actually be healthy. Then again, I, too, would let the bodies drop for him.

"Do you want to go skate?" he asked me.

"Sure, I have only skated a couple of times, and I'm tipsy—this should be great," I told him.

"Should you fall, I will catch you. Shall we both fall, I will fly us high into the sky," he said.

"I do enjoy a nice flight in the sky," I told him.

He interlaced his fingers with mine and pulled me towards the stadium. As we moved through, there were two teams of Drusearons playing against each other. Quite a bit of the cadets had gathered in the seats and were watching, screaming amongst themselves. The teams fought to hit the ball into each other's goal. He pulsed his fingers around mine as we continued walking, the reassurance that he was there.

Once we moved through the stadium, we walked into the flight field. I gasped in awe. I hadn't walked out here yet, and it was pretty beautiful. The entire ground was covered in fluffy snow. There was a large oval area that had been turned to ice. All around the rink was a light blue rope that had loops and knots. The ropes had beautiful, glistening icicles hanging off. All around the field, large fluffy snowflakes were falling. Light orbs danced all around the field, bouncing in sync with the pianist who sat at one end playing.

I could feel the magic that was being used out here. Over the past couple of weeks, I had really focused on what magic felt like. Identifying where it was coming from. Magic from Witches felt different than the magic that Riders and Drusearons used. I tasted metallic when I was in the presence of Witches, while I hadn't figured out the difference between the other types of magic.

We moved to the table where there were metal blades that clamped onto our shoes. Because I was wearing flats, I also borrowed a pair of boots to wear with the ice blades. Once we both got our blades on, we got onto the ice and started moving around. It was right back to being at Winterhand. I moved effortlessly on the ice. I glided forward before whipping around and skating backwards in front of Zane. His eyes opened in awe.

"Only skated a few times, my ass," he mocked.

I let out a laugh. "Did I say only a few times? I might have meant a few dozen."

He picked up his speed and spun me around. He was now skating backwards in front of me. He slowed down and pulled me in closer. He tilted my chin up and brought his lips to mine, less than an inch apart. I moved myself forward to kiss him, and he moved back, but still being close.

"My sweet Anam Cara..."

Then he put his hand on the back of my head, gripping my hair; he pulled me closer, and our lips locked onto each other. We didn't exchange tongues. We just held our lips together, and yet it felt more intimate than when we were feverishly kissing each other.

He pulled back and stared deeply into my eyes, then he picked up his stride, moving us faster around the rink before lifting my arm and swinging me around, letting me skate backwards again. For a brief moment, I had forgotten about what was upcoming, but then it crept in. Anxiety was the biggest fucking buzzkill.

"How long will you be gone?" I asked.

He tilted his head at me slightly. "You struggle with turning it off, huh?"

Before I could control it, a loud laugh escaped my lips. "No, no, I can't. I wish I could. I wish my brain would shut the fuck up sometimes, and sometimes it does, but lately, since being here, it hasn't given me a reprieve. I need to plan and prepare, even if it's just mentally," I told him. I let the whole, barren truth out.

"I wish I could bear some of your troubles for you," he said.

"I have never known my brain to be quiet. I'll adjust. Now, how long are you expected to be gone?"

"Four days."

I gulped down a swallow.

Three days.

That's how long it takes before we start being weakened from the absence of each other. What we didn't know was the distance it took before it started affecting us. Ironic that the fates would have two souls tied together, destined with great power, just to have our greatest weakness be separation.

"I guess we are about to find out what it's like to be separated and lose magic."

"Oh, I forgot to tell you the best part of the plan," he said, his words laced with sarcasm.

"I can't wait."

"I will be granted to leave at twenty-hundred and return to Fort Kalona at zero-five-hundred."

"They are going to allow you to rove back every night?" I asked, confused because it seemed too far-fetched.

"Apparently so. I think this was your father's doing."

"And what if you couldn't rove? What would they have done?"

"I don't know. I wasn't complaining, nor was I asking questions."

"Have you ever been to Kalona?" I asked.

"Nope, on the way there, I will be keeping an eye out and establishing some points to stop. I won't be able to rove the complete distance, it's about the same distance to there as it is to Ashwynd."

I moved to be next to him, skating forward, hand in hand. I let the silence fill the air. Knowing I would be seeing him each night was a relief, and I wanted to let that soak in. I wanted to hold onto that part and forget about him being in a dangerous territory. I stuck my tongue out and caught some of the flying snowflakes—

"You know that's not real snowflakes?" he asked.

"Taste pretty real."

"Stop that. Don't eat the witchy woo-woo."

"I am a Witch, ya' know, with lots of witchy woo-woo."

"I never would have guessed it," he said, giving me a wink.

I stuck my tongue out and caught another one.

"I will give you something real to taste if you need something in your mouth."

"Hmm, maybe later. These taste pretty good to me. You should try it."

"I'd rather taste you..."

"Dirty little Fae," I teased him.

He let go of my hand, wrapped his arm around my waist, and pulled me in closer to him.

"I think we should go back to my room, because every time you stick that pretty little tongue out... well, maybe you should feel," he whispered in my ear.

I stuck my tongue out again, flicking it up super slow, knowing damn well what it was doing to him. The truth was the snowflakes weren't tasty at all, but at first, I did it because he said not to, then I did it because teasing was the best version of foreplay one could do in public.

"MmmMmm," he growled out.

"Does that bother you, Roarke?" Then I did it again. I instantly felt tingles between my legs, knowing I was making him hard, turned me on.

"Hmmm," he moaned out. "Time to go."

In seconds, he let his wings spring free, wrapped his arms around me, and we went up in the air twenty feet, just out of the sight of the other skating cadets. Then the lights flashed stars, and we were in his room. As he lowered me, and my feet hit the floor, I heard the metal skates clink the wood. I reached down and unclasped them from the boots—shit, I would need to exchange these for my flats back.

"Don't worry, your shoes will be perfectly fine," he said. He must have seen my face as I noticed I still had the skates and boots on.

"I hope so, they were one of my favorite pairs," I told him, then smiled at him.

He gave me a devious smile before his lips crashed into mine, and he moved us onto the bed. He kissed me like he hadn't seen me in weeks, like he didn't sleep in my bed every night he could get away with it.

He slid his hand up the side through the slit of my dress, letting his fingers trail on my inner thigh. No matter how many times we devoured each other, it felt like the first time all over again. Electricity shot through my body, and everything rushed with warmth. My nipples tingled, craving his lips to touch them.

His finger moved up and trailed circles around my clit. My underwear was becoming more and more drenched by the second. I dug my head back and let out a moan. Every single touch made me want him inside me, yet I wanted to savor every single touch and the way every movement made my body feel like it was on fire.

He slowly moved backwards off the bed, but never dropping his gaze from mine. He dropped his pants and pulled his suit off. I was perched on my elbows, watching his every move, studying every line of his muscles.

He extended his hand towards me, and I reached my hand to his. I tried pulling him back down on me, but instead, he pulled me to my feet. He turned me around and unzipped my dress, then slid his hands under the shoulders and pushed to slide the dress off my body. It took him some effort, for the dress was very tight on my upper body.

Once the dress hit the floor, my entire body filled with goosebumps, and my nipples stood out. He stood back up and rubbed my arms up and down with his hands, before pulling me close. His lips pressed into mine, and our tongues feverishly caressed one another. He pulled his tongue back in and suck my bottom lip in his mouth. He nipped it and then sucked on it. My head drew back in pure pleasure, and he moved with me, not letting go of my lip.

He gently let go of my lip and started kissing down my neck. My head fell back more, my legs trembled under me. His fingers wandered all over my body, down my stomach, in between my legs, and anywhere that made me squirm more. I reached down between us and gripped his cock in my palms, keeping my thumb on the top. My thumb did lazy circles around the slit, beads of cum hitting my thumb.

"Grrrhmmm," he growled at me, then took a step back. "You don't need to excite him."

"Hmm, but I think I do."

"I want to make you cum twice, and it's hard to do when you've got me this excited."

"Ha ha. One is fine, two is grandeur."

He let out a low guttural groan. "Come here."

He moved to sit down in the chair next to my desk.

"Oh?" I asked him as I closed the gap between us.

"Turn around."

Before I fully turned around, his hands had gripped my hips and spun me around, then pulled me into his lap. His hand reached around and started exploring all of me. His cock was hard, veins showing, cum beading at the top—excited for me. I trailed the tip of my finger all around the tip;

his cock pulsed in excitement. He grabbed my hand and pulled it away, holding it on top of my thigh.

"I'll be the one touching," he whispered in my ear.

"Not fair," I pouted.

"Your body says otherwise."

"My body betrays me," I moaned out.

Two of his fingers slipped inside, moving slowly in and out, thumb rubbing my clit. My head leaned back against his shoulder. All I could think of was how bad I wanted him inside. Sure, his fingers were terrific, but nothing compared to when his cock slipped in for the first thrust.

He pulled his finger out and moved it up my lips and back down in the slowest fashion before coming back up and rubbing my clit between his finger and thumb. The perfect amount of pressure, and—

"Gods," escaped from my lips.

I could feel the heat in my body, like an ember ready to burst into flame. My hips started moving beneath me. I wanted him in me, I wanted him to cum with me, I wanted us to lose control together, but I didn't think I could stop it because I was on the verge of erupting.

I reached down with my other hand and grabbed his hand, making him slow down. I let go and reached down to bring him inside of me. He was right there, waiting for me, wanting me, and why the hell hadn't he already put his cock inside of me?

We both let out moans as I moved, bringing him more inside of me. I ground on him back and forth. He had let go of my other hand and moved it to my breast, his fingers rolling my nipple between them. My vision was getting fuzzier by the second, and I was losing every bit of control I had. I wanted to—I wanted to chase the high of the orgasm, but I also didn't want it to end. I sucked in a breath. I *needed* it to last longer.

I leaned forward, gripping the desk, and started moving up and down faster. He moved one hand to grip my hip, and the other gripped tight onto my ass. I let him take control, moving me up and down. Our breathing was getting more ragged, his moaning was getting deeper.

Then stars exploded. My entire body was on fire, with electricity shooting through it. Moans escaped from me in between gasps for air.

"Fuck. Fuck. Gods. Oh GODDDDS!" he groaned out.

I felt a shock wave and shadows exploded from me—no—from him.

What the fuck was that?

I froze, unable to move. What just happened?

"Auri?" he said.

"What the hell was that?" I shot out.

"What was what?"

"Shadows came from you, not me—you."

He didn't say anything. His heart beat faster beneath me.

CHAPTER 27

I stood up and paced the floor. My brain was running through every scenario of what the hell just occurred. How could *my* shadows come from him?

"I don't know how shadows came from you and not me. I don't know what I did. Oh my Gods. What did I do?"

"Auri," he said calmly, staring at the floor, where my feet paced back and forth.

My heart was racing, and I didn't know if it was from the sex or what just happened or both. Nothing felt right. I closed my eyes—

"Auri, you need to sit down and take a breath."

"I can't. I don't know what happened. I don't know if I am losing control of my magic."

"It wasn't you, it was me."

"What? How? What does that even mean?"

"Please sit down," he said. He stood up and walked to me.

He grabbed my hand and pulled me towards the chair before motioning for me to sit. Once I sat, he knelt, coming eye to eye with me.

"It was me, it wasn't you. The shadows came from me."

"But how?" I cried out. What the hell was he trying to tell me? My stomach burned, the lump in my throat felt bigger, and my knee started to bounce rapidly.

"Remember how you once asked me about what kind of other powers I had?"

"You can fucking wield shadows?"

"Not exactly—"

"But those were fucking shadows," I pleaded.

"Yes. I did, um, wield shadows, but that's not my ability."

"Just fucking say it, Zane, because I'm confused, and I'm getting frustrated."

"Okay. Well, here fucking goes. I am a siphon."

"That wasn't siphoning. You actually wielded shadows."

"I am not like ordinary siphons, I am a siphon manipulator."

"I've never heard of that before."

"Most people haven't. The short version is that I can siphon someone's ability and be able to wield it for a short time. Unlike a siphon, it doesn't actually take anything from the host."

"Well... that... I didn't see coming," Esme purred. I ignored her. I couldn't do two conversations right now. *"Then I'll be here when you need me."*

"But I felt something weird, I don't know how to explain it," I said.

"You would feel it, but most don't know what the feeling is."

"Why haven't you told me?" I could feel eyes welling up. It bothered me that he kept this from me.

"I couldn't," he whispered.

"Don't pull that classified shit on me," I seethed.

He stayed quiet, then he stood up and turned to stare out the window.

"I was scared," he muttered.

"Of what?" I said.

"Your reaction. Saying it out loud. I have been terrified from the moment I figured out what I could do."

"I exploded shadows, and you never batted an eye. Why would you think that I—"

"Because of what I can do. A simple touch allows me to wield whatever it is for several minutes. I can feel the magic someone has," he said, still staring out the window. His shoulders drooped, his chin dipped a little, and his chest moved up and down.

"Who knows?" I asked. I knew he was ashamed; every part of him screamed it, but I was still furious.

"My father. That's it."

"How have you kept this secret?"

"Because I rarely use it, and if they did figure it out, they aren't here to tell anyone about it."

My mouth gaped a little, and my eyes widened. What the hell was I supposed to say to that? I didn't want to ask any more questions, afraid of the truth that he may reveal. At the same time, part of me wanted to know everything.

"Did you kill them because they knew?"

"Um. Yes. No. Well, they were going to die anyway. That is the past, and I don't want to talk about that. Well, I shouldn't."

"Fuck Zane. I feel like I'm finding out about a whole different person."

"I'm sorry," he pleaded. He finally turned back to me and stared at me, eyes narrowed.

"How didn't my dad figure this out?"

"Because I dug it down deep, and I don't know what he would do if he knew what I could do. I don't even know what this power means."

"I think he should—"

"No," he cut me off.

"Why?" I pleaded, I knew that when I first came here, he was the last person I trusted. I was angry at him, but during winter break, it changed between us. He showed me his vulnerability. For the first time, he answered my questions without deflection.

"I don't trust him," he said.

I pursed my lips. I couldn't force him to trust my father, and I understood why he didn't. It didn't change the part of me that broke when he said that. I loved my dad, even when I was angry with him. I *knew* he always had my back, even if it didn't always feel that way.

"I know that's not what you wanted to hear, Auri," he told me.

"No, but I know he hasn't given you a reason to trust him either."

"He hasn't. It's not just that, it's if I tell him, it becomes real. I become a weapon, I become the one they fear. I'm terrified."

His vulnerability hit me hard in the chest. I felt his terror through the bond. We had gotten good at shielding our feelings from each other, but he had let his shield down. My chest got tight, my heartbeat faster by the second, and breathing felt harder.

I dropped to the floor on my knees.

"Auri?" he said

"Shield, please?" I pleaded.

"What?"

"Between, um… your feelings and um, my feelings, I'm… um… overwhelmed."

He knelt next to me and put his hand on my shoulder—then pulled it back sharply.

"I'm sorry," he said.

I heard him take some deep breaths in, and the tightness in my chest loosened.

"You can't be afraid to touch—"

He growled. "I'm not afraid to touch you, I'm afraid that you are."

"I'm not… afraid. I'm not sure what to even feel right now, but I'm not scared of you."

"I'm relieved to hear that, but I don't think it has really sunk in," he said.

He stood up, grabbed his pants, and pulled them on.

"What are you doing?" My head cocked to the side, confused.

"I'm going to go hit the gym, I am… I just really need to get some frustration out," he said, barely looking at me.

"Okay," I said.

"This isn't on you. I'm really angry with myself right now, and I really need to go get it out."

"I get it," I told him, but I didn't. I was angry too for a whole different reason. Betrayal sat heavy on my chest.

He knelt again and kissed the top of my head. "I love you, Auriella."

I looked up at him, our eyes locking. "I love you, too."

He stood up and walked out of the room. I sat on the floor, still naked. I couldn't pull the motivation to stand up or to move. Everything felt hard and heavy. How could it go from such a magical evening to fucking disastrous? Nothing was going right, and it hadn't been for a long time. Was I cursed? What did I do to deserve this?

"Sometimes life isn't always fair, and sometimes the fates put our lives on a specific course to teach us a different perspective," Esme said.

"It feels like they want to teach me too much," I told her.

"You can't self-loathe," she preached down the bond.

"I can, if I want," I told her.

I managed to pull myself up, put a gown on, and climbed into the bed. Tears streamed down my cheek onto the pillow. I didn't even know why I was sad, but then again, I never knew why sadness hit me so hard every time it did, but it was the motherfucker lying in wait to take me down. I would give this the night, but I refused to give it more.

***

Gods. It was so bright in my room, light filtered in from the window. The ones I forgot to draw shut last night. My eyes blinked, trying to adjust to the brightness. Next to me lay the barren spot where Zane usually slept. He hadn't come back to my room during the night. Even though I had been upset with him, I still needed him next to me during the night.

"Are you okay?" I asked him down the bond.

"As good as it gets," he said.

"Where are you?"

"Home," he said quietly.

"Wait, what? Literally?"

"Yes, I roved back to Ashwynd for the day."

"Okay..."

"I just needed to talk to my dad. I'll be back soon, my love," he said.

"I'll be here," I told him.

"We could go on a flight, my little shadow," Esme said. Her voice sounded sweet, gentle, almost.

"I'd rather lie in bed..."

"Yeah, and last night you said you were only letting sadness have the night. So, get your ass out on the flight field, dressed for the cold, and I'll be there," she scolded me through the bond.

"Fine," I told her.

It wasn't like I could argue with her, and if I had, she'd probably land on the top of my wing.

"Correct, I would have made a scene," she said.

I stood up and got dressed, putting an extra underlayer on. Flying during the winter could be brutal if you weren't appropriately dressed. One advantage was the heat from your flier sitting below you.

As I walked onto the flight field, my eyes drifted to Esme. I looked her over, and I swore she had grown some since—

"I am indeed growing. Hopefully, the saddle still fits."

I cocked my head to the side and studied her more. I think she had actually grown two feet.

"Two feet and a quarter," she said, full of excitement.

"I thought the next growth spurt was around thirty?"

"Well, sort of. Most dragons start their growth in the years before that, and most have completed it before that."

"Oh, well, how big are you going to get?"

"I don't know, I can't see in the future."

"Okay, smart ass. How big do they think you will be?"

"Probably close to eighteen." She huffed a small puff of steam at me.

"Oh Gods."

"What is wrong with that? Size is a big deal."

"Gods, please don't say that line ever again."

"It's true, the bigger the bett— yeah, I'll shut up."

Laughter burst out of me.

She crouched down for me to throw the saddle on, and then I mounted her.

"Hold tight, my little shadow,"

"The nickname is..." I didn't finish my thought because, honestly, it wasn't worth it to complain. She would just say it more.

"Where do you want to go?" she asked.

"You're the one who wanted to fly. I am just here for the ride."

"Okay," she said, then she banked a hard right turn. I gripped the pommel tight.

"How are you feeling about Zane?" she asked in her calm voice.

"Is that why you brought me out here?" I asked.

"Maybe you need to talk about it, and clearly, there is no one else you can talk to about it."

"I'm confused, and I feel a little betrayed," I told her.

"Think of it a little differently. What if you had had your powers before you two met? Powers that your father wants kept classified, and you couldn't—"

"Wait. What did you mean by that?"

"About what?"

"About my dad wanting them to be classified?"

"Well, it turns out that shadow-wielding isn't actually considered classified, but it is so rare that it's kept quiet."

"Why say it was then?"

"He may not have known right away, I don't really know—"

"Then how do you know? What the hell do you know, Esme?"

"Can we just go back to the Zane conversation?"

"Yes, after you tell me what you know."

"My mom may have slipped about their recent trip to find the other shadow summoner. Wielding shadows isn't classified, and most shadow summoners end up walking around with shadows encircling their feet, because they can't hide them forever. That's all I know."

"Okay, well that's a conversation for later with my father."

"Now, back to Zane, had you had your powers, and had you been scared of them, would you have been so eager to tell him?"

"When you put it that way... I don't know, and I am scared of them too, you know that."

"I think he might be more scared of his," she said, sadness lacing her tone.

"Whose side are you on here?" I said.

"Always yours, but sometimes being on your side doesn't mean I have to agree with you blindly. I have to challenge your ideas," she said.

"I guess that's fair," I told her.

"Then what makes you angry?" she said.

"I get where you are coming from, but after seeing my powers and after we bonded, he still chose not to tell me. He siphoned my magic."

"What do you think he went home for?"

"I don't know. He said only his dad knew, and then he went home to talk to him."

"Hold on!" she yelped, before diving low.

"What the hell?"

"There is someone else out here," she said. Her head was swiveling around, and her nostrils were flaring.

"Who?"

"I don't know, I smell something."

"Let's get the fuck back to campus," I told her, goosebumps forming over my entire body. Dread took over my whole body.

"I'm trying, but we are in the middle of the mountains, and I need to go higher to move into another valley, or we might end up in the vale."

"I'm sure they will forgive us—well, me—since you're welcome."

"I've already called for—"

A loud screech pierced my ears, and I instinctively pulled my hands to cover them.

"What in the frozen fucks of Yebel?" I said out loud.

Four figures came from behind and four from the front through the fog. My eyes strained to make out what in the hell was flying with us. One by one, they got closer, and I could see that they were griffins—no—something else.

"Hippogriffs—not possible," she said.

"Am I seeing riders on their backs?"

"Yes."

"Go now, Esme, fly high and as fast as you fucking can," I pleaded to her. My heart beat double time, and fear overwhelmed me. Shadows poured out of me, my shimmer locked into place without me commanding it.

"What's wrong, Auriella?" Zane said down the bond.

"Get here now. We're in the mountains. There are hippogriffs? They have riders." I told him down the bond, barely able to get the right words out.

"Coming," he said.

I knew my fear had to be overwhelming him. When my shimmer exploded onto my skin, locking into place, I felt my mental shields also explode. I didn't know what the hell I was looking at.

It was a griffin, but not. It had an eagle head, but there was a horse for the rest of them. The riders on top were all cloaked in complete black robes, hiding their faces.

"Where are you?" Zane pleaded down the bond.

I didn't know. I knew we were in the mountains, enjoying the flight, and then we dipped low into the valley. Now we were so high in the sky, I couldn't see anything but the white sky.

"Tell him we are heading straight south of the Alpha Wing, heading for the campus," Esme said.

Her wings flapped rapidly. I didn't see the other creatures anymore, but I knew they were near. Wing beats echoed off the mountains below us, and they weren't just hers. I relayed to Zane what she said. He couldn't rove to us here, but he could fly.

A loud screech echoed out—it sounded right next—

Then we barrel-rolled, I gripped the saddle tight, not knowing what the fuck was happening. I closed my eyes, took a deep breath in. I opened my eyes and focused on what was happening. I let my shadows roll off my body, letting them be my eyes. Esme roared, then blew a stream of fire at the hippogriff who had locked his talons around her front talons. She roared again, my entire body vibrated, and my ears rang. If they didn't know where we were, they would know then. I rushed my shadows to the hippogriff's neck and wrapped them around, and started tightly squeezing.

It screeched louder than it had before, thrashing beneath the shadows. The rider on its back pulled a sword from its back and swung it towards my shadows, but I wasn't giving in. I sent a tendril at the rider, hitting them in their head. Their head flung back before flinging forward again, and the sword fell from their arms.

"Let fucking go of my dragon," I screamed, "or I will end both of your fucking lives."

Their talons released from Esme, and Esme shot high into the air. The air was thick, making my breathing shallow.

"Are you okay?" I asked her.

"Fine. Pissed," she said, before letting out a low growl.

A roar pierced through the sky that shook my entire chest, followed by lots of wing beats.

"My mother and your father have arrived."

"Yeah, I heard her."

"As well as others."

Another set of wing beats got closer to us, and my head started swinging side to side, watching every angle, until I felt it in my chest. I sucked in my breath and smelled him—I smelled him—holy shit. I knew what the smell was. There was no doubt in my mind that it was him, but I never smelled him like that unless we were inches apart.

Within seconds, he was hovering next to us. Our eyes locked, and electricity flooded every sense in my body.

"We just need to stay straight ahead. We are almost back on campus. Your father, other leadership riders, and fourth-years are taking care of it." Zane said down the bond.

"What the hell are hippogriffs?" I asked him.

"I don't know. Griffin looking things."

"They had riders," I said, still in shock at what the hell happened.

CHAPTER 28

As we got closer to the campus, the bells were tolling rapidly. Active invader signal. The first week we are here, we are taught about the different tolls that may happen. Every hour, there were long tolls, seconds apart. During normal operations, the bells tolled. After twenty-one hundred, the bells didn't toll as loudly until zero-six hundred.

When the school went on lockdown, the bell wasn't tolled until lockdown was lifted. There was one long toll that represented that the lockdown was lifted, and standard bells would toll again. While it only happened twice, if there were any type of intruders either on campus or near campus, the bells would continuously toll rapidly for the first hour. Every hour after that, they would toll twenty-five times rapidly until it was clear.

My chest beat rapidly under my breast. My legs and arms were quaking. My stomach felt like a pit of dread. Nausea crept up my throat by the second. As we got closer to the campus, I could see the chaos ensuing on the grounds. Cadets ran around.

"If an invader signal ever occurs, all first and second-year cadets are to lock down in their chambers. Third and fourth-year cadets are to report to the designated branch area for further instructions."

What Melamora told us flashed back into my head. I could see a group of cadets gathered around the flight field with fliers all around. Esme circled, lowering.

"Please go to your room, and stay safe, my love. I have to report to our assigned area," Zane said through our bond.

"No, you be safe. I'm not done being angry with you yet," I told him, before letting a little chuckle out.

Esme landed hard in the center of the field, jostling my entire body. *"Jeez, Esme."*

"Sorry, you need to get inside, and I am being ordered to the vale, because apparently, I'm not experienced enough. Psh," she said.

I wasn't touching that with any size pole. The agitation laced in her tone was thick. She lowered her leg for me to slide off. As soon as my feet hit the floor and I took two steps forward, she launched into the air.

"Um, the saddle?" I said to her.

"I'm keeping it on, in case we are needed."

"Yeah, they are not calling first-years out."

"If the campus goes under attack, there won't be a choice. Would you rather stay locked in your room in safety? If so, maybe I chose wrong."

"No, you're right. I hate hiding when I know I can help."

"I'll let you know what's happening as I know."

I headed towards Watch Tower One, watching cadets scattering everywhere. Everything was chaotic, cadets tripping over their own feet, running in every direction. We had never practiced for this. Dragons roared overhead, griffins screeched, and phoenixes shrieked throughout the air. Wingbeats beat throughout the air in all directions, from fliers and Drusearons.

I smelt fear in the air, and the magic got thicker and thicker by the second. I walked into the tower and started heading up the stairs. I went straight to the seventh floor to check on my flight. Cadets were running around in sheer panic. Every floor I climbed, I could hear feet shuffling down the hall.

"Auri! Thank the Gods!" Sadie said.

"Is everything okay?" I asked her.

"Yes, Korra said that you were out when intruders came," she said.

"I was, but I am okay. I came up here to make sure everyone is accounted for and okay," I told her.

"Akira, Micah, and Lorenzo are in their rooms. I was just heading in."

"Let's get them and the second squad and go talk," I told her.

I knocked on their doors, and we all went into Sadie and Thora's room. Thora was sitting on the bed, and tilted her head to the side when we entered.

"I'm glad you're okay, Auri," Thora said.

"It was something..." I said, "have any of you ever heard of hippogriffs?"

"I have," Micah said. Everyone else nodded their head no.

"What do you know?" I asked Micah.

"They are basically cousins, just a little different bodies."

"I saw them in the mountains," I said.

"You saw hippogriffs?" he said, eyes wide open.

"Yeah, a bunch of them, with riders on them."

"Oh wow. Shit," Micah said.

"What are we missing?" Lorenzo said.

"I've never heard of them until today, and other than what I saw, that is all I know," I said, "but clearly, Micah was given a different education."

"They are almost myth-like. Believed to be almost extinct and *never* interested in entertaining riders," Micah said.

"I can assure you there were riders," I told him.

"I believe you. I'm just saying that I was taught they never wanted a rider. They didn't want anything to do with teaming up with Fae and went their own way. When they did that, they lost the protection from the other fliers and started dwindling," Micah said.

"What is the angle here? What are they here for then?" Sadie asked.

No one said anything. We just looked around at each other.

"All I know is Esme, and I were out blowing off steam, when eight of them closed in, and then everything went south. One tried to take Esme and me out, and then we got the hell out of there."

"And now the entire campus sounds like a war zone," Akira said.

"Are we supposed to just sit here and twiddle our thumbs?" Thora said.

"That is what they said if we were ever under an invasion. First and second-years are supposed to stay in their rooms," Michalova said.

"When was the last time this happened?" Vida asked.

We all looked around the room.

"I don't believe it has happened in hundreds of years," Erik said.

"We are trained better now—different," Thora said.

"What are you trying to say?" I asked.

"For us to get out there and assist," Thora said.

"Assist with what? We don't even know what's going on?" Michalova said.

"Well, take out anyone who is threatening the college," Thora insisted.

"While I love her enthusiasm, all threats have been either eliminated or captured," Esme said down the bond.

"How do you know?" I asked her.

"My mother, of course," she said.

"We're too late," Thora said, defeated. She had gotten the same information from her Griffin as Esme gave me.

"According to Sylari, we will be—"

Erik was cut off by a long toll followed by a Melamora's voice.

"All cadets report to the stadium classroom immediately," Melamora's voice said.

Every one of us went quiet, eyes widened. It was like she was in our room, but wasn't. It was loud, but had an echo. Projection magic. We all stood up without saying anything and headed for the door. None of us knew what was happening or what we were being summoned for.

Once we walked into the hall, it was complete chaos. Cadets were rushing down the hall towards the Bravo Wing to the stadium classroom. We joined in the chaos of the halls. We all shuffled in and went to our usual seats. Lili was standing in the first row, facing the seats. Standing alongside her were the Wing Commanders and the other platoon leaders. All of them standing, shoulder to shoulder, looking over all of us.

Even though thousands of cadets had piled in, it was quiet. Everyone was on edge, not knowing what the hell was going on. The student leadership for the Riders whispered amongst each other before all of them took a seat except Arya. She walked to the dais and gave General Scullin a nod, then she turned around and walked back to her seat.

All of the other branches did something similar one by one, but to their own Brigadier General. Everyone sat quietly, staring at the dais. The dais was filled with professors and generals. All of them standing tall with worry painted on their faces. They weren't even attempting to hide it.

"Attention," my father commanded. I didn't think it could get quieter, but it did.

"As most of you know, we had an intrusion in our airspace. While we do sometimes get random intrusions that don't sound alarms. This was not random, and nor was it a random person who got lost. This *was* an organized attack. I hate to report this, but the war is here. It is at our doorsteps," my dad said.

Kamban took a step forward to stand next to my dad. "If you hadn't already heard, Nosferatu arrived here on hippogriffs."

Loud gasps filled the room from cadets, including me. I knew about the hippogriffs, but I didn't know that their riders were Nosferatu. Fear filled the entire room, almost overwhelming me. I opened my mouth a little and started to mouth breathe, trying not take it all in. No cadets spoke out loud, and no one was asking questions. Yet, my brain was rapidly firing them.

"This is unprecedented territory. We have never had attacks or wars that have come inland or to our college. When you arrived here, every single one of you went through basic training. Even if you have only been here for eight months, you have been training for this. You aren't children anymore, and you were built for this moment. We don't know exactly how this will play out, but we are sure there is more to come. I need to check our other bases, and in the meantime, every single one of you—yes, even first-years—will be expected to defend this college at all costs. We have the numbers, but they have the experience, so don't underestimate them," my father said.

"All classes are postponed until further notice. There is no schedule. The dining facilities will be open from zero-five thirty until nineteen hundred, with no specific schedule. Eat when you can, at whatever facility you want. This is no longer about which branch you belong to. This is about surviving," Kamban said.

"You should be armed everywhere you go. If you need weapons or supplies, get to the admin office and get them. All Wing Commanders, Platoon Leaders, and Squad leaders, please stay behind for a strategy discussion. Everyone else is dismissed," my father said.

The room burst into muttering, and shoes clattered everywhere. I wasn't even sure what I should do or where to go. The imminent threat was over, yet the danger was knocking on our doorsteps. I decided to head back to my chambers and get all my daggers sharpened.

"When you get done, we need to talk," I said to Zane down the bond.

"I will be there as soon as I can," Zane said.

I sat in my chair, sharpening my blades. It took him a little while to come. By the time he had gotten there, Lili had already come by and let me know that Riders would be given the most up-to-date orders through their fliers, which would ultimately come from Kim or Araydea—Scullin's dragon.

He pulled me into his arms and held me for what felt like forever. I cherished every second of it. I had been angry at him, but I also thought my life would be over hours earlier. It slapped me in the face how quickly our lives could be in danger.

"What do you know?" I asked.

"There were ten hippogriffs, all but one were killed in aerial battle," he said, "of the ten Riders, there are three being held captive."

"Are they saying anything?"

"Not that they have told us," he said.

"You never heard of hippogriffs before today?"

"I had, but they were talked about—"

"Like a mythical creature?" I said.

"Yes?"

"Micah said that as well."

"My dad told us about them, but had only really said they were pretty much griffins, but didn't want to be ridden or work with the Fae. It was so long ago, I forgot about them, honestly," he said.

"How are they letting Nosferatu ride them then?"

"Change of heart? Honestly, I don't know. I want to know why they came here and how many more are here?"

"So, we are both reeling with questions?"

"I think every single person here has endless questions," he said, before rubbing his hand through his hair.

"What the hell are we going to do?" I asked.

"It's never too late to take your dad up on his offer, but you and I both know we don't run from conflict," Zane said.

"True," I said.

"Now that you asked all your questions, are *you* okay?" he asked.

"Yeah, what do you mean?" I asked, confused.

"You were ambushed in the air?"

"Yeah, but I'm fine."

"I felt your fear through our bond. It was almost as bad as when you were injured on the mountain," he said.

"Probably as overwhelming as yours was yesterday..."

He didn't say anything, kept his eyes locked onto the ground.

"I'm sorry, Auri, I didn't tell you sooner. I never wanted you to feel betrayed."

"I never thought you wanted me to feel that way, but it doesn't mean it doesn't feel that way."

"I talked to my dad."

"About?"

"About you knowing, about informing other people."

"And?" I asked.

"He thinks it would be a good idea to let your dad in, but wasn't sure about anyone beyond that."

"Speaking of my dad, turns out our shadow-wielding isn't really classified after all, and can't really be."

"I mean, I kind of wondered why it would be classified, but what do you mean by all that?" he asked, confused.

"Well, when my dad found that guy Genevieve said to find, he told him that eventually my shadows will encircle me full-time. Once that happens, everyone will know," I told him.

"Oh."

"Yeah, oh. Now, I know all these classified abilities, and don't even have a classified one myself... how is that going to look?"

"Your father is the general. It's par for the course that you would know about classified information anyway."

"How does it work?" I asked.

He narrowed his eyebrows. "How does what work?"

"Your siphons?"

"Oh... well, I have only used them a handful of times, and most of those have been accidental," he said, his eyes locked onto the floor.

"And?"

"I touch someone, and then it's there. I don't know how I can use their power exactly, and because it's usually very short, the power I borrow is in bursts. Not exactly controlled."

"Then try it out on me—"

"No."

"Yes," I insisted.

"No."

"Listen, we are about to be at war. What good is this power if you haven't even been able to practice it thoroughly? What you haven't seen is how many times I have been alone that I practiced with my shadows."

"When have you been alone?"

I laughed. "You're not with me every second, ya' know."

"I'm teasing."

"You won't master it if you don't try—"

"You don't understand Auri."

"Tell me then. Make me understand."

"Every time I have used it—oh Gods—I want to use it again. Magic calls to me. I can tell when it's stronger, and the stronger it is, I want it more."

"I see," I said. His raw honesty hit me in the chest.

"See, now you understand why I can't just do that."

"I do, but I still think you should. The problem is, it's like holding stick candy in front of the kid after letting them have a taste and telling them they can't have anymore ever."

"Except that usually giving them the candy would satisfy them, but I'm not sure I will ever be satisfied," he said, staring at the floor.

"I hear that, but you can't live in fear of something you think may happen. I have confidence in you. I trust in you. If you say that you aren't depleting my magic, then it doesn't hurt me."

"Okay," he said.

"Just okay?"

"You make a compelling argument, and you clearly aren't going to take no for an answer on this."

"True. Now what?"

"This was your idea, what do you mean *now, what*?"

"It was my idea, but you're the one who has—"

He reached out and grabbed my hand. Electricity shot through my hand, up my arm to my shoulder, around my shoulder blades, and down my spine. I felt a slight pull at my stomach, and then it released. Shadows slowly came out of his other hand and swirled around his palm.

He took a deep breath and blew it out of his mouth.

"Wow," he whispered. Shadows swirled all around the room—all from him.

"What?" I asked him.

"I'm holding a lot of power, and it's not something I have played with before."

"Command them to get something for you," I told him.

He took in another deep breath and let it out, then he narrowed his eyebrows. The shadows that had been split into tendrils all around the room moved into one shadow. The shadow moved towards my desk and then grabbed the dagger sitting on my desk.

"Impressive."

The shadows moved to his hand in the blink of an eye, and the dagger was gripped in his palm.

"Hmph." I let my own shadows free. "Let's see how good you are."

I used my shadows to grab one of the other daggers and brought the dagger to his throat.

He stiffened next to me, his hand still holding mine. His shadows moved, taking the dagger out of his hand and bringing it to my throat. My eyes widened. I hadn't thought he would actually press the dagger to mine. I pulled the dagger away from his neck and moved it to the center of the room, where the blade swung around. He moved his dagger to mine, where we dueled. Both of us laughed together as we used shadows to have a knife fight.

He adapted to my shadows quickly. He moved them just as fast as I did. He broke them into multiple tendrils and then merged them back with the same speed. While he was quick to figure out the shadow-wielding, we didn't know how it would actually work during any kind of battle. He had to maintain touch to wield them as quickly as I could.

We continued practicing different ways for him to wield. We figured out that the magic was there for half the time held, but the magic started diminishing as soon as his touch left me—

The bells started tolling, loudly and quickly.

"Flight field, now!" Esme said down the bond.

"Okay, coming."

"Esme said I have to get to the flight field now," I told Zane.

"The signal means I need to get to the courtyard. Did she say what was going on?" Zane said.

"Unsure exactly, reports are saying incoming combatants."

"She said incoming, but unsure what exactly is happening."

He grabbed my arms and pulled me close to him. His lips pressed against my forehead.

"My sweet, sweet love, please, please don't do anything reckless out there. I can't live without you. I won't live without you," he said down the bond.

"You took the words out of my mouth. I love you more than you know. Please be safe, I'd hate to have to burn this continent to the fucking ground."

He laughed. "Who's the crazy in love one now?"

"I hate to break up this little love thing that's going on, but you need to start sheathing daggers and get to running," Esme said.

"She is urging us faster," I told Zane.

"We should move faster," he said. He kissed me again and then turned around and headed out the door.

I quickly changed, pulled on my riding leathers, and sheathed my daggers. I took a deep breath in, filling my diaphragm, before slowly letting it out, and then took a step into the hall. As soon as I closed the door, I started jogging down the hall to the watchtower.

The air hit my face as I exited the watchtower into the flight field. The chaos of the cadets running everywhere made me pause for a minute. Riders were running onto the field towards fliers, Drusearons were flying ahead, and Infantry cadets were running in every direction. Esme was crouched on the field, ready to launch into the air.

CHAPTER 29

Two attacks in one day.

"There is a drift of thirty heading our way, all with riders. They will be here in less than ten minutes," Esme relayed to me.

The air was chaotic. Drusearons, griffins, phoenixes, and dragons were flying and launching in the air. For some of these cadets, they had never experienced anything like this. They had come from small communities that had never been under attack. While I was always safe, I knew what happened outside of the walls that protected me.

"Where are you?" I asked Zane.

"Oh, just flying around through hundreds of cadets," he said.

"That doesn't tell me any—"

Wingbeats beat next to me, and my head swiveled to the right. Zane.

"I'm right here, my lady," he said.

I gave him a half smile.

"I'm staying right here, too," he said.

"Are you allowed to do that?" I asked.

"All Drusearons have been paired with a flier-rider pair so we can communicate," Zane said out loud.

"So, we have been told," Esme said, *"They are five minutes out. All first-year riders are to move on the inside, and third and fourth-year riders are on the front line. And aside from Zane, all other Drusearons are paired with their same year."*

We dipped down and flew closer to the school, along with the other first-years. Not every rider had a Drusearon flying next to them, but like Zane, the ones that did flew close to the flier they paired with.

I started to hear faint wingbeats in the distance, my head cocked to the side a little bit. At first, it sounded like it was one, but as I listened, I could hear that they weren't quite in sync.

"I hear them," I told her.

She chortled, *"Really? You hear them?"*

"Um. Yes?"

"They are still three minutes out, and I can barely hear them," she said.

"Erm... my hearing has been really sharp lately," I told her.

"Interesting... well then you know they are approaching—"

Before she could finish that thought, hippogriffs came into view—without riders. My eyes darted all over the sky. The initial reports said that there were riders, and yet there weren't.

"Do you see the riders?" I asked out loud for both Esme and Zane to hear.

"No, a little fucking eerie," she said.

"No, what the fuck is going on?" Zane said.

Ahead of us, fliers and their riders were engaging in aerial battles. Talons locking, beaks snapping. The hippogriffs were no match for the battle that was waiting for them. It made no sense. Why come here to their deaths?

Shouting came from below us. I twisted to the side to look at the ground. Zane also twisted his body and cocked his head. Cadets were running in every direction. My eyebrows furrowed.

What the fuc—

Below us, cadets were being attacked, their necks were being ripped to shreds. The Shapeshifters had shifted into their wolf forms.

Oh. My. Gods.

Nosferatu.

They were here.

"Esme! They are below—"

"I know, I am relaying the message now."

Half of our fliers in the front started dropping from the sky to the ground. The rest of the fliers remained in the sky, taking down the remaining hippogriffs. It was brutal, five fliers against one, piece by piece.

I looked back to the ground, and below us there were cadets—oh Gods—not cadets—Nosferatu. So many of them. At least fifty of them, way more than there was fliers.

"We should drop and help them," I said to both of them.

"No," they both said in my head at the same time.

"They are fucking slaughtering them below us. Are you not watching this?"

"Yes, but I am not leaving you alone, because clearly you will join in, and we were told to stay where we were ordered until told otherwise," Zane said.

Cadets were dropping below us like flies. Infantry was shooting them with arrows, which did nothing. Werewolves ripped off their heads, but there wasn't enough. Nosferatu moved from one spot to another in seconds. Their mouth moved to their necks. Blood spurted everywhere, and cadets went limp in seconds. Leadership and fourth-year cadets were running towards them. Blades slashed through the air. One of their heads toppled to the ground. At the same time, one of them drained another cadet.

"I'm going," I said.

"No," Zane said.

I didn't care what he said. He would follow. I jumped off of Esme. I brought forth my shadows, wrapping them around myself, slowing my fall. Zane was next to me instantly.

"I should fucking rove us out of here," he growled.

"I would be pissed at you—"

"Yes, that's why I didn't, but Gods fucking damn it, Auri," Zane said.

We hit the ground, and I immediately started sending shadows everywhere. I knew that I needed to cut their heads off, rip their hearts out, or burn them to ashes. I pushed my shadows through his chest and clenched it around his lifeless heart, crushing it, and then pulled it out of his chest.

As soon as the Nosferatu dropped to the ground, it was like a beacon for the other Nosferatu. All of the ones near turned their heads towards me, and I knew they were going to be on me within seconds. Zane was next to me, two long swords—one in each hand. They were swinging, and he was on the attack. He, too, was moving around with a quickness. In the blink of an eye, he moved from one part of the field to the other.

My heart beat, and four Nosferatu were surrounding me. Zane was next to my side, his sword swung, and one of their heads toppled to the ground. My shadows branched and had gone into two of their chests.

Her mouth was on my neck as soon as I pulled the hearts out of the other two. My heart sank to my stomach. Her teeth latched into my neck. My blood was draining from me. My shadows clung back to me. My thoughts were racing. I didn't know what do. I couldn't think. Panic took over.

I was going to die.

She was going to drain me and let me drop to the ground like the other cadets.

My eyes started closing. The beating in my heart slowed down. I heard her swallowing mouthfuls of my blood. Stars started shooting behind my eyes.

Then the swallowing stopped. The mouth went slack. Her body slid down my body.

"They're men who traded their souls for blood," he'd said, eyes gleaming with the fire. *"Bodies that don't stay dead, hearts that don't beat, but still they walk. Their teeth are sharp enough to tear through bone, and their thirst never ends. Nosferatu.*

What my father told me when I was little played in my head again. My eyes were heavy, and I was trying to keep them open because this was not the time to be weak. I forced my eyes open. I needed to focus on what was happening. Zane was standing in front of me, his hands held a heart. My eyes dropped to the ground at the Nosferatu that lay at my feet, then I looked at Zane again. He saved me. Of course he did.

My stomach started burning, as if gasoline poured onto a fire. My chest started beating faster. Once slow, now beating hard and fast. Sweat beaded all along my arms, legs, and chest. Every bone in my body felt like it was breaking. Everything was fuzzy.

"Auriella?" Zane sounded muffled.

My eyes strained, and everything in my body felt like it was on fire. Something was wrong. My arms spasmed and twisted in pain. My legs buckled under me, and I dropped to the ground, hitting my stomach.

"What the hell happened, Zane?" my dad's muffled voice filtered in.

"I don't know, sir," Zane said. Even though distorted, I could hear the concern.

"Is that? Is she..."

My ears exploded, and loud ringing took over. Incinerating heat washed over my entire body. I was dying. Was I becoming one of them?

No.

This couldn't happen.

That's not how this worked.

Everything went black.

I heard nothing.

My vision was blank.

My eyes flashed open, and I looked around. My vision was better, but it was worse. My vision was sharp for a mile away, but up close, things were still a little disorienting. Bodies lay all over the field. Cadets and Nosferatu. My father and Zane were both standing around me, their eyes wide, mouths open.

"Is... she... is... what... hell... this... this... isn't pos-pos-possible?" my dad stuttered out, something that rarely happened.

I realized I wasn't standing up, but was on the ground. I looked down at my body—

Oh.

My.

Gods.

No.

No.

No.

This wasn't possible. This couldn't be happening. Oh Gods. I was having a nightmare. This was a nightmare.

Wake up, Auri. Wake the fuck up.

I tried to yell it, but only a growl came out of me. I shook my head. I'm not waking up. I felt the bile rising in my throat. Chest beating, blood pumping faster and faster.

"Auri. You're okay. It's okay," Zane said, except that *he* didn't sound okay at all.

"What's wrong with me? I can't talk," I said down the bond, hoping this still fucking worked.

The ground shook as a flier—no—Esme landed next to us. My head turned to hers, our eyes locking onto each other. She raised her head to the sky and let out the loudest roar I have ever heard.

"Esme, help me," I pleaded with her.

"I can't help you, my little wolf shadow. You are who you are. You are a wolf. It's okay. If you transform back into your regular form, we can fly the hell out of here from the gawkers."

I started to look around, and cadets came to the field from wherever they had been perched. The other fliers and riders landed. There were other cadets in their wolf form on the field, but I was the only one who the general of the military was standing in front of.

"I can't turn back now. They will all know it's me," I told her.

"You can't exactly hop on my back either..." she said.

Zane and my father still stood in front of me in complete shock. Zane's eyes were so wide, I didn't think they could get wider. My dad looked as though he was having a heart attack.

"Zane, I think you need to have my father sit down. He isn't looking well, and I'm pretty sure the heartbeat I hear, that is beating rapidly, is his," I told him, down our bond.

"Okay," he said. Yep. He was in shock, too. There wasn't time for this shit. I, too, was in utter shock. I just transformed into a solid black wolf.

CHAPTER 30

Zane

This was precisely why I didn't want to come to the ground to fight. She fought better than most, hell, she probably ranked top in her whole branch amongst all the years, but that didn't make her invisible. Taking on four Nosferatu was risky, not that she had a choice. They went for her.

I watched one of them latch into her neck. I was there in seconds, and even then it was too long. I felt agony and fear rush through our bond. I heard her heartbeat slow, felt mine racing. My body seared with heat. I punched my hand through the Nosferatu and pulled her heart out. Her body immediately went limp and fell to the ground.

Auri stood there in front of me, her face void of any color, blood seeping out of the two wounds on her neck, slowly pulsing. She had lost far too much blood. She stared at me, but she didn't. Her eyes were glossy, unmoving. It was like she wasn't there.

"Auri," I called to her. Nothing. She said absolutely nothing. If I didn't hear her heart picking up speed, I would have thought she was dead, but she wasn't. Her face twitched, and sweat beads started forming all over her head. It was frigid outside, and I could see that it wasn't just her head that was sweating profusely. Her dad appeared next to me, his face filled with terror.

Her arms twisted out, legs bent to the side, and she collapsed to the snowy ground. Her dad was trying to make sense of what was happening.

She twisted her body, and hair started forming all over her. Her bones cracked and twisted in ways that shouldn't be normal. She fell entirely to the ground, limp but chest moving rapidly up and down. Her entire body shifted from Fae to a wolf.

My mind didn't even know how to explain what I was witnessing. Her fur was jet black and shiny. She flashed her eyes open, bright emerald green eyes with a brown ring stared at me. Stared at her dad.

Holy fucking sinners.

She was a wolf. A Shapeshifter. She fucking shifted into a wolf. It actually fucking happened.

Weeks ago, when we learned that she was actually half Werewolf, neither of us thought she would ever shift because she was two years beyond when one would normally shift. Neither of her parents was a full Werewolf, both being half themselves. Yet, here I was standing staring at her in a wolf form.

Nothing came out of my mouth. I wanted to say something, but it wouldn't escape my lips. Her father stood next to me, stuttering. Her head moved side to side, eyes filled with fear. She dipped her head down between her chest, and when her head came up, she then realized what had happened. She wasn't just a Fae dragon Rider. She was a Werewolf dragon Rider. Her chest started rising and falling faster and faster. She was panicking. She let out a growl, but it sounded more like a cry.

I tried to reassure her, but I knew if I was in shock, she was probably in even more shock. She had made it very clear from the moment she learned about her heritage that she did not want to shift. Her worst nightmare came true. She was living it in front of everyone. Around me, more and more cadets were arriving on the field. The remaining Nosferatu scattered when more and more cadets arrived on the field, and we started dominating.

She pleaded with me through our bond, and I froze. I was relieved to hear her voice, but I couldn't even come up with a thought. She was terrified, and she needed reassurance, but I didn't have any to offer. *Hey Auri, you're a wolf now.* She clearly knows that, so no sense in saying that to her.

General Blackcreek's heart was beating rapidly next to me. I could hear it like it was my own. His breathing was getting ragged, and sweat poured down his face. I wanted to focus on him, but I couldn't—Auri had every bit of my attention.

Esme shook the ground as she landed next to us. She swiveled her head to her and let out an earth-shattering roar. Auri and her stared at each other. Surely, communicating. This was good. Esme somehow always knew what she needed when I didn't. Auri spoke to me through the bond, telling me to take care of her father. I turned to him, and he was getting worse by the minute.

"Sir?" I asked him.

His mouth moved like he was going to speak, but nothing came out.

I placed my arm on his shoulder, and his eyes moved up from the ground and locked with mine. Tears rolled out of the corners of his eye and down his face. I knew he needed more than what I could give him right now. I wasn't sure exactly what was wrong, but something was very wrong with him.

"Auriella, I'm gonna go ahead and take your dad to the menders... something isn't right," I told her, through the bond.

"Please, help him, and then get me the fuck out of this field," she said.

I put my other hand on his other shoulder and gripped down. I really hoped roving with him like this wouldn't jeopardize him worse. I visualized the infirmary and roved him there.

The infirmary was chaotic. Injured cadets and leadership filled the rooms, being mended. As soon as I roved in, my eyes locked with one of the menders, before their eyes moved to the generals. Their eyes widened.

"All available hands on deck!" she shouted.

Menders and Healers all ran from different directions.

"What happened?" the Mender who shouted for help asked.

"Um... well, he saw something that was shocking... I... honestly can't tell you what—"

"Auriella is a *Werewolf,*" he muttered.

"What?" she said, "your daughter?"

"Yeah, we need to get him in the room before he continues talking..." I said. Gods knew we didn't need the whole damn campus to know this.

They ushered him to a room and then rushed the cadet who was in there to another room. One of the menders placed the stethoscope on his chest. He sat there staring past all of us in the room. I really needed to get Auri, but I was also afraid to leave him here alone.

"His heart is beating three times faster than it should be," she stated.

"Move, please," another Mender said.

She placed one of her hands on his chest and the other on the side of his neck.

"Roarke... Braegon get... get... my daughter," he managed to get out.

All the eyes shifted to me, some of them did the subtle look, just moving their eyes, and others fully turned their head. Gods damn it. Not only has he announced Auri's status, but he has also just said my full name. If they suspected it before, he just confirmed it.

I closed my eyes and roved back onto the field.

I froze in place for a brief second, and then I turned to look around. I wasn't sure I roved to the right place. In the fifteen minutes that I was gone, the flight field had turned into a fucking bloody mess.

The cadets that were once dead were rising from the fucking dead. They turned into Nosferatu. The living cadets were fighting for their lives. The only ones that weren't rising were the few Shapeshifters who were dead. My eyes were darting between cadets, trying to find Auri. I could feel her. She was somewhere.

Movement out of the corner of my eye sent me spinning around in an instant. I drew my sword and sliced the cadet's head clean off their shoulders. He was growling with predatory eyes.

Another swift movement caught my attention. I spun around with my sword high in the air. A solid, sleek black wolf—Auri—was staring at me, blood dripped from her mouth. Behind her, bodies lay on the ground, their heads torn off.

"What the fuck happened out here?" I asked her.

"They were dead, and then... Gods, Zane. They fucking rose. They stood up from the ground. Then they started attacking us. I killed them... again... Fuck... Gods... I killed some of my friends," she said down the bond.

I started walking to her. "You did what you had to do. Sometimes war isn't pretty, and most of the time there is death."

As I walked to her, she started walking to me. She rubbed her head against my leg. I reached down and caressed her head.

"We have to go, your dad needs you," I said.

"But there is more to take care—"

"There are plenty of other cadets who can handle it. Your dad *needs* you."

"Okay... well umm—"

"I will rove you to your room, where you can shift back, and then we can rove to his room. Do you think you can shift back?"

"I don't know, I hope so because I am not going to the infirmary like this," she said.

"I've never actually roved... um..." I wasn't sure how to say it.

"With an animal?"

I just nodded my head. Fuck. I felt like I was rubbing salt into her wounds all over again.

"Let's go," she said.

I knelt and wrapped my arms around her. This had to work. I couldn't even think about any alternatives. I didn't allow myself to go down that road. I closed my eyes and thought of her room. The room flashed around me, and then steady ground was under my feet again. My eyes opened, and Auri was there. She was still in her wolf form, but she seemed okay.

"Are you okay?" I asked.

"Other than being this..."

"Just think about your regular form—"

Her body rotated quickly, and there she stood—completely naked.

My eyes trailed down her body, and she followed my eyes and then gasped.

"Oh, thank the fucking seven Gods I didn't do this out in the field."

"Your body is beautiful," I told her.

"Yeah… and only you get the privilege of seeing it. Let me get dressed, and we can get to my father. What was going on?"

"They said his heart was beating too fast."

"I broke his heart… great," she said.

She finished getting dressed, throwing whatever clothing she grabbed onto her body. I grabbed her and held her close to my body. I didn't want to go right away. I wanted to treasure this moment. I wanted to take it in. I thought I was going to lose her. Instead, I closed my eyes and visualized the infirmary, and in a whirlwind flash, there we stood.

It was just as frenzied as when I had left. We walked into the room where I left her father not long ago. He lay on the bed, eyes closed, resting. There were only a couple of menders and Healers in the room now, and it seemed calmer in here than when I left.

"Is he going to be okay?" she asked.

The older Mender stepped towards her. "I believe so—"

"You *believe* so?" she cut her off.

"The heart is a fickle thing, lass. Even menders sometimes can't fix hearts, just like brains."

Auri walked to her dad, and tears streamed down her cheeks. I stayed right behind her, my hand on the small of her back.

"Auriella, I think I was able to mend it before it was too late. We will have to find out when he wakes up."

Her legs buckled, and she started to fall. I grabbed her from behind, holding her up, holding her against me. She started sobbing, gasping for air in between. I held her tightly against me.

"Breathe, my love," I whispered to her.

I heard her take in a huge breath, and she stood steady on her legs. She kept taking in deep breaths, and her whimpering stopped. She stepped closer to her dad and placed her hand on his chest. He stayed sleeping, chest rising and falling. He had to wake up. I don't think she would completely survive losing another parent.

Footsteps approached behind, entering the room. My head spun around, and Professor Gile was standing in the doorway.

"Can I have the room?" Gile said

"I'm staying with my father," Auri said.

"I'm here for you, Auriella," he said.

"I'm staying with her," I said.

"Okay, let me be clearer. Can every Mender and healer exit the room?" he said.

They scurried out of the room, leaving the four of us in there. He pushed the door closed behind them.

He cocked his head to the side. "Braegon, would you do the honors of placing a sound shield?"

"Um... okay?" I let out a big sigh, visualized a sound shield, and felt it lock into place.

"Thanks, cadet," he said. He walked towards Auri and me. I turned my body to put myself between him and her. At this point, I didn't trust anyone.

"You can calm down, son. I'm not... I wouldn't hurt her."

"What do you need? It's been a long day, and as you can see, her father is in rough shape," I said.

"Yeah, I imagine after watching his daughter shift into a Werewolf, he'd be in rough shape with a lot of questions," Gile said.

"Rough shape, he is. Questions... not exactly," she said.

"He knew you might shift?" he asked, his eyebrows furrowed tight.

"What the hell do *you* know?" I shot out at him.

"I know that Auriella is my niece, and I know that there was a slim possibility of her shifting, but I figured she was way beyond that. Her mother was a late shifter, but we believed it was delayed... well, the why doesn't matter."

"She was pregnant with my sister..." Auri muttered.

"You know?" he said. He thought he would be dropping the bombshells, and yet she already knew.

"Yeah, just recently learned," she told him.

"She shifted right after the birth, but then vowed never to shift again, using her magic in some way that was forbidden to mask any wolf part of her."

"Look... I... I have a lot of questions, but my brain hurts. My dad almost died, I turned into a fucking wolf, I had to re-kill my friends, and the whole fucking continent is falling apart. Unless it's life or death, can we just do this later?"

"Your father knows who I am. He just doesn't know all the family secrets. I think it's time to air them all out. Find me when you're ready," he said.

CHAPTER 31

I stood there staring at my dad, part of me trying to will him to wake up and be okay. I spent so many years being angry at him. Every regret poured in. How pissed off I was at him all of last year. In the last few weeks, we had mended so much, and we still had so much more mending to do. I had so many fucking questions that he needed to answer.

Professor Gile came in here and dropped a damn bombshell, one in which apparently my father knew about. Everything made sense. He made a comment about my mother being proud when I had won a sparring match. He was always extra kind towards me.

I was questioning everything I had known about my mother. Was what my father knew the truth? Or did he tell me some bullshit? I always believed that she was adopted as a baby, found on the street, abandoned. I don't think I could handle any more revelations being dropped on me for the rest of the year, and we were only two weeks in.

Gile had left, and a couple of the Healers walked back into the room. They moved to the corner and stared at my father.

"Are you guys just going to stare at him or actually do something?" I asked them.

"We have been ordered to stand in here and make sure he remains safe. Your father has a lot of enemies," the elder healer said.

"By whom?" I asked.

"Major General Kamban," she said.

"Okay. When do you expect him to wake up?"

"We hope in the next few hours."

I sat there for hours. The sun had set outside, and I sat there staring at him. While I believed that the Healers were there to watch him, I didn't believe they could actually ward off an attack if there was one. I wanted him to be awake before I left him. The room was lit with small candles placed throughout. Finally, after seven hours, his eyes flickered open. He looked around the room, looking at the Healers, then looking at me, then at Zane.

"Hi, baby girl," he croaked out.

"Hi, Dad," I said. Tears fell from the corner of my eyes, down my cheeks.

"Are you okay?" he muttered.

"I should be the one asking you that," I said.

He looked at the Healers and lifted his hand in the air, waving them out of the room. They tilted their heads down at him.

"Go," he said.

The three of them who had been posted inside the room turned and walked out of the room, pulling the door closed behind them. My dad cleared his throat and then turned his head and locked eyes with me.

"Are you okay?" he asked me again.

"I'm fine. Are *you* okay?" I said to him.

"You shifted... You became the wolf I had always wanted to be."

"Yeah... that happened."

"I will be fine, Auri. I think my heart was a little stunned that you actually—"

"A little stunned, Father? You had to have your heart mended and nearly died."

"Okay, I was really stunned."

"I'm a Shapeshifter... apparently. Or as Esme called me, a little shadow wolf..."

"You're so much more than that, Auri," my father said.

"Yeah... I'm a Witch too," I said.

"Yes, but you didn't grow up in a pack setting—"

"Whose fault is that?" I cut him off.

"Yes, I'm sorry. I wish things were different, and because of that, you are going to need to learn some things."

"From you? Who never shifted."

"Be nice to me, I just almost died," he said, with a little smile.

"Oh, the pity card, that's below you," I said.

He let out a little laugh. "I always wanted to shift, I never thought I wouldn't when I was younger. I had the traits—superb sense of smell and advanced hearing. Do you want to know what kind of wolf I wanted to be?"

"Uh, no? Isn't there only one?"

"Well, yes, there is only one wolf, but there are different colors. Some are much rarer than others, some signal something greater, and represent what the fates believe to be the next alpha," he said.

"Oh, my Gods... let me guess, Black is rare and believed to be an Alpha..."

"Precisely."

I closed my eyes. Why? Why me? What the hell did the fates have planned for me? Wasn't being a Werewolf-Witch-dragon Rider enough? I mean, the Dragon Rider was enough for *me.*

"I am not being a fucking alpha!" I raised my voice. My father's eyes widened. I rarely raised my voice to him.

"I didn't say... you had to be..." he said slowly.

"Then what the fuck are you saying?" I said. Agitation poured out of me.

"I'm just saying you will be respected—"

I cut him off, "I don't plan to shift again—"

"What? Why?" he said, cutting me off this time.

"Because that's not who I am, what I am. It's the littlest part of me. As you said, I didn't grow up with wolves. Unlike you, I didn't want this. According to my uncle Gile—which by the way—thanks for leaving that part out, my mother never shifted again."

"Your mom had shifted? He came and told you?"

His face told me that I dropped a bombshell on him this time.

"Yeah, he came earlier when you were out. I told him I couldn't handle this conversation right now and to leave."

He blew out a breath between his lips.

"Auri, he probably has more answers that he is probably willing to give you than he would ever have given me," he said.

"Why didn't you tell me she had a brother? I had an uncle?"

"I wanted to, I did, but they were estranged, or that's what your mom said. I don't even know what's true or not anymore," he said, his eyes dropped down. "Was everything she told me a lie?" he muttered.

He was hurt and questioning everything he knew, like I was. He had questions, and I was far from having any answers.

"There is something else..." I said to him. This time, I dropped my eyes to the floor.

"Great... with that look, I'll just go ahead and take a breath, so I don't make my heart fail again," he said.

"Yeah... you probably should... While Zane was rescuing you, I was on the field hanging out in my wolfy form... and... well—"

"Spit it out, Auri," my dad said.

Zane rubbed my back up and down, reminding me he was still here with me. He hadn't participated in the conversation, but stood next to me, taking everything in.

"The dead cadets... they uh... they rose... they... they were alive, but not. They had been turned into—"

"Nosferatu?" he said, finishing my words.

He sat more upright and moved his legs to the side of the bed.

"What are you doing, sir?" Zane said.

"I'm getting the fuck out of this bed," my father said.

"Are we missing something? The threat has been eliminated," I told him.

"Maybe right now, but we have a lot bigger problem," he said.

He stood up next to his bed, and his eyes started darting around the room.

"We're listening," Zane said.

He walked to the table where his clothes lay. "If Nosferatu killed them and they came back to life. They weren't just regular Nosferatu. These are hybrid ones. Remember when I told you that they were experimenting once, and they tried to do it on wolves?"

"Yeah," we both said.

He started pulling his clothing on. "Follow along. When the original Nosferatu were created, they could only turn humans into Nosferatu. They would do this by biting them, draining all of their blood, then, right before they died, they would feed their blood to them. They would then wake up after an excruciating process as a Nosferatu. This didn't work for a Fae or Shapeshifters."

"I didn't see any of them feed them blood. They drained them, let them fall, and moved to the next cadet. None of the Shapeshifters they managed to kill turned either."

"The experiments that I interrupted were trying to turn Fae, make them into Nosferatu. They must have figured out how."

"I thought you said they were doing it on Werewolves?" I asked, confused.

"They were, and on Fae. King Fen is behind this attack. The human continent may be up to something, but this fucking attack wasn't them."

He finished buttoning his clothing and tied his boots.

"Dad, what are you going to do? You almost died earlier today."

"I'm fine. That is the beauty of menders and magic. They attacked us twice in one day. He isn't done. This... what happened today... was just testing what we were capable of. Zane's father and I created the Resurrection for this very moment. We don't have time to sit around and wait for him to dismantle the college," he said.

He opened the door and walked into the halls. Every Mender and healer stopped and stared at him. They were unsure if they should say something. Kamban was leaning forward on the counter and turned his head to look at my dad. Something unsaid was exchanged between them. Kamban pushed off the counter, took a step back, and walked down the hall in front of us.

Zane and I both stood behind my father, unsure if we should follow. Both of us were confused about what the hell was happening, what our roles were, and what he wanted us to do.

"Let's go, keep up," my dad called back towards us.

We both started walking, our pace picking up a little faster.

"What's happening right now?" I asked Zane.

"I don't exactly know. I know we are following your father, and he just told us the King was responsible for all the bloodshed."

"Great. I'm glad we are both just blindly following along," I said.

"What were we going to do, tell him no?"

"Well, no."

He grabbed my hand and interlocked our fingers, then he squeezed my hand. It was the reassurance I needed then. There was so much hanging between us. He watched me nearly die and then shift into a wolf. I was exhausted, yet my adrenaline was coursing through my body. We walked through the halls into the administration part of the building.

Kamban led us into the administration meeting room. My dad was right on his heels, and we were right on my dad's. In the room: Vindex, Melamora, Pascal, Gile, Scullin, Hildegard, Quillet, Foret, and Benning were standing in the room. All of them looked at my father, and then their eyes moved to Zane and me. How did they all get here so fast?

"Your dad has a dragon, who can communicate with a lot of other fliers…" Esme said. She had been quiet since she took off in the field earlier. I know she had a lot to think about, a lot to discuss with the elders.

Vindex cocked his head to the side a little bit. "Should they be here for this?"

"Maybe not, but I want them here," my father said.

"You're in control here," Vindex said.

My father looked around. "Thank you all for responding as soon as Kim was able to pass the message along. I am waiting on one other person, he is coming from a little further away and should arrive—"

Air swished around the room, and Zane's father stood there in front of us.

"If you don't know, this is Duke Braegon of the Veil of Vultures. Glad you came quickly, Roarke."

"Well, when a Rider lands on my property and says you demand my presence, and then says, 'code pineapple'. I can't exactly shoo him away."

My dad smiled and then motioned to the chairs around the room with his hand. "Let's have a seat, we need to discuss strategy."

All of them took a seat except Zane and me. We both stood there, unsure if we should sit.

My father looked up at both of us, squinting his eyes. "Yes, both of you should sit as well."

We both stepped forward and walked to where there were two open seats next to each other. We pulled our chairs out and took a seat. We were still holding each other's hands. I knew we both had a lot to discuss, and we had been through a hell of a day, but we had each other. At the very end of every single day, we had each other's backs—beyond this life and the next.

"If you haven't figured it out, the attacks today had to be King Fen making a statement against us. Braegon, I know you weren't here, but we had two attacks today. Both included hippogriffs and Nosferatu."

"How do you know that wasn't the human continent making a statement?"

"Auriella?" My father said and nodded my way.

"The Nosferatu attacked cadets, draining them and killing them. Shortly later, they rose from the dead," I said.

"Oh," he said.

"Exactly. Not only should that not happen with Fae, but they didn't feed them any of their blood either. The Shapeshifters did not turn. While we are talking about Shapeshifters, I think it's important to share with the—"

"Dad," I said, cutting him off. I knew where he was going with this. He stared at me. Silence between us.

"Auriella, everyone here I trust with my life, and yours. They should know."

"Know what?" Melamora asked.

"Everyone here is aware of my heritage, and I have appreciated every single person in this room keeping that secret. Everyone in the room has also been informed of the mating bond between Cadet Braegon and my daughter. When that happened a few weeks ago, we learned that Lucille was also half Witch and half Shapeshifter. Earlier today, Auriella was attacked and shifted for the first time."

Every single person but my father, Zane, and Gile had their mouths gaping open, eyes wide. None of them was expecting that news today. Zane's father knew that it might happen, but he hadn't thought it actually would since I was now twenty.

"Auriella, are you okay?" Zane's father said, leaning forward on the table, looking at me.

"I'm physically fine, I'm still in utter shock," I told him.

"Isn't she twenty? This is a little late?" Melamora said.

Gile cleared his throat. "She is, but her mother is from the Dunkel pack, and they—"

"Females typically shift later than the rest of the other packs, or when under severe duress," Foret said. He then turned to my dad. "That's why you wanted me here."

"Yes, and because I trust you. You and I grew up together and were friends despite our stupid family feuds," my dad said. "I do wish I knew that little tidbit, though."

"You never asked," Foret said.

"True," my dad said.

"How did you know that, Gile?" Kamban said.

Gile looked at my father. "You didn't tell them about Lucille and my connection?"

"No, I don't like to share Lucille's business," my dad said.

"She was my twin sister," Gile said.

"What!? You never said—she said adopted brother," my dad said.

Every other person in that room went utterly still.

"Lots of dirty laundry being aired at the table, and yet we are no closer to coming to a plan for King Fen," Scullin said.

"Yes, Scullin, we are getting there. I wanted to get some disclosures out of the way first," my father said.

"How many do we have on our side?" Scullin asked.

"Against the King of our continent?" Zane's father asked.

"Everyone who is sitting here," my father said.

"What? Are you kidding me?" Pascal said.

"How am I supposed to recruit people? Oh, hey, do you want to join our movement against the King? That isn't exactly something that will make people eager to join," my father said.

"There are only fourteen of us, and two of them are cadets, Conri," Melamora said, worry lacing her tone.

"We have a college full of cadets, they don't have to know what the actual goal is, they will go where we send them to go," my dad said.

Every head in the room was locked onto my father's. Was he fucking serious right now? I know I was a cadet, but I was different than most of the cadets here. Some of these cadets would be going to their deaths.

"You want to send them to their deaths? We won't be anything, this college will be nothing? We won't have a college, Conri," Kamban said.

"Obviously, we wouldn't take the entire college," my dad said.

"We shouldn't take them under a fake pretense either," Vindex said. He had been sitting quietly in his chair, taking everything in.

"How do you think we should approach that then?" my father said, looking at Vindex.

"Being honest and upfront, if they want to risk their lives, then we take them," Vindex said.

"I propose we only take third and fourth-year cadets," Melamora said.

"The second-year cadets are ready," Kamban said.

"Most of them, yes," Melamora said, "they will be third-years in a few months after all."

"Only Riders, Drusearons, Shapeshifters, and Witches," Pascal said.

"Infantry is ready, and we should definitely take some menders," Kamban said.

"We shouldn't leave the college empty of upper-classmen. There are some menders within the Riders; they will surely join. Leaving all Healers and historians here, we can't leave them completely unprotected," my dad said.

"Do you have officers at Daysn that could come here?" Vindex asked my dad.

"I'd rather ask them to join us in this battle and leave more trained cadets here," my dad countered.

"I know I don't have much pull in this, but I don't think the second-year Drusearons are ready, but they could defend the college if needed," Zane said.

"I concur with that assessment," Pascal said.

"Then let's go back to leaving all second-years here, and any of the upper-classmen that don't want to go," Kamban said.

"Glad we settled that. Now, how do we get all those cadets to Helaoss?" my dad said.

"Drusearons and Riders can fly," Hildegard said. He also had been quiet, adding little input.

"They would make it there much faster than the rest," Melamora said.

"Riders could take on one to two passengers," Scullin said.

"That's brazen to say that all of us will willingly carry extra," Esme chided down the bond.

"I'm betting if the elders said you had to, you would," I said to her.

"Yeah... grudgingly," Esme said.

"We don't have enough fliers for all of them," Quillet said.

"What are our numbers?" my father asked.

"We lost a lot today, sir," Kamban said, his eyes dropped.

I hadn't even thought of how many we lost today. I hadn't had time. I went from killing the fellow cadets that were trying to kill me, to shifting back and being at my father's side for hours. I hoped that my flight was safe, but I broke protocol and dropped to the ground.

"Give me the counts," he said.

"These are estimates of remaining cadets. We believe some cadets weren't counted, as they weren't found dead or alive. One hundred ninety-seven Riders, two hundred forty-nine Drusearons, one thousand six hundred and sixty-nine Infantry, two hundred and twenty-two Shapeshifters, four hundred and fifty-seven Healers, one hundred and fifteen Historians, and one hundred and twenty-six Sorcerers," Kamban said.

"The Infantry has always been the largest branch. They will be the hardest to get there. Most of them don't have magic," my father said.

"We can pair the Shapeshifters and Witches with the Riders," Kamban said.

"How many Riders have teleporting abilities? We could station nearby the palace, and then the Riders could teleport back and bring back cadets?" I asked. I had been quietly listening to them, but we had cadets who had abilities that we could use to our advantage.

"We have a few," Scullin said.

"We also have a handful of Drusearons that could rove back and forth?" Pascal said.

"I would also put any Infantry that has magic with the riders, if there is room," Melamora said.

"I am going to go round up some other close officers that I believe will be ecstatic to join our cause," my father said.

"When do we want to do this?" Kamban said.

"Tomorrow night," my father said, "everyone here needs their rest tonight. We will talk with the cadets tomorrow morning and leave in the afternoon. Kim and I will start recruiting help tonight."

"I have quite a few knights that are loyal to me, that I will go get," Zane's father said.

"What are our plans when we get there?" Gile asked.

"I think it's best to keep our cadets hiding in the forest, and the ten of us have a conversation with him, try to subdue him before we bring in backup," my father said.

"He's going to know as soon as he sees us," Zane's father said.

"Maybe not, I once had made a good rapport with him. He thinks we are good friends," my father said. "We need to be stealthy as we arrive, which is why we will arrive in the evening. We will camp in the woods, and show up at his door for a morning Monday meeting."

"Let's all be honest here, Aldric is no matter for most of us. He doesn't have anything beyond his ability to shift. It's not him I am worried about. It's the army of monsters that he has created that has me a little concerned," Benning said.

Everyone in the room turned their head; he hadn't said a single word before. I had actually forgotten he was even here.

"I know most of you barely know me, but there's a reason Conri has me here, other than my rank. I was gathering inside information at the Palace. Let's just say, I'm a double agent," Benning said.

"He is my cousin, and he can be trusted. The king is unaware of our connection. From what you can tell, Josef, how many are we talking about?" my father asked.

"Roughly a thousand, and they are blindly loyal to him," he answered.

CHAPTER 32

We wrapped up all of the plans for tomorrow, then Zane roved both of us into his room. We both sat on his bed, thighs pressed together. Neither of us had any energy even to speak. It was one of the longest days I had in a really long time, and it didn't look like there would be any breaks for the next several days.

We would be leaving the next day. Helaoss was a small town in central Veskonia. It was around a five-hour flight. The plan was to go around fourteen hundred, arriving in the dark. The Riders who could teleport and the Drusearons who could rove would work on bringing as many cadets as they could. The rest of us would set up camp and prepare for the next morning.

"I'm going to take a shower," I said.

"May I join?" he asked.

I nodded my head yes.

I walked to the shower, and Zane followed right behind me. He reached into the shower and turned on the water, allowing it to get hot. Then he came over to me and started unbuttoning my tunic, then pushed it off my shoulders, letting it fall to the floor. He moved to my pants and pushed them down to the ground.

"Get in," he said.

I walked in as he started to unbutton his clothes and let them fall to the floor. He slowly walked into the shower and moved under one of the streams. He threw his head back, closed his eyes, letting the water pour onto his head and down his back. I stood under another shower head, water pouring down my face and body. I felt like the sins of the day were washing away. I closed my eyes and let the water immerse me.

"You're so beautiful, my love," he said.

I opened my eyes, and he was staring at me with eyes filled with lust. I gave him a little smile. It's all I had, in the quiet of the room and shower, everything from earlier had been replaying in my head. He walked to me and wrapped his arms around my waist, and pulled me close to him. He held onto me tight. I turned my head and pressed my ear against his chest. I listened to his heartbeat. I closed my eyes and focused on it. My eyes started burning, and the tears slipped out of the corners of my eyes.

I took a breath in, I didn't want the little tears to turn into sobs. His finger hooked under my chin and lifted my head, our eyes meeting. He stared into my eyes before he moved his face to mine, our lips meeting. He kissed me tenderly, slowly. We held the kiss for several seconds before he pulled back slightly and kissed me again and again.

"I love you, always," he said.

"I love you beyond this life and the next," I told him.

He pulled me into another hug, squeezing me tightly.

"Let's get cleaned and get to bed. Tomorrow will be another long day," he said.

He lathered me tenderly, then lathered himself, and we left his bathing chambers. We climbed into his bed, both of us completely naked. It was the best way to sleep next to each other, my head on his chest, my leg on top of his. His arm was under me, gripping me tightly. My eyes were heavy, and I could barely keep them open. As I listened to his heartbeat, it pulled me into a deep sleep like the perfect lullaby.

***

I stood on the flight field in my wolf form, which was different. Zane should be back any minute. Esme launched into the air, leaving me there alone with all the bodies. Something caught my attention out of the corner of my eye, so I twisted my head to the side. The cadet lying on the ground, blood all over his neck, sat up. We stared at each other. My head twisted to the side, unsure of what the fuck was actually happening. I was sure he was dead. I watched the Nosferatu rip their throats out. He made a guttural growl at me and then stood up. I stood frozen, unsure of what to do. I was way out of my league here. The dead rising wasn't normal.

He growled at me, flashing me his teeth. His canines were elongated and sharp. He walked towards me. I couldn't speak to him, although I'm not sure he would listen to me. He continued hissing at me, getting closer and closer with each step. He was like the Nosferatu earlier, but slower. He was looking at me like I was food.

I snarled at him, showing him my teeth. He didn't stop. He was getting closer. A deep growl came from deep within my throat. He kept coming. It was him or me.

I lunged for his throat, ripping his head from his shoulders. His body collapsed on the ground, head rolling away. Then another rose and another and another. They all stared at me like I was the best prey they would enjoy. I snarled at them, but they were all coming for me. I heard something from behind me, and I quickly turned around.

Lili stood there—staring at me—hissing at me. No. No. No. This can't be. She can't be dead. I can't kill her. She wasn't on the field. She was in the air. Her head cocked to the side, and she continued to walk towards me.

I didn't want to do this. I didn't want to kill her, but she kept getting closer. She was going to kill me. Her eyes said she was thinking I was the best dinner she would have. She lunged forward, and I lunged at her.

Before I knew it, her head fell to the ground and rolled next to my feet. No. Gods. This isn't real. I lifted my head and howled.

"AURI!" Zane yelled.

I turned around looking for him all over, but I didn't see him anywhere.

"Auriella! Come to me! You're okay," he said.

Everything turned dark and cold, and all the bodies disappeared. I was confused.

"Wake up, love. Come on, open your eyes," Zane pleaded.

My eyes flung open. I was breathing rapidly in and out. Sweat drenched my body. My arms and legs were trembling. I looked around frantically before sitting up abruptly.

Zane was sitting next to me, gently rubbing my shoulder.

"You're okay, it was just a nightmare."

"I was on the field again, and I killed Lili. I mean, I didn't kill her in life, just in my dream, but it was so real. It felt like I was on the field again. They all rose and started to come for me."

"I have dreams like that too..." he told me.

He held me tightly and kissed the top of my head. The reassurance I needed to fall back to sleep. He fell back onto his pillows and pulled me back into his arms, my head on his chest. I listened to his heartbeat again and drifted back into sleep.

The dreams were vivid and random, but they weren't nightmares. We woke up before the sun fully rose in the sky. I wanted another shower because I felt like I was still covered in the sins of killing other cadets. I had ended lives before, but it was when they threatened me or caused harm. These cadets didn't deserve it. They were defending our school and lost their lives—and came back to life.

Zane had roved us back to my room so that I could get dressed appropriately. I put on every dagger belt and sheathed as many daggers as I could.

"For someone who has immense shadow abilities and can be a deadly wolf, you are putting on a lot of daggers," Zane said.

"I don't want to be unprepared. The shadows can use my daggers," I said.

"Whatever makes you feel better."

"What do you think the other first-year cadets are going to think about me going on this mission, and they aren't?" I asked, it had been something that was on my mind.

"They won't know. Remember, only third and fourth-year cadets will be invited, and they will be instructed not to disclose where they are going.

Even if it does spread around, which it probably will, everyone will think you are in your room," Zane said.

"Does it bother you that I am indeed a Shapeshifter?"

"Not really. I mean, I've had a few weeks to get used to the idea. You're still you. The most witty, beautiful wolf I have seen," he said. He flashed me his beautiful smile. The sun in my room hit his blue eyes just right, making them paler—mesmerizing.

"I really needed to hear that, I really did. I had a feeling that it was going to happen... I just—"

"What do you mean?" he asked.

"I wasn't sure if it was from my Witch side, channeling, or what, but my hearing and sense of smell have been very acute as of late. I just... I don't know, I think deep down I knew it was going to happen."

"Why hadn't you told me?"

"That would have made it real, and I wanted to deny it until it happened."

"You know you can tell me, and still deny it, and I'll let you live in whatever delusion you want, if that's what you say you want."

"You are... literally the best," I told him.

"I try to be... for you," he said.

We finished getting ready and headed out to the courtyard. We weren't sure exactly what my father wanted us to do, but I do know he was planning to host meetings with the upperclassmen separately.

Cadets were wandering around. Sundays were leisure days. Cadets did various things, like laundry, extra gym time, and playing games with each other. Some cadets would travel to the nearby town and shop. With the lockdown being over, cadets were spending more time together and gathering items they needed.

This made having meetings both advantageous and disadvantageous; a good number of cadets weren't on campus grounds, but at the same time, there were plenty still here running around. Once we found my father, he told me that all wing commanders were given instructions last night to notify all third and fourth-year cadets not to leave campus.

My dad was strategic and made the meetings happen in classrooms in the wing in which they stayed. He combined the Drusearons and Riders, and then combined the Sorcerers and Shapeshifters, with the Infantry being alone. He asked that Zane and I both come to the two combined meetings. He hoped that seeing cadets would help them make the decision that was in our favor.

He also asked me if I would be willing to share my heritage, as he thought it would help the Shapeshifters and Sorcerers connect better to me—to us. He had hidden his entire lineage from almost the whole military, only letting those he trusted know. Now he was willing to share this secret, let everyone know who he was—what he was.

I admired that, but I was also terrified for him–for me.I also had nothing to lose; they already hated me, what could be worse than that? They kill me. Well, that would be worse, but that wouldn't happen.

Zane and I headed to Vindex's room for the first meeting. My stomach was a ball of nerves, worried this wouldn't go the way we wanted it to go. Zane and I took a seat at the back of the classroom, giving us a way to observe the cadets unsuspectingly. One by one, cadets piled into the room. They looked around, and all of them had a nervousness to them.

I expected that, though, at the front of the room stood my father, Kamban, Pascal, Vindex, and Hildegard. The general of the Military, the general of the school, and teachers who represented both branches were present. I watched knees bouncing as they sat in their seats. Some of them adjusted their collars, others picked the lint that wasn't really on their clothing. All nervous ticks. Once the room was filled, my father cleared his throat, and the room went silent.

"I know that it has been one hell of a few months, and it doesn't seem like we are getting any type of break. With the attack yesterday, it feels like it will never end. I wish I had better news, but instead I'm about to ask something from all of you, something I wish I didn't. We are about to do an organized attack. We are giving third and fourth-year cadets the chance to opt out."

"The Duke must not approve this?" Remus asked.

"This is under the radar, off the books, but it is going after who orchestrated the attacks on our college yesterday," my father said.

"Will this be putting a target on our backs?" Nikolai asked.

"If it goes our way, then no, but I can't give you or anyone in this room a one-hundred percent guarantee."

"What is the mission exactly?" Cassia asked.

"We will be leaving this afternoon, arriving in the dark, and setting up camp. Some of us will try to have a conversation, and if shit goes south, which is highly likely, everyone will move in."

"We're in," a bunch of them said.

"If you're out, which is okay, you will not be judged. Go ahead and leave, while we finalize details," Kamban said.

"Also, this is need to know, so please do not discuss this outside of this room," my father said.

A handful of cadets stood up and left. None of them was in a cadet leadership position. My father and Kamban discussed the details of the incursion. The cadets asked questions here and there, but most of them didn't dive too deep.

We moved to the next meeting, the one I was more nervous about. While I had become friends with several of the Shapeshifters, they were all mostly first-years, who wouldn't be here. If Asmoth was any indication of how much they didn't like Riders or like my father, this meeting could go to shit.

Pascal and Hildegard didn't attend this meeting. Instead, Gile and Foret took their place. Vindex, Kamban, and my father remained. Vindex was popular amongst the entire college, teaching us how to use our magic. We were meeting in one of the Shapeshifter's lecture rooms, one I had never been in.

Some of the cadets muttered under their breath after looking at Zane and me sitting in the chairs in the back. The cadets piled into the room, way more apprehensive than the Riders and Drusearons. There may have been friendly faces standing at the front of the room, but it was clear they weren't going to be as easy to win over.

My father started with the same statement that he had earlier, except the cadets stayed on edge.

"Why do you need us?" one of the male Shapeshifters asked.

"I think that's a simple answer, we need numbers, were you on the field when the Nosferatu took out a large number of your fellow cadets?"

"I was, which is why I am wondering why we would want to go to them," he said.

"They attacked us—" Kamban said.

"Look, this isn't sanctioned by the Duke. If you don't want to help or join, we will hold no ill will towards you," my father said, his voice was cold and calm.

"Why should we trust you?" another Shapeshifter asked.

"I get that you may have been told of the horrors I have done, and there is some longstanding hatred that has developed between Riders and Shapeshifters—"

"You're damn right," several said at once.

"You may be angry, and you may not like me, but I am your commanding officer, and you will *fucking* respect me," my father said.

"What is expected of us?" one of the Witches asked.

"To fight for our college, to fight for our lives," my father said.

"I know that most of the Shapeshifters grew up against the general, but I can tell you there is a false narrative," Gile said.

"Told to you because I was supposed to be the Alpha of the Lupine pack," my father said.

"Blasphemy!" one of the Shapeshifters yelled out.

"It's true, he is half wolf and half Witch, something he has kept very close to his heart," Foret said.

"Then shift," someone yelled out.

"And that is why the narrative has been shifted against me... I, unfortunately, wasn't gifted that ability," my father said. He stood tall, but I could hear the hurt behind his tone.

"Then how do we know you're not up here to deceive us?" one of them said.

I stood up. I had enough of this bullshit. My dad was trying to be genuine. This wasn't why we were here, yet they were putting him on trial. All of the eyes in the room turned to me, and most of them furrowed their eyebrows.

"Why is your daughter even here?" one of them said, before turning to look at him.

He let out a little chuckle under his breath, but didn't say anything.

"I'm here because I can be, because I might be in the Rider's branch, but I am, after all, a born Shapeshifter and a Witch," I said.

I hadn't entirely accepted that part of my heritage, but I sure as hell could fake it for the cause.

"Yeah, your father just said something similar—"

I didn't let him finish before I fully transformed right where I stood. The cadets who were sitting in the front jumped up and moved back. Transforming in the lecture rooms wasn't exactly allowed, due to the size of Werewolves, but I didn't give a damn.

"Holy shit," one of them muttered.

"Now that was wonderful to watch... Um, but do I need to remind you that when you shift back to your mortal form, you'll be naked?" he told me down the bond.

"I think Shapeshifters are actually used to it, but I have a whole other magic trick up my sleeve," I told him.

"Oh, goody, I can't wait for this," he said, before sending a laugh down the bond.

They all stared at me. The whispers amongst them started. I inhaled, and then I pulled my shadows out, surrounding me. I shifted back and then used my shadows to keep myself completely dark and get dressed. I pulled the shadows back within. I took a couple of steps forward and stood next to my father, and then turned around on my heels and faced the cadets. Their faces of pure shock were the exact response I wanted from them.

"As you can see... I have a couple of unique abilities myself. I think it's best to hear my father and Kamban out," I said, then walked back to my seat.

"That was a beautiful little magic trick. I'd like to see it in reverse," Zane said.

I turned my head to the side and smiled at him.

"Now, I'd love to share more about my heritage and how we got here today, but that is not the task of this meeting. I am one of you. I may not shift, but I am part of all of you. We need to wrap this up because I have one more group meeting. Ask questions about the mission, not about me. That's for another day. If you don't want to join this mission, that's okay, but you can go ahead and leave."

More cadets left than at the previous meeting, but not as many as I thought. My dad went over the exact details as he did earlier. After we got done, my dad headed to one of the Infantry rooms. It would be the largest group he would attempt to recruit. Most of them didn't have magic, but they would be valuable, nonetheless. Infantry spent the majority of their time learning how to infiltrate and doing weapons training.

CHAPTER 33

We met on the flight field at the planned time of thirteen-thirty, with a departure of fourteen hundred. My father informed me that he also asked a few of the first and second-year cadets who had specific abilities like roving, telepathic, and teleporting. Which meant Micah and Thora would be joining along. A small part of me was relieved that I wasn't the only first-year out here, but I was also worried about the risk they would be in.

Esme landed in the field next to Veyra—Lili's dragon. Both of them were standing there with their own beauty. The height gap between them was getting smaller and smaller, and Esme would eventually tower over her by two feet, if the predictions of her height are right.

I was being paired up with one extra rider—a Witch—to fly with because Esme was smaller and hadn't completed her full growth. Hildegard was adamant that she should only carry one extra person instead of two or three, like some of the others were doing. She disagreed with their decision, but it wasn't hers to make, and I wasn't getting involved in any of the elder fliers' decisions.

"I could have carried three of you just fine," Esme said down the bond.

"I'm sure you could have," I told her.

Most of the dragons were carrying three cadets—including their own rider—a select few had four total, including my father. I giggled when I saw that. I knew that neither he nor Kim was a fan of letting others ride along. Of course, they would put the mission above all else. Instead of cadets, he had Gile, Foret, and Melamora.

With griffins and phoenixes in the air, we would be moving at the pace of the slowest flier. We would be flying as an extra-large drift. It was decided we would all stay together and fight together. Luckily, we would be mostly in the dark, allowing us to stay mostly hidden. The other professors were told that they had to stay back at the college to direct the other cadets while our group went on the mission.

We launched into the air as soon as the bell clock tolled. All of the fourth-year and professors took the outside of the drift, the small number of first and second-years were in the center, with the third-years being between us. The majority of the Infantry cadets were instructed to be on the field five hours after our departure. It would take hours upon hours for the cadets with the ability to bring them to camp. The fliers were only able to take the Shapeshifters, Witches, and a few Infantry. Griffins and Phoenixes were only able to carry two cadets, versus most of the Dragons, who were carrying three.

"I could have carried three," Esme said. She was still annoyed by being treated like a baby.

"I'm sure you could have done it perfectly, too," I told her.

Willow sat behind me, her arms clutched tight around my waist.

"We could show her a fun time and do barrel rolls," Esme said.

"Absolutely not. Not only are we not killing her, but I'd also like to avoid any scoldings from my father," I told her.

"But you can't control me," Esme purred.

"Esme!" I scolded her.

"I'm just kidding," she said, *"I know better during times of war."*

"Thank the Gods," I said.

We continued flying, and the sun started setting to the right of us as we made our way through the mountains. Willow remained quiet, holding tightly. My thoughts wandered over how the previous week had gone. I barely had time to deal with the information. Zane could siphon my magic. Magic wasn't infinite, while some Fae had stronger bloodlines, which tended to lead to magic that was stronger and didn't deplete as easily. I had barely learned how to use my magic myself and hadn't gotten close.

Vindex had warned us that we would start to feel weak, as if we had physically over asserted ourselves. If we continued past that point, we would start to feel nauseous and disoriented, and then the magic would be gone for a while. He described it as he had personally felt that, and you could see in his eyes that it wasn't something he enjoyed talking about.

"We haven't talked much about me shifting?" I asked her. We hadn't talked about it really.

"What's there to say?" she said.

"You haven't said much of anything, that's the problem."

"It doesn't bother me, it doesn't change anything. I always knew you would shift—"

"Wait. What?" I cut her off, shock-laced tone.

"Have you smelled the other Shapeshifters?"

"I mean, yes, I have noticed that everyone has unique scents," I told her.

"Well, we can also smell all of you, more deeply than Fae can," she said, *"you didn't smell like them, but you smelled different, so I didn't pick it up right away. Then your vision started getting better, and then your sense of smell... I just knew."*

"Why didn't you say anything?"

"You started spiraling as soon as you found out there was a chance. I wanted to give you time to sit with it, and then you shifted," she said.

"Why did you look so shocked? Why didn't you talk to me?" I said, even if she hadn't heard my sadness through my tone, I'm sure she felt it.

"Because it became real. Because the elders would now know that we have an actual Werewolf as a Rider," she said.

"Why do they care?"

"Once upon a time, fliers vowed only to let Fae be Riders. Werewolves are not Fae. They just aren't."

"My father is a—"

"Your father never shifted, and they knew he wouldn't shift. It's like that part of him was never him," she said.

"I'm Fae too..." I said. I knew saying that was part of me trying to convince myself I wasn't just a shifter anymore.

"I know you are," she said, trying to reassure me.

Hours passed by, the sun was gone, and the cold got colder with each passing minute. Willow was silent behind me. I checked on her a few times to make sure she was okay, and she only gave simple answers. She once asked how close we were to camp.

We were relayed a message that we would be landing soon. Most of our saddlebags were crammed full of supplies. Some of the dragons carried canvas bags that carried large canvas tents, which we would be setting up upon arrival. There would be a canvas covering for the ground, and then we had bedrolls to lie on the ground. The Witches would create us contained fire centers for each tent to keep us warm, but not emit a lot of light.

Once we landed, fourth-year cadets were sent to canvas the area. Instead of putting all of the tents in one area, it was decided they would be spread throughout the woods. Zane and several others started to either rove or teleport back to the college to bring cadets here. There were only twenty-two of them in total, and there were nearly six hundred Infantry cadets who needed to come here. While Micah was able to teleport, he wasn't confident in teleporting the distance with someone yet. Instead, he practiced some of his teleporting while we sat in camp.

It took nearly two and a half hours for them to get all of the cadets here. Some of the Riders started feeling weak, and the Drusearons had to pick up the extra when they stopped. Some of them only took four minutes to go and come back, some took six. Every one of them looked completely drained by the time they were done, including Zane. I stood in front of him, looking him up and down. His cheeks were bright red, his eyes glossed over, and he was breathing heavier.

"Are you okay?" I asked Zane.

"I just need a solid night of sleep," Zane said. He leaned forward and kissed my forehead.

"Is that the fix for everything?" I asked.

"Well, it will greatly improve how I am feeling, but what would really help is if I could touch—"

"Shhh–stop," I cut him off, knowing exactly what would come out of his dirty little mouth, and there were wandering ears all around.

"We will be sleeping in different tents tonight," he said.

"Yeah... would be a little weird for you to be in a Rider's tent, or me to be in a Drusearon's tent."

"That it would," he said.

"Hey, you two, get back to work," one of the officers my father recruited said.

"And there are eyes everywhere," he said.

"The good thing is we can always talk, even when we are apart," I said, before tapping the side of my head.

"Yes, I am always here, my anam cara," he said down the bond.

He turned around and headed to where the Drusearons had set up their tents, and I headed back to where the Riders were setting up. Everything was mostly set up, and we had gotten everything done while the Infantry cadets were arriving. As we finished, each group moved to help the Infantry cadets set up, as they had more tents than the rest of us. The fliers were laid all around the encampment.

As the night moved on, we all settled into our tents with our small fires in the center to keep us warm. The bedrolls weren't the most comfortable, but they were better than the frozen ground itself. One by one, we moved from around the fire to our bedrolls, nestling in for the night. The plan for tomorrow was very clear. My father and some of the leadership would go to the palace, and we would only mass when we were called upon. My father was hopeful that they could eliminate and contain any conflict before we were needed, but was also pessimistic enough to believe that he would need our aid.

My mind raced with worry about what would happen the following day and how we would fare. If there were really over a thousand Nosferatu, we would be out of our depth. We would be overrun. My eyes got heavy as my brain was running every scenario of how tomorrow would play out. Deep down, I was terrified. I had been terrified when they attacked us, and it was going to be worse than that if we had to fight.

My eyes flickered, and it was still pitch black out, but something had woken me. I tried to look around. In the distance, I heard something.

Banging? No. Crying? Maybe. Talking? I wasn't sure. I lifted myself, perched on my elbows, closed my eyes, and focused on the sounds I was hearing. Running footsteps and mumbling. Something—no, someone was coming.

"ESME!" I shouted down the bond.

"It's not—there's something in the woods," she said, first annoyed, then worried.

"Wake up everyone!" I told her. I quietly moved out of my bedroll to pull my clothing and daggers—

ROARRRRRRRR

Everyone in my tent moved to their feet in seconds. I hadn't meant for her to sound an alarm, but to silently let everyone know. Outside the tent, footsteps trampled everywhere.

"I didn't mean to wake everyone like that. Now they know we know," I told her.

"It wouldn't have changed anything. They would have wanted us to all wake up and move," she said.

"Well, now everyone is panicking."

"Are you dressed yet? We have orders," she said. Her voice had changed to a serious tone.

"I'm coming. What are the orders?" I asked her. She was rarely serious, which meant whatever she was about to say, she didn't like.

"You won't like it either. Your father has ordered any professor, officer, anyone with a classified ability, Zane, and you to head straight to the palace. He wants us in the sky in five minutes," she said.

"What about here?"

"He has ordered all wing commanders to command, attack, and eliminate," she said.

"Oh."

"We don't have time to mull over what we don't like, why he or my mother makes the decisions they do," she said.

I finished tying up my boots, pulled my knit cap onto my head, and put my gloves on my fingers. I pushed through the canvas of the tent. The cold air smacked my face, momentarily taking my breath away. I started walking to the area behind the tent, where Esme had decided to bed down. She refused to be much further away, claiming her spot as soon as she could.

"Does Zane know?" I asked her.

"I don't know, I don't have a direct line to him, but I know someone who does," she said.

"Yeah, yeah," I said to her.

"Zane, where are you? Have you been told the orders?" I asked him.

"I am making my way to you. Everyone is running around panicking, and I'm trying to give little pep talks on my way to you," he said.

"You can ride on Esme with me, but we need to leave like now," I said to him.

"I'm sure she'll love that. I'm coming," he said.

Within a minute, he was there, and we were climbing atop Esme. He wrapped our arms around my waist and squeezed tightly.

"If shit goes south, and it might, we are getting the fuck out of there—"

"We can't leave the others to fend for themselves," I cut him off.

"You and I will be leaving here with each other, I don't care how that looks," he whispered in my ear, almost a growl.

Once we had fully made it in the air, we connected with the Riders who were ordered to launch. Below us, the bloodshed had started. Battle cries cried out. Shifters shifted and were howling. My father had relayed that they knew we were here, and we would do an aerial drop. My father made it clear that Zane and I would remain near him. If he had been so worried about me, why even have me come?

The palace was massive, much, much larger than the Ashwynd Palace. There were balconies all over, on multiple levels. It was dark, but I could see that there were knights all over the balconies, and moonlight glinted off their metal armor. My father had wanted us to drop onto the third-level balcony. He believed that he would be in the middle of the palace, rather than on the top or bottom levels.

Aerial drops meant fliers would bring their Riders close enough to where they needed to go, and the Rider would dismount in a running jump, usually using their wing. First-years hadn't even practiced that maneuver yet. Zane had decided we weren't going to be practicing out here either, and he would fly us onto the balcony. The fliers would take the outside perimeter and stay near if we needed to exfiltrate.

Esme flew in closer to the building, just as Zane gripped tightly, his wings flexed out hard, and our bodies left Esme as she moved downward. Within seconds, we were on the balcony, and knights immediately started attacking us. Zane drew a sword and went on the defensive. I immediately grabbed daggers for both hands. Both of us were swiping our blades.

I wanted to call upon my shadows and use them, but I knew I needed to save them for when I really needed them, and right now, I didn't need them.

One of the knights rushed and came running at me from my left, and another from in front of me. I was the easy target. I was the short female, but they were wrong. They weren't in sync, though. The one in front of me was moving more quickly. He moved swiftly, and I let my shadows go, just a little to grab him before he actually reached me. I took a step in and spun him in front of me, facing the other knight who had swiped his sword at the same moment. He sliced his arm clean off, and blood spurted everywhere. The other knight's eyes were wide in shock at what he had done. I let the other knight drop to the ground, moved forward, and drew my blade in one fluid motion across his neck. He grabbed his neck, but it wasn't enough. Blood spurted everywhere, and he fell to the floor.

I didn't have time to gloat on what I had done, because another knight was moving in closer from behind me. I spun and threw a dagger, landing directly in the center of his eyeball. His screech joined all the other screeching that was happening all around. Metal clanged against metal. Guttural groans came from every direction. Zane and my father were moving fluidly around, taking down body after body.

We cleared the outer balcony and moved inside the palace. As soon as my father kicked through the door, knights ran towards us. My father held his sword dripping with blood in his hand. He swiped left, severing the knight's head clear off before fully rotating around and doing it to another.

A couple of the knights locked their eyes onto me and came running at me, trying to bypass my father. I stood slightly behind my father and Zane. I didn't need to draw any blood. They had done it all. Knights covered the floor, and we continued moving forward.

"Your dad says that he's either on this floor or above us," Esme said.

I relayed the information to Zane through our bond. There was a reason he told me through Kim, who relayed it through Esme. The three of us moved together, and I was in the center between the two of them. Both of them were slightly angled outward, sometimes taking steps backwards as we moved to the left or right. I heard my dad take a deep inhale before moving us to the right. He had been smelling him.

King Fen is also a Shapeshifter.

It was what my father had told us that night that my powers exploded. Esme pointed out to me that I, too, could smell. I couldn't close my eyes here, and I need to learn to use my senses to my advantage. I inhaled deeply. The metallic smell of blood hit my nose. I could smell Zane. His distinct lavender and pine scent was mixed with sweat. Most of the Drusearon had a flowery smell, all different and unique, but specific to them. I took another inhale, because those weren't the smells I was looking for.

Shapeshifters had a unique musty smell, with a hint of wood. What was different was that each clan had its own unique woodsy smell, but I hadn't figured out where the smells belonged. I had barely figured out that was the difference I was smelling when I was getting the smell.

My dad had a hint of cherry wood mixed with the musty smell. I could smell him when I inhaled, but then it hit me—pine wood. I had smelled that before, but I wasn't sure who exactly, but I had recognized the smell on some of the Shapeshifters on campus.

I inhaled deeply again, this time Zane turned his head towards me and cocked his head.

"Auriella, what the fuck are you doing? That's the third—"

"I think I smell him," I told him.

I tapped my father's shoulder, and he looked over at me. I crinkled my nose at him, hoping he would pick up on what I was trying to say.

"Yes, he said that he does have a smidge of a pine smell," Esme said down the bond.

"A smidge, my ass. It's strong, the strongest I have smelled actually," I told her.

I didn't take deep inhales, but I kept breathing through my nose, focusing on that. I started to walk towards the pine smell. My dad pulled my arm, wanting to go to the left, and I shook my head and nodded forward. Then I tapped my finger on top of my nose. He didn't argue but instead followed my lead. I could hear rustling and metal meeting metal. I didn't know if we were coming out ahead or they were defeating us.

I had led them down a corridor, unsure of where the hell I was going, letting my nose lead the way, which sounded insane. Midway down the hall, there was a door on the right. Not only was the smell the strongest there, but I also heard muffled talking. It was very, very faint, but I heard them.

I nodded to the door that we stood in front of. My father held his finger up, motioning to wait. I cocked my head and narrowed my eyebrows at him, both of us trying to communicate silently.

"Foret, Zane's father, Pascal, Gile, and Melamora will be there within a few minutes," Esme relayed.

I then relayed that to Zane, and he, too, had been standing there confused on why we hadn't breached the door yet. Only moments had passed before the faint footsteps were heard. Even though I knew they were coming, I was on edge. I knew that we were in enemy territory, and I couldn't afford to assume anything.

Once the five of them stood next to us, we all gave each other a nod, and my father and Zane's father took a step forward. They turned to each other, both of them smiled at each other, and then they both nodded at the same time. Legs moved in the air, and both of their feet contacted the door. It flew open, and we all entered.

CHAPTER 34

I had only seen King Fen a few times over the years, but as soon as I saw the male who sat in the middle of the room with dark hair to his shoulders, I knew it was him. He had roughly thirty people around him, all with swords drawn. He stared at my father, at Zane's father, and just shook his head.

"Conri, did you not think I knew you stood against me?" King Fen asked.

"You need to stop this abomination, you can't just create monsters," my dad said.

"I can do whatever I want, I am the King after all," he said.

"We came to negotiate. Talk sense into you," Zane's father said.

"It won't do any good. The military doesn't have enough to handle the human continent—"

"Cut the shit, Aldric. It was you who had been attacking the outpost base, pinning this continent against the other," Foret said.

"Do you have evidence of this claim?" King Aldric Fen snapped. He stood up from his chair, tucked his hands behind his back, and started pacing.

"You surely didn't deny it, now did you?" Foret quipped.

"Hmm... well, whatever I don't do or do is none of your concern, because I *AM THE KING,*" he said.

"Yes, you are—as long as you are living," my father said.

"Is that what this?" he said, before letting out a deep, cynical laugh. "I have you outmatched every *fucking* day of the week."

"Hmm... Maybe or maybe not."

"Look around, Conri, you are outnumbered in just this room. There are only eight of you, and—" He looked past my father and at me, "—one is your daughter who, if I'm not mistaken, is still quite young."

"Go ahead and underestimate that one, I dare ya," my father snarled at him.

He walked around, making his way closer to me. My heart beat harder in my chest as he stared me down.

"Maybe... just maybe I killed the wrong parent that day. Your mom ran her mouth, but it looks like your dad was against me, too," King Fen said.

I cocked my head at him. He was baiting me, and every single cell inside my body knew it, but one more sideways comment and I knew I would be showing him what my father's comment meant. I didn't say anything to him.

"Did your little daddy tell you that he stood about where he is standing and watched me end her life? He didn't do—"

Shadows exploded from me, shot to him, and lifted him into the air by his throat just as I had done to my father weeks prior. This time, though, I was fully in control. I knew what I was doing. I squeezed around his throat tighter. Everyone in the room burst into chaos.

I felt pressure under the shadows holding his throat, but I squeezed harder—then he exploded underneath me and shifted into his wolf form. My shadows struggled to grasp him again and lost their hold on him as he shifted into a dark grey wolf and moved around the room. Several of his guards shifted into a wolf form all around the room. Everything was flashing, my brain was spinning, and I was struggling to focus.

Gile and Foret exploded into their wolf form, and now the room was more wolves than it was Fae. My father was swinging his sword left and right. Zane was gliding around the room.

Melamora was chanting and moving her fingers, dropping bodies—and wolves—left and right. I didn't know where to go or where to start, but Zane and my father had circled me, not letting anyone get close to me.

As I turned, shadows moved around the room. My eyes locked onto the guard who drove a dagger into Pascal's chest, and my stomach turned. My heart crushed inside my chest as he fell to the floor. Blood spurted out as he pulled the knife from his chest, eyes rolled back, and he fell to the floor. This male saved my life once, and now he was gone.

Zane's head swiveled, and I felt his grief wash through me like a battering ram—hard and heavy. One of the guards came rushing at Zane from the other side, and he lost focus. I rushed my shadows out and around the guard's neck, twisting one strand and the other in opposite directions, snapping his neck. He dropped before he even knew what happened.

Fear was gone. I was raging. They took one of our own.

"More than just one, this needs to be ended," Esme said.

I didn't have to ask questions. The urgency and concern in her voice said everything she didn't. We were being slaughtered out there. My father must have gotten the same message from Kim. His eyes widened, and he moved around the room in a beautiful fluid motion, his eyes locked onto the dark grey wolf darting around the room.

My dad was moving through slicing at anyone who came for him. Fen paused for a moment and locked in on my dad. He started darting for my dad. My stomach turned, heart beating double time. My dad drew his sword back on his right side over his shoulder and moved it swiftly down towards his left. Fen jumped on his hindlegs, narrowly missing, and lunged forward, mouth open. He locked onto my father.

My father fell to the ground with deep punctures on his torso. His shimmer flickered around his neck. It wasn't impenetrable. Blood was pooling everywhere. I wanted to run to him, I wanted to stop the bleeding, but instead, my eyes locked onto King Fen.

I let the beast roll out of me, clothes left shredded around my paws. A loud, deep, hungry howl came out of me, and I started running for him. He stood frozen over my father's bleeding body, his eyes locked onto mine. I was bigger than him, and he was fucking mine. I summoned my shadows and wrapped them around all four of his feet. Even if he wasn't standing there like he was staring at a fucking ghost, he wasn't going to move.

My heart thumped beneath my ribs so fast, it should have exploded out of my chest. Inside felt like an inferno. Within seconds, I was at him, and

I opened my mouth wide. He tried to move, tried to jerk, but I held him where he stood, unable to run. My teeth clenched around his throat, and I thrashed back and forth, his blood filling my mouth.

"AURIELLA!" Zane yelled.

I didn't stop. I kept thrashing my head back and forth before I felt his entire body go limp under my teeth. I did one final thrash as hard as I could, letting go of my shadows at his paws, and threw his body across the room.

I looked up at the ceiling and let out the loudest scream from deep within. It came out as a high-pitched howl. The entire room stilled. Every single wolf alive in that room dropped down in submission. They were submitting to me, but I didn't care about that. I looked down at my dad, whose eyes were wild and frantic. Blood continued seeping out of him.

I shifted back to my mortal form and wrapped both of us in shadows. I pressed my hands on the wounds, trying to will them to stop bleeding. His intestines were bulging out under my hands, and I knew he wouldn't make it. Tears fell from my eyes, and I wept so hard, so loud.

My chest felt like it was being crushed, and I was holding down the vomit. He saved me so many times, and I couldn't save him. This wasn't the end of his story. We had so many years left together.

"Auri," he cried out.

I could barely talk through the sobs.

"Dad, I love you. I'm so sorry for being a brat all—"

He gasped for breath. "Auri, I love you. You have been the greatest joy in my life. There is nothing I would change," he said through gasps and sobs.

"I'm so sorry," I pleaded with him.

I felt his pulse beneath my hands slowing down. His eyes started closing.

"No, Dad! Stay with me! Zane can take you to the Mender," I screamed.

His eyes flickered open. "No... time... You two... need to... leave... this... death... trap... I... will... always... love..."

His eyes closed, and nothing else came out. Nothing pumped beneath my blood-soaked fingers. He was gone. Dead. I was a fucking orphan. I was alone.

CHAPTER 35

Zane

I stood there in the room, a wolf between Auri and me, front paws down, nose to the ground. Tears ran down my face. No one in that room moved.

She let out the loudest, most Gods-awful scream I have heard from someone, the shadows she had wrapped around the two of them dissipated, and she lay across his chest completely naked. He was gone.

A dragon roared outside—loud and sad—Kim. His dragon felt his death, as deep as Auri had. The grief that washed over my entire body hit me so hard that I fell onto my knees. It overwhelmed me. I couldn't breathe. I couldn't speak. Only tears rolled down my cheeks. Her sobs were the only sound in that room.

I wanted to grab her and hold her, but I couldn't stand. It was Melamora's movement across the room that broke me out of the trance. She moved towards Auri. She pulled her coat off and wrapped it around her back, covering her up. She knelt and put her arm around her.

It should have been me doing that, but I was in so much pain. I sucked in a breath through the burning pain in my lungs. I closed my eyes and built a shield between her and me. I needed to block her out some. It was the only way I could stand. I took another breath, filling my lungs. I let it out. I stood up, brushing my hands on my pants, and walked to her.

I collapsed next to her and pulled her into my arms. She sobbed so hard, she could barely breathe. It broke a part of me, not being able to fix this.

I wanted to take this pain from her. I would shoulder every ounce of it I could. I, too, had lost Pascal minutes earlier, and yet it wasn't the same. He was a mentor, but she lost her only parent.

I held her tightly against my chest, her tears pooling onto my shirt. I didn't know what to do, and at the same time, I knew we shouldn't stay here. She may have just made every Werewolf in that room kneel to her, but the cadets outside of this room and palace were being attacked. They were none the wiser.

"What the fuck happened in here?" the deep voice said.

My head shot to the doorway, and Benning stood there. His eyes wide, he stared at me, at Auri in my arms, then at Conri's body next to us. Auri remained sobbing in my arms uncontrollably. Everyone in the room but the Werewolves turned and stared at him, but no one spoke.

"Someone *fucking* talk, because from this point of view, the *FUCKING* king and the general of the Military—my cousin—is dead!" he shouted.

He was the second in command—now the first in command. His eyes moved around the room. The Werewolves hadn't moved from where they knelt to Auri after she let out the loudest howl anyone had ever heard. The ground shook in the palace. Surely, it was the reason he was now standing in the doorway.

"Why the hell are they kneeling?" he shouted.

Melamora pulled her hand off of Auri's back and stood up. She had been using magic to try to calm her. She walked towards him.

"It's simple. Fen killed Conri, Auri shifted into—," she took in a breath, "the *most beautiful black wolf,* and then killed Fen. All the wolves, for whatever reason, dropped to their knees at her and haven't moved a muscle since. We are all in shock, mourning our leader and our friends, because if you didn't see, Pascal is also dead," she told him, her voice getting angrier with each word.

"She's the Queen, now," he muttered.

"I'm not exactly privy to how the Shapeshifters' hierarchy works, but *she* just lost her only fucking parent at the ripe age of twenty, can we not say that yet?" Melamora seethed.

"You're right, that's neither here nor there, we need to fucking go, or we won't have anyone left. The cadets have killed quite a bit, but we have also lost a lot of us," Benning said, then cocked his head around Melamora, "—and you need to get her up and fighting, because all of these Shapeshifters that were once loyal to him are now loyal to her."

My eyes widened at him. How the fuck was I supposed to do that? *Hey Auri, I'm gonna need you to forget that you just lost your father and get up and fight.* Yeah fucking right. Gile had moved next to us before I even had a chance to speak.

"Auriella, I need you to listen to me, sweetie. I know everything hurts, and you want to do nothing more but lie here and cry. Right now, you have to get up. You have to bottle that down for the good of the college, your friends, and your fellow cadets. Please, Auri, we need you," Gile said, low and gentle.

I continued rubbing her back, reassuring her that I was there. She sucked in a huge, ragged breath.

"I don't want to," she said, her voice so very broken.

My head shot to the door, to the running footsteps that came down the hall. Benning took a step backwards into the hall. He raised his hand, motioning to whoever was running down the hall.

"Whatever it is, cadets, it's not the time," he told them.

"If you want her to get up and do what she needs, let us in," the familiar voice said—Lili.

"Let them in," I said to him.

It was the first time I had said something since I screamed her name to stop. I didn't want her to kill him and have to live with that, but there was no stopping her. He killed both of her parents, only poetic justice for her to kill him. Benning had moved to the side, and Lili and Alex both ran to the room. Both of their faces were pale, and though their fliers told them her father was dead and she needed them, there was no preparation for seeing the man who was like an uncle to you lie on the ground dead.

Lili knelt beside us. "I know asking you to bottle down another parent's death right now sounds heinous, but Auri, our friends are dying by the dozen right now. We won't have cadets to return if you don't get up," she told her.

"Auriella, you can do this, my love, and after, we will go so fucking far away—wherever you want," I told her, because they were right. Everyone in this room needed to be out there fighting, and she had the power to turn some of them on our side.

"I'm leaving because they need me out there, and I am ordering every person in this room to get the hell up and fight. If she wants to lie here with her father, let her, but everyone else is leaving," Benning ordered. "Now."

Lili looked at me, unsure of what she should do.

"Please, Auri," I pleaded with her again.

She didn't say anything, simply stood up. She wrapped Melamora's trench coat around her. She looked around the room at the floor, eyes cold but lost. Her eyes then locked onto King Fen. She stared deeply, furrowing her eyebrow, before lifting her hand and giving him her single middle finger. She then knelt to where her torn clothes and daggers were. She pulled them close to her chest, and tears fell down her cheeks.

Everyone in the room stared at her, saying nothing. She didn't know it, or maybe she did, but she was in control here. Melamora walked over to her, knelt in front of her, and held her hands out to the clothing.

"May I?" she asked.

Auri handed her the clothing, and within a minute, Melamora chanted something and handed the clothes back, sewn back together. Shadows erupted out of her, wrapping her in solid black. They faded back, but stayed circling her feet. She stood there completely dressed, eyes fixated on the floor—on her father. She knelt to him, grabbed the daggers that were still on his side, and sheathed them in her own dagger belt. She scooted forward a little more and grabbed the necklace that was tucked under his shirt, where a ring was on the chain. She wrapped her hand around it and grabbed it, breaking it free of his neck, and then shoved it in her pocket. She kissed two of her fingers and placed them onto his forehead, dragging her hand down his face, closing his eyes.

She stood up and looked around the room at everyone. Her eyes were puffy and bloodshot red. She was there, but she wasn't there at all. It was like she was leaving part of her soul on the floor.

"Let's fucking go," she said, before turning towards some of the Werewolves in the same position. "I think you think I am your Queen, but I don't know who I am right now, but I need you to do the right thing and take down every Nosferatu that lives. That is my order. I heard you all in my head. That's the only thing I can give you," she said through tears and sobs.

CHAPTER 36

Their thoughts had poured into my mind from the moment I howled after killing King Fen. They weren't Zane's or Esme's. Although they, too, were in my head. I didn't have anything left in me to answer them. I didn't even want to stand, but I knew I had to. I had started walking towards the door before I knew what I had to do. The shadows no longer fully disappeared. I tried to will them in, but they wouldn't.

"Two of you shift back to your mortal form or whatever, and secure my father and Pascal on his dragon, she will be perched on the top of this building," I said to the wolves, before heading back through the door.

"I'll tell her," Esme said.

Esme was waiting for me where I had left her earlier. She had been doing aerial attacks, but returned when she felt my grief. Everyone in that room was on my heels as we all exited.

As we passed a room, guards came running out. At first, I had thought they were coming after us, but they followed along. We neared the balcony, passing the bodies that we fell—that my father fell—earlier. It smacked me in the chest again that he wasn't here. He wasn't leading me—leading us. Tears streamed down my cheek, but I couldn't let this consume me right now. Later. I needed to focus.

"Are there hippogriffs out there?" I asked Esme.

"I don't think I saw any."

"Every cadet who can needs to get on a flier and get in the air. Then we burn everything that remains on the ground," I said.

Benning was in front of me, came to a dead stop, and turned around.

"You know the wolves won't get on the fliers," he said.

"They rode them here," I scoffed back.

"That was different. They are half-feral now, and in full pack survival mode," he said.

"They need to put their fucking pride to the side if they want to live. I'm a half-feral right now, and guess what? I'm about to get on a *fucking* dragon," I said, seething.

"I know you just lost your father, but watch your tone. You aren't in charge of the military—"

"Do you have a better idea? Because where I am standing, Nosferatu can't fly, and we are now down to hundreds out there. The wolves *will* listen to me," I said.

"She's right, Benning. We need to get every cadet in the air, however that looks," Melamora said.

"Fine," he said.

"Esme, tell—"

"Already on it. Kamban and his dragon are almost back to camp."

"Melamora, you can ride with me."

I didn't say anything else and walked out onto the balcony. Esme hovered right next to the railing. She glided in a little closer, and I took off in a run, jumping onto the rail and then onto her neck. I gripped my arms around her and then used the shadows to slide me right onto her back. Melamora stood there staring at me. I reached my shadows out, wrapped them around her waist, lifted her into the air, and behind me on Esme.

"Thanks," she whispered, "not sure I'm as nimble as you youngins'."

"Let's go," I said to Esme, before patting her.

Zane and his father roved the rest of them to the tents. The rest of the Riders who had come to the palace had already left on their fliers. While Kim had been experiencing immense grief, she had told every flier that Fen and my father had been killed, and they needed to retreat and go back to camp.

The morning light started to fill the sky as we headed back to camp. It was only a few-minute flight from the Palace. Below us, Werewolves were running in their wolf forms towards the camp. As we got closer to the camp, Nosferatu were running through the woods towards them. Not to attack, but to meet them—once on the same side. Before they knew what was going on, the wolves eliminated every one of them.

I felt a tinge of happiness watching. It had been a shitty day, but to know they followed the order and were helping us helped. I couldn't let myself go down the path of how we got where we were. I would let it destroy me, but not right this moment.

We flew over where the camp was. It was chaotic below us. Esme flew lower, allowing us to get the best sight advantage. I could still see cadets running around, and Nosferatu. I needed to get down there and help get these cadets in the air.

"I would strongly advise against it, but you'll just jump again. So, I will land," Esme said.

"I'm landing to help, you can stay on her back if you want," I told Melamora.

"No, I will assist, as that is my duty to protect all cadets," she told me.

Within a minute, we landed, the ground shaking below her. I dismounted with grace. I pulled one of my daggers out, making sure to leave my father's sheathed. I started running full speed at the Nosferatu that was on top of a cadet feeding on them. One swipe through, and he left his head rolling on the snowy ground.

"Why the hell are there so many cadets still on the ground, Esme?"

"I don't know, the order was relayed, but we can't telepathically talk to the Infantry cadets or Shapeshifters."

That explained the chaos. I looked back at Melamora, who was trying to take down the two Nosferatu who were attacking her. Not today, mother fuckers. I bolted to her, my shadows rushing ahead. I pushed my shadows into the chest of one and pulled out their heart, crushing it with my shadows. Melamora briefly looked at me before driving her dagger into the other's chest.

"I need you to amplify your voice and tell every cadet to get on a flier, and I don't care which one. They have minutes before we take the sky and scorch this place," I told her.

She nodded before closing her eyes and rubbing her fingers together. She opened her eyes and stared at me.

"Every cadet needs to get on whatever flier they can, NOW!" She projected across the entire courtyard.

The cadets and Nosferatu on the ground went frantic. A group of fifty or more turned their way to Melamora and me. Shit. They looked at us like we were the beacon in the dark, running in our direction.

"Zane, I need a little assistance," I said down the bond.

Within seconds, he was next to me.

"It's time to show the world just what we can do," he said.

"What? What does that mean?" Melamora muttered.

Neither of us answered; instead, he interlocked his hand with mine, and we stepped forward as one. We both had shadows streaming out of us. Melamora gasped behind us. I broke my shadows into many tendrils, sending them towards the hearts of the Nosferatu coming at us. Zane did the same thing. The most tendrils I had been able to do were ten, but all at once, all ten of them entered a chest and pulled their lifeless heart out. Zane had only been able to break his into five, but he got six today, and six bodies dropped. We didn't celebrate. No, we kept going for all of them. After all of them fell, we moved deeper into the woods. Dropping Nosferatu after Nosferatu.

Cadets stared in shock. Professors stopped in their tracks, mouths agape. Most of them had learned what *I* could do, but they hadn't seen what *we* could do. Zane and I, hands held tightly, had shadows all around both of us, shooting from both of us like spider webs.

Among all of the dead Nosferatu, there were also dead cadets everywhere. Some of them had risen again, and if we waited too long, they would all rise, and even Zane and I couldn't handle that.

We stood in the center of the camp, taking down any Nosferatu who came for cadets trying to get on fliers. The ground shook as each flier launched into the air. Some of them had four and five cadets, holding on for their lives. Some of those fliers lost their own Riders and still chose to save the cadets that remained.

Zane and I kept going after the Nosferatu, but my shadows weren't reaching as much. I lost two of my tendrils, and he had lost four of his. I knew I was taking too much. I kept pushing myself. My entire body started sweating. The shadows dissipated from Zane. Gone. I only had one. I could do this. There were only a few cadets and fliers left on the ground. My entire head spun. Vomit spewed out of my mouth. Fuck. Zane let go of my hand.

"They're almost all in the air. Get back here. They can fight for themselves," Esme said down the bond.

I looked at Zane and told him, before he grabbed me and pulled me into him and roved us back to Esme. Melamora had been standing near her with two cadets—one was in rough shape.

"I'll take him," Zane said, before grabbing the injured one.

I helped Melamora and the female on Esme's back before I started to climb up her—

Esme blew out a huge fireball. Melamora grabbed the cadet in front of her tightly. I turned around, and two Nosferatu lay on the ground, charred.

"Thanks," I said, then climbed onto her. Every ounce of my body ached. Shadows no longer circled my feet.

She launched into the sky with the three of us. Once in the sky, all the Phoenixes and Dragons started burning the entire ground below us. We hoped every cadet who was alive got out, but we didn't know for sure. There were wolves on the outer edges that ran deep into the other direction. They weren't cadets and refused to get on with a flier. They all knew, get out or be charred.

Once the ground was nothing more but ash, we started flying back towards the school. The cadet and Melamora stayed silent. Completely silent the entire five and a half hours it took. Some of the fliers moved much more slowly this time around, most of them having more cadets on them than when we arrived. We had no idea how many we lost. We had no idea what we would be going back to. Zane had roved the cadet back to the campus, and then roved back and flew alongside Esme and me.

"What are we going back to?" I finally asked him, we were about thirty minutes out, and I finally decided I needed to know.

"Actually, it's not bad. They were attacked, yes, but it looks like they held their own well."

I felt a huge sigh of relief lift off my shoulders.

"Esme, I'm not staying there."

"I know," she said.

"How?" I asked.

"I know everything."

"Then where are we going?"

"You guys haven't decided yet?" Esme said.

"Are you coming with?" I asked her.

"I'm offended you would ask that?"

"It's complicated for you," I told her. It wasn't just about following me wherever we went. She had Lakung, and he was bonded to a rider. She would be abandoning her Vale.

"No, it's actually not. Knoxx didn't make it during this last attack. Lakung will follow wherever we go, and fuck the Vale, I do what I want."

My heart skipped a beat. Fuck. Lili was going to be sad. She really liked him, and she would be learning about his death when we arrived back. It also ached for Lakung. Losing a Rider was catastrophic to the flier.

"I don't want to stick around for good-byes. I can't be here. I don't want to be here. My father told me to get the hell away from here, and for once in my fucking life, I'm listening to him."

"Okay, whatever you want. Wherever you want..." she said.

We landed in the chaotic flight field. I think every healer and Mender was standing outside, running to anyone who looked injured. They may not have known of our plans, but it was clear they knew something now.

I helped Melamora and the cadet off of Esme. I was weak. My legs and arms ached. Sleep was calling my name. I wasn't just physically tired. I was emotionally tapped.

"It's time to take me far away from here as you promised," I told Zane down the bond.

"I know," he said.

My legs were buckling beneath me, my head rushed with heat, and my stomach churned. This was burnout.

"Esme, we will be at a very small coastal village, at the very Northeastern edge of Yebel. Nearly cut off by the sea. I am roving us there, she's expended too much," he whispered so low, I barely heard it.

She moved her head up a little and let out a little puff of steam at him. She then moved her nose to me and pressed it into my chest. She moved her head very gently.

"I'll see you soon, my little shadow wolf," she said down the bond.

"I... love... you," I told her, before my legs collapsed below me.

Before I hit the ground, Zane grabbed me into his arms, and the world went dark.

CHAPTER 37

Zane

I roved us right outside of Northhold Outpost, and then to the cabin outside of Erlösung. This cabin belonged to our family. When my father would travel to see the villages on this side of the continent, we would often stay here. It was right off the sea, hidden amongst the mountains. It is nearly too treacherous for anyone to access by land without flying in or having extreme mountain climbing abilities. There was boat access, but not many people boated this far north.

My father chose this spot because it was safe and unknown. When I had gone home to talk to him, right before the Nosferatu attacked the first time, we discussed sharing my ability with her father. I also asked him about this place, asked him if we needed a place to leave and start over, could this be it?

He didn't ask any questions and instantly said yes. I didn't have to explain—hell, he didn't even want me to tell him anything else. He wanted to have plausible deniability. The military would be in shambles, and while most of them knew we were alive, most of them also heard her father's last pleas for her to get out of there. While we had both signed up and agreed to go there, we weren't actually conscripted to be there, like the majority of them were.

It was a beautiful two-story cabin, built of Cypress wooden logs. It backed up against the mountain, and in the front, there was a covered porch. Inside was simple, a living area with a stone fireplace, dining room, kitchen, an office, a small bathroom, and a small library. Upstairs, there was a primary bed chamber with a bathroom suite and three smaller rooms. As a child, it was one of the few places where we shared rooms. None of us complained. We spent nights playing silly games on the floor.

When we were here in the summer, we spent every hour the sun was out swimming. The water was calm here and beautiful. Once you stepped off the porch, the most beautiful white sands lined the ground until you hit the sea. There was a small rock bluff that extended out from the mountainside, which my siblings and I would jump off of. Although during winter, the ground was usually covered in snow.

Auri remained unconscious as I laid her in the extra-large custom bed in the primary bed chambers. My father had it made for him and my mother to accommodate their wings. She looked so small in the bed. I sat in the chair next to the bed and stared at her, memorizing every single freckle on her face. Her chest rose and fell, slowly. I didn't know how long she would need to rest. I was in uncharted territory.

I went and sat on the porch in the rocking chair. When my father had the cabin built, he had them build log rocking chairs. They sat on the porch overlooking the sea. It was quiet here. Peaceful. I sat there watching the sun set until the stars took over the sky. She remained asleep.

I tidied the house of the dust that had accumulated. I wanted to boat into town and get the necessities for the house, but I couldn't leave her until she woke. I finally crawled into the bed behind her and pulled her body into mine. I propped up on my elbow and stared at her. I gently moved her hair from the side of her face back. I studied her crescent and star birthmark behind her ear. It wasn't often that I got to study her. We usually fell fast asleep in each other's arms. The small candles that lit the room were the perfect amount—illuminating her face.

Every part of me hoped she would be fine, but I knew she wouldn't. I knew that she would go through immeasurable grief once it really set in. I wasn't there when she lost her mother, but I knew that it took parts of her that she never got back.

Morning came way too fast, light filtering in from the outside. She had barely moved while she slept. I checked her breathing multiple times because she was so still. I slowly left the bed, tucking the blanket around her. I went downstairs to the library to find some paper to write her a letter. I needed to get us food, soda water, and juice.

My Dearest Auri,

We are in a very secluded cabin in the far Northeastern part of Yebel, in the Drusearon Mountains. If you wake up before I return, I have gone to gather food and supplies. Be back soon.

Zane

I placed it next to her on the nightstand before I left in the small boat that was docked. I wanted to get us plenty of supplies, since the cabin had been unoccupied for the last few years. The small village wasn't far down the shoreline. It was a small and quaint village. There was a square road, with little shops around. Most of the Drusearons lived above the shops they owned. It was the only village with shopping in this little arm. The Drusearons that lived up here wanted seclusion, welcoming it, living in the mountains, flying where they needed.

As I paddled to the shore, I tied the little boat to one of the open docks. Someone walked towards me, eyes squinting, wings hung high behind him. He tilted his head to the side a little bit. I walked towards him. He looked familiar, but I didn't know who he was.

"Little Braegon?" he asked.

"Whose asking?" I said.

"I'm a friend of your father's. I haven't seen you since you were a little boy."

"Oh, sorry, I don't remember—"

"I run the little butcher store on the corner," he said.

"Oh, I think I remember you. Sorry, it's been a while. You will be seeing me around a lot more. I'll be in the shop shortly," I told him, before smiling at him.

"I'm down here taking a little break, but if I'm not back, my wife is in there."

I gave him a nod before walking up the little bank from the docks and into the village. It hadn't changed much since I had last been there. There was a little general store on the right-hand corner that was filled with various foods and beverages. Next to them was a small bakery, baking daily sourdough bread. Every day, they baked something extra. It alternated between cakes, muffins, fruit pies, cookies, or whatever they dreamed up. There was also the butcher shop, blacksmith, a tavern, and a postal store.

I got us enough food, drinks, and supplies like toiletries and oil for the lanterns to last at least a week. I wanted to minimize going into the village, although I knew most of the people wouldn't know us, I didn't want to risk any of them if anyone came looking for us.

She was still sleeping when I arrived back home, in the same position as I left her. I threw away the letter I had left and put away all of the groceries. Just as I had finished grinding the green beans for coffee, something shook the entire outside ground. It startled me, before I quickly made my way to the porch. As soon as I opened the door, I saw her—Esme. She sat on the snow-covered beach, fluffy snow all over her legs and neck.

I gave her a nod. I wished I could converse with her as Auri did. I know that she could hear me, but I needed to know what to do with Auri. I walked out to her, just as I got close enough, she shook like a dog and threw snow all over me.

"She hasn't woken yet. I don't know why, though," I told her.

She moved her head in a serpentine way.

"I don't know what—"

Another set of loud wingbeats was approaching, sending my eyes to the sky, looking around.

"Expecting company?" I asked her.

Her eyes blinked a few times too fast before she lifted her head up and down. Well, I guess she could answer me in some way.

It wasn't just one set of wingbeats. It was two dragons flying side by side. Fuck, Esme. Only Esme and Lakung were supposed to know our location. I recognized the large grey with black dapples. Her mother. Right behind her was a navy-blue dragon with a Rider on their back.

"You know the less that knows, the safer we are?"

She blew a puff of steam at me.

Within a minute, Kim and the navy-blue dragon—Veyra—with Lili in tow landed next to Esme. Between the three of them, they took up most of the shoreline.

"Oh, Lili, you're not supposed to be here," I told her.

"For all intents and purposes, I'm not. I refused to let Esme leave—well, that's not completely true because I don't control her, of course—but you know what I'm saying. I wanted to know where you two went."

"We were disappearing, she wasn't supposed to tell you," I said, before giving Esme narrowed eyes.

"Yes, but don't you think she needs her best friend while she goes through the unimaginable?"

"Maybe... but I'm not sure when she will wake—"

"What do you mean?"

"She burnt out," I said, my eyes dropped to the ground.

"When? How?"

"When we were fighting the Nosferatu. She gave it everything, and then she collapsed once we got to the college. She has been asleep since," I said.

"Oh," she said.

"What do you know about burnout?"

"I haven't experienced it."

"I didn't ask that," I snarled at her.

"If someone hits that point, they may be out for several days... or longer... Kim says that when Conri burned out once, and he was asleep for five days," she said.

"Gods..." I mumbled.

"Yeah, not only did her magic deplete, but she also went through serious trauma," she said.

"You don't—no, you can't stay here."

"Well... Zane... There really isn't a college to return to right now."

"What do you mean?" I asked, confused.

"It is complete chaos, and no one knows what is happening. There isn't a king of our continent, no general of the army. Professors are dead. We were all told to go home and wait to be summoned to return. I then convinced Veyra to convince Kim and Esme to bring me to her."

"I see..."

I didn't realize what happened or what would happen following so many leaders falling. All the Dukes were probably hashing it out to appoint the next King. Not that I actually cared about any of that, or what was happening outside of what was happening in that room.

"Where is Lakung?"

She looked at Esme, eyes filled with sorrow. "There is a small Vale south of here, he went there... to mourn."

"I'm... um... sorry, Lili," I told her, remembering that Auri had told me that she and Knoxx had gotten close.

"It sucks..."

"Um... well... I guess you can stay in one of the rooms. And the dragons—" I looked around her and at all three "—can stay here..."

"Thanks for the hospitality, Zane," Lili said.

***

Six days had passed since we arrived at the cabin. Lili had taken up residence in one of the rooms my sisters used to stay in. We both spent most of our days reading in the library, hopeful to come up with some quicker way to wake Auri up. She slept profoundly, barely moving from the spot I had placed her. She spiked a fever for a couple of days, her body sweating profusely. Lili and I alternated staying in the room with her. We both talked to her, reassuring her that she was okay.

The day prior, the temperature started rising outside. Lili had decided she would head into the village today to restock our pantry. She opted to take the boat instead of riding Veyra, trying to minimize people knowing about us. The dragons had come and gone throughout the days. Lili had said Esme was anxious, but could feel Auri's presence getting stronger each day.

"Hey!" I heard Lili shout from outside.

She arrived back, and I assumed she needed assistance carrying groceries. I left the library and walked onto the porch.

"By all the fucked stars," I mumbled under my breath.

Next to the little boat was a Keelboat that had two Drusearons in it, but that wasn't what really got my attention. It was the fawn-colored cow that had a fawn-colored calf at her side. It was the crate that I could see fowls in. It was the two sheep—one white and one brown—standing in the boat. It was the three goats—one buck, one doe, and one baby—standing there looking at me.

I stood frozen on the porch—speechless. What the hell were we to do with all of these? How the hell did she get this? What did she barter for this?

"You gonna come help?" she shouted, staring at me.

I left the porch and started her way. I recognized one of the males as the one who owned the butcher store in town. The younger male must have been his son. He was a near twin of him, but younger.

"What have you done, Lili?" I exclaimed.

"Oh, Sir Braegon, I thought your wife—"

"No, not wife, not anything, just a friend," I cut him off.

"That's what they all say," his son muttered.

"His future wife is in the house, so what he says is true," Lili said.

"Oh, sorry for assuming," he said.

"It's alright... now tell me what my dear friend has brought back," I said, giving Lili a look.

"She played some hard bargains and stated that you guys needed some livestock for the homestead. I couldn't exactly tell the lady no," he said.

"I guess we could use some livestock," I said. I was so far out of my comfort zone. I saw plenty of animals growing up at the market, or at my friend's farms, but we never had anything other than horses.

"I got groceries, hay, and ground grains, as well as some wood to build shelters," Lili said.

"And don't forget the living animals," I said, letting out a nervous chuckle.

"The cow is in milking, she will give us fresh milk and feed her calf, which we can butcher later on—"

"Wait, you want me to raise it—no, no, no—you want Auri to raise this calf and then eat it?" I let out a full laugh.

"She might not be able to, you'll have to," she said.

"No." In no part did I want to be on the bad side of Auri's.

"Well, anyway, the cow has milk in addition to what the calf is eating. The sheep have wool, the goats are—" she let out a laugh, "—good eating. Of course, the dunghill fowl for eggs," she said.

"While this has been fun watching you be in shock, we need to get this unloaded and get back to the shop to help Ma," the butcher's son said.

"Okay, well, let's do this then," I said.

He grabbed a small wooden ramp and fashioned it to the boat, and then to the dock. They wrapped a rope around each one and led them up the ramp, onto the dock, and onto solid ground. We carried all the materials from their boat and Lili's up to the house.

All the animals except the calf, buckling, and dunghill fowls had small bells fashioned around their necks. As they moved all around the land, little bells sounded. It was different, but peaceful at the same time, watching them move around. Hopefully, Esme didn't think they were her snacks.

After I got everything put away, I headed up the stairs to check on Auri. I knew she was still sleeping, but it hadn't stopped me from checking on her several times during the day. As I walked into the room, I stopped in my tracks.

Shadows swirled around her ankles. She had moved a little since I had last checked on her. She was still sleeping, but this was a good sign. I sat in the chair next to her and grabbed her hand. It was warm again, but not feverish.

After her fever had broken, her skin cooled down and stayed that way. Kim assured all of us that this was normal and the way the body protects itself. While I hadn't wanted Lili to be here, I was grateful to have someone who could communicate with Kim and Esme.

"I sure hope you like farm creatures. Your friend brought a bunch home. Apparently, we need to be self-sufficient," I told her, before letting out a laugh.

It was then that the hand I held in my hand squeezed mine back. My heart skipped a beat or three, and my stomach felt like a thousand butterflies were moving about.

"Auri," I pleaded to her.

Gods. I wanted her to be awake, to be okay. I had prayed every night to Betha to let her be alive and well. She squeezed my hand again. Oh, thank the Gods.

Her eyes moved under her eyelids, and I knew she was trying to open them. I let go of her hand and pulled the curtain closed in the room, making it a little bit darker. I didn't know if it would help, but I was willing to try anything to see her emerald eyes. I grabbed her hand and squeezed her tightly.

"Come on, love, I'm here. Lili, Esme, Kim, Lakung, and Veyra are here, and you are now the owner of eleven animals."

Her eyelids shot up, and she stared at me with her wild and wide-open green eyes.

CHAPTER 38

Eleven animals. My eyes burst open. I wasn't sure if I was dreaming him saying that or if I actually heard that. My eyes burned from the light, even though he had made the room darker. I squinted at him, trying to focus on him. I stared into his baby blues as he stared back into mine. One small tear escaped the corner of his eyes and ran down his cheek.

"How long have I been out?" I asked, my voice sounded rough and crackly.

"Six days, it's Sunday," he told me.

I didn't say anything. My throat was on fire. My eyes finally stopped burning, and I could open them widely. I dropped my gaze and started to look around the room. We were not anywhere I had been before. The room was large, but not oversized like at his home. It was simple. There was a bed, small night tables, two dressers, two chairs in the corner, and three doors—two of them were closed and the other open. There was a little hall with more doors.

"I need water," I told him down the bond.

He leaned over and grabbed the water-filled jar that sat on the nightstand.

"Here," he said, placing the jar in my hands.

I gulped the water down quickly. It felt so cool and soothing on my throat. Everything was groggy and confusing.

I cleared my throat. "What happened?"

"You burnt out," he said softly.

"Where's Esme?"

"Either flying here or outside, staring at your new animals like a meal," he said.

"I'm outside, and well, they do look yummy, but I wouldn't," she said.

"Where are we exactly?" I asked.

"A small cabin in the far Northeastern part of Yebel, in the mountains," he said.

"Oh," I said.

I wasn't sure what to say or how to respond or even how to feel. I closed my eyes to try to remember what had happened. It all flashed back—me killing the King, my father dying beneath my fingers.

"My dad is dead," I said, and tears fell down my cheeks.

"I'm sorry, Auri," he whispered. His gaze never left mine. He stared at me like the times I was in the infirmary.

I didn't have words. It hit me hard in the chest, and cries poured out of me. What was I going to do? My family was gone.

"You have family, we are all here for you," Esme said.

I *knew* that was true, but it didn't make the emptiness that had settled deep in my gut feel better. I was an orphan, and the same person killed both of my parents. I *killed* him, and I didn't feel bad about it. I'd do it again and again. He deserved it.

Zane reached up and wiped the tear from my cheek with his thumb. I could say I was okay, but I wasn't—I was far from it. I closed my eyes and just let the tears fall down my face.

"How about a shower? It's not as grand as either of mine at campus or my home, but it is nice," he said.

I nodded my head yes. It was all I could offer him. He swooped me up into his arms and walked to one of the doors that had been closed. There wasn't a handle. He pushed the door with his foot, and it swung open. There was a shower on one wall, and a large oval tub next to it. It wasn't grand, but both were still nicer than most of the bathing rooms I had growing up.

"Think you can stand?" he asked.

I nodded. He gently lowered me down, and my feet hit the cold wood floors. Putting weight on my legs felt weird. Like I had worked out too hard, or when I had gotten injured during the pass. They trembled underneath me. He kept one of his arms around my waist as he reached in and turned on the hot water.

Steam quickly filled the air, my tears slowed down, but didn't stop. He pulled off the gown he had dressed me in at some point while I was out. He walked me into the shower, his clothes still on. He stood behind me, his arms wrapped tightly around my torso.

He didn't fill the space with conversations, just letting me take everything in. My eyes closed, and I drifted back in time, where my father held me tightly and rocked me to sleep from the nightmares. When he brought me on so many rides with Kim. When he helped me exact my revenge against my assailant. When he chased guys out of my room. When he chased Alex from my room, or the times he used his ability on me. All the memories—good, bad, sad, and funny rushed in.

My legs gave out, and sobs escaped my mouth. Tears poured out of me. The hot water washed down my face. Zane held me tightly, then moved us to sit on the bottom of the shower. He pulled my hair back away from my face and caressed my cheek with his thumb.

I sobbed for a long while in the shower before the tears stopped, and I was able to breathe. I became numb. I stood up on my own, washed my hair and body. Once I stood without support, Zane stripped his clothing off, throwing them in the bathtub. He helped me get out and get dressed. Lili had brought all the things from my room. I pulled on my black leather riding pants and a black long-sleeve shirt.

"I'm ready," I told him.

I wasn't really, but I knew that if I sat here alone, I would just cry. I wasn't even sure there were any tears left in me to cry. My head floated in a space of pain.

I walked out of the room, taking everything in. The layout of the cabin. I made my way down the stairs, and the door outside was across from the staircase. I turned my head to the right, where a large library filled with books and empty canvases on the paint stands. To the right was the sitting room where chairs were placed around a table.

I opened the door and walked out. Sitting in the rocking chair staring at me was Lili. She smiled at me, the one where I knew she was happy to see me, but she knew I was heartbroken. The pity smile.

"Hey, Lil," I said.

"Hey," she said softly.

I looked out the porch and gasped. It was breathtaking. All you could see was water. Mountains surrounded the other three sides. The snow melted off the sand. At the water's edge, Esme stood there, next to her mom. I continued taking everything in, including the cow and her baby roaming around, the goats and their baby, the two sheep, and the four dunghill fowl running around.

"Eleven animals, Liliana? I think you have elevated your animal gifting," I said.

She shrugged.

"What does that mean exactly?" Zane asked.

"Oh... she didn't tell you? Well, when my mom died, she brought me a goose," I said.

"Yeah... her dad didn't approve and made us rehome him because he chased him around," she said, before she let out a laugh.

A small laugh escaped. I remembered that day vividly, and then a full burst of laughter rolled out of me so hard. Jim was his name, and he thought I was his mom, and he chased my dad anytime I wasn't around. As I recalled, my father running all around outside from Jim, I laughed harder and harder. Zane and Lili both joined me in laughing.

I let out a sigh of relief. "I needed that memory, that was funny."

"I opted out of a goose this time, didn't want a repeat with Zane."

All three of us burst into laughter again.

"Thanks for that, but what are we going to do with them?"

"I don't know. Feed them, and they shall reward you with food in return," Lili said.

"I can't raise them, and then eat them, Lili," I told her. She was crazy if she thought that. I had never had the heart to hurt an animal.

"I told you," Zane said.

"What will happen to them when we leave here?" I said.

Both of their heads dropped to the ground.

"What?" I asked

"I didn't have plans for us to leave here, unless you wanted, but this is our home," Zane said.

"There's something else?" I asked.

"The recent newspaper suggests it's best to stay here for a long while. They are looking for you. You killed the King."

"What else does it say?" I asked.

"I'll go grab it..." she said, before standing up and walking inside.

It didn't take her long before she came back and handed me the newspaper.

The King and General of the Army are dead!

The details of what happened are unclear; however, it has been confirmed that King Aldric Fen and General Conri Blackcreek have been killed in some type of conflict. It is believed that Conri Blackcreek's daughter, Auriella Blackcreek, murdered King Fen. Several other professors and cadets from Sandorg War College, guards, and nearby residents also lost their lives. The state of Sandorg War College is currently unknown and has been temporarily closed while the 7 Dukes confer and decide on another king. King Aldric Fen left no surviving spouse, parents, or children. General Blackcreek only left his surviving daughter, Auriella Blackcreek.

I read the last line over and over again. It was the visual reminder that I was alone. The letter didn't say anybody was looking for me directly, but anybody who was loyal to Fen might want to take their revenge against me.

"At least it isn't a wanted person ad," I said, before handing the paper back to her.

"Always looking for the positive," Lili said.

"Where's my father's body?" I shot out. Zane and Lili shot each other a look before looking at me.

"Kim left Pascal at the college, but she took your father to the Lupine Pack," Lili said.

"But I... didn't... get to say goodbye and they hated him," I muttered.

"Regardless of how they felt, he was one of them. They will bury him and put up a small headstone. We can go visit there, if you want," Zane said.

"I would like that," I said. I took a deep breath, and the tears burned in the back of my eyes, but I needed to hold them in. "Let's see all these new responsibilities I have."

Both of them stood up, moved off the porch, and walked towards the fawn-colored cow and her calf.

"This is Daisy," Lili said, patting the cow on her head.

I burst out in laughter. "Did you name her?"

"No," she sighed.

"Hmm... okay then," I said, then reached my hand out to Daisy, "hi, Daisy."

"You can name the calf. It's a heifer," she said.

"I'll go with Milkshake," I said, before kneeling and reaching my hand to the little calf. She stepped forward and nuzzled her wet nose into my hand.

Zane let out a laugh. "I hope our children get... umm... strong names," he said.

"What children?" I asked, deadpan. His eyes widened. Lili let out a small chuckle under her breath. "Just kidding."

Lili took me to the other animals. I knew how to milk cows, thankfully, but I didn't know how to shear sheep. Lili reassured me that the butcher said he would stop in and give Zane and me lessons on the things we didn't know. The little calf followed me all around as I met the other animals. There was something so sweet within her. I reached down and wrapped my arms around her neck, and she let me hold onto her for way longer than she should, before she pulled back and ran back to her momma, kicking her little back legs into the air. It was the peace I needed in that moment.

***

We had been there for several months. I had spent every night crying myself to sleep for two weeks. Zane was patient, holding me through every sob and all of the tears. Lili went back home after a week. Kim came and went, as she had her own mate she needed to be with. She would come and stay a couple of days, and I would often climb up her and ride her over the open seas. She was the little piece of my father I needed, refused to give up, and she knew it. I think I was her little piece of him that she couldn't give up.

It had been quiet out here with only the animals, Zane, and me. His dad had stopped in several weeks after we were here to check in on us and brought some of Zane's personal belongings. He looked at me with sorrowful eyes, the eyes that watched me lose control and lose my father all in one day. The village of Erlösung had become our peace. They knew who we were and what I had done, but they were loyal to the Duke and didn't care about any of that.

We had been sitting on the porch watching the sea waves crash onto the dry land, Milkshake was frolicking around, when someone appeared on the beach. One second, they weren't there, and the next, they were. Zane and I both shot each other a look before immediately standing up.

"I'm coming," Esme said. She had been out hunting with Lakung.

Zane and I started down the stairs and towards the person—Genevieve. She stood there staring at us, my gaze dropped from her eyes to her growing baby bump.

"What are you doing here?" I asked.

"Pardon me. Hi sis, welcome to our home," she said.

"Well, not that you're not welcome, but no one should know where we are," I said.

"Well, I was worried. I astro-projected into your room, as I said I would, and everything was gone. Then I heard what happened," she said, rubbing her belly.

"How did you find us then? Should we be worried—"

"No. No. I used a locator spell, and since we share blood, it made it easier," she said.

"What are you doing here?"

"Always so many questions, still no welcomes," she said.

"Sorry, I'm just... You just caught me—us—off guard," I said,

Esme landed on the banks, shaking the entire mountainside.

"I told you to be gentler in your landing. We don't want to cause an avalanche," I said to Esme. She blew an icy breath at me, something she had been doing a lot since her second gift came.

"There's nothing wrong, Auriella. I was worried about you, and it took me a little while to put everything together and find you. I wanted to see you and wanted you to know that I am here for you," she said.

"Oh, I see... Is it safe for you to travel like that?" I asked, looking at her bump.

"I have a couple more months. It's not ideal, but I needed to make sure you were okay," she said.

"I'm doing better with each passing day, some days it hits me harder than others, but I have the animals, the sea, and Zane, of course," I said.

I motioned to the house, to the porch, for us to take a seat and for her to rest. There was peace in getting to know her more, learning about how she was raised, and where she came from. She finally disclosed that she was living near a little village—Moonwood—in Cliana. She swore me to not share with anyone where she or the rest of her Sarradet clan was, and I wouldn't. She was clear across the continent, which is why it made it a little harder for her to locate me.

Genevieve stayed with us for a week before she headed back home. Knowing that I still had family, I still had someone who was part of my mom, gave me the peace I needed to move forward. I didn't know what would happen in the years to come. I knew that the Werewolves had bowed to me, had sworn their allegiance to me that day, but I wasn't ready for that. I didn't want that. I wanted what I had right then. I wanted Zane, I wanted peace, I wanted a beach, and I had all of that. I didn't want anything else.

ACKNOWLEDGMENTS

This book would not exist without the love and support of so many people.

To every single person who picked up Black Wing and Shadows and loved it and demanded more. Thank you.

To every single one of my children who have been the best cheerleaders, going to my signing events, and helping me pack books. To my adult children who buy my books to sit on their shelves. I wouldn't live in a world where you all didn't exist.

To Sara and Jessy, who have been some of the most amazing ARC/Beta readers an author can have, and have more faith in me than I do in myself.

To all the many other ARC and Beta readers who read my book, gave me feedback, and cheered me on along the way. I appreciate you more than you know.

To all the small bookstores, taking a chance to stock my books and letting me do book signings.

About the Author

J. L. Rosenauer is an author who loves letting her mind go wild and spill onto a keyboard. When she's not writing, you may find her floating down the river and spending time with her family. She lives in Missouri with her family, where she proudly answers to both "Mom" and "Gigi". She aspires to travel more and dreams of living near the East Coast one day.

Throughout her life, she has endured hard challenges, and writing has been a powerful outlet for her. Black Wing and Shadows is her debut novel. Of Shadows and Siphons is her second book, and the second in the series of The Sandorg Chronicles.

9 781969 797101